I0819929

PRAISE FOR *THE LAST CON*

"Bartels interweaves the story of an ex-grifter trying to go straight with the historic tale of a man and a group seeking ultimate power. I was quickly drawn in and kept turning pages."

—**RICHARD L. MABRY**, BESTSELLING AUTHOR OF *MIRACLE DRUG* AND *CODE BLUE*

"A tightly written page turner!"

—**CARRIE STUART PARK**, AWARD-WINNING AUTHOR OF *THE BONES WILL SPEAK* AND *A CRY FROM THE DUST*

"Rich in legend, deceit and thievery, along-side a story of family, grace and forgiveness. The struggle between doing what is right and doing what you want resonates. The characters are both lovable and frustrating, and always highly relatable. And of course, Bartels throws in a twist at the end that will leave readers stunned."

—***RT BOOK REVIEWS***

"With the same intense intrigue as *The DaVinci Code*, *The Last Con* is a novel that spans the globe and leaves the reader hungry for the next twist in the story. From Italy to Detroit and even France, Zachary Bartels' latest suspense includes artifacts, museums, security guards all wrapped up a puzzle that no one will see the answer to until it is far too late. Dig into Fletcher's story and get lost in the details of *The Last Con*."

—***CBA RETAILERS & RESOURCES***

"Zachary Bartels is the King of Snark, the Emperor of Twists, the Caesar of the Page-Turning Story. *The Last Con* had me neglecting housework, ignoring emails, and staying up well past my bedtime. I simply had to find out how the whole thing would play out. Life is short, reading time is precious. Still, *The Last Con* is a novel I plan to read again."

—**SUSIE FINKBEINER**, AUTHOR OF *A TRAIL OF CRUMBS* AND *A CUP OF DUST*

Spoiler Warning

The book you now hold in your hands is a sequel to *Playing Saint* (2014, HarperCollins Christian Fiction). As such, be warned that it contains major spoilers to that story. And, while we believe a reader could enjoy this second book without having read the first, we highly recommend you get ahold of a paperback or ebook of *Playing Saint* and save this read until you've enjoyed that one. Together, these stories are more than the sum of their parts.

Also, Kevin Spacey's character is Keyser Söze and Bruce Willis is dead the whole time.

Playing Saint | All Souls' Day

Published by Gut Check Press
P.O. Box 10003
Lansing, Michigan 48901
www.gutcheckpress.com

Published in association with KD Enterprises.

Also available in hardcover, ebook, and audio book formats.

Library of Congress Cataloging-in-Publication Data

Bartels, Zachary
Playing saint | all souls' day / Zachary Bartels.
p. cm
ISBN 978-0-9830783-9-5 (pbk.)
ISBN 978-0-9830783-7-1 (cloth)
1. Christian Fiction I. Title.

Library of Congress Control Number: 2017903326

Publisher's Note: This novel is a work of fiction. Names, places, and incidents are either products of the author's own imagination or used fictitiously. Any similarity between characters in this book and real people, living or dead, is purely coincidental.

For the Gut Check Army

I Can Gib 'em to Ya

"God creates out of nothing. Wonderful you say. Yes, to be sure, but he does what is still more wonderful: he makes saints out of sinners."

—Søren Kierkegaard

Prologue

People died screaming in here.

You'd never know.

From without it looked like an unremarkable backyard shed, the garish blue paint—fashionable forty years ago—slowly peeling and dropping to the ground among the autumn leaves, the shingles curled under decades of sun and snow. It was nothing to look at. Unremarkable. Unless one looked deeper.

Inside, there were no lawnmowers or hedge clippers. No gardening equipment or bicycles. Rather, twin antique lamps illuminated the fresh drywall, a toile rug, and a few pieces of Colonial Revival furniture.

Near the back wall stood a man, also unremarkable from the outside. He removed his jacket and tie, carefully laying them on an oak dresser. From one of its drawers he withdrew first a long leather robe, which he pulled onto his frame, tying it with a belt around the waist, and then a leather hood, which hid his face completely, save for two eye holes corresponding perfectly to the spacing of his own eyes—yet another confirmation that this was all God's will.

The musty hood smelled of mothballs, sweat, and sulfur, but the odor quickened him. The thought of the history, the men who had worn this garment before him, filled him with a zeal he had otherwise not felt in decades. Not since his former calling had petered out. But now, there was new work to be done.

Now, the Tribunal was in session.

He'd purchased the robe and hood at a gun show out in the sticks three months earlier. Jewed the guy down from a grand to $320. He'd used that word too, just because he could. Because it was one of the few places one could still speak freely. You could say anything at that sort of gun show (so long as it leaned toward the right side of the socio-political spectrum) without ever drawing a reprimand from the thought police. The same vendor of curiosities was selling authentic Nazi armbands, as well as china and ashtrays etched with swastikas. No one even blinked. The Tribunal had no use for such garbage, but the atmosphere of no-questions-asked was vital.

Two booths down, he had purchased an active—or so the wheezing slob had insisted—Claymore antipersonnel mine, the kind with the words FRONT TOWARD ENEMY embossed across the plate. The Slob had pulled it from a gunny sack beneath his folding table and handed it over in a plastic bag bearing a 1980s Sears logo. Surreal.

It had taken a few weeks of research to confirm that the mine was authentic and indeed active. He had done far less research on the dry, cracking leather robe and hood. They matched the basic drawings he found online for the correct office in the correct era, but short of conferring with experts and running chemical tests, there was no way to know for certain. Besides, whether a true historical artifact or a costume reproduction, it was real enough now. He had made it real.

Naturally, the man recognized the absurdity of someone with his convictions—not to mention his vocation—donning the vestments of the Grand Inquisitor, the ancient office by which the Medieval Roman Catholic Church had brutally snuffed out dissenters and adversaries. But that was the beauty of it. There was something monumentally fitting about it, both on an ironic, poetic-justice level and in a more straightforward way. This was needed, now, in a world where the most effective weapon the powerful could yield was to accuse their adversaries of being motivated by fear, even while using fear to control them.

He would show them what fear was.

The man struggled to tie the lace (a modern replacement—his own) at the back of the hood. His fingers were not as nimble as they had once been, and there was no mirror in here. This was not an oversight, but by design. He did not like the sight of himself in the hood. There was something silly about it, although experience told him that it did convey terror, which was the primary point of the thing. Still, he felt overly dramatic, like a supervillain in a comic book. The title "Grand Inquisitor" didn't help, conjuring images of a spandex outfit covered in question marks. For that reason, he eschewed the title and had slowly begun to think of himself *as* The Tribunal while wearing the ancient vestments.

And that was their real purpose. He did not wear them primarily for the way they looked, or even the way they made him feel, but for how they delineated things for him—a tie to the past and its relentless drive to purify and punish, and a reminder that, while he alone may have been The Tribunal, this Inquisition of his and the justice it dispensed was infinitely bigger.

Stooping down, he rolled the rug back from the corner, about six feet, revealing a trap door in the floor of the shed. It had taken months to carefully excavate and prepare, to soundproof and secure. But now things were moving quickly. He unlocked the trapdoor and swung it open, revealing a steel mesh staircase, which he descended, slowly, relishing the dull echo of each footstep and knowing the terror they brought to the accused.

The smell of blood and urine hung in the air down here. A flick of his finger brought a set of fluorescent lights to life and his eyes struggled to adjust. An old workbench, its surface pockmarked and oil-stained, bore a variety of tools—pliers, knives, saws, and corkscrews; tools to flay, burn, and destroy the flesh—as well as rolls of various tapes and bandages.

The Tribunal glanced past these instruments of torture and interrogation to the newspaper article affixed to the wall above: "Local Minster's Congregation Going Strong a Year after Tragedy." Perfectly centered in the sea of text beneath that headline, the date, November 2 had been highlighted in yellow-green. He felt a churning inside, anticipation and anxiety. It was fast approaching.

The Tribunal turned his attention to the center of the small room, to the metal frame of an old La-Z-Boy chair, stripped of its upholstery and stuffing, and to the man tied down to it, bleeding and gagged. As soon as their eyes met, the wretch began to thrash against his restraints, his voice rising, ragged, from his throat, all but disappearing into the wet fabric of the gag. The Tribunal snatched up the end of the noose that hung around the man's neck and slowly tightened it until the condemned man fell silent and slumped back against the metal of the chair.

It was time to execute another sentence.

The Tribunal steadied his shaking hand. In for a penny, in for a pound. He'd done this before. No time to lose his nerve.

Reaching down, he cranked the lever hard, pulling the chair roughly back into a full recline, leaving his victim prone and exposed. The chair itself was a frightful and cursed relic from The Tribunal's past and it was beyond fitting that this was where hypocrites—four of them now—came to die.

A pathetic whimper arose from the man's throat. His eyes begged for mercy.

The Tribunal, his own eyes inscrutable, spoke calmly. "Your pleas fall on deaf ears. The Inquisition finds you guilty. If you still believe in your God, you'll probably want to make peace with him. But you will not have it. You will never have peace."

PLAYING SAINT
All Souls' Day

ZACHARY BARTELS

GUT CHECK PRESS
Lansing, Michigan • Jackson, Tennessee

1

Corrinne never wore heels.

Even at her wedding, it had been flats. Who could see them anyway under all that overblown dress? Just seemed stupid to risk tripping and falling on her face while cellphones recorded the event from every angle. And she certainly didn't wear them at work. Already on the tall side, they offered no advantage in that department. And everyone agreed that Corrinne exuded power and confidence without *click-clacking* everywhere she went.

In fact, she only wore heels when she was a hooker. And that was happening less and less these days. Corrinne had mixed feelings about this.

That morning, as the briefing came to a close, the captain from vice had announced, "Senior detectives can sit out the solicitation sting if they like." The comment was meant for her, she was certain. For one thing, he was looking right at her when he said it. And she knew that Vivien Allen—the only other woman in the room besides her own captain—would absolutely be going undercover tonight, walking the street, approaching cars, waiting for the johns to say those words that would bring out the handcuffs.

Senior detectives. She realized it was probably her imagination, but it seemed like the captain had put an odd emphasis on the word "senior." A little more like *senior discount.* Or *senior citizen.* Real or not, this slight had guaranteed she'd be out here tonight, in character, gathering in a fall harvest of scumbags to be processed and prosecuted.

At forty-seven, she was the oldest of the five false prostitutes—by more than a decade. But she was nowhere near ready to begin fading into the background. Sure, she'd be captain herself one day, but she had a very specific timeline in mind, and that was a ways off. Tonight, she was a hooker.

Checking her reflection in a cracked and taped window, Corrinne wondered if perhaps she'd overdone it. Earlier, while shimmying into her go-to streetwalker outfit, it had struck her that perhaps the captain had a point. Her trendy-but-professional hairstyle, her toned arms, her alert gaze, the slight crow's feet in her otherwise smooth and moisturized skin—they all screamed "cop." Or maybe "principal" or "consultant." But definitely not "prostitute."

And so she'd caked on the makeup, crop-dusted the restroom with hairspray, and switched out her usual streetwalker shirt for a bright orange tube top that reminded her of those aerobics videos she'd done every morning throughout much of the Eighties. And, of course, she'd squeezed her feet into these four-inch heels, knowing full well that getting from point A to point B while wearing them was outside of her skillset.

"Got one approaching," came a quiet, scratchy voice from inside the vinyl purse. "Silver Benz. M-Class. Dang, nice ride." She reached into the purse and clicked off the radio, letting her hand run along the cuffs and Ruger 9mm pistol tucked inside. A moment later, the SUV appeared around the corner, slow and quiet, searching. It was a few years old, but in pristine condition.

Corrinne overrode her usual impeccable posture and pushed her hip out of joint, letting her mouth hang half-open in the kind of glazed-over, detached sneer she'd seen on the faces of innumerable prostitutes during her early years as a beat cop.

The Benz pulled to a stop a few feet from her and the tinted window came down, revealing a fake-baked man a little older than Corrinne leaning lazily behind the wheel. He wore a Hugo Boss suit and tie, clasped with an obnoxious gold chain. The man smiled broadly at Corrinne, revealing a mouthful of comically capped teeth ringed by a meticulously shaped beard.

"How are you this evening, baby girl?" he oozed, squinting creepily at her.

Baby girl? Corrinne swallowed down some bile and leaned partway into the car, which smelled like old cigarettes and new leather. She glanced toward the back. She could see no one else in the vehicle, but the seats were all down, which turned her stomach.

"Oh, I'm good," she purred. "What can I do for you?"

The man's fading smile confirmed her fear: she was coming on too strong, too confident. A real prostitute would approach a car this nice with apprehension, even if she knew the driver, beat around the bush a little.

She squinted back at the man, suspiciously, trying to save the collar. "Wait—you a cop?" she asked, going on the offensive. *Ugh!* She dug a stiletto heel into her calf. Why on earth had she said *cawwwp* with some kind of Boston wharf accent? This was Grand Rapids, Michigan, perhaps the most Midwestern city in the Midwest. She could feel her backup watching and listening from beyond the reach of the streetlights, muttering to each other about the out-of-practice *senior* detective who still insisted on playing dress-up in the midst of their sting.

"Am I a *what*?"

"A *cop*," she enunciated. "You look like a pig. Don't see a lot of cars this nice in this neighborhood, ya know?"

He nodded, but in a way that said *No*. "You haven't seen this car around here before? Because I'm down here all the time."

Once a haven for crime and prostitution, Division Avenue had been slowly gentrifying over the years, pushing the criminal element back into a relatively short stretch of debauchery. There was only one reason a man like this would be a regular down here. Corrinne needed to take this creep down.

He glanced off into the distance, eyes searching for nothing in particular, his interest spent. He was going to drive off scot free, probably head back to his wife and his home theater and his cushy job where everyone respected him.

Corrinne reached into the car, around the steering wheel, and turned off the ignition, then forced herself to place her hand tenderly on his knee. "How about I get in so we can talk?" she said.

The man wrenched her hand away. "Get lost," he growled.

"Sweetie, what did I—" A sudden jarring and Corrinne felt the concrete connect with her back and skull. The memory of the scumbag shoving her registered only after she landed, and the first clear thought to enter her mind was that, if it hadn't been for these stupid heels, she wouldn't be lying here, staring up at the moon and dreading how sore she'd be tomorrow. She laughed angrily and gave her head a shake. Assaulting an officer was a felony. She reached for her cuffs.

Oh no! The purse. Her gun, her handcuffs, her badge. Where was it? The john must have grabbed it when he pushed her. *Nice job, Senior Detective.*

The sound of the car's ignition roused her. She could hear the gentle purr of the engine and the electric whir of the window beginning to close, cutting off access to the contents of that ugly black purse. Corrinne kicked off her heels and, with a burst of speed and energy, was back on her feet, closing the space between them. Her left hand darted into the car, reaching again for the ignition.

She felt the chunky smartkey for just a second before the man's fingers locked tightly onto her wrist. Then she felt the window closing against her upper arm, clamping her in place, apparently right where a major branch of nerves brought a stream of information from arm to brain. It was only bringing one message in this moment: pain.

Looking in through the tinted glass, she could barely make out her own hand a few inches from the man's face. Feeling strangely disconnected from it, she commanded a sharp snap from her elbow, driving the heel of her palm into his nose. A crunch and the spatter of warm blood.

"Grand Rapids Police," she shouted, smacking the roof of the car with her free hand. "Roll down the window! You're under arrest!" She silently prayed he would obey. Her backup was undoubtedly closing in and Corrinne did not like being rescued.

The man's lips curled into a wicked smile. Then the car began to move.

Corrinne padded along awkwardly next to it, her sheer stocking-clad feet slapping along the blacktop.

"Stop! Now!" she shouted, grabbing for the man's face. He clutched her wrist again, harder this time, and pinned it to the steering wheel. Then he sped up a bit, smiling broadly now. Corrinne missed a step and felt an explosion of pain up by her armpit, where the car window was biting into her flesh like a dull knife. She recovered her footing.

Looking down, she cursed the German engineers for not including a running board—a perch on which she could ride this out. She pushed herself to keep up, ignoring the potholes and broken glass beneath her feet and frantically assessing the situation. There might be enough of an opening to allow her other hand access to the window controls or, failing that, the driver's throat. But such fine motor skills were not an option while trying to stay upright as the car picked up even more speed.

She momentarily lost her footing again as the man turned right onto Baker Street, jerking her wrist along with the steering wheel and bringing another spike of pain. She looked in helplessly at her limp arm; with no leverage, she couldn't even fight for control of the car. Besides, for all the guy's compounded crimes, he was gripping the wheel—and Corrinne's wrist—at precisely 10 and 2.

With a sudden surge of gas, the SUV jerked forward, pulling her off her feet. It felt as though the window was now slicing through her flesh, right down to the bone, although she knew that was impossible. With a desperate kick, she snagged the ledge of the rear window with her nylon-covered toes and launched her lower body up onto the roof, clutching the luggage rack with both legs in an awkward scissor lock.

Half upside-down, her head a few feet from the concrete below, she tried to estimate how fast they were going. Forty, maybe? Fifty? Her free hand groped, blindly on the roof of the car, finding a bungee cord stretched across the luggage rack. She wrapped it twice around the meat of her hand and gripped it tightly. She could imagine skis and suitcases up there, which filled her with renewed rage for some reason. Streetlights were zipping by above, like a blinking bulb at the end of the tunnel—the kind warning you *not* to walk toward the light.

Tires squealed as the Benz took a sharp right, and Corrinne slipped a few inches closer to the ground. The tight skirt was keeping her legs from gaining a solid grip. Turning her hips over, she locked a foot under the rear brace of the luggage rack. She could imagine exactly what sort of a *crunch* her ankle would make as it broke into pieces should the john slam on his breaks or crash into a parked car. It was worth it, though, to protect her shoulder from a far worse fate. She shuddered at the thought of her body flying through the air at sixty miles an hour as her arm remained firmly locked inside with this sleazebag and his gaudy tie chain.

The faint sound of a siren approaching met her ears as the Benz ran another red light. Corrinne consciously kept herself from thinking the words, *I'm too old for this.* She wiggled the fingers of her left hand, now going numb and tingly under the driver's death-grip, and began to form a plan.

First thing, she needed a better hold on the roof. Against every instinct, she let go of the bungee and reached down—or was it up?—to her skirt, jerking the fabric and tearing a few more inches into the slit on her right leg. That should free her up enough. Shifting against the roof rack, she felt a sense of dread settling in. The skirt wasn't the problem. It was the rack itself—too low to permit any more of her leg beneath it. And her left thigh was now spasming involuntarily, prelude to a full shut-down.

God, I don't usually bring you to work, but I'll die if I fall from this car. I need some— Wait. The baton. She reached to her inner thigh, drawing the collapsible baton she had concealed there. She flicked her wrist, extending the weapon from seven inches to twenty-one with a satisfying *schick.* The satisfaction quickly faded, though. Now what?

Newer batons came equipped with a special cap—ceramic pins that would shatter safety glass with one firm rap. Not this one. It was outdated. A senior baton. She would need some power, some leverage if she hoped to break the glass. Pinned as she was, hanging off the top of this SUV, she had neither. Besides, knocking out the side window would only cause her to drop to the concrete below, probably cracking her head open like a melon. If she could get the car to stop, though, even for a second, she could probably drop down and free herself.

Another upswelling of pain as her shoulder, knees, and ankle flared. Red brake lights illuminated the road behind them. And then a turn signal. The guy was actually using his turn signal. She ground her jaw and internalized the pain, saving it for later, and again anchored her right arm on the bungee, ready for the SUV to take the corner.

Glancing ahead, she saw two lanes closed off by orange barrels—a common sight this time of year—and a backlog of vehicles funneling down to one lane. The Benz slowed to maybe ten or fifteen miles an hour as the driver cut through an alley, searching for open road on the next block.

As he cranked the wheel, Corrinne's arm was again yanked across the dash. She felt blood vessels bursting where the window had her trapped. Then she felt something small and plastic in her left hand. She blinked, hard, and peered into the car.

It was the end of the gear shift lever.

Corrinne pinched it as tightly as she could with two oxygen-deprived fingers and a stiff thumb and did not let go as the man straightened the wheel, pulling her hand with it. She felt the lever tip up and a button click under her index finger, and then another swell of pain as the car jerked to a stop amid the grinding shriek of the transmission. The man's grip on her wrist released.

Her stocking feet were suddenly on the ground again, gravel digging into her arches. With a swing of the baton, she shattered the window, releasing the Benz's hold on her. She brought the baton back down against the driver's nose with a *wumph.* Reaching around the steering wheel, she finally got ahold of the key, pulled it out and chucked it into the darkness of the alley.

"You're under arrest," she rasped between labored breaths. The department-issued vinyl purse was barely visible on the floor of the passenger seat, still latched closed.

"Out of the car—now," she ordered. "Hands where I can see them." Her own left hand was completely numb, but responding to her repeated commands to open and close, which was a good sign.

The john behind the wheel looked her in the eye for the first time. He was high on something—she could see that—and the wheels were turning in his mind as he sat there in his erstwhile getaway car, now safely shifted into park. Then, without so much as a blink, he shifted gears as well—from flight to fight.

The door came slamming into Corrinne's hip, pushing her back three feet, and the man in the fine suit came roaring out, fists swinging, teeth bared. Her baton was rolling under the SUV. No matter. Corrinne didn't need it.

She caught him in a wrist lock and took a long step backward, dragging him with her, throwing him off-balance, then struck the knife edge of her numb hand against his arm, just above his elbow, raking it up along the protruding bone of her wrist. Pivoting, she dropped her weight hard and brought him to the ground in a heap, turning him onto his stomach.

"Hands behind your back!"

Like a defiant toddler, the man yanked his free hand in under his chest. "You have no idea who you're messing with!" he shouted.

Corrinne smiled. *Right back at ya.* She wedged her foot into the back of the man's knee, actually wishing she was wearing heels for the first time in her life. Grabbing him around the ankle, she folded his leg down savagely, knowing the burst of pain this would bring to his tibial nerve. High or not, he'd tap out quickly.

Flashing blue lights filled the alley just as she was pulling the man's wrists together behind his back. *Not too old for this,* she thought as two uniformed men rushed to her side. Cold metal cuffs came out of a rookie's belt and did their thing.

The rookie shook his head at Corrinne in disbelief, mouth hanging open. "You okay, ma'am?"

She lifted her left elbow above her head experimentally. The shoulder ached like fury, but was not dislocated. Giving her arm a fill rotation, she nodded. "Nothing's torn. I'll be fine."

The rookie breathed an expletive, then shook his head again. "I can't believe that just happened!"

She squelched a smile. They'd be talking about this one for a while.

"Believe it, kid," she said, rising and walking toward the squad car. Not a bad night's work, even for a senior detective. The john was in cuffs, undoubtedly headed for a long stretch in lockup. She was in one piece—banged up, but nothing broken or even bleeding.

And most importantly, no one had saved her.

2

In the movies, cops were always wryly complaining about all the impending paperwork, even as they drew their guns or prepared to give chase. This always annoyed Corrinne. In real life, the paperwork came as a sucker punch every time, an unpleasant little after-the-fact surprise. Even after decades on the job.

Corrinne grumbled and tossed another pen across her desk. The department had switched suppliers a few months earlier, or maybe just downgraded which model pen they ordered. It was a miracle to get through a single page without the thing quitting. She pushed the paperwork aside, leaned back in her chair, and rolled the sour grapes around for a few seconds, savoring the taste. It was nearly midnight.

Four desks over, a small pack of young male cops crowded around Vivien Allen. Like Corrinne, she was still dressed in her hooker clothes, and yet, simply by walking into this place and reassuming her role as detective, the clothes seemed to somehow morph into stylish and acceptable—if a bit quirky—workplace attire. By contrast, Corrinne felt ready for a costume party, despite having gone to town on her face with a dollop of cold cream and donning a white cotton button-up to cover the ridiculous tube top. Her heavily sprayed hair had doubled in volume during her ride on the SUV and it refused to come back down.

She caught herself sneering at the gaggle of laughing officers. Her eyes met Vivien's for a moment and she forced a friendly smile. It wasn't that she disliked her colleague. Vivien was kind enough, if a little aloof. What irked Corrinne was the way the younger woman had swooped into the Major Case Team two years earlier and cut in line. Corrinne had been the only woman on the team back then, and one of the most respected detectives on the force. Everyone knew she'd had to claw her way to her present position and if they happened to forget she reminded them.

Then there were two. And Vivien was younger and faster and had a magnetism she seemingly couldn't shake, despite her best efforts. She was effective, too. Brought in nine johns tonight, two of whom had resisted arrest, and none of whom had managed to separate her from her badge and gun.

An hour earlier, upon Corrinne's return to headquarters, an audience had spontaneously formed before her, wanting to hear all about the one-vehicle car chase. But it was a surprisingly short story to tell and the group had summarily dispersed, inevitably falling back into orbit around young, pretty Det. Vivien Allen. Corrinne suddenly craved a cigarette despite having quit years earlier.

Vivien's soft chestnut skin and careless, short natural curls defied any attempt to pinpoint her age. Corrinne had referred to her hair as an "afro" when they first met, while clumsily trying to compliment the detective, which hadn't made the best first impression

Vivien was laughing now, in a laid-back, half-committed sort of way that showcased her white teeth and caused her hair to bounce playfully, as if it were trying to excite her into a real laugh. Corrinne instinctively pushed a hand against her own voluminous hair and felt it crunch beneath the pressure. She sighed and started pawing through her purse—her real purse—for a better pen.

"Hey, Evel Knievel," Det. Troy Ellis called out, uncomfortably loud, as he filled the large room with his presence. "There's a sketchy-looking guy here to see you. Claims to be your husband. Shall I tell him to get lost?"

Walking in behind Troy was a handsome man in his late thirties, wearing a tailored suit and a grin, accessorized by a stock-photo-quality dimple. The weight evaporated from Corrinne's sore shoulders as she watched him blow right by Vivien and her groupies and stride up to her desk.

"Hello, Reverend Saint," she said, rising from her chair.

"Hello, Mrs. Saint." He delivered a quick kiss, all she would permit in a professional setting, and gave her thigh a surreptitious squeeze. "I brought you chicken shawarma and tabouli."

Troy was hovering. At 6'3" and at least 295 pounds, the trek from the elevator had left him winded. He stood there awkwardly, just inside the couple's personal space, huffing a bit, until they released their embrace.

"Mrs. Saint, huh?" he said with a raise of his eyebrows. "So you did take his name, finally?"

Corrinne shrugged. "Not officially, but I told him he could call me that if it makes him happy." She smirked at her husband. "Anyway, *I* proposed to him; he's lucky I didn't make him take my last name."

Parker echoed her shrug. "And I couldn't really expect her to take my name when I wasn't sure what it was."

"Oh right," Troy said. "You were going back to—what?—Bernie? Bernie Saint?"

"Brian Parker."

"Right, right." Troy nodded. "I knew it was something like that."

"How is Bernie Saint like—"

"Anyway," Troy boomed, suddenly employing an outdoor voice again, "I like Parker better. Bernie sounds like a used car salesman."

Parker opened his mouth to object, then thought better of it. He turned his attention instead to his wife's appearance. "So what happened here?"

"I'm fine. It's not that bad."

"I don't know about that," Parker laughed. He poked at her inflated hair and then began sticking the many discarded pens into the stiff nest of hair and spray.

She laughed along for a moment before slapping his hand away.

Parker took a step back. "Wait. What do you mean, 'It's not that bad?' Are you hurt?"

Corrinne pulled back the white cotton shirt to reveal the angry-looking bruise protruding from her left armpit and following several meandering lines down under the orange tube top.

"Oh! Honey!"

She pushed his hand away again and replaced the shirt. "Not as bad as it looks," she said. "I've had worse. You should see the other guy. All that stuff."

"Speaking of the other guy," Troy said, reinserting himself, "I've got his file for you."

Corrinne folded her arms. "Tell me about my john."

"Well, his name's John—"

"Of course it is."

"John Slocum." Troy perused the file for another moment before handing it over. "He's a lawyer at a pretty big firm downtown. Adler & Clark."

Corrinne flipped through the folder's contents, grinning. "Well this just keeps getting better."

"Been talking our ears off down in lockup. *We don't know who we're dealing with. He knows important people. He'll have everybody's badge.*"

"Never heard that before."

"Another thing I'm not gonna miss," the big detective said.

"Finally retiring?" Parker asked.

"What do you mean, *finally*?'"

"No, I just mean—"

Troy laughed. "Yep. Tomorrow's my last day. Got a place on the lake and a pontoon boat."

"Good timing, I suppose. Ya know, since this John guy was about to take your badge anyway."

Corrinne snorted. "Nothing more intimidating than big talk from a guy handcuffed to a table."

"Might not be all talk," Troy said. "Slocum used his phone call to dial up Max Van de Burg. The city councilman. Knew the number by heart. Sounded like the guy took his call."

"Great." Corrinne stood and began buttoning the white shirt, although the Day-Glo tube top showed easily through it. "I've got to go talk to this guy, hon," she said to Parker. "Thanks for bringing dinner. You didn't stay up just for me, did you?"

He shook his head. "Nah, I've been going over my sermon. And the big announcement—I want it to be just right. How late do you think you'll be?"

She glanced at the mountain of paperwork. "Don't wait up."

Parker leaned in and she gave him a preemptory peck on the lips.

"Oh," he said. "You may want to, um . . . " He pulled an ink pen out from her hair, then another, and tried unsuccessfully to flatten it back down.

Corrinne felt the weight returning.

"Just think," Troy said, his voice booming again, "after tomorrow, you'll be the most senior detective on the team."

* * *

"I hope you made more coffee," Corrinne called out, emerging from the bathroom amid a cloud of steam. "Because I'm gonna need a third cup." Her hair washed and tamed, she wore a cream blouse and pencil skirt. "Do you think this is okay?"

Looking up from his cereal, Parker's eyes traced her form from top to bottom, then back up. "Looks more than okay to me."

"I'm serious! I've gotten looks and little comments from Ruthless Ruth three weeks in a row. Last week, it was my stockings."

Parker smiled and nodded. "Ah, the fishnets . . . "

"They weren't fishnets. They were—never mind. I'm gonna change."

"You look fine," Parker assured, rising from his chair. "And I did make more coffee. Have a seat."

Corrinne wavered for a moment before plopping down at the table. She rolled her shoulder around for the tenth time that morning, wincing at the pain and glowering off into the distance. Her hand trembled slightly, troubling the shallow pool of coffee in the bottom of her GRPD mug.

"A refill, ma'am?" Parker sidled up to the table, carafe in hand. "Need a warm-up, miss?" Her trance didn't break. "Detective!"

Corrinne snapped to and suddenly noticed her husband holding out the coffee pot. He gestured with it. "Well?"

"Oh, sorry," she said, and clinked her mug against the carafe. "Cheers."

"I take it you didn't get much sleep last night."

"Got home an hour ago and squeezed in a twenty-minute power nap. Why?"

Parker laughed, steadying her roving mug and refilling it.

"Because why would anyone do 'cheers' with a coffee pot?"

"Oh. Right." She took a long sip of the dark roast and then chuckled weakly. "A little out of it, I guess."

"You know, Charles asked me what you and I are doing for our three-month wedding anniversary."

"When is that?"

"It's the day of the Church Unity Revival," Parker said. "I guess I'll be busy."

"That's fine. The three-month anniversary isn't even a real thing, am I right? Let's see if we make it a year." She laughed. "Sorry. That's not funny. I'm not on my game today."

"Why don't you go back to bed, hon? People will understand if you miss one week."

"No, I'm fine."

"Well, drink up, then. If you show up, you'll need to be *on*. We're singing your favorite song again."

"The prostate one?"

"Prostrate."

"I know. We sing it like every week."

"Hey, I don't pick 'em."

Corrinne sighed. "Of course not. Ruthless Ruth does. And she always sings *prostate.* Loudly."

Parker laughed. "Yeah, you've got to make sure you hit those Rs in that hymn. And not just with *prostrate.* In the last verse, if you're not careful, you can 'join the yonder, sacred thong.'"

"I didn't say *thong."*

"I know what I heard." He smiled. "We should leave in about ten minutes. You sure you're coming?"

"I'm not missing your big announcement. You worked so hard for this and I'm proud of you."

Parker shrugged and raised the carafe above his head. "Okay, then. To prostates."

Corrinne raised her mug. "And thongs."

"Cheers."

Sunday, October 22

* * *

Rev. T. Charles Watkins slipped into the back of the auditorium and sidled up to Corrinne. "Did I miss it?" he whispered.

She smiled at the older minister. "No, you're just in time."

At the pulpit, Parker was speaking. "Before we close today, I have an important announcement. As most of you know, this congregation went through a tough time, financially, a few years back and lost our original building." His tone was even, unreadable to everyone but Corrinne. "To our great dismay, it was purchased by a group who saw fit to turn it into a night club." There was a collective shudder from the older members of the congregation, gathered in pockets throughout the sanctuary, as they experienced anew the shock and helplessness of the loss, still fresh after the better part of a decade.

Parker furrowed his brow and nodded his agreement. "These past few years, Rev. Watkins and Holy Ghost Temple have been kind enough to let us use this worship space. But we've imposed long enough." The four hundred worshipers waited in tense silence for their pastor to indulge in a dramatic pause. "It is with great joy and excitement that I announce that the night club was a rousing failure and, as of last Friday, we are once again the owners of the historic Hope Presbyterian Church, where my father pastored and my grandfather before him." The last few words, Parker had to shout in order to be heard over the cheers and applause.

When it died down, he added, "It's going to be some hard work restoring the facility to its former grandeur, but we can do it, can't we?" More cheers, and whistles. In that moment, one would hardly have known they were Presbyterians. "Amen!" he shouted, signaling the organist.

As the postlude filled the auditorium, a mob of parishioners met Parker in the aisle, halting his descent with slaps on the back and attaboys.

"Let's go congratulate him," Charles said.

Corrinne surveyed the yonder sacred throng and shook her head. "I'm not fighting that crowd. I'll congratulate him at home."

Rev. Watkins laughed. He had the most genuine laugh she had ever heard. He gave her shoulder a little squeeze, not knowing the pain it caused, and began wading upstream toward Parker.

Corrinne watched him disappear. She knew that, with all the benefits the new-old building would bring, the downside would be distance from Parker's mentor and friend, Rev. Watkins. While their offices had been ten feet from each other, the older pastor's gentle guidance, counsel, and even rebukes had been invaluable to Parker, as he re-adjusted to life as a parish pastor—no longer the televangelist and megachurch celebrity. He'd also helped and encouraged Corrinne as she rediscovered her latent faith. Sure, they'd still see Charles, but nowhere near as often. She would miss that smile, framed by barely-graying hair and deep brown skin that still refused to produce a single wrinkle.

"Exciting news, hmmm?" The voice came from behind Corrinne, but she knew from the condescending tone whose it was and that it was directed at her. She turned and faced the speaker. Ruthless Ruth. "Pastor Parker is just full of surprises." Parker had decided not to revert to his birth name of Brian Parker when he realized that his old congregation and more recent following, both called him *Pastor Parker*, the former out of formality and the latter in familiarity.

"Yes, very exciting." Corrinne's eyes searched quickly through faces in the distance, trying to find someone who would rescue her from this. In certain, utterly unbearable situations, she was okay with being rescued.

"I knew Pastor Parker would pull that off," said Ruth's friend, whose name escaped Corrinne at the moment. For some reason, despite her ability to identify suspects and fugitives with ease, she couldn't keep these women straight. When she'd first started attended Hope Presbyterian, more than half of the older women were named Ruth, which made it a pretty safe bet to call an unfamiliar face by that name. But now all the Ruths had gone the way of all flesh. All but the queen bee: Ruthless Ruth.

"I had hoped, though," Ruth said, "that the news would be about an addition to your family."

Corrinne laughed, a little louder than she intended.

The other older woman drew down her brow. "Don't you want children?"

"Well, um, . . . " *Grace!* Her name was Grace. "I may be a little too old for that at this point, Grace."

"Marty," the woman said.

"What?"

"My name is Marty."

"Oh. Sorry."

The disapproval took a moment to melt off Marty's face. "How old *are* you?"

Ruth shot her friend a sharp sidelong look. "Honestly, Margaret," Ruth chided. But then the two just stood there, staring expectantly at the pastor's wife.

"I'm forty-seven," she finally answered.

Ruth gasped, as if "forty-seven" were the name of some terminal disease. "I was a grandmother at forty-seven."

Corrinne opened her mouth then forced it closed again. "I think I'm going to go congratulate Parker."

* * *

They were partway through dinner when the doorbell rang. Corrinne made no move to answer it, her feelings on dinnertime calls—whether by phone or in person—no mystery whatsoever. But Parker couldn't stand letting a phone ring or a knock go unanswered.

"Whoever it is, I'll get rid of them," he said, scooting his chair back.

When he opened the door, a boyish young man smiled and waved, half-heartedly. "Me again," he said. The man's red hair was swooped up in a cartoon coif and his cheeks bore clusters of freckles, although they were semi-obscured by a fake tan.

"I know we've met," Parker said, apologetically. "Remind me where."

"Jeremy McLean. I'm with the *City Beat Paper*," he said, "your alternative press." He held out a business card, which Parker did not take.

"Oh, right. The pushy guy."

Jeremy smiled. "It's the job of the press to be a little pushy."

"Showing up at my door on a Sunday at," he consulted his watch, "six fifteen is more than a little pushy. I told you, I'd be happy to schedule an interview to talk about my church, my upcoming book, or the Church Unity Revival, which I'm headlining, by the way. But I'm done talking about Daniel Paul Ketcham and murder and corruption and all the rest."

The young reporter scratched his head. "All due respect, Rev. Saint, but how can you be done with something when you never started?"

Parker glanced back at their dining room. Even from behind, he could read Corrinne's body language as she sat, impatiently, waiting for him to return before resuming dinner. "Did you get an advanced copy of my book?" he asked Jeremy.

"Yes, I did. I even read most of it."

"Well, I talk about the murders and the investigation and the effect they had on me in the book. It comes out a week from Wednesday." He began closing the door, but for some reason he couldn't click it shut until the conversation had reached a real conclusion.

"The book is vague at best," Jeremy said. "The first third is about your grandfather and your father and how great of pastors they were, the next is about your TV persona, and the rest is a bunch of religious jargon."

"Well, maybe you're not the target audience," Parker said, "but I've got to get back to dinner." He forced himself to shut the door.

"Call me if you change your mind," he heard the man shout from outside. "You have my number!"

3

T.C. Barrett fished the Grand River every morning, right downtown amidst the bridges and skyscrapers. Since retiring four years earlier, almost every day had been the same: up before dawn, brew a pot of Maxwell House, read the paper (although it was much less substantial than it used to be), and then drive to Fish Ladder Park, where he'd pull his waders from the bed of his truck and onto his legs, ready his rod and reel, and wade out to the middle of the river where Jim and Russ were already at it.

Although the name Grand Rapids seemed to describe raging white waters that might drag a man under at any moment, the river flowed relatively calm and lazy downtown thanks to the dams. Installed more than a hundred and fifty years earlier, these walls of concrete effectively tamed the rapids by concentrating most of that potential energy into a single fifteen-foot drop. T.C. and his friends fished just south of the Sixth Street Dam, where the water foamed white with fury. The resulting roar made casual conversation all but impossible, but that was fine for T.C. In fact, he preferred it that way.

The river was shallow here, but full of holes and trip hazards. Still, by taking careful steps and keeping his wits about him, T.C. had never fallen in eight years of fishing the same spot.

He'd missed most of the morning today. Doctor's appointment. They were becoming far more frequent. The sun was already well above the city skyline when he headed out toward Jim and Russ.

"Morning," he called, as he waded out toward them. He checked his watch. Yes, still morning for a little while longer. The men nodded a greeting, eyes on their lines as they danced in the current. He smiled and readied his rod. He'd stay later than normal today—make up for lost time.

Everyone at Steelcase had thought T.C. was nuts when he announced that, rather than move to Florida or buy an RV and tour the West, he planned to spend his retirement right here, catching fish that he wouldn't dare eat, exchanging no more than a few words each day with his companions. But to T.C., it was heaven. After decades in human resources, he was sort of done with humans. Now, he dealt with steelhead, salmon, brown trout, and smallmouth bass, all of which were far more reasonable. He took a deep breath and held it in his blackened lungs for a moment before releasing it in a contended sigh. The October air was cool and crisp.

That's when Jim actually spoke a full sentence. Shouted, in fact. "T.C., look out!"

T.C. cranked his head back toward the churning water of the dam to see a massive round object, maybe seven feet across, barreling over the dam, all speed and mass, bearing down on him as if it had singled him out as its target. He dove out of the way, avoiding a collision by inches. Frigid, funky water was suddenly all around him, above him, in his eyes, up his nose, filling his waders from the top-down. He quickly got his feet back under him and stood upright. The object was racing down the river now, disappearing into the distance.

T.C. rubbed the water from his face and squinted at the thing, trying to focus without his glasses, which had disappeared somewhere beneath the surface. It looked like a big round wooden platform, riding low in the water with at least two feet visible above. And lying on top of it appeared to be a man, shirtless. Lifeless. His face, upside-down, had stared vacantly back at T.C., before going fuzzy and out of focus, rotating away. He was black all over. Not brown—black. Like he'd been dipped in used motor oil.

But that couldn't be right. T.C.'s eyes were playing tricks on him. He needed his glasses.

"You okay?" Jim asked at his side.

"Yeah."

"I'll call 911."

"I said I'm fine," T.C. insisted.

"Not for you. For the body."

* * *

Monday, October 23

Monday was Troy's last day and he had planned it out in detail. He showed up at 6:30 AM in cargo shorts and a Hawaiian shirt, which struggled to contain his massive torso, and spent the morning floating from desk to desk, reminiscing about cases worked and experiences shared over the years, confusing everyone with manufactured sentimentality and protracted goodbyes that fit him about as well as the shirt. At about ten, he'd invited the Major Case Team into the break room, where he unveiled a large sheet cake—brought in by Troy himself—that read "Enjoy Your Retirement, Detective Ellis, you will be missed" above bad frosting art depicting a pontoon boat cutting lazily through a lake.

By 10:30, it had all been consumed and Troy had made a show of turning in his gun and badge. And yet he remained, making small talk. When he had gathered a large enough audience, he pulled a bottle opener from his pocket and popped a beer, which he sipped until the captain told him to dump it or she'd put him in a cell. As noon approached, he rolled over to Corrinne's desk on his one-time desk chair, and planted a massive elbow.

He sighed. "End of an era, partner."

"We already did this, Troy," she said, not looking up from her paperwork.

He chuckled. "There's a box of stuff on my desk. Must be the new guy's."

"It's not your desk anymore."

"Yeah, I know. You met him?"

Corrinne closed her laptop and sat back. "No. You?"

He nodded. "I don't like him. Guy's a hotshot. Worked homicide in Chicago. People are saying he's got his sights set on the chief's office."

She almost challenged, *What people?* but then remembered that he'd spent the morning chatting up half the station.

He raised his eyebrows obnoxiously. "I just mention it because I know you've got designs for that post yourself."

"Right." She opened her laptop back up and turned her attention to the screen.

"Oh, and I forgot," Troy added, "the captain wants to see you."

* * *

Captain Hillary Dunleavy had been promoted ten months earlier, when the department tied the entire Daniel Paul Ketcham affair around the old captain's neck and forced him into retirement. Corrinne had sort of assumed they would offer her the job, but ultimately she too was a little too close to the controversy, having been Ketcham's go-to guy during the entire investigation. New blood was needed. Apparently, when a senior detective turns out to be a serial killer, the whole division is tainted. Who knew?

Corrinne found the captain in her office, talking with a short, compact man in a tailored suit, his longish hair pulled up into a nub at the top of his head.

"Come on in, Kirkpatrick," the captain called. "Reese, give us the room a minute."

As the man turned, Corrinne saw the shield hanging around his neck and realized this was the new detective, whose desk would be right next to hers for the foreseeable future. She disliked him even before he caught her eyes and gave a slimy little half-nod, half-wink that made her want to take a shower.

"Shut the door," the captain ordered, "and have a seat." She waited a moment for Corrinne to get comfortable, then stared at her with piercing green eyes until she was thoroughly uncomfortable. "How's the shoulder?" she finally asked.

"Fine. Levison looked at it this morning. I'm cleared for duty."

"A little reckless, don't you think? How would I explain losing a detective during a routine prostitution sting?"

Corrinne folded her arms. Capt. Dunleavy liked putting her cops in the hot seat, but she didn't have the discipline to sustain it. Corrinne had learned long ago that the key was simply weathering the first couple of rounds. "He was high on something," she said. "Tried to pull me into the car. So, yes. It was reckless. On his part."

"Well, I'm glad you're okay," the captain said, her tone nowhere near glad. "I've got some bad news, though, and I need you to receive it with professionalism."

Corrinne leaned back in her chair. "We'll see."

"John Slocum is not being charged."

"What?" Corrinne stood involuntarily.

"Sit down, detective."

She obeyed, taking a deep breath and trying to keep the image of Slocum's smug face from forming in her mind. "Not being charged with what?"

"With anything."

"You need help coming up with charges? I've got some for you: solicitation, resisting arrest, assaulting an officer, assault with a deadly weapon, reckless driving, reckless endangerment. Shall I go on?"

The captain was doing her Easter Island impression again, which only served to further infuriate Corrinne.

"What about drugs? Did the tox screen come back?"

The captain's lips barely moved as she said, "We never sent one out."

"Help me understand this."

"Slocum claims you failed to identify yourself as a police officer. He was lost in the wrong part of town and stopped for directions, he claims. When you reached for his keys, he thought it was a carjacking. I've reviewed the tapes and they're . . . inconclusive."

Corrinne rubbed her shoulder, which had suddenly begun to ache again. "I don't believe this nonsense."

"I don't believe him either. But there are a lot of moving parts here. I got a call from the deputy chief this morning, ordering me to bounce Slocum from lockup immediately. He must be connected."

"Yeah, he wouldn't shut up about it last night. Works for Adler & Clark, the big law firm. Ellis says he called Councilman Van de Burg after we processed him."

Dunleavy nodded. "Van de Burg. That's a name I've heard a few times this morning." The stone mask parted for a moment and she scowled. "City politics. It's half the job. Anyway, I wanted you to hear it from me first. He's not being charged. You're not to follow up with him in any way. We pretend the whole thing never happened."

"Oh, sure," Corrinne said. "It never happened. Hey, I wonder why my shoulder's all black and blue." She undid a few buttons and pulled her blouse back to reveal the bruise. "How strange. It almost looks like some psychopath dragged me all over town on the roof of his car a couple nights ago."

"That's enough, Kirkpatrick."

She felt the fight dissipate inside of her. "Fine. Am I dismissed?"

"Not yet." The captain stood and beckoned to someone outside. "Reese, come back in here."

As the door opened, Corrinne turned her back and began frantically rebuttoning her blouse.

"Corrinne Kirkpatrick, this is Jackie Reese. He's taking Troy's desk."

"Nice to meet you," she heard the man say. She could almost feel his proffered hand waiting behind her, but this second button was stuck. "You okay?" he asked.

"Yeah." Screw it. She turned and gave his hand a confident two-pump shake. Corrinne had long ago mastered the art of squeezing first when greeting a man. Just enough pressure on just the right tendons and his hand was immobilized like a little felt Muppet hand. Yes, it was petty to try to win every handshake. But men were petty at every turn and she'd gotten where she was today by meeting them there. Beating them there.

Reese's eyes flicked down to Corrinne's chest and then back up. She could feel the air on her skin and wondered just how ridiculous she looked. Then again, after last night's wardrobe, anything was an improvement.

"Up here," she said, pointing at her face.

He looked at the captain instead. "So, uh, should I get settled in?"

"Kirkpatrick will show you around and introduce you to the team. We've got a light load now, so it's a good time to get your feet wet." She looked at Corrinne and said, "Loop him in on your cases. Dismissed."

"Yes, ma'am." Corrinne skipped the difficult button and fastened the rest. "Let's go." Reese followed her out of the office, trying to come up next to her in the narrow hall.

"Was that a test back there? Or what?" he asked.

"Yeah, it was a test. You got an F-minus. Room for improvement." They emerged into the bullpen and she walked him over to Vivien, who was eating a salad and locked into a game of Tetris.

"Detective Allen," she said, "got a minute?" Vivien paused the game and spun in her chair.

"This is Jack Reese. New detective on the MCT."

"Jackie," he corrected.

"Really, though? You don't look like a Jackie."

"What, because I'm not a woman?"

"Because you're not six years old."

He grinned, obnoxiously. "What about Jackie Robinson? Ya know, sports hero, full-grown man?"

"You're not serious," Vivien said, eyeballing his carefully assembled hair bun. "You're more Onassis than Robinson, I think."

"I'm from Chicago," he offered, defensively.

"That's cute," Vivien said. "I'm from Saginaw—no El Train to carry you safely over the bad neighborhoods. Anyway, welcome aboard. We're like a family, blah, blah, blah." She spun back in her chair and resumed her game and salad.

Jackie ignored the hint and settled in, leaning against her desk. "You're a little snarky. I like that."

"Keep walkin', Jackie O."

Corrinne punched his shoulder. "Come on, I'll introduce you to the guys on Team II."

As they walked away from Vivien, he lagged a bit. "So what's her deal?"

"No idea what you mean." They approached a group of men, all surrounding Detective Ellis (Retired), listening to another hyperbolized story from the Good Old Days. "Let me cut in here a minute," she said. "This is Ragsdale, Clancy, Hamrick, and you already know Troy, who is at this moment quite full of crap." She addressed his audience. "I was there, guys. It wasn't cocaine in the ventriloquist dummy. It was black market Canadian cigarettes."

They made a full circuit of the bullpen, meeting most of the detectives and ending at Troy's old desk, now topped with Jackie's effects, still in box.

"So, this is me," she said, "and this, of course, is you. Do you have any annoying habits I should know about?"

"I'm always right," he said.

"No, that's already taken."

He laughed. "I'll find something else." He looked at his watch. "So you taking the new guy out to lunch or what?"

A jolt went up her spine. "Oh, crap!" She checked the time. 12:17.

"I mean, we don't have to if—"

She grabbed her keys. "No, it's this funeral thing at church. I signed up to help with the luncheon. I was supposed to be there half an hour ago."

"Sounds like a nightmare."

"You have no idea. Rain check on lunch." She grabbed a couple file folders off her desk and dumped them on his. "You got a login?"

"Yeah."

"Good. Have a look at these cases. They're not much, but pickings are slim the last couple months. We're all working cold cases. See you in an hour or so."

She took off running, thinking how stupid it was that she could stare down her captain without breaking a sweat, but was tied up in knots at the thought of disappointing Ruthless Ruth.

* * *

Parker was no good at funerals. He knew this. During his TV ministry days, he'd only done a couple. But since returning to Hope Presbyterian, they were an almost weekly occurrence. Sadly, all this practice had done nothing to help improve his performance. He couldn't understand why; as a preacher he was natural and articulate and engaging—the darling of conference dais and religious TV alike. But wheel a body in and he practically went to pieces.

"I've known Beverly Donavan," he was saying, "since I was an associate pastor here, under my father, many years ago. I mean, I guess I didn't really *know her*. Beverly had an injury when she was a young woman, which resulted in her not being able to talk. But, I understand she was incredibly kind, cared a lot about people." He paused and looked at his notes. He'd gotten way off track. Where was he supposed to be? Someone in the congregation coughed. Then someone else.

Parker looked at Stephen Donavan in the front row—a long-time family friend who had also been his neighbor two-doors-down for the past three years. He deserved better than this, as did his late mother. "I really only got to know her through her son, Stephen. Earlier this week, we sat down together and he shared some stories about Beverly, including one that I thought was very funny and really summed her up most appropriately."

He looked down at his notes again. *Neighbor's Poodle/Baseball Story*. Parker blanked. What was that story again?

* * *

Corrinne burst in the front entrance of Holy Ghost Tabernacle and down the stairs to the basement. She'd made it from the station in seven minutes without even using the siren. As she entered the social hall, though, she could see that all the preparations were complete. The food was neatly lined up on the long buffet at the front and the tables were all stocked with silverware, salt and pepper, sugar and creamer. She entered the large kitchen.

"So sorry I'm late," she said to the four women, standing in a circle, chatting.

Ruth regarded her with a dash of judgment. "We got it done without you."

"I'll stay after and help clean up," she offered.

"Believe it or not, we do have a system," Ruth said. "Another group comes to clean up. In fact, it was your late mother-in-law who developed it. It's a shame you never met her. A very sweet and remarkable woman."

Corrinne felt like walking right back out, but couldn't let the old woman win. "Are you telling me that, when it comes time to clean all this up, two extra hands *won't* help?"

Ruth half-shrugged. "I suppose you can stay if you want."

"Okay. And again, I'm sorry. It was work."

"When we sign up for things," Ruth said, her tone that of a mother addressing a small child, "we need to make sure we can follow through. Allison here is a stay-at-home mother, which is a job as well." She paused and gave the young woman an empowering nod. "And she got a sitter beforehand so she could be here on time to minister to this grieving family. I don't mean to lecture, but this is just a very important issue for me."

"Well, it's not quite the same thing," Allison said. "Corrinne's a police officer. She probably had an emergency. For all we know, someone got murdered."

Ruth raised her eyebrows. "Is that what happened?"

Just then, a flood of people spilled down the stairs and into the social hall. The funeral luncheon had begun.

Her help with the meal itself unneeded and unwelcome, Corrinne spotted Parker and sidled up to him. "How did it go?"

"Ugh." He shook his head. "It was—"

"It was wonderful," Stephen Donavan said. "How are you, Corrinne?"

"I'm all right. Again, I'm so sorry for your loss."

He nodded. "Well, in some ways I've been saying goodbye to my mom since her accident. She was never really herself after that. But I very much appreciated your card."

"Card?"

"It was from both of us," Parker said.

"Your support has been—" His eyes locked on someone in the crowd descending the stairs. "Oh, you have got to be kidding me," he said. "How dare he?" He set his jaw and marched across the room.

"That's a jerk move," Parker said.

"Who is it?"

"Don Caraway. He's the guy suing the city council about the opening prayer at their meetings. Donavan represents the city."

"Wait, you mean the guy with the shoes?" Corrinne had heard about the high-profile lawsuit brought on by some crusading atheist group and had heard the name Don Caraway, both on the news and from their neighbor. The two men seemed to be in the midst of quite a public feud. In her mind, Don Caraway was some kind of hulking mob boss figure, as the name seemed to imply. Instead, she saw a tall and lanky middle-aged man with a bushy red-brown beard, wearing a three-piece suit and bright blue Converse sneakers. He strode into the social hall, two women walking close behind him—one with pink hair and the other with blue. Caraway's eyes scanned the crowd and seemed to light on Donavan, who was stalking toward him like a torpedo through the waves. Caraway smirked and held out his hand.

In the same moment, he said, "My condolences," and Stephen said, "You sick son of a—" He seemed to remember his surroundings and stopped short. "What are you doing here?" he demanded.

Parker rushed over, the hysterical peacemaker. "Guys, let's not do this here. It's not the time or place."

Caraway ignored him. "Look, just because we're on opposite sides of a civil case doesn't mean we can't be civil. I harbor no ill will, Stephen. I came to offer my sympathy at the death of your mother." He gestured around him. "I even walked into a church."

He wore a gaudy metallic lapel pin, emblazoned with the letters FAR. Corrinne tried to remember what it stood for. Forget All Religion? Fools Are Religious? Friendly Atheist Revolution? She approached the budding confrontation and noticed that the two women with the neon hair were filming it with their iPhones.

"Leave," Donavan said. "Now."

Manufactured offense spilled over Caraway's face. "But I thought churches were open to anyone. Are you saying I'm not welcome here?"

"Yes." The veins in his neck were pulsing. Stephen Donavan was in his mid-sixties at least, but he exuded a sense of youth and power. And, at that moment, rage.

Corrinne stepped in, lifting her badge six inches from Caraway's face. "It's time for you to go sir."

"Fine, we'll leave," he said, biting down a smile. "I guess Jesus isn't for everyone after all. What a shock."

At the word "we," Donavan looked beyond the taller man and saw the iPhone documentarians.

"What is this, some kind of stunt?" Donavan shoved him. Caraway took a long, involuntary step back, bumping up against a table.

"That's assault!" He pointed, broadly, as if he needed to call the attention of the room—already silent and gawking—to the skirmish. "Arrest this man!"

Corrinne pulled back her jacket and rested her hand on her gun. "Sir, you need to keep your hands where I can see them."

Caraway smiled, triumphantly, and nodded his approval. "No self-control," he muttered.

"I'm talking to you, Mr. Caraway. Hands where I can see them."

"Me? What are you, joking?"

She unsnapped the retention flap on her holster. "Last chance."

"You getting this?" he asked the two amateur videographers, as he placed his hands on his head. Both *uh-huhed.*

Corrinne reached inside the man's jacket and pulled a compact Kel-Tec handgun from an inside-the-waistband holster. There were gasps around the room.

"I have a permit to carry that," he said.

"Are you a licensed PI?"

"No, I'm a citizen of the United States! I have a right to bear arms!"

"Not in here you don't. Michigan law designates all houses of worship gun-free zones unless the presiding official permits concealed carry. That's you, Parker. What do you say?"

Parker opened his mouth, but no words came out. He turned to Donavan, eyes questioning.

"Don't look at him," she said, a little more brusquely than she intended. "It's your call."

"Isn't Rev. Blackwell the presiding official?" Parker said. "I mean, they own the building."

Corrinne rolled her eyes. "You're presiding here. At this funeral."

"He needs to be locked up," Donavan said. "We've never allowed guns at Hope."

"Quiet, please." Corrinne put a hand on Parker's shoulder. "You need to make a decision."

"Just get out of here, Mr. Caraway," Parker said, looking past him. "This is a funeral. It's meant to be a place of healing and comfort. We don't need guns and handcuffs and big public stunts."

"I'll walk you out," Corrinne said.

As they ascended the steps, Caraway said, "He did assault me, you know. We have it on video."

"And you can feel free to bring that video when you file a complaint," she said. "For now, take this circus off church property." Outside the door, she removed the magazine from his gun and handed it to Caraway, followed by the pistol itself.

"I have a right to protect myself, you know," he said. "I've had threats on my life since bringing the case against the city."

"Did you file a police report?"

He scoffed. "Let's just say, in this town, I don't put much faith in the police."

"Sorry to hear that. Now, on your way." In her peripheral she could see Donavan standing just inside the glass doors of the church, surrounded by a small crowd of mourners. If this blew up again, she doubted she could contain it. "For what it's worth," she added, "I don't think they should open government meetings with prayer either. But you don't have to be a jerk about it."

Corrinne heard the door open behind her and Donavan come roaring out, apparently feeling free to curse once outside the walls of the church building. He was ranting and pointing out at the drive, where a news van was entering the parking lot. He rushed Caraway; Corrinne had to hold him back.

"I know you think nothing is sacred," Donavan said. "I know that's your whole *thing*, but this is ridiculous! You are ridiculous. It's my mother's funeral!"

Caraway looked up at the approaching van, confusion on his face.

"I had nothing to do with that."

"Oh, they just showed up, I suppose! Just randomly?"

Corrinne inserted herself more firmly between the two men. "It doesn't matter, because there will be nothing for them to report on. Right?"

"Yeah," Caraway said. "Let's go." He climbed into the back seat of a Ford Prius and was chauffeured away by the two women. Corrinne addressed the small group milling in front of the church. "Go back inside." When they hesitated, she added, "It's over," in a tone that did the trick. When the lawn was empty, she walked over to meet the news crew, piling out of the van, gathering cameras and microphones.

"Can I help you with something?" she asked.

"We're here for the press conference," the young field reporter said.

"I think you have the wrong address."

The reporter tried to furrow her brow, but the thick layers of makeup kept it firmly unforrowed. "Tim, do you have that press release?"

A giant of a cameraman sorted through a stack of disheveled papers. "Here it is. Says the city council prayer thing is going to be settled out of court, right here at 12:45."

Corrinne wished she'd just cuffed Caraway when she had the chance. What a dirtbag. "Sorry, but this is a prank," she said.

"Seriously?" The reporter's face fell.

"Afraid so."

"Ugh!" She dumped the microphone back into the van. "There is nothing going on in this town."

Corrinne's phone bleeped. A text from Detective Alvarez. She read the message and looked up at the defeated news crew, climbing back into their van. "Chin up. I'll see you guys in a little while."

She entered the church and descended the stairs. In the social hall, Allison was re-stocking a tub of vegetables while two other volunteers poured punch and doled out cake. Entering the kitchen, Corrinne saw Ruth leaning against the counter, reading a book called *Amish Country Romance, Vol. 19*. She quickly set it down and began filling the sink.

"Need something?" she asked, watching the water pour in.

"Just wanted to tell you I can't actually help clean up today." She waited a minute for the older woman to meet her gaze. "Someone has been murdered."

4

Corrinne was the last one on the scene. She hated that, and she blamed Ruth. And Don Caraway. And Channel 8 for not knowing a fake press release when they saw one.

She parked in a university satellite lot and trudged down toward the river. It was a cat's cradle of crime scene tape—undoubtedly the overzealous work of a bored beat cop—and standing outside of it were Vivien Allen and Jackie Reese. Vivien was thumbing her way through something on her phone, transparently unhappy.

"What's the matter," Corrinne asked, "cops won't let you in? They can be so mean."

Vivien pocketed the phone. "Jackie O. insisted we wait for you," she said. "Not sure what that's about."

Jackie straightened his jacket. "Captain said you'd want to take lead on this. Allen here thinks she's just trying to make up for some bad break you got last night."

"Yeah, probably," Corrinne said, ducking under the tape. "But, thanks."

"I still can't believe her first name's really Hillary," Jackie said. "That's too perfect."

"How so?"

He grinned. "Ya know. The pantsuits and all the—" He made an angry face. "Right?"

"No," Corrinne said.

"But you have to admit that—"

"No," Vivien said, following Corrinne under the tape.

Jackie paused before following them into the crime scene. "So it's gonna be like that with you two?"

Vivien shrugged. "Guess so."

"Like I joined a stinkin' sorority," he grumbled.

Jackson Island was only an island by the most basic definition and then only sometimes. The city had purchased the hundred-foot-wide strip of wooded land just off the bank of the Grand River a few years earlier with the express purpose of declaring it off-limits to everyone. This year the river was low, drying the stretch between the island and the west bank and rendering it no longer an island in any sense. They crossed the dry riverbed and climbed up onto the island proper, where a number of uniformed cops stood in a clump.

"Who's in charge here?" Jackie called.

A tall blonde lieutenant approached them. "I am."

"No, you're not," Jackie spat. "She is. Detective Kirkpatrick. So listen up."

"Ignore him," Corrinne said. "How you doing, Craig?"

"Not bad. Magen's pregnant again."

"Seriously? What is that, four?"

"Five."

"Sheesh. You could start your own basketball team. You've got the numbers and the height."

"No coordination, though."

She laughed. "So what do we have here?"

"One body. Seems to be . . . male."

"And . . . ?" Jackie prompted.

"And he's dead. That's about all I can tell you."

"Approximate age? Race? Cause of death?"

"No idea," the lieutenant said. "On any of them."

"Where do you find these people?" Jackie looked from Corrinne to Vivien to Craig. "Just show us to the stiff."

"Right this way." They followed him north along the edge of the island to the spot where the river veered to the east of the island. There, another ribbon of police tape surrounded a huge wooden wheel, seven feet in diameter. Chained to the top of it was a man, his flesh burned and blackened, his mouth stretched wide, frozen in a scream.

Vivien nudged Jackie. "Okay, new guy: age and race. And if you say black . . . "

Jackie swallowed something down and approached the corpse, tearing the police tape away. "How would this even . . . ?"

Corrinne examined the body closely. "I don't see a bullet wound, but who knows what happens when a body cooks like this. Might close back up. Obviously, we'll have to wait on the autopsy for cause of death."

"You okay, Jackie O.?" Vivien asked. "You're a looking a little green."

"I'm fine. Look at this. Guy's wearing a Rolex." He put his ear close to the watch. "I think it's dead."

"Tells us something about the killer, though." Corrinne said. "That he didn't take it."

Vivien jotted some notes in her pad. "More than that. Look at that watch: shiny and clean. Every inch of this guy is charred, and yet not a smudge on the watch. No soot, nothing."

"Maybe it washed off in the river," Jackie offered.

"No, he was up, out of the water," Corrinne said. "It looks like maybe the watch was fastened on his wrist after he burned up. Like the perp's trying to send us a message."

Vivien stopped writing. "Like what—he didn't kill the guy for his money?"

Jackie shook his head. "Seems like there are . . . less complicated ways of doing that. I mean, what's with all this? You kill a guy, burn him up—"

"Let's hope it was in that order," Corrinne interjected.

"—and then chain him to this massive *thing* and float him through downtown in broad daylight. That's a huge risk."

"So it's either an idiot or a psycho," Vivien said.

"How do you figure?" he asked.

"It's possible someone killed our guy here in a fit of rage, then tried to do away with the evidence via fire. When that didn't work, he chained him to the biggest object he could find—whatever this thing is—and dumped him way up river, in the woods, not factoring in the, uh, buoyancy of wood."

"Or . . . ?" Jackie said.

"Or we're dealing with a world-class sicko who wanted to parade his handiwork right through the middle of town, for all to see."

Jackie clicked on a small flashlight and began peering down through the wooden spokes of the wheel. "There's something down here." Reaching a latexed hand into the void, he struggled for a moment. "It's wedged in there. Wait, I got it." He gave a hard pull and then produced a black leather briefcase, the bottom half of it soaked.

Corrinne took a step back. "We should call the bomb squad."

"Yeah," Vivien agreed.

"Let's just see if it's locked," Jackie said, popping open the two latches. "I think we're good. I'm having a look inside. You girls want to take cover?"

"We need to wait for the bomb squad," Vivien repeated. "Step away from the case. And if you call me 'girl' again, the rest of your meals are coming in through a straw and going out into a bag. Understand?"

Jackie smiled, unfazed. "Fine, we'll do it your way. But you've got to admit, there's a real exciting tension between us. We're going to need to work that out at some point."

* * *

The briefcase, it turned out, contained no bomb. Jackie did not gloat about this, nor did he need to. His perma-smirk said it all: these timid *girls* had wasted time while the killer was getting further away from the point where he'd launched the wheel into the river with every passing minute.

"No prints on the case," he announced. "And none on the Rolex. But have a look at this." He pointed at the watch's face with an ink pen. "At first, I thought the thing had just died, maybe in the water—help us establish a time of death. But it's got the wrong date too. Off by five months and change."

Corrinne had to put on her reading glasses, which she hated doing. The watch's time read 11:44, just ten minutes before the fisherman had called in the body. The date indicated May 16. "That's weird," she said. "I'm starting to think someone killed this guy just to jack with us."

"I'm going to open the briefcase now," Jackie said. "Everyone okay with that?"

Corrinne pulled him back by the collar. "No. Allen and I are going to look in the case. You stand over there." She boxed him out and opened the lid.

"It kept the water out," Vivien observed. "That's good news. Looks like a wallet and a book or attaché of some kind." She carefully removed the brown leather billfold and cataloged its contents. "We've got a Platinum card—matches the Rolex, I guess. Michigan Driver's License for one David Michael Cates, born December 12, 1968. Lived right here in town. Seventy-four dollars. And what's this?" She carefully slid an unlaminated card, bigger than the ID, from one of the sleeves. "St. John, Pray for Us," she read. Corrinne and Jackie peered over her shoulders. A painting of a bearded, berobed man, holding a crucifix in one hand and a palm branch in the other. A halo surrounded his head.

"Guess he was religious," Jackie said.

Vivien returned the card to the sleeve. "Maybe. This whole thing was pretty carefully curated—the watch, the case, the wheel. Whoever floated this guy even put his wallet in here so it wouldn't burn up or get wet. We need to triple-check every little detail with the next of kin."

Corrinne removed the leather-bound book. "It's a planner," she observed. "One of those high-end types. Looks like he ripped out every page up through today." A heavy X had been drawn over the whole day, in black magic marker. She flipped to the next page. Also crossed out. And the next. She began thumbing quickly through the remainder of the year.

Jackie chuckled. "Between this and the watch I'm gonna go out on a limb and say this guy had no idea what day it is."

Corrinne stopped flipping at November 2. No big red X—just the words "ALL SOULS' DAY" written in a manic hand and underlined several times. She turned the page. November 3 was crossed out, as was every subsequent day to the end of the year. At the back of the book, a newspaper was tucked into a leather pocket. She pulled it out and unfolded it. The religion page of the *Grand Rapids Press*. Saturday, October 21. She stared in disbelief. Front and center, above the fold—the article about Parker and Hope Presbyterian.

"That's it?" Vivien asked. Corrinne nodded.

Jackie was thumb-typing on his phone. "I think I found him. David Cates, Financial Manager for Winslade and Associates. He held up the profile picture, next to the man's charred face. "Yep! Perfect match."

Vivien laughed, then said, "That's not funny."

"I'll call over there," Jackie said, "see if this David showed up for work today."

When he was out of earshot, Vivien said, "I don't hate him."

"Yeah," Corrinne said, "but I kind of wish I did."

* * *

Parker lingered by the coffee pot. He never knew how long he was supposed to stay at these things. His instinct was to eat a couple of crackers with cheese, convey his final sympathies to the family, and get out. But whenever he did that, he felt guilty the rest of the day.

After the incident with Don Caraway, the crowd had been abuzz, prompting everyone present to, one at a time, tell Donavan just how inappropriate and tacky they thought the stunt had been. Most then assured Parker that he'd done all he could to defuse the situation with the subtext that he shouldn't feel too bad for his ineffectiveness. Seeing that Donavan was now unengaged, Parker approached him to try and lay an exit plan.

"Stephen," he said, holding out his hand, "I'll be praying for you, my friend."

The older man gripped his hand and pulled him in close. "I do wish you'd been a little more decisive earlier," he said. "I know you were in a tough position, but what that man did . . . " He shook his head. "Oh, well. Thank you for the service. It was lovely. I wish you'd known mother before her accident." He still hadn't released his grip on Parker's hand and elbow. "She loved your family, you know. She was your grandfather's secretary when he was pastor of Hope." He went silent, gazing into the distance.

"Well," Parker said, "if there's anything I can do, you know where to find me."

Donavan snapped out of it. "Yes. Two doors down." He smiled. "I appreciate you." He finally released his pastor. As Parker made for the exit, Ruth intercepted him.

"Nice job today, Pastor," she said. He could see in her eyes that she had something else on her mind. Probably something critical.

"Thanks very much," he said, quickening his pace.

"And tell Corrinne not to worry. We'll get everything cleaned up. It will just take a little longer."

He stopped. "I thought she was on the setup team?" Ruth was notorious for mapping out overcomplicated systems for every lunch, potluck, and reception, involving no fewer than three separate teams. Apparently, this was a hallowed tradition, going back at least a generation.

"She was," Ruth said, her ever-present frown deepening. "But she switched. And then she left."

"Well, I'm sure it was something urgent."

"You're probably right. I guess that comes with being a policeman."

"Well, she's not a police*man*."

"I'm sorry," Ruth said, her tone not-sorry. "In my day, that's all we had."

Parker almost answered her, then thought better of it, nodding first at her and then at nothing in particular, before retreating down the hall to the church office. He slid in behind his desk, feeling a sense of reprieve. An introvert at heart, he'd had enough interaction with people for one day. Time to check his email. Maybe schedule a few tweets. His stomach quivered a bit at the sight of the new message. It was from booking@thegospelallianceconf.com. He opened it.

Dr. Rev. Saint,

Thank you so much for your willingness to speak at our Gospel Alliance Conferences. We have been following with interest and joy the evolution of your ministry over the last year and are very excited about your forthcoming book, which we plan to stock in our conference bookstores.

Unfortunately, we have booked our next two years' worth of conference speakers in advance and are unable to fit you into our roster at this time. We will keep you in mind should someone need to back out.

Wishing the best for you and your ministry,
The Gospel Alliance Conference Planning Committee.

Parker's vision wavered—bad horizontal hold. He clicked Reply and began to type.

Dear Committee,

I understand where you're coming from, but I think you should reconsider. My platform is still quite large and could help expose many in the "word-faith" movement to the biblical Gospel, if you were to add me to the ticket. I am still speaking at major events. For example, the Church Unity Revival here in Grand Rapids on November 2, which is expected to draw as many as twenty thousand people. I'm actually the keynote. I just don't want you to miss out on a prime opportu

He deleted the draft, his spirits in freefall. Book release day was a week away and things were not coming together like they should. And they truly should. When his ministry had been shallow and self-serving, full of platitudes, it had grown steadily without much more than a nudge here and there from Parker. But now, he'd done the right thing. He'd repented, given up all he'd built to come and rescue a tiny, broke congregation, circling the drain. Why wasn't he being rewarded more abundantly?

Parker thought of the reporter at his door. Maybe he should have given him that interview. He wasn't exactly in a position to turn down any publicity at this point.

* * *

Father Michael rolled his carryon bag forward another five feet. "We're supposed to be able to skip all this," he said, looking around at the mass of humanity, slowly shuffling slowly through the maze, toward customs.

"The first shall be last," Father Ignatius droned. He was never much for complaining.

"Well then we should let someone else be last. Right? That'd be the polite thing to do."

The older priest harrumphed. "Are you really in such a hurry to reach the conference?"

Father Michael sighed. "Good point. You know, when I joined a secret order, I never thought I'd be spending three days at a time attending workshops and plenary sessions. I hate this stuff."

"New pope, new requirements." Ignatius spat the word *new* like it was something rotten stuck to his tongue.

Michael examined his ticket as they rolled forward another few feet. "Looks like we're laid over in Detroit on the way back. Maybe we could meet up with Parker. Have lunch or something."

"I don't see why not."

"Really? I thought that would be a hard sell with you. You don't *like him*, do you, Father Ignatius?"

"He's not horrible. For a Protestant."

"Michael Gretzgy," a woman called from one of the desks.

Father Ignatius scowled. "That name is bringing undue attention to us. I wish you'd be more careful with your identities."

Father Michael grinned and wheeled his bag up to the customs agent. But the grin disappeared almost immediately. He had a sudden sense of déjà vu. His last trip to the States. All the murders. The demonic possession. The death of Father Xavier. A deep sense of disquiet embedded itself in him, like a grain of sand in an oyster.

"What is the nature of your visit?" the young woman asked. "Business or pleasure?"

"Diplomatic," Father Michael said, and slid her the documents.

5

Parker watched the 6 o'clock news on a small under-the-cabinet TV every morning while making breakfast. He was just wilting the spinach for the frittata when he heard it.

"And local minister Parker Saint reportedly helped to quell a conflict between activist Don Caraway and attorney Stephen Donavan yesterday. The confrontation took place after a funeral at a large west side church. We received this cellphone footage from a viewer."

A shaky and chaotic video materialized on the screen: Donavan shoving Caraway and Parker tugging back on his sleeve. Parker felt a dump of dopamine as he heard his name and saw his image on the news. It cut back to the anchors just as Corrinne inserted herself between the men. "Caraway and Donavan have been embroiled in a very public dispute over FAR's court challenge to the city council's practice of opening each meeting with prayer—a dispute which has at times gotten rather personal."

"And speaking of Parker Saint, Sheila," the male anchor segued, "you may remember that he was present when the Blackjack Killer was apprehended, one year ago last week, after murdering eight people in the Grand Rapids area. And now a charred body washed ashore on the bank of the Grand River and many are experiencing some unwelcome déjà vu."

Parker felt a sense of shame dampening his elation, as he realized he was smiling at the description of a grisly murder. But to be mentioned twice, in one newscast. And, of course he'd invited the press to the official re-opening of the historic Hope Presbyterian building later this morning. Not to mention that they'd have to name him again, later in the week, as the revival approached. It was shaping up to be a huge affair. This might be some real momentum. He knew he had to leverage it, but had no idea how. His assistant, Paige, had handled that sort of thing before she was killed. Perhaps he should call a publicist.

The sight of his wife walking across the frame, behind a line of police tape brought him back to himself. He looked down to find that the spinach was blackened, ruined. He thought about his wife, getting ready for her day in the next room, and how she wouldn't care one whit that she'd been on the news twice that morning. He dumped the spinach. Perhaps a simple omelet would be better this morning.

Just as breakfast hit the table, Corrinne appeared from their bedroom wearing a fitted skirt and jacket.

"Wow, you look nice today," he said.

"How do I usually look?"

"No, I mean, you don't generally wear a skirt to work. That's all."

She shrugged. "May have to talk to the press about this homicide." She showered her eggs with salt and pepper. "Apparently, they're going nuts over it. News has been slow lately; now there's chum in the water."

"I saw you Channel 8 this morning," he said. "Sounds horrible."

"Yeah. Guy was burned up. Potter's doing the autopsy this morning. By the way, do you mind giving me your opinion on something?" She reached for her briefcase.

Parker looked down at his uneaten omelet. "It's not, like, crime scene photos, is it?"

She laughed. "Don't worry. It's nothing graphic." She extracted a file folder and dug through it until she found a photo, which she slid across the table. A prayer card bearing the words, *St. John, Pray for Us.* "Found that on the victim," she said.

"Is it okay for me to see this?"

"Hey, you were never officially let go, so as far as I'm concerned, you're still an expert consultant for the Major Case Team in the area of religion and the occult. This is religious."

"Oh, right." Parker smiled a bit, pleased with this idea. "Let's see. It's a holy card, also called a prayer card. This would probably be his patron saint or his go-to saint. I'd guess he's Roman Catholic or Greek Orthodox, right?"

"Anglican," she said. "Church of the Holy Spirit."

"Yeah, that makes sense." He picked up the picture and looked closer. "The guy on the card almost looks like John Calvin, but I'm guessing it's John the Apostle. If you want, I can ask a friend for a real expert analysis."

She snatched the photo from his hands. "No thanks. I think I know who you'd call."

"Why don't you like him?"

She returned the folder to her case. "Seriously?"

Parker's phone began ringing with an annoying *beep-boop-beep*. He glanced at the display and flashed Corrinne a goofy smile. "Father Michael!" he answered. "We were just talking about you, my friend."

"Parker, buddy! Good to hear your voice. What's it been—three, four months?"

"Almost three months. Since our wedding."

"Oh, right. How's that treating you by the way? Good? Or did I dodge a bullet with the whole 'vow of celibacy' thing?"

"No, it's going well."

"Have you used the fondue set?"

"Um, not yet."

Corrinne stood. "I think I'll get going."

"Is that the missus?" Michael asked. "Tell her I said hi."

"Father Michael says hi, honey."

She grunted and brought her plate and glass into the kitchen.

"What'd she say? Did she say something?"

"Not really," Parker said.

"She doesn't like me, does she?"

"I don't know if I'd say that. I think you just bring up some unpleasant memories. When you showed up at our wedding, the last time she'd seen you was the night you killed her partner."

Corrinne breezed back into the room and slipped the strap of her bag over her head.

"And saved your life," Michael added. "Is she really mad at me for that?"

"Tell your friend I can hear him," Corrinne said, "and that I'm 'mad at him' for crashing my wedding."

"She means our wedding," Parker amended.

"Crashing? I got an invitation."

"I know. It was just a little . . . distracting. And she was already kind of on-edge. You know how brides are."

She shot him a lethal look.

Michael laughed. "Dude, you didn't run the invite list by your bride in advance? Not a strong move!"

"Oh, I did," Parker said. "It's just . . . I don't think she expected you to come all the way from Rome."

"It's called being polite," Corrinne raged. "Like how you invite out-of-state family and casual coworkers and Vatican agents, even though you know they won't come."

Parker added, "Plus, she was there when Homeland Security told you never to step foot on American soil again."

The priest laughed again. "Oh, they tell me that all the time."

"Anyway," Parker said. "I'm glad you were there." He heard the front door close. "How have you been?"

Michael let out a ponderous sigh. "Horrible. I'm at this conference in Baltimore. It's just like PowerPoint, PowerPoint, PowerPoint. I'm going to hang myself."

"Sounds terrible," Parker said. He loved conferences more than almost anything.

"But the good news is, we're laid over in Detroit for like three hours on Friday. We could grab some lunch if you want to make the drive. I know Father Ignatius is dying to see you."

"Sounds great. What time?"

"Our flight comes in at ten to eleven."

Parker tapped the appointment into his phone. "Alright. See you then."

"Right. If I survive three more days of workshops and presentations and priests trying to be funny."

"I'll pray for you."

* * *

At 9:30 AM, Parker stood on the steps of the historic Hope Presbyterian Church. Dr. T. Charles Watkins stood to his right, with a couple members of his leadership team. They were surrounded by a smattering of Hope Pres members. Only two people stood in the place he'd reserved for press: a thoroughly dispassionate woman from the *Grand Rapids Press,* who kept checking her watch, and young Jeremy McLean from the *City Beat Paper*. He nodded at Parker, encouragingly.

Parker swallowed his disappointment and announced, "Welcome everyone. We're here today to celebrate the re-acquisition of this historic building by the congregation who built it more than a hundred years ago." He had struggled to put together fitting remarks for the occasion. It seemed foolish to let the event pass unmarked, but the actual ribbon-cutting would come later, when the building had been restored. And, of course, the ground was already long-since broken. So, these brief comments and a short prayer were it.

He extolled Dr. Watkins and Holy Ghost Tabernacle for hosting the congregation the last few years, praised the people of Hope for keeping hope alive (which had seemed far cleverer on paper), and mentioned his forthcoming book twice. When he finished, he looked to the two reporters and asked if there were any questions.

The woman from the *Press* pocketed a digital recorder and shifted her weight impatiently. Jeremy raised a finger and said, "I heard your name mentioned on the news this morning, Pastor Saint. Do you think there's any connection between the body they found yesterday and the killing spree last year?"

"I meant questions about the church, Mr. McLean."

"Oh." He folded his notebook shut and pocketed an ink pen.

"Well then," Parker said. "Thanks so much for coming." He realized after the words were out that they sounded bitter and sarcastic. The small crowd broke up immediately, heading for their cars. Parker shook Charles's hand once more and then entered the building for the first time in a year.

The sight brought on a flood of emotion. Memories from his childhood, running up and down the halls; from his early years of ministry, as associate pastor for his father; and most recently, memories of the night he and the Jesuits Militant had skulked through the church-turned-nightclub, looking for a long-lost holy relic. Despite the overwhelming amount of work that lay before him, Parker felt nothing but peace as he surveyed the building. This is where he needed to be.

Striding down a side hall, he opened the door to the pastor's study. It still bore a sign that read "VIP Room," reminding Parker of the heartbreaking, stomach-churning sight of the sacred defiled. He ripped the sign down and tossed it to the floor. Stepping into the spacious office, he was relieved to find it almost empty. A chair and a gaudy glass table remained.

A sudden wave of inspiration hit Parker. He could yet mark this day the right way by having his office furniture moved here. Today. Forget the timeline he'd laid out; this would be his office from now on. Sure, there was no internet, no copier, no working phone. But it didn't matter.

This place represented a new chapter, and that's what he needed. Parker was nearly forty and he feared that, wherever he was when he hit that milestone, that was as high as he would climb. He needed a platform from which he could relaunch, and what could be more fitting? The poetry of it was palpable.

He looked around the room, seeing the art materialize on the walls: portraits of his father and grandfather to honor the past, stills from his dad's TV program and his own. The cover of his book over there, nicely matted and framed. And something on this wall to represent the future. But what?

* * *

Corrinne found herself back in the captain's office that morning. "This whole thing is a mess," Dunleavy was saying. "The press is all over it like flies on trash. The stupid timing—almost a year to the day after Ketcham goes down, another gruesome murder." She heaved a heavy sigh that seemed to transfer her stress across the desk to Corrinne. "People are panicking. You know I had to bring in temps to help answer calls from concerned citizens?"

Corrinne sat back, passively. She'd been in here nearly ten minutes and hadn't said a word.

"Look, I want all three of you on this thing. Okay? You and Allen are my best and Jackie's got a fresh perspective for us—might come in handy. And I know you're the senior detective on the team now, but part of me thinks Detective Allen should oversee the investigation."

"What? Why?"

"It's not that Vivien is better than you, per say. But it looks good, with the press. The black thing. You understand. Plus, she was nowhere near that whole fiasco last year." When Corrinne didn't respond, she added, "Besides, if I'm being honest, she actually is better than you at a lot of it."

Corrinne still said nothing. She wouldn't beg for her own job. And honestly, if she had to answer to any other detective on the force, it would be Vivien, hands down. Still, though . . .

Capt. Dunleavy gave her a long, assessing look before asking, "You really think you can handle this?"

"Of course."

"Alright," she said. "You and Allen split your other open cases between Alvarez and Hamrick. You can take the lead for now. But I want you using both of them to the full extent. Including Reese. None of this hazing, *earn-your-way-into-the-inner-circle* crap, you understand me?"

"Yes ma'am."

"Take 8B."

"How fitting," Corrinne mumbled.

* * *

Corrinne could not help but be transported back in time to the previous October, when she, Troy, and Paul had dubbed this room "The Command Center" and spread their investigation all over the walls. This was also the place where she first got to know her husband. They'd be better memories if the killer they were hunting hadn't been running the show.

Just as she finished pinning up the last of the photos, Jackie entered the room.

"Just met with the medical examiner," he said. "It's worse than we thought."

"Hold on a sec," Corrinne said. "Vivien," she called out to the bull pen. "You got a minute?"

When they were gathered around one end of the conference table, she gave Jackie the floor.

"The fire was not an attempt to dispose of the body," he said. "At least not after the fact. Cates was burned to death."

"Savage," Vivien said.

"And his tongue was cut out. Because *that's* something people do."

"Ech," Corrinne said. "Before or after he was cooked?"

"M.E. said before or during."

"Anything else?" Corrinne asked.

"Yeah, he confirmed the watch was not on his wrist during the fire. The burns are consistent down the arm, onto the hand. Also means he wasn't bound by chains until after the fires were out."

"Does the wife know any of this?"

Jackie shook his head. "The tongue thing? No. She knows they had to use dental records to confirm his identity, but nothing more."

"I'll go talk to her today," Corrinne said. "What do you have, Allen?" she asked, nodding at a paper in Vivien's hand, scribbled full of notes. It drove Corrinne nuts how the young detective seemed able to keep perfect order in a constant swirl of chaos—scrap papers, sticky notes, and files, piled high everywhere.

"I tracked down the source of the wheel," she said. "It was a custom reproduction of a sawmill water wheel being built by a carpenter in Kentwood as part of a renovation up north. A little tourist town called Clinch Rock."

"Never heard of it," Corrinne said.

"Me neither. Contractor's name is Ken Digman and the client is a Brian Green. It was stolen about two weeks ago. The guy filed a complaint with Kentwood PD, but then just started building a new one. Never thought we'd locate it, I guess."

"To steal something that big," Jackie said, "you'd need a pretty good-size truck."

"Good point," Vivien agreed. "And probably more than one person to move it. Thing's heavy."

Corrinne processed this for a few seconds. "Okay, Jackie, you get everything you can on this grand theft water wheel. Look for any connection to Cates. Vivien, why don't you reach out to this Digman guy and feel him out."

She could see Vivien balk at the direct order.

"Guy's a dead-end," she declared.

"You talked to him?"

"No, I can just tell. Anyway, aren't we overlooking something here?"

"Like what?"

"The newspaper. It was the religion section of the *GR Press*. Nine articles on it." She flipped the paper over. "Four of them mention November 2. We got a piece about Parker Saint. There's something about the installation of a new Lutheran Bishop. St. Isidore's having a big fundraiser for Puerto Rico. And there's some concert at Calvin Seminary that day." She looked up. "None of them mentions 'All Souls' Day' specifically, but I'm planning on looking into each of these this afternoon."

"What is that anyway?" Jackie asked. "All Souls' Day?"

"Wikipedia says it's a Christian holiday for remembering the dead," Vivien explained. "Mexicans call it the Day of the Dead. No idea what it means to the perp or the victim."

It occurred to Corrinne that Jackie had no idea that she was married to Parker Saint. And while Vivien almost certainly did, she was being discreet about it, which was greatly appreciated. Keeping her private life locked down and out of sight was almost as important to Corrinne as never being rescued. Still, the feeling of gratitude was quickly snuffed out by the memory of her conversation with Captain Dunleavy, who had been so ready to give Allen lead on this case.

"I'll look into the paper," Corrinne said. "You check on Digman. If you have time, get in touch with Cates's priest. See if he can tell us anything about the prayer card." She stood. "Captain told me she wants quick results on this, so let's move." Jackie pocketed his notes and phone and cleared out.

"You looking for some company interviewing the widow?" Vivien asked.

"No."

Vivien hesitated. "What am I picking up here, Kirkpatrick? Did I do something wrong?"

"Not in your whole life," she said, heading for the door.

* * *

Corrinne couldn't help but think Julia Cates looked like someone straight out of Central Casting for the role of Rich Widow in a low-budget cable crime show. She sat on a leather sofa in slacks and a designer top, heavy diamonds pulling on her earlobes, the day after her husband's murder.

"I understand you spoke with some policemen last night," Corrinne was saying, "but I'm heading up the investigation into your husband's murder and I'd rather have you repeat some things than for us to miss them altogether, okay?"

The woman nodded. She was clutching a wad of moist Kleenex.

"First of all, can you think of anyone who would want to harm your husband? Anyone at all? A colleague, neighbor, family member?"

"Sure," she said. "The man who lives two doors down never liked David. A few people at work. I can think of plenty of people who might have wanted to hurt him. But no one who would light him on fire." She grimaced at her own words.

"I see." Corrinne glanced at her notes. "The wooden wheel we found him chained to—it was on its way up to a town called Clinch Rock. Do you know if your husband had any connection with that town or if he was investing in any of the renovations up there?"

She shook her head. "I don't know. He never brought work home with him. That was our arrangement." She wrestled down a wave of tears. "I'm so sorry."

"That's quite alright," Corrinne said. "We'll interview his co-workers as well. What I'm most curious about is two particular dates and what they might mean to you. First off, May 16."

Julia tugged at her lip while she thought. "That's our nephew's birthday. He turned three."

"Anything else?"

"I don't know. I don't think so."

Corrinne retrieved a printout from her bag. "That date was on a Rolex we found on your husband's wrist. Do you recognize this watch?"

Julia nodded. "I bought it for him. For our twentieth."

"Did he wear it often?"

"Every day. All the time. He loved that watch."

"What else did he love?" Corrinne asked. She'd learned long ago that open-ended questions would often produce better information than specifics.

"He loved me. I know that," Julia answered before yielding to an upswelling of tears. When she recovered, she said, "He loved God. David was very religious."

"It's interesting you bring that up," Corrinne said. "The other significant date we found referenced in his effects was November 2. It was marked as All Souls' Day. Does that mean anything to you?"

She shook her head. "I went to church with him on Christmas and Easter, but I've never been very devout or anything. He always asked me to go, but he never pushed it."

"November 2 is a Thursday. Would it be odd for David to attend church during the week?"

"Not at all."

"And he belonged to the Church of the Holy Spirit, correct?"

She nodded. "He used to be really involved at a different church, but they had some kind of controversy there and he wound up leaving. That was a few years ago. He didn't like that sort of thing." She looked at her own high-end wristwatch and said, "I'm sorry, can we finish this another time? I'm not really feeling up to it right now."

"Sure. Just one more question. Have you ever seen this card

before? It was in your husband's wallet." She handed her the picture of the prayer card.

"Maybe," she said. "It seems like something he would have. I don't really pay much attention to the religious stuff."

"Okay," Corrinne said. "Get some rest, Mrs. Cates. I'll be in touch soon. In the meantime, if you think of anything, here's my card. Feel free to call me day or night."

As she drove home, Corrinne pondered their lack of decent leads. She'd been through enough dead-end cases to know one when she saw it, and this was starting to shape up that way. The wife was useless—a woman of few words and certainly not involved in the murder. The motive was completely inscrutable, and the list of viable suspects nonexistent.

And her gut told her that Vivien was right. Their best lead was probably the newspaper, as a sort of key to help decode the rest of it. She did not need to follow through on her promise to analyze the relevant articles because she'd already done it, many times over, looking into each and every local interest story. It all led her to an undeniable and very troubling conclusion: if it was Cates's killer who placed the newspaper in that briefcase, there was a very good chance that all this had something to do with Parker. Not only had that article been facing up when she pulled the page from the planner, it was the only one to reference November 2 in any sort of significant way: the Church Unity Revival at the Van Andel Arena.

Her phone chirped the arrival of a text. "This is Jackie . . ." Corrinne rolled her eyes. How had he even gotten her number? Then she saw the rest of the message: "We've got another one."

6

Combined, the three detectives had worked hundreds of homicide cases—in Chicago, Flint, and Grand Rapids. And yet, they just stood there, shoulder to shoulder, silently taking in the scene for a good two minutes.

They were at Hasselbring Park on the east side, also ensconced in crime scene tape, which cordoned off the park's elaborate fountain and another dead human being. The man looked to have been spray-painted white, clothes and all—the Yang to yesterday's Yin—and somehow lashed to the highest tier of the fountain. His face was dotted with little red dashes, pointing every which way. Corrinne couldn't tell from down here if these were wounds inflicted after the paint had dried, or just more sick decoration. A noose of black rope encircled the man's neck, hanging down like a necktie.

Vivien finally broke the silence. "How long has he been here?"

"At least two days," Corrinne said. "Probably longer. We've got uniforms going door-to-door in the neighborhood, asking when they first noticed it. Everyone just thought it was bad art." She gestured at the forest green plaque mounted on the lowest level of the fountain, which read "Official Artistry Entry" in large white letters across the top. Beneath it, a block of smaller text read, "Ode to Margaret: This piece is a tribute to all the righteous, whitewashed tombs, the white-toothed grins, and the black hearts within. To vote for this piece, download the Artistry app on your smart phone. Help everyone enjoy this art; please do not touch." In a small font at the bottom, it read, "This work completed on May 16."

It was not hard for Corrinne to understand how this body could hang here in plain sight while visitors to the park came and went without taking much note. This was the Artistry season, after all—a citywide art contest that had begun almost a decade earlier, drawing hundreds of thousands of visitors to the city, its winners chosen both by popular vote and a panel of expert judges. Every year, there were a few dozen majestic and moving paintings and sculptures to be seen both indoors and out. But for every beautiful three-story mural or elaborate mosaic there were ten barely-photoshopped cellphone pictures, creepy clown figurines in diorama, or what looked like a chalk-white mannequin with measles, crowning a public fountain. Seeing the familiar, official-looking placard, members of the public had undoubtedly just shaken their heads and moved on. Only this morning, when the man began attracting flies, did someone think to call the police.

A couple of techs tipped an extension ladder carefully against the pinnacle of the fountain and one began to climb.

"It's going to be a while before they get him down," Corrinne said, gesturing around them. The crime scene photographer was still getting every angle and the evidence collection had barely begun. "In the meantime, here's what I want . . . "

"Hold up," Vivien said. "If you're lead on Cates, what makes you think this is your case too?"

"Isn't it obvious? It's the same perp. Charred black corpse, now a painted white corpse? Macabre, horror-show public presentation of the body. It's the same investigation. Besides, I've got a little experience with this kind of thing." Vivien said nothing, but looked less than convinced. "Shall we call the captain?"

"I think you two should fight over it," Jackie said, smiling. They both ignored him.

"You really want it?" Vivien said. "Go nuts."

"Okay. First thing, I want this plaque analyzed. It's a pretty good likeness to the official signage. Even has raised lettering. Wasn't printed out in someone's basement. So who made it? Jackie, you find out who supplied the real signs. Vivien, call every printer in the city, every Kinko's—is that still a thing?—anybody who might do this kind of sign and see if they've had any weird orders lately. And let's do some deep cross-referencing between both our vic and May 16th. Same date as on Cates's watch, by the way. That's obviously not a coincidence."

"And what are you going to do?" Jackie asked.

"I'm going to keep an eye on the nerd herd here. And the moment we have an ID on our victim, I'm going through his life with a fine-toothed comb."

"Looking for what?"

"Anyone named Margaret."

* * *

Parker was monumentally pleased with himself. It had taken more than three hours, but he had actually gotten the old intercom system working again. He remembered the day it was installed in the mid-Nineties, during a time of break-ins in the area, and how futuristic it had seemed. The secretary could not only talk to visitors at the church's front door, but see an image of them on a small black and white screen before deciding whether to buzz them in. The apparatus was still mounted on the outside of the building, but Parker had found the monitor and handset stuffed into a box on a closet shelf in his study.

He savored the little thrill of accomplishment, which was only heightened by the *ding-dong* of the intercom filling the office. His secretary not yet aware of the effective change in home base, Parker scrambled back to the desk, feeling a little silly for it. The image on the screen was fuzzy and small and backlit by the sun. It was a man, probably in a button up shirt.

Parker grabbed up the handset and asked, "Can I help you?"

"It's me. Stephen. Can you see me?" He waved his hand in front of the plastic bubble guarding the camera.

"I sure can. Just fixed the intercom this morning. First step in restoring the whole place."

"That's the spirit." He shifted, awkwardly. "I don't suppose I could come in?"

"Oh, right." Parker buzzed him in.

By the time he found Parker in the pastor's study, Donavan was ghost white. He lowered himself weakly into a faux velvet chair full of iffy stains—a relic of the night club. His voice cracked as he said, "I had no idea it was this bad." He looked up at Parker, holding back tears. "Did you?"

"Sadly, yes. I actually visited once while the nightclub was functioning. Thought I was going to throw up. Compared to that night, the place looks great. I mean, we need new pews, we need to rebuild the chancel, give everything a new coat of paint. It's going to take some money and some hard work, but I bet we can reconsecrate this place and move the service here within three months."

"I think that's a little optimistic."

Parker laughed. "It's a lot optimistic. And we'll make it happen."

"I'm sorry I missed the dedication this morning. I had a client meeting. Just wanted to stop by and have a look at things." His eyes made a circuit of the room while he spoke. "My goodness, I have a lot of memories of this place. Of your father." He pointed back toward the main church office. "And I remember sitting right out there as a little boy while my mother met with your grandfather."

"Speaking of, did you get the advanced copy of my book?"

"I did. I'm five or six chapters in. It's quite a hagiography of your ancestors."

"Yeah. I had to tell the publisher you might blog about it to get you that copy. I didn't mention it was a legal blog."

Donavan chuckled. "I'm sure I can accommodate that. How's your wife, by the way? I saw her on the news, talking about that murder. Horrible stuff."

"I assume she's fine. She's a rock—keeps work at work for the most part."

"I knew him, you know."

"Who?"

"Dave Cates. The man who was murdered. He was a client and a friend. I hope they catch whoever did it."

"If anyone can, she will."

Donavan stood and again surveyed the room, this time smiling. "I can't believe we got her back. Well done, Pastor. I just wish I had more time to help get this place back in shape. Maybe after this case is over. Anyway, I'll let you get on to the next thing, whatever that is." They shook hands and Donavan let himself out.

Parker looked at the disgusting chair his friend had just vacated.

The next thing would definitely be renting a dumpster. The bigger the better.

* * *

"We've got an ID on our victim and some preliminary notes," Corrinne said. She'd assembled her team in the conference room once again. Jackie and Vivien took chairs on either side of the table, leaving empty the seat at the head. Corrinne opted to stand. It was probably a power play, but she didn't care. She handed a small stack of printouts to each of the others.

"Leslie Doane," Jackie read. He arched an eyebrow. "Leslie?"

"Right," Vivien said. "Instead of trying to solve the murder, let's giggle because the victim had a girl's name, *Jackie*."

"Touché."

"He's a real pillar of the community," Corrinne said. "Had a rough past—addiction, a bit of a rap sheet—small-time stuff. A little jail time. But the last twenty years, he's run a nonprofit, gives presentations about," she consulted her notes, "'sobriety and positive change.' His website is chock-full of testimonials about how his work has changed people's lives. I followed up on a few and they seem legit."

"Well, somebody didn't like him," Jackie offered.

"So what's his dark secret?" Vivien asked.

Jackie rolled his eyes. "Why assume he's got a secret? Could be random. Could be someone from his old life, just got out of the pen and wants some kind of revenge. Who knows?"

"The sign," Vivien said. "It mentioned whitewashed tombs. That's a quote from Jesus. 'Woe to you, teachers of the law and Pharisees. You are like whitewashed tombs.'"

Jackie chuckled. "Didn't peg you for the religious type."

"You don't know anything about me. Anyway, add the reference to a black heart and the fact that this guy was literally painted white, it's safe to say our perp knows a secret that Leslie was trying to hide."

"You may be right," Corrinne said, flipping to the next page. The others followed suit. "Doane had no convictions after 1993," she said, "but in 2007 he got scooped up in a prostitution bust at the Lazy T Motel. At first, the woman was going to cut a deal and testify against Doane, but then she changed her story. Said it was consensual."

"Let me guess," Jackie said. "Hooker's name was Margaret?"

"Nope."

"You find any Margarets connected to him?" Vivien asked.

"Only one. A former secretary who retired eight years ago and died last June. I want to dig a little further, but I really don't see anything there. We get anywhere on the placard?"

Vivien shook her head. "I talked to twenty-two print shops and sign manufacturers. Nothing."

"Could have ordered it online," Jackie said, "from anywhere in the country. I assume the lab will check for printer stenography?"

"Yeah. On rush. This case is priority one. Potter's doing the autopsy at 4:30. Should be a real treat, considering the victim's been baking in the sun for at least two days. One of you want to go?"

"I'll do it," Vivien said.

"Thanks. I'm anxious to hear cause of death on this one."

"Fifty bucks says he was hung from the neck until dead," Jackie said.

"I don't think so," Corrinne countered. "According to preliminary notes, his spine is unbroken and there doesn't seem to be any rope burn or contusions around the neck. Although that may have been obscured by paint."

Vivien gathered her things. "I never eat after an autopsy, so I'm going to grab a bite now and head out."

She made her exit quickly, leaving only Corrinne, towering over Jackie.

"You think there's going to be more of these?" he asked.

"How would I know?"

He shook his head. "Crazier than anything I ever saw in Chicago. Both of these. And on my first two days on the job."

The captain popped her head into the open door and said, "Kirkpatrick, I need you in my office."

Corrinne sighed. "Again?"

"Excuse me?"

"Nothing. Sorry, ma'am. Be right there."

"You want me to come too, Captain?" Jackie asked.

"Yeah, why not?"

The two suits waiting in the captain's office may as well have had "Fed" tattooed on their foreheads. The man was mid-forties with a dad body, twenty-year-old glasses, and an ill-fitting button-down shirt that bloused out around his waist. The woman was a little younger and very muscular, wearing a sharp tailored pantsuit and a practiced scowl. She reminded Corrinne of Xena, the warrior-princess of Nineties television fame.

Captain Dunleavy gestured at the man. "Detective Kirkpatrick, this is Agent—"

"Special Agent Wilson," he interrupted. "And this is Agent Bertuzzi. We're with the Bureau." He made no move to shake her hand.

"Good for you," Corrinne said.

"Detective . . . " the captain warned.

"What? I'm just waiting to find out why they're here." She flopped down in one of the chairs opposite the captain's desk. No one else sat. She chuckled dryly. How quickly these things reversed themselves.

"It's come to our attention," Wilson said, "that you've had a string of very unusual murders here recently and—"

"A *string*? You mean two, right?"

"Two is how it starts," Wilson said. "That's how it started last October, am I correct?"

"You mean there were two before there were more than two? You're right." She gasped. "That's uncanny, now that I think about it."

He ignored the barb. "And now, one year later, a similar situation has come up in your otherwise quiet city. We thought you might want a bit of help, that's all. We have a world class criminal profiler and—"

"I think we've got it covered," Corrinne said. "And I wouldn't call it a similar situation. Except that we took care of it then, and we'll take care of this too."

Wilson flipped through some papers in a green file folder. "I don't know if I'd say you *took care of it.* The perpetrator, Daniel Paul Ketcham, turned out to be one of your own—the detective in charge of the investigation. Is that correct?"

"You know it is," Captain Dunleavey said.

The agent kept his gaze on Corrinne. "Your partner, I understand."

"No. Not officially."

"Unofficially maybe?"

Corrinne said nothing.

He tipped the folder toward her, revealing a report full of black Sharpie redactions. "It's hard to piece it all together based on what Homeland Security gave us."

"Get a higher security clearance, I guess," Corrinne said.

Wilson smiled, revealing crooked teeth. "Right. Why don't you help me sort out the rest of the details? Your husband, Parker Saint, is the man Ketcham was trying to murder when he was shot and killed by—"

"He wasn't my husband then." She could feel Jackie gaping at her from behind. Why was he even in here?

"Yes, I see. And now a newspaper clip about your husband was found on a murdered man floating down the Grand River. Do you think perhaps you're just a little too close to all this?"

By way of answer, Corrinne leaned forward in her chair and reached for the agent's thigh. He sputtered and shuffled awkwardly as she grabbed the top of a long sticker and yanked it from his pants. It said "38 x 32" about twenty times down its length. "Sorry," she said, "that was driving me crazy. They're nice pants though. Most guys can't pull off pleats in 2017." She rolled up the sticker and tossed it in the trash. "I'm sorry, what was the question?"

Before he could recover, the captain said, "Let's cut the crap. You act like the FBI is offering all these resources out of the goodness of your collective heart, for us to use at our leisure. But we all know how this works: we let you in the side door and you'll take over the investigation."

"We'd be cooperating with your department, looping you in; but yes, we think it would make the most sense if we had command."

"Do we have a choice?" the captain asked.

"For now."

"Then I say no. For now."

The two FBI agents exchanged a look and Wilson retrieved several business cards from his pocket. "If you change your mind, give me a call," he said to the captain, handing her a card. "And Detective, if you think of anything—"

"Nope." Capt. Dunleavy intercepted the second card. "You talk to me. Don't contact my detectives."

"Good enough," Wilson said. "We'll be in touch." Xena nodded at the captain and then Corrinne as she followed Wilson out.

"What a tool," Corrinne mumbled.

"He's not wrong though," the captain said. "This is looking bad for us. I need you to make some progress. Today would be nice."

"Yes, ma'am." As they left her office, Corrinne could still feel Jackie gawking at her.

"What?" she said.

"Nothing. I mean . . . I have no right to know."

Corrinne sighed. "Yes, you do." She checked the time—4:15. "You want to get a drink, Jackie?"

7

Parker finally located the pull string and brought a dull, dusty light into the attic. As a kid he'd played up here, among the old banners, hymnals, and poorly produced set pieces from productions gone by. The smell was familiar and comforting and, as his eyes adjusted to the light, he felt a thrill of discovery. It looked as though the proprietors of the night club had moved half the missing stuff up here, rather than toss it. There was the altar, the cross, and the stand where the visitors' book normally sat. And all around them were boxes and boxes containing who knew what else.

No, he decided, there's no way the night club people did this. Someone at the church had the foresight—and faith—to pack it all away in the attic, awaiting the day the church building might be theirs again. Like a giddy child he dug into the boxes. He spent half the morning methodically making his way through them. He found old black and white photographs, ancient newsletters and bulletins. And then, behind a stack of boxes, the greatest treasure of all: the pulpit—or at least part of it.

Parker felt tears of joy and recognition threatening to burst forth. His grandfather had always preached from behind the imposing wooden pulpit, as had his father, for a time. It was only when Parker had joined the staff and the TV program was really taking off that they had banished it to the dust heap up in the rafters in favor of a more modern-looking Plexiglas lectern. He picked through the pieces of the pulpit, some assembly required. It seemed to be all there. Feeling a drive he hadn't known in at least a year, Parker knew what he'd do next. He'd bring this massive furnishing back down into the church and reassemble it.

His grandfather's pulpit.

His father's pulpit.

His phone rang.

"This is Parker."

"Good morning! It's Stephen Donavan."

"Stephen! I was just thinking of you. I'm up in the church attic and I found some old pictures with your mother in them."

"I'd love to see them sometime."

"Yeah, I'll bring them by."

He heard his friend take a deep breath on the other end. "Look, Parker, I wanted to touch base with you today because I'm thinking I might call you as an expert witness."

"Really? Expert in what?" Parker grinned, despite himself.

"In things religious. You've opened the city council meetings with prayer, and you're well known and respected in the community. I think you could help. I could also mention how you'd been an expert consultant for the GRPD. Would really give you some credibility. If you're willing, that is."

"Sure, I'd be happy to," Parker said.

"And when you're up there, I'll bring up the gun, how Caraway brought a gun into a church and almost got arrested."

"But what does that—"

"If you'll just acknowledge you saw it, their attorney will object and I'll withdraw, but the jury will see him for the bully he is."

"That's sounds a little iffy, Stephen."

"Oh, people do that kind of thing all the time in the courtroom. It's theater really, at the end of the day. And it's the truth. Groups like FAR abuse the legal system, forcing their secularist agenda on hard-working Americans, scaring school boards and local governments into rolling over—"

"Yeah, I know."

"—and acquiescing to all their demands."

"Stephen, I know. You're preaching to the choir. I just don't know if it's the best—"

"And thank God our fair city decided to end the madness and put up a fight. We've got to do this Parker. We owe this to the people, don't you see?"

"I'll think about it, okay?"

"Your father would do this."

"I said I'll think about it."

"Your grandfather would do it."

"Goodbye, Stephen," Parker laughed.

"Alright. I've got to go, anyway. I've got a meeting with a beautiful woman."

"Well, I hope that goes well."

* * *

Donavan ended the call and walked into the police station. A man greeted him from within a circular information kiosk. "May I help you, sir?"

"Yes, I have an appointment with Detective Corrinne Kirkpatrick."

"Your name?"

"Stephen Donavan."

The cop consulted a list and handed him a temporary guest pass. "You'll find detective Kirkpatrick on the second floor. There's a desk sergeant just outside the elevator, who can help you."

Corrinne greeted Donavan a bit tersely and led him into the conference room, noting with dread the thick folder he carried. He probably wanted to talk about Caraway and the gun. He wanted to press charges. Or perhaps he wanted a sworn affidavit about the incident, to bring up in his high-profile civil case. Whatever the case, she did not have time for it. Donavan was a friend, neighbor, and fellow church member. And, sure, the city council lawsuit was important, she supposed, but not as serious as murder. She would give him a couple of minutes and lose him as gently as possible.

"So, what can I do for you, Stephen?" she asked, leaning forward in her chair. She noted the time out of the corner of her eye. 9:42. He had till 9:44.

The lawyer began to open the folder, then paused. "Let me first say that I realize what this will look like coming from me. I understand. Hopefully you will understand why I had to report it. Granted, it's a long shot, but who knows?"

"Sure. What have you got?" She was doing a bad job of hiding her impatience.

"As you know, I've been representing the city in FAR's lawsuit regarding the practice of invocation prayer."

"I know."

"It's really quite absurd," he said. "The city has opened it up to any group who wants to sign up. They've had an imam, a rabbi, a Wiccan. Even a secular humanist 'prayed' one week. Still, Don Caraway's not satisfied."

"I'm going to stop you right there, Stephen. I do care about your work—I really do—but the pressure is really on me to solve these two homicides and—"

"This relates to the homicides."

"Really." Corrinne was suddenly interested.

"You see, I've been on this case for more than a year now, and that whole time, I've been archiving FAR's website and social media, trying to put together a pattern of abuse and harassment to present to the jury. I print everything out because Caraway changes things up a lot."

Corrinne's interest began to wane once again.

"At any rate, when I read the name of the second murder victim in the paper this morning, I just about had a heart attack. I immediately went back into my files and found this, from FAR's website." He slid a printout over to Corrinne.

The heading at the top read, "The Shellfish Registry." Beneath it was a brief paragraph explaining that all Christians were hypocritical, by nature of picking and choosing which aspects of their sacred text they wanted to follow, but that this list was the worst of the worst in the Grand Rapids area. What followed was a catalog of several dozen names. Two were highlighted: David Cates and Leslie Doane.

"So what are you saying—Caraway killed them?"

"I'm not saying anything. Except that both men were on this list. I couldn't very well keep that to myself. Besides, you'll notice I'm on the list too, just below Cates. Presumably because I dared provide him legal counsel, which is his constitutional right. I'm a little worried for my own safety, to be in such mortal company."

"You defended him when?"

Donavan sighed, sadly. "It was about ten years ago. David was on the board of a parachurch ministry. It was called the Saving Faith Network. It came out that there had been some sexual abuse and several of the victims charged that the board had intentionally covered it up and kept the information from the police. Honestly, it was one of my least favorite cases. We won, but it never really sat well with me. Between you and me, those board members were culpable."

Corrinne couldn't believe she hadn't uncovered this herself. Then again, they'd had less than a day to focus on Cates before the next body turned up.

"I'm not saying the next body will be on that list," Donavan said. "I pray there is no next body. I just thought you should know."

Corrinne nodded. "I appreciate it very much. May I keep this?"

"Of course," he said, rising from his chair. "We're both busy, so I'll take my leave."

Corrinne shook his hand. "Thanks again, Stephen," she said. When he'd left, she sat and studied the page. Having seen the bad blood between these two men play out at the funeral, she was more than a little bit skeptical. Then again, there it was in black and white. And she didn't exactly have anything else to go on.

She picked up the phone on the conference table and punched in Jackie's extension.

"This is Reese."

"It's Kirkpatrick. I've got someone else for you to look into."

***

Parker had one more stop on his afternoon errand run. He'd already been to Home Depot, where he picked up a bunch of screws, some wood glue, and an electric nail gun. He'd been meaning to become a little handier for years, and this church renovation was the perfect opportunity. Now, for the matter of Corrinne's gift.

Snagging the parking spot right in front of the door, Parker grabbed the manila envelope and fairly bounced his way into Weber

Frame and Engraving. He was in a sensational mood, high on possibilities—new beginnings and old ones resurrected.

"How can I help you?" the ancient man behind the counter asked.

Parker pulled his and Corrinne's marriage license out of the envelope and placed it on the glass counter. "I'd like this framed," he said. "And matted. A real nice job."

The man inspected it. "Newly married, huh?"

"Pretty new. It'll be three months next Thursday."

"I see. Fifty-two years for me."

"Congrats. Anyway, my wife thinks it's stupid to celebrate partial-year anniversaries, so I thought it would be funny for our three-month if I had our license framed and gave it to her then."

The man scratched his head. "So, this is a gag gift?"

"No. I mean, it's a real gift. It's just sort of funny. You know."

The man shook his head. "I don't."

Parker laughed nervously. "Can you do it? Mat and frame it? In a week?"

"Of course. We'll do a great job. Your wife will love it."

"Not likely." Parker laughed again.

The man gave him a pitiful look.

* * *

Jackie wheeled over to Corrinne's desk in a single push from his own. "I've looked into this Caraway guy," he said. "No adult record. Looks like he was in the juvie system, but that's all been sealed. I'd need a court order to get a look. Otherwise, he's pretty clean. Sues a lot of people, but who doesn't these days? What's got him on your radar?"

Corrinne showed him the list.

"This is the best lead we've got," he said. "Which is saying something, 'cause it's not a great lead. But still. You want me to try and unseal the guy's juvie record?"

"Why not? I mean, I doubt any judge would go for it. This is the thinnest of circumstantial evidence. I don't even really know what to do with it."

"I do," Jackie said. "You and me go find this guy and show him the list. See how he reacts. I can read people, CK. We put this in front of him, I'll tell you based on his reaction whether he's worth pursuing as a suspect."

"I don't know . . . "

"Come on! Let the techs do their analysis and the grunts dig through all the world's Margarets, looking for a hit. I'm ready to interview a suspect already."

"You know what? You're right."

* * *

Bridgewater Place was a reflective-glass skyscraper on the west bank of the Grand River—one of the tallest buildings in the city's skyline. It housed retail units, apartments, a hotel and, at the top, two law firms. One of them, Adler & Clark, sublet space to FAR, Inc. Corrinne flashed her badge to the security guard at the desk and she and Jackie boarded the elevator.

Only when the doors parted on the seventeenth floor did Corrinne remember. John Slocum was a partner at Adler & Clark. She prayed she would not see his smarmy face, doubting she could control her tongue. The law firm's receptionist directed them down a wide, high-traffic hall, lined with offices, which would apparently spit them right out at the FAR headquarters.

They were within sight of a small sign bearing the FAR logo when a familiar voice boomed, "What is *she* doing here?" Corrinne wheeled to see Slocum, flanked by young women in form-fitting business skirts that terminated three inches above the knee. "Don't tell me you're still a cop." His cake-eating grin was begging to be knocked down his throat.

"Your eye," Corrinne said. "It's healing nicely. What happened?"

The grin faltered a bit. "Didn't you get the message from the deputy chief?" he said. "I'm untouchable to you."

"Untouchable?" Jackie asked. "Then where'd you get that shiner?"

Slocum frowned. "If you two know what's good for you, you'll—"

"Look, I'm new in town," Jackie said. "Just transferred in. I don't know the history here and I don't know the deputy chief, but I do know when I hear someone threatening two police officers. How about you move along before I Tase you where you stand and let your girlfriends watch you flop around, foaming on the floor. Think you'll look like a big man then?"

Slocum glared.

Jackie pushed. "Did they know a woman did that to your face? Or is that news too?"

The lawyer uttered a few choice words and walked away.

"I didn't need your help with that," Corrinne said.

"I know. It was an empty threat anyway. I don't even carry a Taser."

Corrinne laughed. "I'm trying really hard not to like you, Reese." They continued down the hall.

"Just give in," he said. "I'll wear you down eventually."

FAR, as it turned out, was comprised only of Caraway, the two women with the iPhones, and a young receptionist with a Hitler Youth haircut. The nameplate on his desk simply read TANNYR.

"We're here to see Mr. Caraway," Corrinne told him. "We called a while ago."

Tannyr managed to arch an eyebrow suspiciously at the detectives without looking up from his iPhone. "You have an appointment?"

Jackie inserted his badge between the screen and the receptionist. "Yeah, here's the confirmation number. Tell him we're here."

The kid rolled his eyes and scampered off behind a cubicle wall. A moment later, Caraway emerged. He'd added bright red socks to the blue Converse sneakers, yet still buttoned his jacket like Don Draper as he walked. When his eyes fell on Corrinne, he stopped and made a broad improv face that said, *Oh, I see what's going on here.*

"Mr. Caraway, my name is Det. Kirkpatrick. This is Det. Reese. We're with the GRPD."

"I remember you," Caraway said. "Is this about Mr. Donavan the other day? Because I still have that footage and I haven't ruled out pressing charges of my own."

"No, it's not. Is there somewhere we could ask you a few questions?"

He sighed. "Sure, we have a conference room. Follow me." He took them back behind the cubicles into a cramped little room lit with Edison bulbs. The reclaimed barn wood table barely fit and Corrinne found it difficult to insert herself into one of the six chairs around it.

"Do you want to disarm me before we talk?" Caraway asked, smirking.

"No, just keep your hands on the table. And just for future reference, when you interact with a police officer, you need to let them know at the outset if you're carrying."

"Good to know." He furrowed his brow. "Hey, should my lawyer be here for this?"

"Did you do something illegal?" Jackie asked.

"No. But he's just down the hall. Maybe I should call him."

"Let me guess," Corrinne said, "John Slocum."

"How'd you know?"

"It just fits. You can give him an excuse to bill you if you want or we can just chat for a few minutes. If I ask you anything that makes you uncomfortable, we can hit pause and you bring in the attorney. Sound good?"

"Sure."

Corrinne handed him a copy of the "Shellfish Registry," the two victims' names highlighted, and let him sit with it for a moment.

"Seriously? This is why you're here?"

"You target twenty-six people there," Jackie said. "Now two of them are dead. How do you think that looks?"

"I didn't *target* anyone," Caraway said. "This is about shaming people who use shame as a weapon. It's not a threat; it's just a list of scumbag hypocrites."

Corrinne tried to lean back in the chair, but it wouldn't budge. "Did you just call two recently murdered men 'scumbags?'"

"Because they were. I'm sorry they're dead—I don't wish anyone dead—but the fact that they are doesn't suddenly make them saints."

"I'm curious: what did they do to land on your list?"

"Cates covered up a sex scandal, and not the consensual kind. He was the chairman of the board that swept it all under the rug. Told the parents involved just to *forgive* the guy and then moved him to a new city with a new group of kids. Does that sound like a good person to you?"

"And what about Leslie Doane?" Jackie asked.

"Oh, right. Mister Positive. Mister Shoot-for-the-Stars. Mister Put-Two-Prostitutes-in-the-Hospital."

"Tell me about that," Corrinne said.

"I talked to one of them. Nicole Something. Saunders? It's in my files. When he wasn't promoting clean living, Leslie liked getting rough with women. Especially addicts, because they'd always trade their silence for money to feed their habits." He raised an accusing finger to Corrinne. "I called you people, by the way. Told you where he'd be, what he'd be doing to that poor girl, and he was back speaking in middle schools the next day." He laughed. "You know what? I changed my mind. I actually am glad he's dead."

"Do you really want to say that?" Corrinne asked. "Considering what happened to the guy and your connection to him?" She indicated the paper.

He pointed to the URL at the bottom of the page. "You know what the first W in WWW stand for? Worldwide."

"That's actually the first two Ws," Jackie corrected.

"Because it's worldwide. This was a public list. Anyone could have seen it and decided to act on it. That doesn't make me guilty of anything. I didn't encourage violence. I didn't even put their addresses out there. I'm not ashamed of what I did."

"Then why'd you take it down?" Corrinne asked.

"Your friend, Stephen Donavan. He sent me a Cease and Desist. It wasn't worth the trouble of fighting him on it. He was just trying to spread us thin because we've got a small operation here and he's got the whole city behind him." He slapped his hand down on the paper. "You know, guys like Donavan abuse the system, trying to force their religious agenda on everyone, throwing their muscle around. But the tide is turning. That guy's a dying breed—he and his minions." He looked at the two detectives, as if just realizing who they were. "You know what? I think I do want my lawyer here—*because* I didn't do anything wrong."

"Don't bother," Corrinne said. "We've heard enough. Appreciate your time, Mr. Caraway."

* * *

The Tribunal descended the stairs to the basement. The train of his robe followed a few steps behind. He knew this task would be easier without the vestments, but he couldn't start blurring the lines now. Even though the man was already dead and there was no one to frighten down here. No one to impress. No one from whom to hide his identity. Still, it mattered.

He walked differently while he wore the hood and robe. Every step slow, careful, grim. He felt his heartrate increase as he approached the old chest freezer in the corner, audibly chugging along to keep the body cold. He opened the lid and looked down into the frostbitten eyes of the condemned man. Frozen blood crystalized around the wounds in his chest.

"Rise and shine," he said. "It's your big day."

8

Corrinne was in the office before seven Thursday morning. She hadn't been able to sleep, thinking about what Caraway had told them. From his point of view, both victims were practically subhuman. Being dead didn't make them saints, he'd said. And yet, everyone else she'd spoken to, and all the news coverage she'd seen, had portrayed them as exactly that. There was something there. She couldn't help but think it might be the key to the whole investigation.

Her gut told her Caraway had nothing to do with the death of those two men. Not directly. The man stood firmly—obnoxiously—on principle and the absolute assurance that he was in the right in every given situation, but not like a narcissist or a sociopath. He was grounded. Caraway might have been a jerk, but he wasn't a psycho.

Whoever burned one man alive and hung the other as a trophy in a public park had both a deep vendetta and a screw loose—perhaps a victim of the kind of hypocrisy he or she now sought to expose? One thing was clear: the two victims had not been chosen at random. She shuffled a few papers and re-read the inscription from the bogus Artistry placard: "Ode to Margaret: This piece is a tribute to all the righteous, whitewashed tombs, the white-toothed grins, and the black hearts within." These were the words of a self-righteous ideologue.

Corrinne had already tracked down the victims in the scandal that Cates had helped cover up, although she was not sure what she'd do with the information. Did it make sense to force those people to relive such a dark chapter in their lives, while implying that they might be the monster in the present equation? Victim-blaming had always been something for which Corrinne had zero patience.

And then there was the matter of the two prostitutes Caraway had mentioned. Nicole Chandler was the name of the woman arrested with Doane at the motel. Most likely the same Nikki he'd mentioned. That was a lead worth following and, at the moment, those were few and far between. Lab results—rushed by order of the chief—were now coming in at more than a trickle and, so far, nothing had moved the ball forward. Jackie was analyzing ATM and traffic cams in the area and combing through geotagged pictures on social media, but they couldn't even determine exactly when the body had appeared, let alone find a clue as to who put it there.

At the thought of Jackie, Corrinne smiled to herself. He had arrived only ten minutes after she did this morning and handed her an Americano—her drink. She was starting to warm to the guy, despite herself. He was single-minded, sarcastic, driven, and married to the job. A year ago, that would have perfectly described her. Happily married to the job. Back then, she'd have made Jackie work for her respect, at least for a couple months. Then they would have dated for a while, before mutually deciding it had run its course. She'd been there before. Now she was married. To a pastor. *What?*

A new e-mail bleeped in.

> FROM: hdunleavy@grpd.grandrapids.gov
> TO: ckirkpatrick@grpd.grandrapids.gov
> SUBJECT: Update on Cates and Doane Homicides
>
> I'm meeting with the chief this afternoon. Please provide me with a summary of where we stand on these investigations. Allen mentioned that you and Reese interviewed a suspect yesterday. Anything there?
>
> -Capt. Dunleavy

Great. So now the captain was talking directly with Vivien about the case. Corrinne felt a migraine coming on. Today would be the day. She'd track down this Nicole Chandler and sort out exactly what had happened. She'd put together a working motive. Material evidence may be a Mardis Gras of dead ends, but her intuition had solved plenty of cases in the past when all else had failed. She just needed a day with no new bodies, to get some momentum and carry it around the corner.

That's when the call came in.

Thursday, October 26

* * *

East Beltline Avenue, one of only two major north-south arteries through the city, was once the home of several sprawling orchards. But the proliferation of new strip malls and chain restaurants had crowded out all but one, and even it was shrinking a bit each year, continually trading land for another season to try and recover the magic. This was the peak time, when families flocked in from all around for games, hayrides, and a front-row seat to the magic of the apple press.

Thankfully, before the first hayride of the morning left the barn, a farmhand had taken a four-wheeler out to inspect some ailing trees and happened upon the dead man with the stakes in his heart, propped up in the branches. He looked to be mid-sixties, a little chubby, with a thin beard.

"World's Greatest Dad," Vivien read, from the man's T-shirt. "Oh good. I was hoping this would get sadder."

"I'm no doctor," Jackie said. "But I think he might have been stabbed to death." No one so much as chortled. Four large wooden dowels, about three feet long, were buried in the left side of the man's chest.

"So this is like a daily thing now," Vivien observed. "I guess I should cancel my weekend plans."

"Seriously," Corrinne said, "none of us gets a day off until we've got someone in custody. Jackie, you were first on scene. We got an ID?"

"Name's Garrett Appelt. Retired CPA, serial grandpa."

"What?"

"That's what it says on his LinkUp page. 'Retired CPA, Serial Grandpa.' He went missing ten days ago."

"That doesn't ring a bell," Vivien said.

"Yeah, he lives in Lansing," Jackie said. "I mean, he used to."

Corrinne chewed her lip for a moment, making a decision. "We're getting spread too thin here," she said. "Allen, you take this scene. Jackie, get with LPD—whoever was on the missing person case. We need to know whatever they knew. Today, this guy is your only concern. Both of you."

"And what are you going to do?" Vivien asked.

"I'm going to find me a prostitute."

Corrinne tried for three hours to locate the current address of Nicole Chandler. The Secretary of State had her in a basement apartment in Heritage Hill, which was now occupied by four college kids. Consumers Energy last showed her living on Diamond Street. Again, no dice. Corrinne burned through four phone numbers, all disconnected.

She knew what she had to do. Sure, she dreaded the thought, but she'd already wasted a chunk of a day with nothing to show for it. Picking up the phone, she dialed the number for FAR.

"You've reached FAR, protecting your freedom from religion. This is Tannyr. How may I help you?"

"This is Det. Corrinne Kirkpatrick. I need to speak with Mr. Caraway."

"One moment."

At least three minutes later, Caraway's voice filled her ear. "Detective." He sounded oddly gleeful. "How are you today?"

"Not great. Look, I need—"

"You know, I decided to talk to my attorney about our conversation. It turns out he knows you. According to him, you tend toward excessive force."

"I didn't call to talk about John Slocum and what I did to his face while he was resisting arrest," she said. "I called to ask for your help with something."

"Always happy to help the cause of law and order. What can I do for you?"

"You mentioned that you met with one of the prostitutes Mr. Doane allegedly assaulted. Nicole Chandler. Any chance you still have contact information for her?"

"We probably do, although that was a year and a half ago and she did seem like the kind of person who might relocate frequently. I'll ask Gwen to dig that up and send it your way."

"Thank you, Mr. Caraway."

"My pleasure."

As she hung up, Vivien walked up and dropped a file folder on her desk. "Here's what I've got so far, if you want to have a look."

"Thanks. Anything jump out at you?"

"Appelt was an ordinary guy, except that he was practically a saint. He took in a bunch of orphans and stuff. But look at this." She flipped open the folder. "The guy disappeared on Monday afternoon. When we found him, his phone was in his pocket and there was a call made yesterday morning."

Corrinne perked up. "To who?"

"Georgio's Restaurant, in Alger Heights. I found the hostess who talked to him. Appelt—or whoever it was—made a reservation for Saturday night, for twenty people. Asked about big meals they might serve for the whole table. Apparently, he kept saying it was going to be a 'real feast.' Weird, right?"

"I don't know," Corrinne said. "At this point, weird is normal."

* * *

Parker sat in the living room, trying not to look at his watch. He knew his wife was under loads of pressure—more than he could understand. But this was date night, an almost sacred pact they'd made six months earlier. Corrinne had proposed marriage on a Thursday night and they had promised each other Thursday nights would always be dedicated to spending time together. Parker had a reservation at Leo's for 6:00. It was now almost 6:20.

The door burst open and Corrinne came chugging in, her bag over her shoulder and several folders in her hand. "Hi," she said absently as she walked past him into the office they shared.

"Um, hi?" He got up and followed her into the office. "Everything okay?"

"Not really." She was scanning through the contents of one of the folders, a page at a time. "Vivien just dumped all this stuff on me. I don't know if you heard, but we had another one today."

"I did," Parker said. "Look, if you want to call off date night, I understand. Seems like you have a lot on your plate."

"Date night!" Corrinne mashed her hands into her face. "I forgot. I'm sorry. Oh, and look at you; you're all dressed up."

He shrugged. "It's okay. Want me to order a pizza?"

"Yes, that sounds good. We can have date night here, okay? Just give me, like, forty-five minutes to go over this. An hour, tops."

"All right. No hurry."

"That was good," Corrinne said, adding an uneaten crust to the three already on her plate. "Better than that tilapia you would have ordered at Leo's. Admit it."

"Yeah, right." He reached over and squeezed her hand. "I really am sorry you're under so much pressure. Is there anything I can do to make things easier for you right now?"

"No, I'm alright. I'm just . . . The captain's thinking of giving the case to Allen. She's got the chief and the mayor and the FBI breathing down her neck and she's paying it forward."

"The FBI? Seriously?"

"Yeah. They mentioned you, by the way."

He laughed. "Of course they did."

She fiddled with the pile of crusts. "We just can't catch a break with this case. We've got giant wheels, corpses as modern art, grandpas staked through the heart like vampires. But no traction. Then Ruthless Ruth called me today, and told me I was to come to her place for tea tomorrow morning. That really clinched the day for me."

"Yikes."

"Yeah, like I have time for that. But I don't want to make things harder for you."

"Maybe she wants to bury the hatchet," Parker suggested.

"Or bury three stakes in my heart." She winced at her own joke. "I don't know. It's clear to me that I'm not up to snuff as a pastor's wife. People like Ruth have all sorts of expectations. But I used to be able to tell myself, at least I'm good at my real job. Now I'm afraid I might—" She actually choked up.

Parker froze. He'd never seen his wife cry before. And she wasn't really crying now. He could almost see her pushing the lump in her throat physically back down into her body, cartoon-style. She dabbed at her eyes with a napkin and recaptured her composure.

"Sorry," she said. "You don't need all this on your shoulders with everything at the church and your book coming out and everything." Quieter she added, "Maybe just pray that God will hand me a breakthrough in the case soon." With that, she stood up, gathered their plates, and said, "This was nice. But I have to get back to work."

* * *

Parker lay in bed, waiting for his wife to fall asleep. It was no mystery when it happened, as her breathing always went ragged and loud the moment she drifted off. In fact, it was less drifting and more like driving into a brick wall. He slowly, carefully, got up out of bed and made his way around to Corrinne's side. The floors were old and creaky and he seemed to be finding all the loudest possible footfalls. There, next to the bed, was her bag. He lifted it carefully to his shoulder and made for the landing.

From the doorway, he looked back at her. She was still breathing deeply, but her brow was furrowed, as if even the reprieve of sleep could not offer a break from her troubles. Parker descended the stairs, as quietly as possible, and entered their home office. He had to do this quickly, both because Corrinne might wake up at any time and because he knew it was a stupid thing to do and he was afraid common sense would get the better of him.

Opening her bag, he pulled out several folders, flipping through the contents of each until he had determined which three represented the current wave of murders. He got a little light-headed at the sight of some particularly graphic crime scene photos. Still, he pushed ahead. He couldn't stand seeing his wife like this, stuck in a horrible situation, about to break.

It couldn't just be a coincidence, he had decided. The night after his notoriously private wife bears her soul and shares her struggles with this case, Parker would be hooking up with the Jesuits Militant in Detroit. It was providence, he told himself, as he began to copy each photo and document on their all-in-one printer. Of course, Corrinne would never agree to let Father Michael weigh in on the case. As they say, it's sometimes better to ask forgiveness than permission.

He would just let the Vatican agents have a quick look at the evidence. They'd have a fresh perspective and, of course, elite training in investigating. Then he'd shred all of the copies and burn the shredded documents in the fireplace. Best case scenario, they'd notice something everyone had missed—something that would help Corrinne blow the whole case open. Worst case scenario . . .

Parker stopped thinking and just kept making his copies.

9

Father Michael enveloped Parker in a bear hug that threatened to break him in half.

"So good to see you, buddy!" He gave Parker the once over and then patted his belly, adding, "Looks like the wife's cooking is having an effect on you."

Parker laughed. "I don't think Corrinne has ever cooked a day in her life."

Father Ignatius shook his head sadly.

"You want to get some coffee?" Parker asked. "I passed a Starbucks on the way up here."

"That I do, my friend," Michael said.

Parker and Michael ordered lattes, Ignatius a cup of English Breakfast tea, and the three of them spent half an hour ping-ponging between reminiscing about the events that had brought them together and catching up on the latest. Michael asked a lot of questions about married life and talked at length about how boring the conference he'd just attended had been.

"I am happy to hear about your church," Father Ignatius said. "I've woken up more than once in a cold sweat, thinking about the sacrilege we saw there. If only I could have had some time with the men who did that."

"And the book," Michael added. "We want signed copies. And none of this 'Best Wishes' crap. Something personal."

Parker laughed. "You got it."

"How about the wife? How's her career going?"

"Now that you bring it up," Parker said, reaching into his briefcase and retrieving the fat manila folder full of photocopies, "I actually wanted to get your take on something."

* * *

Corrinne stood outside Ruth's door for at least ninety seconds before ringing the bell. There were so many reasons she didn't want to be here. First, she didn't have the time. Three homicides demanded her attention and who knew when the next body would drop? Secondly, she didn't like Ruth, who was always quick to deliver a poison dart wrapped in a cloak of politeness and concern. Mostly, though, the whole thing felt like a trap. Her detective's intuition told her to draw her gun and be ready for anything. She overrode it.

The door swung open and a wall of heavy perfume came floating out. "Hello, Corrinne," Ruth said. "Come on in. I've got tea and cucumber sandwiches in the dining room."

Corrinne hated cucumbers. And she wasn't big on tea. "Sounds delightful," she said.

* * *

"And it says here that they actually cut the guy's tongue out." Parker shuddered and handed a copy of the autopsy report to Father Michael. He'd been handing him pages, one at a time, for the past twenty minutes, as they talked through the first crime scene.

"Just give me all of it." Michael held out his hand.

Parker hesitated. As long as he was in control of the documents, he felt better about this. "Um, okay." He slid the folder across the table.

Michael began flipping through the documents, handing each, in turn, to Father Ignatius, who also studied them. "I want another latte," he said. "Be a champ and get me one, would you?"

When Parker returned with two more drinks, he found the priests quietly talking, pointing here and there at different documents spread out on the table. "Well," he joked, "did you solve it?"

"Yes," Father Ignatius answered.

"That may be an overstatement," Father Michael said. "But we definitely found the pattern the police have missed."

Parker felt a rush of excitement. "Tell me!"

He held up the police report for David Cates. "St. John of Pomuk," he said. Pointing at a picture of Leslie Doane, he said, "St. Margaret of

Cortona." And to the third victim, "St. Jude Thaddeus."

"Huh?"

"Look, it was right in front of them the whole time. This prayer card is St. John of Pomuk." He found the photo of the card and moved it to the top of the stack. "See the stole he's wearing? That's the sign of a confessor. And he's holding a palm branch, meaning he was martyred. And, of course, the five stars around his head for the stars that appeared in the sky the night he was killed."

"Right," Parker deadpanned. "No idea how they missed that."

"Look," Michael said, "everything about this crime screams John of Pomuk."

"You're going to have to fill me in here, guys," Parker said, laughing. "I've never even heard of him."

"Well, that makes sense," Michael said. "I mean, he's the patron saint of discretion, so he tries to stay on the DL."

"John of Pomuk," Ignatius explained, "was a priest in Bohemia, in the Fourteenth Century. The royal family were among his flock. When King Wenceslas began to suspect that his wife was having an affair, he demanded that John divulge the secrets of the confessional. When he refused, the king had him arrested and brought to the dungeon beneath his castle. There, the king tortured him with fire for days."

"Wait, you don't mean Good King Wenceslas, like the song?"

Michael shook his head. "This is, like, *bad* King Wenceslas. The Third."

"Wenceslas IV," Ignatius corrected.

"At first it was a carrot versus stick type thing," Michael said. "Do what I say and I'll give you riches and glory. Don't and you'll be slowly burned to death." He took a sip of his drink and Ignatius jumped back in.

"When John proved himself unwilling, the king cut out his tongue and set him ablaze. Then, to try and cover his crime, he had the priest chained to a large iron wheel and dropped from a bridge into the River Vltava." He sifted through the papers until he found a handwritten report. "The date on Mr. Cates's watch: May 16. That's St. John's feast day."

Parker pulled a pen from his breast pocket. "Okay, can you say all that again? Only this time, slower."

* * *

"This is a lovely home." Corrinne practically gagged as she forced another cucumber sandwich down her throat.

"You already said that, dear."

"Oh. Sorry."

Ruth sipped the last of her tea and set the cup on the saucer with a clink. She looked up at Corrinne, smiled apologetically for a moment, and then said, "I believe in the value of forthrightness and honesty. Don't you?"

"I . . . suppose."

"Good. As the Scriptures say, *better is open rebuke than hidden love.*"

"Here we go," Corrinne mumbled.

"So I'm going to be honest. I wanted to have you over for tea because, frankly, I'm afraid our pastor may be unequally yoked."

"What? No. I mean, he's eccentric in certain ways and it's kind of weird how he completely freaks out when he sees a spider, but he's not crazy."

Ruth smiled patiently. "You see, that's just what I'm talking about. A real Christian would know that 'unequally yoked' describes a believer marrying a nonbeliever. It's from Second Corinthians."

"Oh."

"I'm not accusing you of anything, mind you. I'm just concerned. For example, I understand that you did not attend church much before you came to Hope." When Corrinne didn't answer, she added, "just a few months before the two of you were married."

Corrinne took a deep breath and steadied her voice. "Well, I'm there every week now. Several times a week."

"And are you attending for yourself or for Pastor Parker?"

"For God," Corrinne said, sarcasm dripping.

Ruth grasped her head, as if having an epiphany, careful not to muss her hair. "I just realized it." She smiled and squeezed Corrinne's hand. "There's precedent for this. Ruth did the same thing."

"Are you seriously talking about yourself in the third person?"

"No, in the Scriptures. The Book of Ruth. She went with her mother-in-law back to Bethlehem and told her, 'Your people will be my people. Your God will be my God.' And, of course the name Ruth means *friend*."

"I would not have guessed that," Corrinne said.

Ruth poured herself some more tea. "You did the same thing," she said. "You followed your husband from whatever heathen background and now you're in our midst. I should be more understanding. Of course you aren't going to fit in right away. It's not fair for us to expect that of you."

Corrinne bit her tongue.

* * *

"St. Margaret is just as clear," Michael said. "For starters, the sign says, 'Ode to Margaret.' That's a big one. And her feast day? Also May 16, like it says on the sign. Plus, she preached against vice, just like this Leslie Doane guy did. And you even see her life reflected in this guy's death."

"How's that?"

"Margaret was very lascivious as a young woman," Ignatius said, shaking his head sadly. "When she was converted, she joined the Franciscans. She was so haunted by her past sins that she wore a noose around her neck as a sign of public penance and would frequently have to be restrained from cutting and mutilating her own face. She did not want to be beautiful because she thought she would cause men to lust after her."

"Like the noose and the red marks all over Doane's face." Parker wrote down the basics, double-checking the spelling of Cortona. "This is great, you guys. I mean, I have no idea what it means, but I'm sure it will help Corrinne narrow her search. Bizarre stuff. What about the last victim?"

* * *

"Maybe I could take you under my wing," Ruth said. "Show you what's expected of a pastor's wife."

Corrinne balked. "That's nice of you to offer, Ruth, but I'm afraid I don't really have any extra time at the moment."

"Did you know that a number of single women left the church when Parker married you? They were here for the wrong reason, I suspect. Maybe you were too, at first. But now you're here to stay and we should embrace you. So you didn't take your husband's last name. And you don't know how to play the piano. And maybe your clothes are a little," she wavered, "worldly. All the same, you're what we've got." She beamed at her guest, as if they had just shared a major victory.

Corrinne felt something snap inside of her. "Are you friggin' kidding me?" she demanded. Her voice echoed through the dining room. "You're just insulting me over and over again while pretending that you're accepting me. I'm so sick of this. I'm sick of you."

Ruth fanned herself with her napkin for a moment, her mouth hanging open.

"Oh, what?" Corrinne said. "Are you gonna get *the vapors*?"

"I don't appreciate your language or your tone," Ruth clucked.

Corrinne stood. "I don't care. Because clearly nothing I do or say will be good enough for you. So why hold back? You like honesty and forthrightness? How's this for open rebuke: you're a miserable old woman! And you try your best to share your misery with everyone else. Oh, and these sandwiches are terrible. What, are they held together with caulk?" She hesitated for a moment when she saw the tears brewing in the older woman's eyes. "I'm out of here," she said, clomping out the door.

The moment her feet hit the front porch she felt a massive wave of regret. She'd have given anything to take back the past thirty seconds, being perfectly aware that most of what she'd just unleashed on Ruth had nothing to do with the old woman. Rather, it was the breaking of the dam. She couldn't yell at Captain Dunleavy. She couldn't yell at

Vivien. It was pointless to yell at Jackie. Sure, Ruth was a passive-aggressive chore of a woman, but mostly she was just in the wrong place at the wrong time.

Turning back toward the door, she toyed with the idea of trying to make amends. No. She wasn't built for that. Apologizing, sharing her feelings, explaining why she'd said what she'd said. Besides, there were plenty of things awaiting her attention that were far more important than this.

* * *

"Father Ignatius spotted St. Jude," Michael said. "It's a little more subtle."

"Subtle?" Parker said. "The guy was hanging in an apple tree with three stakes through his heart."

"I mean the connection is more subtle."

Parker rubbed his chin. "I'm still trying to figure out how nobody at all noticed this and called in a tip."

"There are hundreds and hundreds of canonized saints," Michael said, shrugging.

"And you know all of them?"

"No," Ignatius said. "Father Xavier knew all of them."

The three men were silent for a moment, thinking of the priest who had lost his life a year ago while trying to save Parker's.

Finally, Parker spoke. "I'm surprised they haven't replaced him yet. Didn't you say you guys always work in teams of three?"

"Not anymore," Michael said. "Looks like the Jesuits Militant are being phased out. Even with a Jesuit pope. I mean, this guy doesn't have the stomach for what we do. He's all puppy dogs and rainbows."

"Michael," Ignatius reprimanded, his eyes harsh.

"Sorry." Father Michael made the sign of the cross. "So your last guy, he was killed with three javelins to the heart. Considering that he was found in a tree, I first thought it might be a reference to Absalom, King David's son."

"Right," Parker said, "caught by his hair in a tree and speared to death by Joab."

"Exactly. But Ignatius saw this thing with the phone call." He dug out a copy of a report. "Whoever killed him used his phone to make a reservation at a restaurant for tomorrow. October 28. Apparently, he specifically said it was a *feast*. Reiterated it more than once." He looked at the page. "Whoever wrote this has really nice handwriting."

"Focus, man," Parker said.

"Sorry. The feast of St. Jude Thaddeus is October 28."

Parker smiled and wrote down a few more notes. "Corrinne is going to be thrilled, you guys." He pointed at Michael. "She might actually start to like you."

"Oh, you're too kind."

Father Ignatius nudged his fellow priest. "Don't look now," he said quietly, "but we are being hunted."

Parker wheeled his head around.

"I said *don't look*. Judas Priest, Protestant."

"Sorry," Parker said.

"Who we got?" Michael asked, pretending to be sorting through the papers.

"Father Sacha and, I believe, one of his Knights of Malta."

"They run this town," Michael said. "We should have gotten the okay even to layover here."

"Never," Ignatius said.

"The Knights of Malta?" Parker asked, accepting the papers from Michael and returning them to the folder. "I thought you guys were on the same side."

"Same shape," Father Michael said, "but it's a polygon, man. Many-sided. There's some bad blood there."

"They have not spotted us yet; I will flank them," Ignatius said, furtively moving from the table, out into the chaos of foot traffic.

"Well, this has been fun," Michael said. "Let's do this again soon. If your wife really does warm up to me, you should come out to Rome. The Vatican will blow your mind. I can bring you into the secret archives of the library if you sign an NDO." He reached for the folder. "You mind if I take this with me? I've got a ten-hour flight ahead of me. I might find something else."

"Um, I'm not sure."

"Wait, your wife *did* clear this, right? You showing us all this stuff?"

Parker panicked a little. "Uh, yeah, it . . . was cleared," he said. After all, even Corrinne had said it: having never been released, Parker was still an expert consultant with the GRPD. Still, he knew it was still a lie and he felt the guilt immediately.

"All right then." Michael stuffed the folder into his carry-on, just as Father Ignatius walked up and placed a hand on his shoulder.

"We're needed elsewhere, my son."

Michael drained his coffee and slid his athletic frame from the booth. He gave Parker the briefest of hugs, more a chest bump and whack than a real embrace.

"Good catching up. Tell the wife I said hi. And let me know how this thing works out."

Parker offered his hand to Ignatius, who clasped it firmly and resisted his attempt to shake. "Christ be with you, Protestant," he said. "And good luck with the serial killer."

"You say that like it's normal."

"As long as I've known you, it has been."

* * *

The Tribunal pulled open the trap door and descended the staircase. He could hear whimpering below. It filled him with doubt. This time was different. A woman. Somehow, that didn't seem right. Then again, it was certainly not right for the Inquisition to discriminate. The whitewashed monsters came in all sizes, shapes, and sexes. Plus it was 2017. Time for equal pay.

He flipped the switch and the woman squeezed her eyes shut against the harsh light.

"The Tribunal finds you guilty, Bibiana," he said. She tried to shout something, but the gag in her mouth swallowed the words. "You have something to say in your defense?" he asked from behind the hood. "It's too late. You've already been condemned."

The woman's voice dropped in volume, but she continued trying to speak.

"Or maybe you have some last words. I suppose that should be allowed." As he removed the gag from her mouth, he said, "Just remember what I told you. No one can hear you down here. No need to shout."

"My name's not Bibiana," she pleaded. "You have the wrong person. I swear."

"The wrong person? I know of six innocent children who would beg to differ." Her face went chalk white and she gaped for a moment before beginning to sob.

"Yes," he said. "You should weep and wail. Because true justice has finally caught up to you."

10

Parker knew it was going to be a good night. He prepared Mahi Mahi tacos, one of his wife's favorite dishes. He had all the ingredients laid out by 3:45 and so spent the next hour on Wikipedia, researching the three saints Michael had mentioned and writing up as formal and professional a report as he could about the connections between each crime scene and its patron saint.

Corrinne arrived home at 6:15, digging her fingertips into her left shoulder, with a pained expression on her face.

"I have had the worst day," she said.

"Well," Parker said, "I think I can help you have a really, really good night."

Corrinne dropped her bag on the couch. "Oh, honey. I'm sorry, I'm just too tired."

"No, no. I'm making dinner. And I have some big news. Why don't you sit down and have a glass of wine and I'll let you know when it's ready?"

As they ate, Corrinne walked Parker through her day, including the blow-up with Ruthless Ruth, although she was scant on details when it came to what exactly she'd said to the woman before storming out. Before long, the tacos were mostly eaten and the wine was refilled and Corrinne finally looked something like her usual laid-back self.

"This is nice," she said. "Having someone to come home to and unload." She tipped her head and smiled at him. "You know, I'm feeling less tired already."

Parker grinned. "I like where you're going there, but first I have to tell you something huge."

"Oh, right! Let's hear the big news. Is it about your book? Are you gonna be on *Good Morning America*?"

"No, actually, it's about your case."

"What do you mean?"

"Well, as you know, I spent some time with Michael and Ignatius today." Corrinne's face fell from a hopeful smile to a defensive snarl. "I know. I know you don't like him. But we wound up talking about some of these murders and that card you showed me and—"

"Parker, that's confidential. You shouldn't be discussing that with anyone."

"I know," Parker said. "But you're going to be so happy when you hear—"

"I'm in hot enough water as it is, between the captain and the stinkin' FBI. What were you thinking?"

Parker squirmed a bit. "I mean, most of the stuff we talked about was on the news anyway. Kind of public knowledge."

"*Most* of the stuff?"

"Well, I mean, there was the prayer card and . . . "

Corrinne drained her wine and slammed the glass down. "This is not okay, Parker. Boundaries!"

"You said yourself I was never let go as a police consultant. I was just—"

"You're not going to charm your way out of this."

Parker plopped the report he'd typed onto the table. "Don't you even want to see what they found?"

She grabbed it and skimmed the first page. "*Saints*? Parker, this isn't like last time. There are no crosses, no pentagrams, no whatever-you-call-those-things tattooed on victim's bodies. Okay? I don't need priests. I need for me and my team to focus up and do some police work without worrying that my husband's blabbing confidential information to some Vatican stooge who's not even supposed to be in the country!"

Their landline rang. Corrinne grabbed it off the cradle. "Hello? Uh huh . . . Yeah, the inspector's right here." She held the handset out to him. "It's for you, Lestrade. I'll see you later."

Parker covered the mouthpiece. "Where are you going?"

"Back to work."

"On Friday night?"

"Crime has no weekend," she said.

He put the phone to his ear and practically yelled, "What?"

"Rev. Saint, it's Jeremy McLean again. From the *City Beat Paper*. I figured it was safely past dinner hour. Wondering if you'd like to get together for an interview. I know your book comes out Wednesday. Just so happens we have an issue hitting stands that day; I could squeeze you in if you want. Anything I ask you would be couched in the context of the book. What do you say—you ready to get back in the spotlight?"

"Sounds good. When do you want to meet?"

* * *

Corrinne finished reading Parker's summary for the third time and set the four stapled pages down on her desk. She was still mad at him, at least intellectually, but the rage in her gut had been replaced with pure excitement. There was no denying it: this was the breakthrough she'd been waiting for. It accounted for every weird detail, everything on the Artistry sign, even the odd dates, although it didn't explain the reference to All Souls' Day. If it had been All Saints' Day, which fell on November 1, that would have made more sense.

She Googled each of the three saints in turn and began jotting her own notes. Despite the undeniable connection, she still had no idea what it meant. And then she saw it. John of Pomuk, Patron Saint of Discretion. He hadn't disclosed something and he'd paid the price. Just like Cates had buried the sins of two men in the Saving Faith Network and had now seemingly been killed for it. She clicked back over to an entry on St. Margaret. She was patron saint of the falsely accused, the mentally ill, single mothers, and despairing prostitutes.

There it was. She'd been on the right track, trying to locate Nicole Chandler. Caraway's assistant had e-mailed her the contact info from his records that afternoon and Corrinne had left a message in what seemed like a functioning voicemail box. Tomorrow, the three detectives would not rest until they found her and heard her story.

The last guy, though. Garrett Appelt. She wasn't sure what was going on with him. Jude Thaddeus was the patron saint of lost causes.

But the old guy seemed like anything but. Vivien had even referred to him as a saint. Corrinne dropped her pen. Don Caraway's words echoed in her head. "Just because they're dead doesn't make them saints."

She'd officially removed Caraway from their list of suspects when she found that Appelt was not on his "Shellfish Registry" list of hypocrites. But now, he was back on her radar.

* * *

The nice thing about Saturdays was that they had the bullpen to themselves. Alvarez was on call and Irvine was looking into an overnight shooting. The rest of the team was enjoying the weekend.

Corrinne texted both Vivien and Jackie at 6:30 AM, telling them to be in the conference room by 8:00. Vivien walked in at 8:05.

"The reason I've called you here to the Command Center," Corrinne began.

Jackie burst out laughing. "*Command Center?*"

"This guy Ketcham used to call it that," Vivien explained. "Of course, he turned out to be a serial killer, so . . . "

"I gave it the name," Corrinne said. "Me. Now listen up, because I'm about to blow your minds and explain every little detail of these three murders in less than fifteen minutes." She clipped an icon of St. John of Pomuk to the white board and opened her notes, which she'd finished polishing up at about 3:30 AM. As she walked them through the first crime scene, the two detectives digested the information without a word. When she finished, Jackie just sat back in his chair and said, "Whoa."

"Yeah," Vivien said. "Where did you find this stuff?"

"My husband's a preacher," she said coyly, "I know these things."

"What about Leslie Doane?"

Corrinne smirked. "We wondered who Margaret was. Meet St. Margaret of Cortona." She popped an icon of the sainted woman over the image of John. "Patron saint of despairing prostitutes. That's right, we're bringing in Nicole Chandler today. Whoever finds her gets to do the interview. I want to know every prostitute this scumbag may have led to despair, and I want to know today."

"Scumbag?" Jackie said. "Correct me if I'm wrong, but we're supposed to be solving this guy's murder, not trying to convict him."

"We're getting inside the perp's head," Vivien said. "It's our best shot." She nodded at Corrinne, who nodded back, but couldn't help but wonder if Jackie was on to something. "Scumbag" is what Caraway had called Leslie Doane. Perhaps she needed to take a step back and regain some perspective.

"So what saint is my vic?" Vivien asked.

"Let's see. . . St. Jude Thaddeus."

The perma-smirk disappeared from Jackie's face and his hand went to his throat.

"What is it?" Corrinne asked.

"Nothing."

"I will beat it out of you," Vivien said.

Jackie sighed and unbuttoned his collar. He reached down into his shirt and pulled out a silver chain with a small charm on the end.

The two women crowded in, trying to make out the tiny inscription. Corrinne tapped out. She'd need her reading glasses.

"Jude Thaddeus," Vivien read. "Pray for us, St. Jude."

"He's the patron saint of the Chicago PD," Jackie explained, a bit defensively. "We all wore these. Everybody."

"He's also the patron saint of lost causes," Corrinne said.

"So you've got two reasons to wear that thing," Vivian said.

"Well, if Jackie didn't do it, I'm not sure of the connection with this one," Corrinne said. "You learn anything new, Allen?"

"A couple things," she said. "First off, according to his obituary online, Appelt took in more than thirty-five foster kids and wound up adopting eight of them. In addition, he and his wife had three natural children."

"World's greatest dad, indeed," Jackie said.

"Oh, and he taught Sunday school for forty years."

"*That's* the other thing?" Jackie asked.

"No. The M.E. says he can't give an exact time of death because

Appelt's body was frozen, postmortem."

"Now that's just friggin' weird," Jackie said.

"Just keep it in mind," Corrinne said. "As we go forward, anything in Appelt's life that looks like a lost cause could be key to establishing motive. She set three copies of the e-mail from Caraway's office down on the table. "Okay," she said. "We're going to call, threaten, bribe—track Nicole Chandler down, however you can. But nobody's going home tonight until we've had a talk with this despairing prostitute."

Corrinne peed before pouring another cup of coffee and settling at her desk. She'd put in enough time chasing Nicole Chandler. Only fair to let the others have a head start. She checked her e-mail. One new message. *You have got to be kidding me.*

TO: ckirkpatrick@grpd.grapndrapids.gov
FROM: FrMikeyMikeSOJ@gmail.com
SUBJECT: Don Caraway Juvenile Record

Corrinne,

Hey, it's Father Michael. From your wedding? Parker shared some aspects of your current investigation with us and it looked like you wanted to have a look at Donald Caraway's sealed juvie record. Luckily for you, the Knights of Malta owe us a couple favors and a guy in the Justice Department was able to get the attached digital copy. Have a look and see if it's worth the hassle of petitioning the court to officially unseal it.

Happy to help!
-Father Michael

P.S. If you need any more help, feel free to call me at 410.555.5450.

Corrinne's blood boiled. She could actually feel it boiling inside of her. She pulled out her cell and dialed the number.

"Go for Michael!"

"What do you think you're doing?"

"Who is this?"

"Corrinne Kirkpatrick."

"Oh, hi!" he said. "Did you get my e-mail? I thought you'd be interested in that."

"How did you even know about the sealed record?"

There was a pause and then, "Oh, no. Parker said he had your permission to share some stuff with us. Tell me my boy wasn't fibbing."

"Oh, he absolutely did not have permission to share anything. And you're a priest. Is that really called 'fibbing?' How many Hail Marys for 'fibbing?'"

"Yeah, I'm pickin' up what you're throwin' down. I think he was just worried about you, though. Wanted to help. His heart was in the right place."

"Don't tell me about Parker's heart."

"Did you at least look at the PDF?"

"No, I deleted the e-mail!" She looked up at her computer screen and saw the message sitting there open, very much not deleted.

"Okay. Well, it does tie your Mr. Caraway to one of the victims. So, you may want to see it."

"Michael, this whole thing makes me look shady."

"If you're worried about e-mail archives, I know some people who can scrub it off the server, like it was never there. Want me to make some calls?"

"No. Especially not to me. Ever. Okay? Lose this number."

"But *you* called me," Father Michael said.

"Lose my e-mail too."

"If that's what you want. Hey, I was wondering, did I remember to put the gift receipt in with that fondue kit?"

Corrinne hung up, fuming. Her anger yielded to curiosity, though, and she opened the attachment. The document was dated September 10, 1989, and bore the seal of Ingham County, Michigan. She read the two-page report and then reread it, thinking her eyes might be playing tricks on her. According to this, Don Caraway was one of the foster kids taken in by the Appelts. He had lived there for two years. Then, when he was sixteen, he set fire to their house. After spending a few months in a juvenile offenders' home, Garrett Appelt had had a change of heart and petitioned the court to let him go and seal his record.

The implications sunk in. This tied Caraway to all three murders.

"You guys!" she shouted.

Jackie wandered up, his coat on and keys in hand. "Vivien left already. Said she knew right where to find this Chandler lady."

Corrinne quickly minimized the document. No reason to raise questions.

"Well then, no use in all of us chasing after her. Tighten your man-bun, Reese. We're making an arrest."

Jackie smiled. "About time."

* * *

Jackie drove like the wheel man for a bank crew. By the time they reached Caraway's East Grand Rapids home, Corrinne felt positively sick. They pounded on the door of the dark house until a neighbor called over from her yard that Caraway always worked on Saturdays. In fact, he was almost never home.

"Give me your keys," Corrinne said. "I'm driving."

As they made their way back toward downtown, Jackie said, "So what's going on here? We didn't arrest this guy two days ago. What changed?"

"Did you file the request to unseal Caraway's juvenile record?"

"Yeah. Haven't heard anything back."

"Get on that." Corrinne looked down at the speedometer. She was going faster than Jackie had. "Let's just say I know what we're going to find. A little birdy, etcetera."

Jackie grinned. "You're something else, Kirkpatrick."

Bridgewater Place was far emptier on a Saturday morning. As they entered, Jackie pointed out an Artistry entry in the lobby—an attractive mixed-media piece portraying two young women walking down a wooded path. Corrinne didn't even notice them anymore.

They took the elevator up to the seventeenth floor. As soon as the doors parted, they saw the problem. Caraway's offices were back behind the law firm's, and the law firm was closed. Dark. Doors locked.

"I'll go find security," Jackie said.

"Thanks." As she waited, Corrinne began to doubt herself. Why was she here, looking to arrest Caraway, instead of out building a case against him? This was foolish. She'd let that priest get her all worked up and then made an impulsive decision. If she were a man, it would be perceived as bold, decisive—loose-cannon at worst. But as a female detective, if this came back to bite her, they'd say she was overly emotional, impetuous, PMSing.

Luckily, she'd come to her senses. When Jackie returned, they would question Caraway, bringing up Garrett Appelt to see if he would admit to the arson on record. That would eliminate the need to unseal the juvenile record.

Corrinne sat on a bench and waited. Jackie was certainly taking his sweet time. Maybe he was unable to find building security. Or maybe they were giving him some lip. Or perhaps it was an attractive female security guard and he was trying to get her number. She was about to call him when she saw Jackie approaching from the other side of the glass, walking Caraway past the law firm's reception desk. In cuffs.

He shoved Caraway into the crash bar on the inside of the door and the two came spilling out.

"I went up the freight elevator," Jackie explained. "And would you believe this guy failed to disclose to a police officer that he was carrying a concealed weapon? That's an arrestable offense." He turned casually to Caraway. "Oh, and I almost forgot: you're also wanted in connection with three homicides."

"I'm invoking my right to remain silent," Caraway said. "These are the last words you'll hear from me without my lawyer present."

11

Parker stopped by Martha's Vineyard, his favorite wine shop, followed by a high-end florist, a block away. He'd been texting Corrinne all afternoon, but she hadn't responded. This worried Parker. Sure, they'd had a few fights before, but never like this. Corrinne hadn't come home until after 3 AM, and then she'd crashed on the couch and left again before Parker got up. The mess of blankets and pillows was the only proof she'd even been back. And now she wasn't returning his texts.

When she got home tonight, he'd apologize. He'd wow her. He'd recapture that wonderful moment from last night when they connected over dinner and she had actually forgotten her troubles for a few minutes. Parker had her favorite kind of flowers ("yellow") and a lovely Sauvignon Blanc. And he'd order in Thai from Corrinne's favorite takeout place.

He firmly believed she was wrong. He *could* charm his way out of this hole. That is, if Corrinne ever came home.

* * *

As they brought Caraway in for processing, Corrinne and Jackie received a text from Vivien, who had located Nicole Chandler and was bringing her into the station for questioning. By the time they entered the observation room for Interview D, Vivien was already seated across from the woman, pouring Coke into a plastic cup.

"Anything else I can get you?" Vivien asked.

"No, I'm okay." She looked to be in her mid-forties, although Corrinne knew her to be only thirty-one. Her matted hair and disheveled clothes gave the impression she'd been out partying all night.

"You're not under arrest," Vivien assured. "We just have some questions for you about Leslie Doane." The woman nodded.

Jackie grunted. "So, Allen plays the good cop, huh?"

"Not always," Corrinne said. They watched through the one-way glass as Nicole took a long drink from the cup.

Finally, Vivien spoke again. "It says here that you were offered a deal if you testified against Mr. Doane. No prostitution charges and you'd walk. And you took the deal initially."

"Yes," she practically whispered.

"Then you changed your tune. Even though you had a broken nose and bruises on your ribs and back. Why risk going back to jail for a guy like that?"

Nicole was silent for a minute.

"He's dead, sweetie," Vivien said. "He can't hurt anyone anymore."

"I know."

"So why'd you back out of the deal?"

"Because I knew what he was capable of. What he did to me, that was nothing compared to what he did to my friend."

"Your friend Margaret?" Vivien asked.

"Oh, smooth, Viv," Corrinne said under her breath.

"No. My friend Kim."

Corrinne turned to Jackie. "Did I not explain who Margaret was? She died in like 1300."

"What happened to Kim?" Vivien asked. "Take your time."

She took another long gulp of Coke. "He supplied her with Oxy," she said. "In exchange for . . . you know. Whenever he'd hit her, he'd just give her more dope and she'd forget all about it. Then one night, I got home and found her lying on my floor. Dead. They ruled it a suicide."

"But you think it was something else?"

"I don't know. But if she did kill herself, it was just to get away from him. I completely understood."

The door to the observation room clicked open and Captain Dunleavy glared in at the two detectives. "Kirkpatrick, I need to speak with you. Now."

"Yes, ma'am." To Jackie, she said, "Tell me what I miss."

Once in the hall, the captain said, "I just came in to check on the case to find that you've arrested a rather high-profile suspect."

"That's correct."

"And what do you have on him?"

"For starters, he publicly targeted the first two victims on his website some months ago."

"Yeah, I've got that," Dunleavy said. "What else?"

"We're waiting on a court order to unseal his juvenile record. I have it on good authority that it will tie him to the third victim as well."

The captain looked up to the ceiling as if it might explain what she'd just heard. "You're telling me that, after you had a confrontation with this guy—on the *news*—he's now occupying a cell, based on what some thirty-year old juvie record *might* contain, if in fact you can get it unsealed."

Corrinne stood her ground. "I can lean on him in here. Break him. His lawyer is on the way. When he arrives, I'll put the screws to him. You know how I—"

"Oh, no you won't. You know who his lawyer is?"

"Yes."

"I promised the deputy chief I'd keep you far away from Mr. Slocum. Remember that? That direct order?"

"Yes, ma'am."

"You're on thin ice, Kirkpatrick. Use your team. Get me something else on this guy by tomorrow. Because after forty-eight he walks. And if that happens, well, Allen said she'd be happy to take over."

The door to the observation room opened again and Jackie came sauntering out. He looked from Corrinne to Capt. Dunleavy and said, "Everything okay here?"

"Worry about yourself, Reese," the captain spat. "And roll those sleeves down. Or I might see that stupid tattoo on your arm, mistake you for a perp, and throw you in lockup."

"Whatever you say, Hilary," he mumbled.

"What was that?"

"I said *yes, ma'am.*"

* * *

Saturday, October 28

Parker had the flowers in a vase, the cartons of food arranged perfectly on the table, and Corrinne's favorite Pandora station playing when she arrive home.

The moment she was in the house, he greeted her. "Hi, honey. I hope you don't mind, but—"

"What gives you the right?" she demanded.

"Sorry?"

"How did you even know about Caraway's sealed records? Did you overhear me on the phone or something?"

"I don't know. I think—"

"Shut up, Parker. Anything you hear because we happen to live together is confidential. Do you get that? Cases are thrown out of court for this sort of thing. Murderers walk free!"

"Father Michael's not going to say anything. He was headed back to Rome."

Corrinne pinched the bridge of her nose, squinting. "That's beside the point. Look, Parker, I don't tell you how to do your job. Okay? Please just let me do mine."

"Okay." He waited a beat and then said, "I got Bob Thai for you."

She looked at the table, covered in cartons—enough food for five people.

"Thanks," she said, grabbing a couple containers. She headed for the door.

"Where are you going?"

"Back to work. I just needed to have this conversation in person. I can't stop now. Thanks to you and your friend, I've got—" she looked at her watch, "forty-five hours until my main suspect walks. If that happens . . ." Her face clamped down, locking out tears once again. "Don't wait up," she said, heading out the door.

***

Corrinne boxed out all thoughts but the case at hand. The custodians were hard at work when she arrived at the station, but soon they had left her in mostly-dark solitude. She wandered into the Command

Center and made a few circuits of the room, surveying the photos, reports, and theories tacked up on the walls.

The icon of St. Margaret of Cortona gazed back at her, full of peace and tranquility and just a tinge of sadness. A new note was pinned up, in Vivien's hand: "Kim Ashland. Deceased, 1/19/07. Ruled a suicide." The despairing prostitute. She thought of Leslie Doane, who had gotten away with everything through intimidation and then of John Slocum, another sleazy john who had somehow kept himself out of a cell and in a corner office of a high-end law firm.

Slocum's face morphed in her mind into Caraway's. Back in 1989, the secular crusader had apparently maintained that the fire in the Appelts' home was accidental. And now there was no one left to ask. The Appelts had divorced a few years earlier and the ex-wife had moved back to England, where she seemed to be living in some sort of commune or something with no phone.

Lying down on the conference table, she stared at the ceiling. The saint thing fit at every angle, but what was the point? Why saints? Was Caraway making a wry observation, via murder, about how the most upstanding Christian citizens were actually hiding dark secrets? Or was it something else? Her thoughts turned to the newspaper clipping and the date in Cates's planner: All Souls' Day—the two things that the priests' theory failed to explain.

She felt a twisting inside. What if *that* was the point? Saints—Parker Saint? Was he a potential target? Or maybe Parker was just in her head. Somehow, he'd even followed her here.

* * *

Parker dialed Michael's number. He answered on the third ring.

"Hey, man."

"What happened, man? Corrinne freaked out on me!"

"I'll tell you what happened: you lied. You said she was okay with our involvement. News flash: she is *not okay with it.* She made that super-clear."

"You should have called me, not her."

"Why? You're not a cop. That makes no sense."

Parker was pacing. "I need to fix this. She's so mad at me. She's in trouble at work now. What should I do?"

"I don't know, Parker; I'm not a licensed marriage counselor. Father Ignatius is, though. You want me to put him on?"

"What? No! I mean, what should I do about the problem we caused?"

"'*We?*'"

"We, you . . . whatever. What would you do in this situation?"

"You need to back off," Michael said. "Your wife's a sharp lady. She can handle it."

"That's not what I asked. What would *you* do?"

"I'd do things you can't, Parker. I wish I could help you, but we got stuck in Detroit for a night, and now Father Ignatius tells me we're headed to Panama."

"So just tell me what you'd do. I'm not going to try to be you. I'm just curious."

Michael sighed. "Well, I looked into this Caraway character. He runs a small operation. I'd probably have a peek at his files. Plus, I'd bet he only has a couple copy machines. I'd have a look at those hard drives. If he was sloppy, you might find something there."

"What do you mean, hard drives?"

"Modern digital copiers have drives that store every print job, every copy that you make, like, forever. It's actually an identity thief's dream. Con men have been known to buy second hand copiers and mine the hard drives for sensitive information. More than once, I've brought a drive duplicator into an office and dubbed their drive."

"But people don't print things out anymore, right? They mostly just e-mail."

"You'd be surprised how many people are using hard copies these days. Federal law says you have to keep e-mails in perpetuity. Business servers automatically file them away. A letter, on the other hand, can be burned or shredded once it's been read. But again, you've got the copy on the hard drive."

"Oh, that's good," Parker said. "Do you just dress up as a repairman or what? I need to get one of those metal clipboards."

"No, Parker. Just tell your wife. She can get a search warrant."

"She doesn't want me talking to you about this. Besides, he's threatening to sue her for harassment already. It's this whole thing."

"Just trust her, okay? You wouldn't know where the hard drive is or how to copy it or anything. You need special cables. It's not as easy as it sounds. I'm sorry I brought it up."

"No, I'm glad you did."

"Don't you have something else you can focus on? Aren't you in the middle of like renovating your old church building?"

"You're right," Parker said, thoughtfully. "Our offices need a lot of work. Maybe it's time to set up our new copiers. That way I can get really familiar with them."

"Parker, don't try to—"

"Gotta go, Mike. Have fun in Panama." He hung up.

* * *

Corrinne was completely lost in her thoughts, stretched out on the conference table when she heard the click of the door. She sat bolt-upright, her hand on her gun.

"Don't shoot," Jackie said. He chuckled. "I didn't know you lived here."

She laughed. "Just putting in some extra time. What are you doing here on a Saturday night?"

He shrugged. "What else do I have to do?"

Corrinne made a pouty face. "Aww, are the kids not being nice to you at your new school?"

"Hilarious. Vivien actually asked me to go through all these calls from the tip line. There were sixty-two. Most of them useless."

Corrinne grimaced. What was Vivien doing giving the new guy orders? Had the captain already initiated the transfer of power?

"There was one call worth looking into, though," he said. "You want to hear it?"

"Sure, why not?"

Jackie pulled up a chair and logged into his laptop. He clicked through a few folders and opened a sound file. It was a young female voice. She said, "I don't know who else to call. I think you need to do something about the Heritage Pride Church. There's something going on. I think they're going to hurt some people." There was a click.

"That's it?" Corrinne asked. "She doesn't even mention the murders or any of our vics."

"Yeah, I thought the same thing. But then I started looking in to these nutters." He opened a web browser and clicked on a bookmark. "Check this out: It's the pet project of this guy Jay Anders. His 'church' meets in a pole barn behind his house." He clicked through a few pictures on their Facebook page. "Looks like about forty people attend, and more than half of the people tagged have the same last name. But they've got over 10,000 followers."

"Yeah, I've heard of that clown," Corrinne said. "Got semi-famous in the Nineties, picketing funerals of AIDS victims. I thought he'd kind of faded away."

"No chance. They've been shoving their message into every crevice in the Internet." He clicked through several tabs of social media accounts. "This guy hates the pope, hates the government, hates established religions, hates Democrats and Republicans. And look at this: Facebook, Twitter, Instagram, tons of followers. He updates his blog every other day."

Jackie scrolled down a blog post to reveal 481 comments.

"His *blog*?" Corrinne said. "What is this, 2002?" She tipped the laptop toward herself. "Dang, that's a lot of comments."

He laughed. "They're trolls. They like to get a rise out of people."

"Well, apparently it works." She scrolled down the thread, divided equally between those condemning Anders and those praising and defending him.

"Absolutely. For every status, post, or picture there are dozens, sometimes hundreds of responses—giving this guy exactly what he wants."

"Does he have a record?" Corrinne asked.

"He did two years for tax evasion in '09. That's probably when he fell off your radar. Claims he doesn't recognize government above the county level. His brother-in-law, who also lives in his little commune with him, has two DUIs. But it gets better. I cross-referenced these gents with our victims' names. Got a couple hits."

Corrinne hopped off the table and took a chair next to him. "Let's have a look."

"First off, commenting on this tasteful post called 'Thank God for IEDs,' a familiar name has some choice words for our man Anders." He pulled up a screen shot.

> **@DavidCatesSFN**: You are an ignorant buffoon. I'm ashamed to live in the same city as you. Protesting funerals is for cowards and sickos.

"I think he showed great restraint," Corrinne said.

"Right. And here's another."

> **@LeslieDoanePositivity+:** Miserable, hateful, bigoted people like @PastorJayAnders will never be anything but miserable. They hate and hate and their hate consumes them.

"Anders has also been waist-deep in a public flame war with our buddy Don Caraway ever since the whole church council kerfuffle began."

Corrinne folded her arms. "Sounds like the guy's a pariah though. If thousands of people have posted about him, it's less significant that a couple of our vics did."

"There's one more thing, though," Jackie said. "And this one's harder to explain away." He opened another screenshot.

> **PINNED TWEET:**
> 11.2.2017. A day you will all remember. #fireandbrimstone #judgmentday

Corrinne felt the little hairs on her arms standing at attention.

Saturday, October 28

* * *

"You realize they're going to bill you double, right?" the technician asked.

"That's fine," Parker said.

"As long as you're cool with it. I get plenty of maintenance calls late on Saturday nights, but this is the first installation I've done." The man was portly and unkempt, wearing a polo shirt bearing the Foster Print and Copy logo and a name badge that identified him as Ned P.

"I just really want to have it all up and running for tomorrow morning."

Parker had called Foster, by far the largest copier sales and service firm in the area, as soon as he hung up with Michael, requesting immediate installation of two photocopiers—the highest-end machines they had on hand. The list of up-charges, weekend rates, evening rates, and fees they'd rattled off seemed designed to inspire a postponement of the installation, but he had readily agreed to all of it.

Ned P. walked him through every aspect of copying, printing, and scanning on the machines, which he repeatedly called "babies."

"You have any old copiers you need us to dispose of?" he asked as he seemed to be preparing to leave.

"No, we've been sharing a building with another church, using their equipment."

"Alrighty. And it's just these two? Are we adding more later?"

"Nope, this is it. Small job. You guys probably do a lot of really big setups, though, huh?"

"You wouldn't believe how many networked machines I set up at Steelcase in one day."

"What about downtown?" Parker prompted. "Some of those high-rise office buildings would be a challenge, I imagine."

"We service Amway," Ned said, "and the law firms at Bridgewater."

Parker smiled. That was his *in*. He knew from Corrinne's files that FAR was subletting their office space from Adler & Clark, at Bridgewater Place. Even if they owned their office equipment outright, a

Foster Copy technician moving around the building wouldn't stand out as strange.

"Can you show me where the toner goes in one more time?" Parker asked.

Ned flipped open a door and indicated a long plastic tube. "Right down here."

"Hold on, let me get a picture of that. Keep pointing." Parker took out his phone and aimed it at the toner drum. He then zoomed out until Ned's shirt and name badge were in the shot.

* * *

"A day you will remember," Corrinne read. "Does he post that sort of thing often?"

"No, this is the only time he's hinted at Judgment Day coming," Jackie said.

"And it's All Souls' Day."

"Right? And look what's happening that night." He typed in a URL and brought up the website for the Church Unity Revival. "When it comes to Stuff Fundamentalists Want to Burn Down, I imagine that a bunch of different stripes of religious people—all playing nice together—is near the top of the list."

At the bottom of the screen, Corrinne saw the words "Our Speakers" and the name "Rev. Parker Saint" half visible.

Jackie stood. "I know it's a bit of a stretch, but like I said, Allen asked me to go through the tip line calls. And since tomorrow's Sunday, I was thinking of popping in at their little 'church' and asking a few questions, especially about this Judgment Day post."

"I can't let you go out there alone," Corrinne said, absently clicking back to the Heritage Pride Church website. She thought about the opportunity to avoid Ruth—and Parker too, for that matter—by skipping church. "It says here that their service starts at 10:00," she said. "We can show up at 10:15, get a look around while they're occupied. Huh. Look at this." She pointed to a graphic on the side of the page, depicting Don Caraway with devil horns and a pitchfork photoshopped in.

"You realize," Jackie said, "if Anders was involved, we've got the wrong guy in lockup."

In response, Corrinne put her head down on the keyboard. Jackie rubbed her shoulders gently for a minute.

"It's getting late," he said. "You want to order in some food?

She sat up. "Next time. I'm going to go home and get some sleep. I'll see you at church tomorrow morning. Wear something nice."

12

Corrinne and Jackie met at a Marathon station half a mile up the road from Anders' property on Kraft Road, just inside the Grand Rapids city limits. She did a drive-by first, surveying the land. The open field, weathered farm house, and rusty outbuildings stood in stark contrast to what was clearly a trend of frantic development all around.

As Jackie stepped out of his newish Chrysler, Corrinne doubled over in laughter. "What are you wearing?" she called out the open window.

Jackie looked down at himself—tan three-piece suit, turquoise bowtie, and matching pocket square. "What? You said wear something nice. I don't know; what do people wear to church?"

"I was kidding, Reese. It was witty banter."

He grinned. "You mean flirty banter."

"Just get in."

He slid into the passenger seat of her Expedition and they pulled back onto the road. "Sorry," Jackie said. "I thought we were going to, like, blend in."

Corrinne laughed again. "Blend in? In that? We're not in Montgomery, Alabama. These people are probably wearing overalls and straw hats."

A small, hand-painted sign near the entrance to Anders' property read "Heritage Pride Church, Private Congregation." A swinging metal gate had been pulled open, allowing access to the drive. Other signs marked the way up to the farm house: "Our Lives Matter," "White Pride," and "Muslims Turn Back or We'll Pick Your Virgins" among them.

"Welcome to the Fundie Farm," Jackie said. "Get it? *Fundie Farm*?"

"Why do I have a sense we're being watched?" Corrinne asked.

"Me too. From before we even turned in."

Corrinne pulled up under an enormous, gnarled weeping willow about fifty feet from the house and they got out, cautiously approaching the wraparound porch.

"Wait," Corrinne whispered. "Look over there." On the far side of the house, they could see the back doors of a large delivery truck bearing the logo of Fresco Food Service.

"Think it's stolen?" Jackie asked.

"I don't know. Get the plate. Thing's definitely wide enough to fit that big wheel."

Jackie scribbled the plate down in his notepad and the two of them mounted the stairs to the porch. The front door was open and, through the screen door, they could hear talking and clinking inside.

When Corrinne hit the doorbell, all noise inside came to a sudden halt. After some brief whispering, a woman came to the door. She appeared to be about Corrinne's age, with incredibly plain features, no makeup, wearing an ankle-length frock. She regarded the detectives wordlessly through the screen.

"Good morning," Corrinne said. "I'm Det. Kirkpatrick, this is Det. Reese. We're with Grand Rapids . . . " The woman turned and walked briskly away, out of sight. "Oooookay."

Jackie walked over to the north side of the porch nearest the pole barn and peered around the corner. "Looks like she's getting the man of the house," he said.

"Hello," Corrinne said. A girl, perhaps fifteen, perhaps nineteen, was peering around the corner where the woman had disappeared. "My name's Corrinne. May we come in? We just want to talk to you." The girl nodded timidly. "Come on, Jackie," Corrinne said. "We've been invited in."

Once in the foyer, Corrinne had to coax the girl out like a frightened animal. "What's your name?"

"Esther." Her voice was small and babyish. The detectives shared a look. This was almost certainly the person who had left the message on the tip line. "We were making lunch. For after service," Esther said.

Corrinne met the girl halfway, entering what had originally been a formal dining room, but now looked like an AA meeting about to happen.

A double-decker Bunn drip maker—the kind you'd find in a truck stop—sat on a buffet table, surrounded by foam cups, filling the room with the irregular heartbeat of bad coffee brewing. The place hung with the oily stink of machine grease, which mixed with the coffee, reminding Corrinne of a tire joint waiting room.

"Esther, can you tell me something?" Jackie said, surprising Corrinne with a tender tone. "How long has Mr. Anders had that big truck parked next to the house?"

"A few weeks," she practically whispered.

"Do you know why he bought it?"

"Jackie," Corrinne said, nudging him and pointing through the doorway to the living room, where an antique gun cabinet was filled with modern assault rifles—AK47s, AR-15s. A dozen of them.

"What is this?" a deep voice boomed through the house, followed immediately by its source, an older man in a bright red turtleneck beneath a tweed jacket charging up from the back of the house. "You're trespassing!" he declared.

Jay Anders. Corinne recognized him immediately.

Another woman, similar in appearance to the first, but much bolder in countenance, followed behind him. "They're cops," she said. "And they shouldn't be in here." She looked Jackie in the eye. "You got a warrant? Let me see your warrant!"

He nodded at the girl. "She invited us in."

"Well, I'm inviting you to leave."

"I'm afraid it's not as simple as that," Corrinne said. "Because now we've seen those rifles, out in plain sight. If I'm not mistaken, Mr. Anders, you're a felon. Which means you can't own a firearm in the State of Michigan. Unless it's been three years since the end of your parole. Has it?"

"Those are mine." Another man, younger and bigger than Anders, filled in behind him. He wore a yellowed button-down shirt with faded blue pants and a tattered sport coat of a very different blue.

"You must be Timothy Philips," Jackie said. The live-in brother-in-law.

"That's right," the man said. His stance and tone challenged, *What are you going to do about it?*

"Mr. Philips, you've got a couple DUIs under your belt, am I right?" Corrinne said.

"Misdemeanors."

"I assume you have the documents to prove those are all your guns?"

Philips snarled, "This is our property. You should leave. Now."

Anders reached smoothly into his jacket and pulled out a compact revolver, levelling it at Jackie. Corrinne stayed her hand. She couldn't draw. Not with the girl there.

"No, they're going nowhere until we figure this out," he said. He turned to the woman at his side. "Honey, why don't you head back into the meeting and lead the flock in some singing? Something loud." The woman backed out, glaring at Corrinne—a look that stole her breath for a moment.

"Calm down," Jackie said, raising his hands. "We just came in here to talk. Let's not escalate things." Philips was now holding a gun as well, although Corrinne didn't remember him drawing. She couldn't focus on anything but the girl, standing between her and the gunmen.

"It's a little late for that," Anders said. "FBI's been watching us for weeks. Just waiting for a chance to burn us down, like Waco. They hate freedom and freedom fighters. And I'd bet green money the ATF is on their way as we speak. But let me tell you what—it won't be like Waco. I got a barn fulla people who would follow me anywhere. And 10,000 more online who will appear out of the woodwork if I give the call. We go down in a blaze of glory, we're bringing you all with us. All of you."

"We'll work this out," Corrinne said. She could feel her own gun, snugged into a shoulder holster under her coat. It was not a quick draw by any stretch. "First, though, why don't you let this young lady leave? I know you don't want her to get hurt."

Anders looked down at the girl with contempt. "You called that number, didn't you? What did I tell you would happen? *Huh?*" He knocked her to the ground with the back of his hand.

We're going to die today, Corrinne thought. *And no one will know what happened.* Sure, it was on the log sheet that she and Jackie were planning a visit here, but with all this land and all the willing accomplices in the next building, their bodies would disappear, along with her vehicle. Anders could claim they'd stopped by for a short visit and then left, their questions all satisfactorily answered. It was stupid coming out here with no backup.

"Take his gun," Anders ordered, his own trained on Corrinne. The brute took a long step toward Jackie and buried a fist in his gut, doubling him over. He then pulled the tail of his jacket over his head, revealing the 9mm on his hip, which he yanked free with a woodblock hand.

"Where's your backup piece?" he demanded.

"Don't have one," Jackie grunted.

"Don't play games with me."

"I'm not! I'm a detective. I haven't drawn my weapon in twelve years!"

"What kind of cop doesn't have a backup piece?" Anders said. "I guess a cop who dresses like that. Tell ya what: you're gonna take off those fancy clothes and show us. Down to your skivvies."

When Jackie hesitated, Philips whacked him in the ear, knocking him down to his hands and knees. Struggling to stand, the detective complied, removing his jacket, vest, shirt, and pants, until he stood there in his socks, shoes, and silk boxers.

"Look at this guy," Anders chortled. "What a pansy. You're everything that's wrong with America, rolled up into one." He turned his attention back to Corrinne. "Your turn," he said.

She froze. There was no way she would follow this order. If she was going to die today, it would be with dignity, standing up straight and fully clothed. If only the kid wasn't still in their midst, eyes wide with terror, she'd take off her jacket and pull her gun in the process. At least then she could take this sicko out with her.

"What are you waiting for?" Anders demanded. "You hiding something down there, lady cop? Or should I call you Mr. Lady Cop?" He belched a cruel laugh. Both men leered at her like patrons at a strip club.

Corrinne closed her eyes and prayed. *God, I know I should be at church right now and everything. And I know I don't talk to you as much as I should. But I need help. Right now.* She opened her eyes to see Jackie shove the distracted Philips's considerable bulk into Anders.

"Run!" he shouted. "Call backup!"

She wanted to grab the girl, but she knew there was no time. This was the only window for someone to get out and call for help. She jumped right through the screen in the door and hit the porch, crouching low, clearing the stairs in a single bound. Her gun was in her hand now. Muscle memory. Even from this distance, she could hear the beating that Jackie was taking in the house—the dull packing sound of fist against flesh.

Weaving back in a serpentine pattern, she kept her silhouette to a minimum. Entering the cover of the willow tree's branches, she stopped short. A woman was standing next to her car, hand resting on a holstered gun. Corrinne took aim at the woman's chest and barked, "Hands! Now!" even as she recognized the woman.

It was Xena. Of the FBI.

Corrinne lowered her weapon. "They've got my partner," she said. "We have to get him out."

"I already called Agent Wilson," the warrior princess said.

* * *

Parker despised distractions to his preaching. Up until a year ago, he'd been dealing with wait-list crowds—an audience that knew they were lucky to be there, and likely to be televised as they sat enraptured by his message. No longer. Real congregations included squirmy kids, bored teenagers, and senior citizens who thought they were whispering quietly while everyone for five pews in either direction understood every word.

But that was nothing compared to this. Where was Corrinne? She'd slept on the couch again after coming home in the wee hours of the morning and left Parker a note that simply said, "Can't be at church. Have a lead in the case." What kind of lead couldn't wait a few hours? Now Parker stood at the pulpit, stumbling over his words, having lost his place yet again.

He tried to re-focus, but his mind wandered to Paige. Beautiful, devoted Paige, who had been at every single preaching engagement, no matter what was going on in her life. He'd always known, deep down, that he'd marry Paige eventually. It made sense on every level. But she was gone now. So was Corrinne, for that matter.

Trying not to feel too sorry for himself, Parker moved on to his final point.

* * *

"You know, when you said we were going to Panama, I pictured something different," Father Michael said. Their rental car eased past the "Welcome to Panama, Indiana" sign at exactly the 25 MPH speed limit. Father Ignatius was at the wheel.

"Yes, you still need to work on your assumptions," he said.

"So, that was like a test or something? To teach me—what? Ask more questions?"

Ignatius shrugged. "If that's what you need to learn." They made their way slowly down the village's main drag, passing a post office, a medical marijuana dispensary, and a number of empty storefronts.

"This is the cross street up here," Michael said. On one corner, a hot dog stand called Coney Heaven was doing a brisk business. On the other, St. Michael the Archangel Catholic Church looked all but deserted.

As the priests pulled into the parking lot, a couple dozen people emerged from the church, heading to their vehicles. They all looked somber and subdued.

"What's the parish priest's name?" Michael asked.

"Bryer," Ignatius answered. "Father Mark Bryer." They parked the car and entered the church, finding a tall, bespectacled priest greeting the last few worshipers as they left.

When he saw the Jesuits, he immediately broke off his conversation and rushed over to them.

"I'm Father Mark," he said, offering an oversized hand. "Are you the men from the Vatican?"

"No, we're here to look at the backflow regulator on your boiler," Michael said. "We just dressed like this to be funny."

"I apologize for my young colleague," Ignatius said. "He does not travel well."

Father Mark nodded, confused. "Let me see to my robes and then I will meet you in my office." He pointed at a hallway. "It's just down there, on the left."

Ten minutes later, the three priests were crammed into the office.

"I'm so happy you made it," Father Mark said. "I was told you'd be here yesterday. When you didn't show up, I feared something more important had claimed you."

"It was this whole thing," Michael said. "We were headed to Rome, but then the Knights of Malta kind of hijacked us and then they sent us here, but our luggage went to Rome, so we had to go pick it up in Indianapolis. But we're here now. So fill us in."

"Well, for starters, I've only been here a little more than a year," the local priest said. "It's a small parish, as you undoubtedly notice, but we usually have about twice as many as we had today. The problem is, they've all heard the stories."

"What stories?" Ignatius asked.

"That this church is cursed. Haunted. Possessed. What have you." He paused for a beat and then half-shrugged. "Apparently, back in the mid-1800s there was a Catholic boys' school here, and one of the boys poisoned a bunch of his classmates. I don't know if it's even true, but people talk about it a lot. Then, of course, we've had the recent death of one boy and the disappearance of another, with," he hesitated, "very suspicious circumstances. And now they're talking about the curse again, saying it's back to claim more children. Attendance is down, just when people need the Church most. Many have told me their faith is shaken. And now reports of these strange occurrences."

"Back up," Michael said. "We didn't get the usual dossier on this case. Tell us about the missing boy and the dead boy. Then hit me with the strange occurrences."

"It began with young Brady Miller. He was twelve years old when I arrived here. A month later, he was diagnosed with lymphoma. For a time, it looked like he might pull through, but I'm afraid he died in August. The town was still in mourning, when another boy, Griffin Matthews, disappeared early last week. From right here in this church."

"During the service?"

"No. Griffin was a good friend of Brady's and had been spending a lot of time in the church, praying for him, lighting candles, sometimes into the night. His parents, bedrock members of the parish, allowed it. It seemed like a relatively healthy way to deal with things. Since Brady's death, Griffin had been coming less frequently, but still multiple times a week—praying for the boy's parents and for his own grief." He shook his head. "Such a nice kid. I just—" His throat seemed to close up.

"When you say he disappeared from here," Ignatius said, "do you simply mean that this was the last place he was seen or that there were witnesses to an abduction?"

"Somewhere in the middle, I guess," Father Mark said. "There were unmistakable signs of a struggle. And blood, which they tell me matches the boy's. The police believe two or three men took him and then set about defacing the sanctuary of the church."

Ignatius's face hardened further. "Defacing, how?"

"They destroyed the crucifix, completely shattered the statue of Our Lady, and spray-painted all sorts of occult symbols throughout the church proper. The fear is that Griffin came upon them, in the act, and they attacked him. We're not allowed to meet in there, but I don't imagine we would anyway. We've been using our small chapel in the meantime."

Ignatius's eyes, which had been steadily darkening through this report, were positively murderous. "What do you think happened?"

Father Mark let out a sigh. "I don't know. A lot of people pass through this town. The highway is a major trucking route. But I still pray this was born of boredom, not true evil. Perhaps local teens blowing off steam in a post-Christian world. Although, that does not explain Griffin's disappearance."

"Maybe he ran away," Michael suggested.

"I've heard that. But it sure doesn't sound like him. He was very studious, always reading, learning. And very polite. Such a good kid. And there's also the matter of the blood."

"What about the 'strange occurrences?'" Father Michael asked.

"Yes. Well, the police first reported it. Around the altar, where the blood was found, electronic devices will simply stop working. There have also been unexplained noises. Teenagers are now daring each other to run in and touch the altar. And someone posted the events on a paranormal chat room online, bringing thrill-seekers and hobbyists who want to chronicle their visits so they can brag about their adventures. I didn't know what to do, so I called the bishop, who contacted you."

"Thank God," Father Ignatius said.

13

"What were you thinking?" Agent Wilson raged.

He had arrived with a dozen feds in windbreakers about twenty minutes after Xena—whose real name turned out to be Agent Rosa Bertuzzi—made the call. They had pulled back to the road and established a barricade.

Corrinne liked Rosa and decided immediately that she should be in charge. And yet, here she stood being chewed out by Agent Wilson.

"Don't you already have a suspect in lockup?" the agent demanded. "How many are you planning to collect? Could you do me a favor and maybe warn me if any of the others happen to be the subjects of deep, longstanding federal investigations?" He stared at her expectantly, eyes manic, for a moment, as if the question had been sincere. "This one was a joint FBI-ATF task force. By my count that's two federal agencies you've screwed over today!"

He closed his eyes and pushed his fingertips together, breathing out his nose in some sort of improvised Zen move. When he opened them again, he said, "Here's what we're dealing with: these guys have been looking for a source to buy a whole lot of C4 for a while now. One of our undercover agents made contact last month, claiming to have stolen government ordinance. They had a meet set up for tomorrow." His face began to re-redden. "We were *this close* to taking them down at the buy, without all this collateral! Without them having the homefield advantage in their homemade bunker with an arsenal of God-knows-what!"

Corrinne stood impassively through all of this. When he finally stopped to breathe, she interjected, "All due respect, Agent Wilson, but do you think we should try and get my partner out of there first and then bring the hammer down on me later?"

"Don't worry," he said. "I'll get him back. Agent Bertuzzi and I are about to make first contact, get a lay of the land. My tactical team should be here within the hour."

"You got a negotiator coming?" Corrinne asked.

He pushed his chin out and wagged it back and forth. "The United States government does not negotiate with terrorists."

"Then I'm going with you."

He laughed. "I think you've helped enough. Leave this to us."

"Wilson, I made 'first contact' more than half an hour ago. I know the players, I know the layout of the house, I know which kid he was using as a human shield."

The agent rolled this around for a moment. "Fine, you can come. But follow my lead. I do the talking. Understand?"

"Sure."

Wilson rubbed his chin. "Now our profiler says that, in this case, if we cut off the head of the snake, the rest will just flop around. They're mindless followers. Keep that in mind."

Agent Wilson gathered his feds together—save for the two snipers he'd deployed into the field behind the house—and briefed them. They were to be ready to breach at any moment, on his command, but he planned to be in and out.

"We keep our weapons holstered," he said, looking at Rosa and Corrinne, "but we keep our weapons. If it goes down, I've seen Agent Bertuzzi draw and drop three hostiles before they even saw it coming."

They reached the door, now closed, and Agent Wilson pounded on it. "FBI," he said. "Let's talk terms." He glanced at Rosa and shook his head conspiratorially.

The door opened and Corrinne saw Esther, standing there with tears streaking her face. Behind her, Anders had holstered the revolver and held an AR-15 to the back of her head.

"Whattaya want, fed?" Anders demanded.

"I just want to come in and talk a minute," Wilson said. He showed his empty hands. "You've got the gun. You've got the power."

"Come on in then," he said. "One wrong move, you get to see what's inside this girl's head. And I don't mean her thoughts and dreams."

Agent Wilson opened the screen door, the broken mesh hanging down where Corrinne had burst through, and held it for the two women. As they entered the house, they saw Philips hanging back in the corner, taking aim at them with another assault rifle.

"First things first," Agent Wilson said. "I'm obligated to ask you to release the girl. Show us you don't want this to end badly."

"Why do you assume I don't want it to end badly?" Anders grinned, producing a deep dimple. "Anyway, it's you feds who have a history of turning religious minority communities into human barbeques."

"It doesn't have to go that way," Wilson said, "but I'm not going to lie to you; you're in a world of trouble. You've opened Pandora's box and now it can't be closed. Why don't you just put your guns down and tell us where you have the detective?"

"They didn't have a warrant."

Wilson laughed. "We're way past warrants. Det. Kirkpatrick was invited into your home and saw what she believed to be illegal weapons in plain sight, and now you've taken a law enforcement officer captive. This day ends one of two ways: with you two men in a cell or in body bags."

Corrinne bit her tongue. She hated this kind of macho brinksmanship. When men started one-upping each other, the odds of unnecessary loss of life increased tenfold. She glanced over at Rosa. Her expression was inscrutable.

"You forget," Anders said, "the Lord is on our side. He is mighty and full of righteous wrath. Unless you want to see someone die right now, why don't you go think about that?"

"I'm going to give you one more chance to do the right thing," Wilson said.

Anders raised the stock of the rifle to his shoulder and said, "Timothy, I'm gonna need you to go get me another girl from the meeting. This one's about to be used up."

Esther cried out.

"You got it," Philips said. Corrinne saw him walk through the house and out the back door.

"Someone younger!" Anders called out after him.

"Fine." Wilson said. "You like hellfire and brimstone? I'll bring them down on your head. Let's go." He led the way out the door and down the steps, hand on his gun, eyes on the doorway. When he'd cleared the front steps, he picked up the pace.

As Corrinne descended the steps, she saw the broken screen door closing slowly on its hydraulic arm. Somehow, she knew: that door was closing on Esther's life. And Jackie's. If she walked away, that was it. She pulled her gun from its holster and tossed it onto the lawn.

"Hang on to that for me, Rosa," she said, and re-mounted the stairs, two at a time.

She heard Agent Wilson behind her, shouting, "Get back here! You hear me, Kirkpatrick? That's an order!"

"Be right back," she called over her shoulder, before gliding through the door, just as it was about to shut, hands above her head.

* * *

"The police were very clear," Father Mark said. "We're not allowed in here until their investigation is over."

"This is a church," Ignatius said, ducking under the crime scene tape. "Emissaries of His Holiness are always 'allowed' here."

Michael followed him in and, a moment later, the lights came on. "God have mercy," was all he could say. He felt like he'd been hit in the stomach with a baseball bat. The nave of the church was mostly untouched, save for the symbols spray-painted on the walls in glossy white: the inverted cross, Baphomet pentacle, enneagram.

Beyond the altar rail the sanctuary was pure chaos. Every item on the altar was upturned and paired with a small cardboard reference number placed by crime scene investigators. On the floor beneath it, a small pool of dried blood was also marked.

The shrine on the Gospel side of the church had been savaged, the Blessed Virgin reduced to fiberglass shrapnel, and a glass display case smashed open. But worst of all was the crucifix. Three quarters of Jesus' head lay on the floor, at the foot of the cross.

"Let's start with these symbols," Michael said, recovering. "Pretty basic Google-search stuff. This could all be a distraction from someone grabbing the kid."

Father Ignatius nodded his agreement. "Does the child live with both parents?"

"Yes. They're very happily married. The police asked the same thing. No one could come up with anybody who would have reason to take Griffin."

The Jesuits began making their way around the nave of the church, inspecting each symbol, Ignatius a few steps ahead.

"Look at this one," Michael said, pointing to a simple circle with a dot within. "Ancient pagan symbol of sun-worship." He glanced over at Ignatius, who was transfixed, gazing at the next symbol on the wall. "What is it?" He walked over to where his friend stood and took an involuntary step back.

On the wall, precisely halfway up the side of the church, was scrawled a dingir—the ancient Sumerian symbol of deity that had factored so deeply into their last visit to the States.

"You're sure you killed him?" Father Ignatius said, softly.

"The detective? Oh, yeah. He's five kinds of dead. Whoever was inside, though . . ."

Ignatius grunted. "This is looking less and less like a distraction."

"Agreed." They finished their circuit of the nave, bringing them back to the altar. "This is where electronics are supposedly acting wonky?" Michael pulled out his cellphone. "Looks to be working okay," he said. "I only have two bars, but then again, we're in the middle of infinite cornfields."

Father Mark finally ducked under the crime scene tape and joined them near the altar. "I forgot to mention," he said, "that this morning I found that about half of the consecrated hosts were missing from the ciborium in the tabernacle."

Ignatius locked eyes with Michael. "Are you thinking what I am thinking?"

"That thing in Port-au-Prince?"

"What thing?" Father Mark asked. "What happened?"

"The desecration of a church," Ignatius said. "And the pilfering of many consecrated hosts for blasphemous occult use."

They were all silent for some time. Father Mark finally cleared his throat and said, "This is also where one of the policemen—one of my parishioners—reported hearing strange, unsettling noises. Scraping and such. Muffled voices."

"Is there a cellar or basement beneath the church?" Ignatius asked.

"Yes, this way."

They made their way down creaky wooden stairs to a sparse dirt-floor basement. Father Mark found the pull-string, illuminating the immediate area.

"Do people come down here often?" Michael asked.

"Not anymore. Only to turn the boiler on in the fall and off in the spring. Haven't needed it yet this year with how hot it's been. Apparently, one of my predecessors in the early aughts kept a lot of notes and books down here, but they were destroyed in a flood, so we steer clear of using it for storage these days."

Michael and Ignatius did a thorough search of the basement, finding nothing.

"Am I the only one feeling a presence down here?" Michael asked.

"No," Ignatius answered, fingering his crucifix. "Father Mark, I think your parishioners may be right; something sinister is at play here."

14

Parker dialed his wife's number for the fourth time. It went right to voicemail.

"Where are you?" he hissed. "I made lunch plans and now you're not here. This does not make either of us look very good, honey." He sighed heavily into the phone. "Just call me as soon as you get this, okay?" He hung up.

"No luck?" Ruth asked. She was smiling, which bothered Parker intensely. They had been standing in the lobby of Holy Ghost Tabernacle for the past twenty minutes, while Parker made calls and sent texts.

"She must have gotten called to an emergency," he said. And he wanted to believe it. Still, it was horrible timing. The rift between Ruth and Corrinne meant overwhelming grief for Parker. He wanted—needed—to help them reconcile. That's what this lunch was about. He hadn't told Corrinne because he feared she'd back out if she knew.

Is that what was happening? Had she caught wind of this lunch and chickened out?

* * *

"Don't test me, woman," Anders warned. He was still pointing the AR at Esther, who was now sitting in a chair beside him.

Corrinne made eye contact with her. "Don't worry, Esther. Everything is going to be okay."

"Don't tell her that," Anders said. "You don't know that!"

"I thought you were their pastor," she said. "Their shepherd."

"Sometimes a sheep has to die for the good of the flock."

"I've never heard of that. But I can see that you're not a very wise shepherd—pointing a gun at your own lamb instead of the very real danger five feet away."

He snorted a laugh. "Danger? I got two unarmed women in here with me. I think I'll be alright."

"But use some judgment. Who's the greater threat, her or me?"

Anders smirked. "You really want me to point this gun at you? Fine." He swung the barrel in her direction.

Corrinne stepped quickly toward him, catching the barrel of the gun in the web between her left thumb and index finger, pushing it up toward the ceiling. Grabbing on with her other hand, she circled around him and slammed the barrel of the gun into his temple again and again.

"Run, Esther!" she shouted. Anders stumbled back, in shock. Corrinne slammed her knee up into his groin—the ultimate equalizer when fighting a male perp. He cried out in pain, but kept his grip on the gun, now exerting his superior strength. She felt her grip weaken. The kid hadn't moved.

Corrinne circled hard to the left, driving with the gun, using the momentum to connect the barrel with his face once more. Seeing an opening, she stepped between his legs, and lurched into him, throwing all of her weight into his upper body. Anders tripped backwards and she landed hard on top of him.

It suddenly occurred to her that the gun had not gone off during all of this. Or had it? She couldn't remember. The barrel wasn't hot to the touch. Was it jammed? Was it even loaded? She yanked out the clip and threw it over her right shoulder.

"Esther, you've got to go!"

Men were coming. She could hear them, shouting and running toward them. FBI? No, it was from the back of the house. They would be here in moments.

Wait. Something had changed. They were no longer fighting for the rifle. She looked down at it, gripped tight in her hands, too close to Anders even to use the one round in the chamber. Then she saw his revolver, clearing the holster. Not too close to use that.

All at once, the smell of the sub-Sanka coffee hit her anew, like it was calling to her. She reached out, snagging the orange handle of the carafe with her finger tips and slamming it down hard on the bridge of Anders' nose, creating an explosion of near-boiling liquid and shattered glass. He shrieked and dropped the gun, bringing his hands up to his burned and lacerated face, shards of glass poking up from it like stalactites.

Corrinne dumped the AR and snatched up the revolver, taking a step back from Anders' contorting form. In her peripheral, she could see the screen door once again closing slowly on its arm—Esther was gone. And then a huge, ruddy bear of a man burst in from the rear of the house, pump shotgun in hand. She fired two shots, center mass, and the man went down, sending the shotgun skidding along the hardwood floor.

Philips rushed in behind him, holding his own gun in one hand and Jackie's in the other. His eyes went immediately to his companion, face down on the ground, bleeding and still, and then to Anders, disarmed, disfigured, and writhing. He dropped the guns and raised his hands. Two black-clad men in FBI windbreakers burst in through the front door and slammed Philips to the ground.

Corrinne hopped over them and rushed out the back, the revolver still locked in her hands. A few dozen civilians in their Sunday best were pouring out of the pole barn, hands up, at the behest of a pack of FBI agents. At gunpoint, they were ordered to their knees. Men. Women. Kids.

She broke right, homing in on a smaller shack of rusting corrugated metal. The door was open a crack and Corrinne threw it wide, filling the dim interior with sunlight. A young man, maybe seventeen, shielded his eyes with one hand. In the other, he held a Glock.

"Drop it," she ordered, drawing back the hammer of the pistol. He obeyed. "On your face!" She buried her knee in his back and clicked her handcuffs onto his wrists, a little tighter than necessary.

A few feet away, blindfolded and tied to a thick eyehook sunk into the concrete floor, was Jackie, still in his boxers. His face and ribs showed signs of a beating. Corrinne fished the folding knife from her pocket, cut him free, and pulled away the blindfold.

"You're okay," she said.

It seemed to take a moment for him to recognize her. Then he wrapped his arms around her neck like a toddler and pulled her in close. Her first instinct was to push him away, but she decided against it. The poor guy probably thought he was going to die in here. The least she could do was indulge him.

Corrinne endured the embrace for half a minute, before firmly separating from him. "Thanks for the opening back there," she said. "Took some stones. We'd have been dead otherwise."

"Thanks for saving my life," he said. His signature smugness was nowhere to be seen.

"Sorry about that," she said. "No male cop wants to be rescued by a woman."

He smiled, weakly. "I kind of liked it."

* * *

"They take your gun?" Detective Alvarez asked.

Corrinne was back at the station, anxious to get in a room with her suspects. This was the third time she'd been stopped. For a Sunday, there were more people around than usual.

"The perps?"

"No, the brass. I shot a guy a couple years ago and they took my gun," he said. "I had to use a loaner for two weeks while mine was at the crime lab."

"I found a loophole," she answered. "Used one perp's gun to shoot the other."

Alvarez laughed. "Nice." Then he went suddenly serious and asked, "You okay?"

"Yeah. It's not my first time. I'll write my statement, talk to the shrink, put it behind me."

"Good for you. By the way, I got your perp on ice in Interview B."

"Which perp?"

"Phelps?"

"You mean Philips," she said.

"Yeah, the other guy's handcuffed to a bed at down Butterworth. Needed some stitches and a whole tub of burn ointment." He whacked her on the shoulder and walked off, grinning.

On the way down to the interrogation room, Corrinne powered her phone back up. She had four new voicemails and six texts—all from Parker. Had he heard what was happening? The poor guy could be out of his mind with worry. She opened the most recent message: "Never mind, I guess. I'll just tell Ruth I don't know where you are. Which is the truth." She turned the phone back off and buzzed herself into the interrogation room.

Philips was cuffed to the table, his upper body slumped over it, fingers drumming.

Corrinne sat down and monkeyed with some papers for a moment, as if she didn't even notice him there. She'd grabbed them off her recycling pile. It always helped to remind the perp that they were in your territory now. She scribbled a few nonsense phrases down and then slid the papers into a file folder, before finally looking up at her prisoner.

"Your brother-in-law's going to be well enough to travel in a couple days," she said, "at which point I imagine they'll bring you both to a federal facility. When that happens, this will be out of my hands. No more deals to be made, no special consideration for your cooperation. If you want to make things better for yourself, now is the time to start talking."

She could see him swallowing, hard and slow, his Adam's apple like an elevator going down to the basement and back up to the penthouse. He'd talk.

"Let's start with something easy," she said. "When did you get the Fresco Food Service truck?" He stared at the table. "I can just look it up. It's not that hard. Did you steal it?"

"No," he said. "We bought it. About three weeks ago."

"What for?"

He fiddled with the chain of his cuffs, said nothing.

"Look, Timothy. You're obviously not the brains of this operation. It's your brother-in-law we really want. You help me out and we can make a deal. Now tell me: what have you got planned for November 2nd? Why is that a date people will remember?"

Philips squeezed his eyes shut and, for a moment, looked like he might cry. Then he opened them, bloodshot and wet, and looked right into Corrinne's. "He's been planning it for months."

The door buzzed and swung open. A desk sergeant offered, "Sorry, detective," and walked away, leaving John Slocum framed in the doorway.

"This is over," the lawyer announced.

"*This man* is your attorney?" Corrinne asked. Philips shrugged.

"Jay Anders' wife contacted me an hour ago," Slocum said. "I'll be representing both of them. If you have something to say to them, you say it through me."

"Do you even have experience in federal court?"

"Not your concern. Out you go."

"Fine." Corrinne gathered her papers. As she passed Slocum, she craned her neck, gazing at his right eye. "Are you wearing makeup, Mr. Slocum?"

"Do I have to call the councilman?"

"No, I'm just saying . . . that's foundation, right?" She stepped out into the hall. "You're wearing more makeup than I am. Are you covering something up?"

He gave her that smug cake-eating grin and slammed the door.

Corrinne allowed herself a chuckle, out in the hall. Then the door to the observation room opened and Capt. Dunleavy stepped out.

"Kirkpatrick, we need to talk."

* * *

"I just don't understand why God would allow this, Father." Gloria Matthews mopped the tears from her eyes with a Kleenex. "Griffin had just lost a friend. He was just starting to heal. We all were. And now *this*?"

Father Mark had put the Jesuits Militant in contact with the missing boys' parents an hour earlier. Ignatius suggested they approach them in plainclothes, as investigators, arguing that the clericals would encourage existential conversation rather than a rehearsal of the bare facts of the case. Father Michael had overruled him, but was now regretting it. They'd been sitting in the Matthews's immaculately curated living room for two hours discussing a wide variety of topics and continually getting off track. The McMansion, positioned fifty yards back off the road, stood in stark contrast to the older, dilapidated homes around it.

"I have kind of an odd question," Michael said. "Was there anything suspicious about Brady Miller's death? Anything that didn't quite seem right?"

"When a twelve-year-old boy dies, that never seems right," Cliff Matthews said. "But suspicious? Not really. He had cancer."

Ignatius nodded. "Was Brady as involved in the church as young Griffin?"

"No," Gloria said. "I mean, I don't know. They were Seventh Day Adventists, so they went to a different church. But he and Griffin had been close friends, especially this past year. And Griffin doesn't make friends easily." She began to weep again.

Ignatius fixed Michael with a look that said, *Let's get out of here.* Michael couldn't agree more. He felt nothing but compassion for these parents, but this well was dry. They could do more for them by moving on in their investigation.

"Thank you so much for your time," Father Michael said, standing. "We'll be in prayer for you and we'll contact you with any developments. They shook hands all around and the two priests returned to their rental car.

When they were back on the road, Michael asked, "So what are you thinking? Cover-up?"

"I'm not sure. I noticed something about our friend Father Mark. The way he spoke of the missing boy—"

"The past tense thing? I noticed it too. 'Griffin *was* studious, he *was* a good kid.'"

"Yes," Father Ignatius said. "Either he's lost all hope or he knows something we don't."

* * *

The captain would not stop looking at Corrinne like that. Like she was looking at a one-legged puppy. "Are you *sure* you're okay?" she asked for the third time. They were in the Command Center, surrounded by crime scene and evidence photos

"Yes, ma'am."

"It would be completely normal to take you off active duty while you get some counseling."

"No need, ma'am. I'll be fine."

The look faded a bit. "Good. Because frankly I can't spare you right now. We're just coming off this thing with the recorded phone calls and now three murders and a—" she dropped her voice to a whisper, "terrorist."

"We took down the terrorists," Corrinne said. "I don't see how that hurts our image."

The captain shrugged. "It's all *optics*, I guess. I don't even know what that means. Anyway, that FBI agent wants a word." The look of concern washed back over her face. "But we don't have to do this now. We can wait until you're up to it."

"It's fine. I'm fine."

"They're not happy," the captain warned.

"Are you kidding me?" Corrinne's voice rose, involuntarily. "I saved them another Waco, for crying out loud. That guy was determined to go down in a hail of bullets and take innocents with him. But thanks to me, no one got hurt!"

The captain shrugged. "They don't see it that way."

"You mean Wilson doesn't see it that way."

"Like I said, we can do this another time."

"Oh, no. Let's go have a chat with the FBI."

The two agents were waiting in the captain's office, Wilson sitting behind her desk. Corrinne glanced at the captain, unable to gauge her reaction.

"Agent Wilson," Corrinne said, taking a seat across from him.

"It's Special Agent," Rosa corrected, her expression hard.

Special Agent Wilson tipped back in the captain's desk chair. "Tell me something, Captain Dunleavy, does this woman always disobey orders?

"Not always."

"Not good orders," Corrinne added.

He glared at her. "We got lucky today, Kirkpatrick. Do you realize that? Your recklessness could have—" His phone began to ring in his pocket. *Livin' la Vida Loca.* He scrambled to silence it.

"Nice choice," Corrinne said. "That's a classic."

He turned to the captain. "We offered you our help with this murder case because your detectives are clearly in way over their heads. You declined. Had it all under control, you assured me. Now, in the course of that dumpster fire of an investigation, you've somehow unraveled an unrelated case we've been building for eight months!"

"It's unfortunate, yes," the captain said, evenly.

"Tomorrow!"

"I'm sorry?"

"*Tomorrow* we were going to make an arrest!"

"So you got them a day early," Corrinne said. "What are you complaining about?"

Wilson was turning purple. "It would have been low-risk, Kirkpatrick. And we were going to have a nice, gift-wrapped, slam-dunk charge of domestic terrorism."

"You've got a whole smorgasbord of charges you can hang around their necks now. He's in custody; what more do you want?"

He waved at Corrinne dismissively, as if he could cause her to disappear with a mere gesture, and addressed the captain again.

"I'll tell you what more I want: I want you to bench her. Take her off this murder case before she does any more damage."

"No," the captain said. "Not unless the chief orders it. What I will do is put another detective in charge. Vivien Allen. Detective Second Grade, highly decorated. One of my best."

He sneered. "You said *she* was one of your best." He gestured broadly in Corrinne's direction.

"How about you take it easy, Wilson. She's had a rough day. And get out of my chair."

"I'm so sorry. I didn't realize the little snowflake was having a hard day." Bertuzzi snorted a laugh. Wilson vacated the chair and straightened his suit jacket. "Just be glad none of my people got hurt as a result of your Dirty Harriet crap, or this would be a very different conversation." At the door he paused and said, "Oh, and we're taking your prisoners. First thing in the morning."

When they were gone, the captain resumed her chair. "That pompous prig messed with the lumbar support."

"Am I dismissed?" Corrinne asked.

"Yeah. Take the rest of the day. Think about taking a little time tomorrow as well."

Corrinne nodded and retreated to the ladies' room. She splashed some cold water on her face and dried it with a coarse brown paper towel. Looking into the eyes of her reflection, she realized she felt nothing, just dead inside. She almost wished a flood of tears or rage or anything would come to the surface. But it didn't. She'd never been good at that sort of thing.

The door opened and Vivien popped her head in. "There you are," she said. "You okay?"

"Yes. I'm fine," she said again. "Congratulations, by the way."

"For what?"

"It's your investigation now."

Vivien shook her head. "No, it's still *our* investigation. And we've got another body. Just now."

"Seriously?"

"Afraid so. You want to sit this one out?"

"Absolutely not."

Vivien smiled. "Good to hear. We're already down one man. Or, Jackie O. anyway."

15

The Grand Rapids Public Museum was one of the oldest in the nation, although its current building was an architectural ode to the Nineties. The building sat perched on the bank of the Grand River, in the heart of downtown, with a pavilion jutting out over the river itself, in which children could ride an authentic 1920s-era carousel. Detectives Allen and Kirkpatrick were carefully climbing their way under this pavilion, where five pillars held it up from the rocky grade beneath.

Tethered by her wrists to one of these pillars was the latest victim.

"Her name is Hannah Goodwin, 46, of Byron Center," Vivien read. "Last seen shopping at Aldi two days ago."

The woman wore mom jeans and a white T-shirt, the back of which was tattered and stained a dark crimson.

"Looks like she was caned or whipped or something," Corrinne said. "Ugh."

"That's a lot of blood," Vivien said, climbing closer to the body, hunched over against the steep incline. Corrinne followed.

"And not much left of the back of that shirt," she said. "Someone took their time with this. Who found her? And when?" These were the questions that had plagued Corrinne the whole way here. She had two suspects in custody, one of them for twenty-four hours. If this body had turned up today, that meant neither suspect was the perp.

"A photography student from Kinsey was taking some pictures from across the river this morning. When she got home, she dumped it all on her computer and started going through them. She thought it was just a trick of the light until she zoomed in and got a good look at our vic."

"Probably have some pleasant dreams tonight," Corrinne said. "Any idea as to time of death?"

"Not yet." She seemed to read Corrinne's concern. "But she could easily have been here since yesterday morning. Only when the sun is at just the right angle can you even see her from the river, tucked way up under the pavilion like that."

"Yeah, I guess."

Vivien's phone buzzed in her back pocket. She dug it out and answered, "Hello . . . Oh, hi, Captain . . . No, she's here with me . . . Can I ask why? . . . I really don't think there's a need for . . . No, I'm not. No, ma'am. I'll tell her . . . Okay, goodbye." She hung up and told Corrinne, "Captain says you need to take the rest of the day off or she'll put you on leave." She shrugged. "Sorry, Kirkpatrick. Not my call."

"I know." Corrinne could feel her insides in freefall. The last thing she wanted right now was to be home with nothing to do but think about what she'd seen and done today. The captain had allegedly been an actual cop at some point; how did she not understand that?

"E-mail me what you find," Corrinne said. "I'll do some research from home, see if this fits with the whole saint motif."

* * *

The Tribunal stood motionless against the wood siding of the house. The sun had not yet gone down, but the deep horizontal shadows hid him well enough. Next door, all the blinds were drawn. They were away for the weekend; he'd made sure of it. Another house over, Parker Saint was pacing back and forth just inside the picture window, pathetically unaware of how close the danger was.

He was wearing the hood, but not the robe. A compromise: maintain the integrity of the Inquisition without standing out or slowing his movements. From the pocket of his heavy coat, he retrieved a slot screw driver and opened the telephone interface box affixed to the side of the house. It still bore the logo of the long-defunct Michigan Bell company, but contained a state-of-the-art fiber optic connection.

In the early days of home security systems, the alarms were connected to a phone line, which automatically called the police or alarm company. Back then, a burglar could simply cut the line where it met the house, simultaneously taking out the alarm and the homeowner's ability to call for help. Lately, a new breed of do-it-yourself security systems had positioned itself as beyond all that. In the age of Internet, Bluetooth, and Wi-Fi, everything is completely wireless, they claimed. The Tribunal laughed to himself. How did people think the Internet came into their homes? One nice big fat cable. At least the old, professionally installed systems had ear-splitting sirens inside the walls, to draw the attention of neighbors, should the call not go through. Nothing like that here.

The Tribunal unplugged the cable, simple as that. No need to even cut the line. Pinch a tab, pull down a half-inch, and the lawyer's house was unprotected. After quickly screwing the box shut again, he replaced the screwdriver in his coat pocket and gingerly checked the opposite pocket. The syringe was intact. He felt butterflies in his stomach.

* * *

Parker saw Corrinne's Expedition pull into the driveway at almost five. But she didn't come into the house. She just sat there, behind the wheel. He felt his ire rising. What had he done to push her away, other than trying to help? Maybe he should just back off and give her what she wanted, leave her to deal with things all alone.

No, that was wrong. Marriage meant picking each other up when one falls, but more importantly, holding one another up so no one fell in the first place. Corrinne could sleep on the couch, live at the station, and box him out. He wouldn't give up on her.

The door opened with a jingle of keys and his wife stood, just inside the house, her brow drawn down, mouth a hard, straight line. When she came no further into the house, Parker went out to meet her in the foyer.

"Where were you?" he asked.

Her eyes darkened for a moment and her face clamped down all the harder. Then her lip began to quiver, like a child's—the precursor to unrestrained tears. Parker covered the space between them in a second and enveloped her in his arms. She sobbed into his chest, drenching his shirt, breaths coming in irregular hiccups.

A few minutes later, the tears let off and she stepped out of his embrace, wiping her face on her sleeve.

"Do you want to talk about it?" Parker asked.

"That's the last thing in the world I want to do."

"Okay. But . . . are you okay?"

Disgust flashed across her face, swallowed up by a blank Zen. "Yeah, honey. I just need some time by myself. If that's all right with you. I think I'll take a bath."

"Sure," Parker said. He wished they were still locked together, even if it meant more tears, but he would give her the space she needed. "Anyway, I've been meaning to bring these old pictures over to Stephen," he said. "Might actually find him home on a Sunday afternoon."

Parker stuffed his feet into some loafers and grabbed the stack of old photos off the table by the front door. They were Rockwellian—black and white images of church life in the late fifties, all of them featuring Donavan's late mother. The prize of the bunch was a posed photo outside of the church office. Parker's grandfather and Beverly Donavan beamed at the camera, comfortably close. He'd scanned it and was considering blowing it up to be framed and hung in his study.

The warm glow of nostalgia evaporated the moment he mounted the steps to Donavan's front porch, replaced by an icy sense of foreboding. Something wasn't right here. The front door was open, which was not unusual for a pleasant autumn day like this, but loud music was wafting from inside—a soft rock channel, cranked up like death metal. Parker tried to imagine Donovan choosing this music or this volume and came up empty.

He almost called Corrinne, but thought better of it. To interrupt his wife's bubble bath of solitude with nothing more to go on but that hideous ditty about Jack and Diane would only drive the wedge between them deeper. Instead, he knocked loudly on the storm door. No answer. He rang the bell and waited for thirty second before ringing it again. Nothing.

"Hello?" Parker called, opening the door. He stepped inside. Over the past year, the two men had established walk-in neighbor rights, the kind of friendship where you grab a Coke from the fridge instead of asking for one.

The music was coming from the living room, a high-end stereo that had only ever known the likes of Mozart and Brahms. Parker turned it down. What was that sound? The slamming of a door? It had come from the back of the house.

"Hello? Stephen? It's Parker." He forced one foot in front of the other, bringing him through the dining room, toward the kitchen. Toward the sound he thought he'd heard.

Then he saw his neighbor, flat on his back on the kitchen floor, his eyelids sagging, his breath coming ragged.

"Stephen!" Parker rushed to his side. "Are you okay? Did you fall?"

Donavan shook his head forcefully. He opened his mouth to speak, but seemed unable to form words. A stroke? Parker pulled out his phone and dialed 911. He asked for an ambulance, gave the address and symptoms, and then hung up, despite the operator's insistence that he stay on the line. He needed Corrinne. Because Donavan was miming something now. And it looked an awful lot like a syringe being jammed into his thigh and the plunger pushed down.

Hair still wet, Corrinne burst through the front door not two minutes later, gun in hand. Parker told her about the radio, the sound of the door, and Donavan's charades. Ordering him to stay put, she did a sweep of the house, during which the ambulance arrived.

The EMTs asked a series of rapid-fire questions. "His pupils are dilated," one of them said to the other. "This guy's on something." They strapped him to a gurney, wheeled him out, and loaded him into the back of the ambulance.

When they'd gone, Corrinne called to Parker from the back door.

"Look at this," she said, indicating the damaged doorframe. "Someone pried it open."

"You think he was attacked?"

She nodded. "He was definitely telling us he'd been injected with something. And he was loopy. If I had to guess, I'd say you scared off the attacker by coming into the house."

"But who would do that?"

"Hello? Dad?" The voice came from the front of the house.

"It's Connie," Parker said. "Stephen's daughter. She sometimes comes over on Sunday nights."

"She can't come in here," Corrinne said. "This is an active crime scene."

"I'll bring her outside and explain what happened."

* * *

"The lengths you'll go to," Vivien said, "to avoid a day off."

Corrinne had called her shortly after the ambulance left. In itself, the break-in probably didn't fall under the Major Case Team's purview, but Vivien, who had just been leaving the crime scene beneath the museum, agreed to assume the case.

They stood in the kitchen and rehearsed what had happened, with help from Parker. Then Corrinne sent him home, ordering him to double-check the locks and throw the deadbolts.

"This doesn't seem like a neighborhood with a lot of break-ins," Vivien said, pushing the foot pedal to open the trash can.

"Donavan's got more than a few enemies," Corrinne answered. "He's representing the city council in that lawsuit."

"I've got something there." Vivien reached a gloved hand into the garbage and withdrew a plastic syringe, depositing it carefully in an evidence bag. "Strange that the perp would leave—oh."

"What is it?" Corrinne followed Vivien's gaze into the trash and immediately saw it. A card, about three inches by four, upon which was printed the likeness of a young man with soft features, wearing a fur-trimmed robe, and the words, "St. Thomas More, Pray for Us."

Their eyes met. It was instantly clear what this meant. Hannah Goodwin's body was not proof-positive that the perp was still on the loose, but if the same man who had killed Cates and all the rest left a prayer card in Donavan's kitchen, that did the trick.

"Okay," Vivien said, "we need to tighten it up going forward. You and Jackie arrested Caraway and went after those militia guys without me. No more of that. We do this whole thing as a team."

Corrinne nodded. She felt a suffocating weight pushing down on her shoulders. It was like the feeling she had at Ruth's house only a hundred times heavier. After all, she expected to bomb as a pastor's wife. That was no surprise.

But she was a great detective.

Or had been.

16

The two men from the Marshals Service reminded Special Agent Wilson of a couple high school football coaches, which were among his least favorite kind of people. They were just climbing out of a black SUV at the Kent County Jail when he and Agent Bertuzzi arrived in a more or less identical SUV. It was a little after five, Monday morning, and the parking lot was mostly empty.

Both men wore long-sleeve T-shirts, hugging tight to muscular frames, and battered blue jeans. Wilson scoffed. Hardly the uniform of professionals. He was well aware that a single bad encounter with a deputy U.S. Marshal years earlier had soured him to the whole enterprise, but this morning he didn't really care. Nothing else could go wrong with this case.

"Gentlemen," Wilson called, approaching the marshals, who were strapping black Kevlar vests emblazoned with the word POLICE onto their torsos. "I'm Special Agent Wilson, FBI." He flashed his credentials. "Anders and Philips are my prisoners. We've got a nice quiet hole to throw them in back in Detroit."

The taller of the men peeled off a heavy Velcro strap from the vest and refastened it, tighter. "Copy," he said. "We'll sign them out. You can follow along behind."

"Not happening," Wilson said. "This is a joint FBI-ATF operation. So far, the ATF has done squat. Then local PD shows up yesterday and blows the whole thing to pieces. We're not dealing another agency in. We sign these guys out together, perps ride with us, you can follow along behind."

"That's not how it works." The deputy marshal refastened the same strap again, as if he were trying to crush his own ribcage with it. "We cover federal prisoner transport."

"Not today," Wilson said. "You want to stand outside all day and make calls, I'm game. We can take it up to the director and the U.S. Marshal for the State of Michigan for all I care."

The two armored men looked at each other and shrugged. "If it means that much to you, be our guest. We've got auto restraints."

"We brought our own," Wilson said. "We're taking no chances."

Thirty-five minutes later, the prisoners were shuffling toward the FBI vehicle, their cuffs attached to their leg irons by short chains that kept them hunched over like a couple of Igors. Bertuzzi loaded them roughly into the back seat and buckled them in.

As he slid in behind the wheel, Wilson announced, "Enjoy the sunshine, boys. It's the last time you're going to see it for a long, long while." He started the SUV and turned off of the service drive, onto Plymouth. "Whole different set of rules for terrorists in custody." He looked back at Anders' face, full of stitches, scabs, and red patches. "Looking handsome, by the way, Jay."

Traffic was sparse this early. He glanced in the rearview mirror and saw the marshals following close behind.

"What's that?" Bertuzzi asked. She was pointing at the road ahead of them. "Why is the pavement wet?"

"I don't know. Maybe it rained."

"It didn't rain. Slow down a minute."

Wilson shot her an impatient look. "It's nothing. Fire hydrant maybe."

"Look!" She pointed again, this time at the silhouette of a man standing on the freeway overpass, just ahead of them. Wilson punched it and crouched down in his seat, just in case.

The man on the overpass tossed down a bottle, a flaming rag protruding from its mouth. It pancaked against the ground and suddenly there were orange flames everywhere.

Now Wilson eased on the brake.

"What are you doing?" Rosa demanded. "Gun it! Go through!"

The SUV lurched forward, passing unharmed through the flames and a curtain of thick black smoke. Just as they came out of it, back into the morning air, they saw the delivery truck, blocking both lanes. Too late. The words Fresco Food Service filled their vision, and then there was broken glass. Twisted metal. The powdery *boomf* of the airbags. Then it was silent. Behind them, the fire was already burning itself out.

To Wilson's right, Rosa was unconscious, slumped forward in her seat, bleeding from her nose and a gash on her forehead. With much difficulty, he cranked his neck to look behind them. The SUV containing the deputy marshals had embedded itself in the back third of their own vehicle.

He commanded himself to draw his weapon, but the order was lost in the shock and trauma of the crash. Anders was leaning back in his seat, craning his neck, looking for someone or something outside.

Then the driver side window exploded. A hand reached in and hit the power locks. Wilson looked up at the tall, broad-shouldered man who was now pointing a Glock 17 at him. He recognized the man—one of the forty people he'd corralled out of the pole barn the day before. He hadn't given the guy a second look or a second thought.

"Just take them," Wilson mumbled.

"We will," the man said, grinning ear-to-ear. Then he pulled the trigger.

* * *

The captain gathered the whole team together, first thing, and informed them of the escape.

"We've got two dead deputy U.S. Marshals, a dead FBI agent, and another in critical condition," she said. "They now have all the resources of those agencies focused on tracking them down. I predict these two men and their accomplices will be in the morgue by dinnertime. For now, though, be vigilant. Watch each other's backs. I highly doubt they'd hang around town, but just in case. Remember, it was two of ours who made the bust to begin with, and these guys seem to hold a grudge. All right, dismissed."

As the group broke, the captain called out, "Kirkpatrick, a word."

Corrinne followed her into her office. It was practically habit at this point.

"A couple things," the captain said. "First, I see Reese is back today. I want your opinion: is he ready to get back out there? Or do I put him on a desk?"

"I'm not sure. He was pretty shaken up by what happened yesterday. Anyone would be. I'll keep an eye on him."

"You do that." She sighed. "The other thing: we're bouncing Caraway this morning."

Corrinne just nodded. "Makes sense."

"We've got the thing at your neighbor's house, while Caraway was in lockup. We've got the new victim by the museum. M.E. thinks she died late Saturday night. And then there's this." She turned her laptop to face Corrinne.

It was a selfie of a young woman holding a smiling baby at Hasselbring Park, the fountain visible in the background. "Fun with Logan at the park, #MommyLove" the caption said.

"This was taken a week ago Saturday," the captain explained, "at 7:30 PM. No body on display." She clicked the right arrow, bringing up a screenshot of a Tumblr page called "Worst of Artistry." A series of photos—first a wide shot, then a close-up of the man's face, and finally the counterfeit Artistry sign—were accompanied by the text, "If this is art, please stop the bus. I want to get off. #whitemangroup #odetomargaret #odetotacky #wtf."

"This was posted the next morning," Capt. Dunleavy said. "Now we know when the victim was placed in the park. Only problem is, Caraway was in Tallahassee for a week-long conference and only flew back in Sunday night."

"So he couldn't have placed the body," Corrinne said, stating the obvious.

The captain's eyes went soft again, the return of the patronizing mother figure from the previous afternoon. "Allen dug this up for me," she said. "This is the kind of basic police work you should have done before arresting him. I expect a lot from you, Kirkpatrick."

"I know. Sorry, ma'am."

"I need you to steer clear of Caraway. This Slocum slimeball's his lawyer and they're rattling my cage about a harassment lawsuit, not to mention the deputy chief still breathing down my neck because of his connection to Max Van de Burg on the city council. We don't need this now. Give them all a wide berth."

"Yes, ma'am."

"Everything okay with Allen?"

Corrinne nodded. "Just fine. Stephen Donavan is finally lucid this morning. I'm interviewing him and the three of us are comparing notes this afternoon."

"Okay," the captain said, waving a hand. "Bring this psycho in."

* * *

Parker and Corrinne converged in the halls of Butterworth Hospital, right in front of the uniformed cop sitting guard.

"Hey, honey," Parker said. He planted a kiss on her cheek. He'd adopted a pretend-everything-is-normal policy the night before and it hadn't backfired yet.

"Hello." She glanced at the cop and added, "I'm working right now."

"Me too." He lifted his Bible. "Pastoral hospital call. It'll be nice to work together again."

"Right." She pointed at the badge on her belt and told the guard, "We're stopping in. Shouldn't be more than ten minutes."

"Why is there an officer outside?" Parker asked as they entered the room.

"I asked for him," she said curtly.

"And the saints come marching in," Donavan announced. He was sitting up in the bed, smiling weakly.

"How long have you been saving that one?" Parker asked.

"A while," he admitted. "Hi, Corrinne."

"Good morning." She pulled up a chair to the bedside. "Listen, Stephen, you mind if I ask you a few questions?"

"Right to the point," he said. "I like that. I wish I could get back to work myself."

Parker wagged a finger. "You need to take it easy."

"Hey, I will when you do," he laughed.

Corrinne looked impatiently from one man to the other, pen poised over pad, until they both stopped smiling. "Could you tell me what you remember about the incident yesterday?"

Donavan slumped back in the bed and fixed Corrinne with a disappointed look, as though by bringing up the attack she had shattered the alternate reality he'd created where it never took place.

"I was washing the dishes," he said. "I didn't hear him come in, but he pulled a—maybe a pillowcase?—over my head and then I felt this sharp pain in my thigh and I could tell it was a syringe. I could feel the contents going into my leg."

"You're sure it was a man?"

"Had to be. He was so strong—dragged me down to the kitchen floor and held me there. I guess he was sitting against the fridge. I tried to fight him, but within maybe thirty seconds I started feeling groggy. The will to fight disappeared. There are bits and pieces after that, but the next thing I really knew, I was lying here." He turned to Parker and declared, "Someone wants to stop the work I'm doing for the Lord. They're trying to scare me out of doing my duty."

"It may be something a little more troubling," Corrinne said. "They're doing bloodwork to determine exactly what was injected into you, but it's probably the same stuff they found in the syringe in your trashcan: a cocktail of Fentanyl and Propofol."

"Is that supposed to mean something to me?"

"They found traces of both in David Cates."

He chuckled, drily, as if it all made sense now.

"There's more," Corrinne said, retrieving the prayer card from her jacket pocket. "This was found with the syringe. Have you ever seen it before?"

He shook his head.

"St. Thomas More is the patron saint of lawyers," Corrinne said. "I can't tell you too much, but suffice to say this fits with the serial killer's methods. He's been targeting seemingly upstanding and beloved citizens and killing them in ways that bring out their dark secrets—sometimes things that happened decades earlier."

"What are you saying?" Parker asked.

"I'm saying someone thinks Stephen has some sort of hypocrisy in his past." She turned to him. "Something related to you being a lawyer—and they were going to drug you, drag you out your house, and . . ." She hesitated. "And kill you."

"Thank God I happened by," Parker said.

Donavan nodded.

"Is there anything I need to know?" Corrinne asked. "Whatever may have happened in your past, I won't judge you and it really could help us find this guy before he hurts someone else."

"Isn't it obvious? I defended David Cates and the other board members. I won the case for them."

"Right, but that just doesn't seem like enough—this connection to one of his previous victims. I mean, he hasn't gone after anyone else's lawyer."

Donavan looked hurt. Betrayed.

"Don't get me wrong. You're the victim here; no one's denying that. I'm just trying to figure out—why you?"

Parker caught her eye and practically whispered, "Hon, maybe we should just—"

"If you're uncomfortable with this, you can wait outside. This is my job, Parker."

He sat down in the window sill, chastened.

"Well, Mr. Donavan?" she prompted.

"*Mr. Donavan*? I don't know what you want me to say. It makes perfect sense to me that I could be targeted by someone with the kind of issue you describe. I was quite vocal at the time of that case, defending this institution. And I was raked over the coals by the press. You can easily find the news archives." He sat up straight and looked Corrinne in the eye. "Am I completely at peace that the Saving Faith Network board got off scot free? No. But I do stand by what I said: that case was part of a broader assault on religious institutions. And Don Caraway was instrumental in getting it off the ground.

"The reality is that people of faith are easy targets for predators because we're trusting. Sure, it's a flaw, but it comes from the right place. After all, we see the best in people, not the worst. And so the

Caraways of the world go after churches and ministries rather than try to help equip them to guard against being infiltrated." He lay back in the bed, defeated.

There was a light knock at the door and the cop ducked his head in. "Sorry to interrupt," he said, "but Mr. Donavan's got another visitor."

"We're not done," Corrinne barked.

"Oh," the uniform said. "It's just, he's kind of a VIP. Max Van de Burg."

17

"I'll just be a moment, officer. I promise," a voice said, out in the hall. Then the door swung open and in walked Councilman Max Van de Burg, he of the practiced squinty smile and double-breasted suit. Corrinne breathed a curse.

"Max!" Donavan brightened immediately. "Good to see you. Hey, do you know *this guy*?" He poked a thumb toward Parker.

"Why, Parker Saint. Been a while." He gave Parker a two-handed shake.

"This is my wife, Corrinne Kirkpatrick."

"*Detective* Kirkpatrick," Donavan put in.

"Oh, yeah?" The councilman's smile froze in place, but he looked down at Corrinne with a mixture of surprise and disdain. He definitely knew the name. His eyes lingered on her a moment longer before he turned back to Donavan. "So how long are they going to keep you here? The city council needs you fighting for us, Stephen."

"I don't know. It was a scary thing, Max. A dangerous man was in my house. If he would have come half an hour later, my daughter would have been there with me." He shuddered.

Corrinne stood. "Why don't you take my seat?" she said. "Parker and I have to run out a minute. You two visit."

"Well, if you insist," the councilman said. As they shuffled past each other, her eyes met his, which now contained only a genuine smile. She grabbed Parker's hand and pulled him out of the room.

"What are you doing?" Parker asked. "I didn't even get to pray with him."

"Do you have a minute?" Corrinne asked. "For me?"

"For you, of course." He looked at her with concern. "Everything okay?"

"I just need to talk. They have a decent café here; you up for a latte?"

"Always."

* * *

They ordered their drinks and settled in at a corner table of the hospital's small cafe. At first, neither of them said anything. Then Corrinne pulled her badge off her belt, held it up for him to see, and slid it into her pocket.

"What does that mean?" Parker asked.

"We were both working up there. Pastor and cop. Down here, you're working and I'm not."

"I don't get it."

"It's weird," she said, "but you're my pastor. It's weird, right? And I need you to work something out for me."

"Okay?"

"Starting with that phony up in Stephen's room. You know him?"

"The councilman? Not really. From the old days, the TV gig. We ran in similar circles. He's a decent guy."

"Depends on who you ask. I've heard nothing but praise about the man from Donavan. Like he's a saint or something, always ready to stand up to the forces of darkness. But he also shut me out of an investigation. Remember last weekend? My shoulder? The guy who did that—the *lawyer* who did it—walked because Van de Burg threw his weight around. Oh, and that same lawyer represents Caraway in personal matters. I doubt Stephen knows that."

Parker nodded slowly. "That's a little messed up."

"Not unusual though. That's the thing, Parker. It's become normal in the last couple weeks. All the people who seem to be one thing on the surface, sparkling clean, if you ask the right person you get the real story. Yesterday, I raided a church service and the preacher held a gun to a girl's head. And this whole—"

"Wait. That was *you*? Anders, that Michigan militia nutburger and the other guy who escaped—you arrested them?"

"Yes, but that's not my point."

"They could be anywhere now." Parker looked around the café, as if the men might be hiding beneath a nearby table.

"I'm sure they're many miles away. But the point is that this whole case . . . at every turn I'm seeing how all the upstanding, *righteous people* who supposedly love God and their fellow man are hiding horrible secrets. They're not saints. They're just playing saint and everyone's buying it."

Parker nodded, but with confusion fixed on his face. "So you want me to explain . . . ?"

"What does the Bible or the right theology or whatever have to say about that? Because if all this Jesus stuff is just an act at the end of the day, I don't need it. Six months ago, when you baptized me, it felt very real. Now? Not so much."

"Well, first of all, Jesus told us that we'd always have these people. The phonies. He called them 'whitewashed tombs,' squeaky clean on the outside, but full of filth and rot inside. We'd have wolves in sheep's clothing, pretending to be harmless, while they preyed on the innocent. He warned us not to listen to them."

Corrinne nodded slowly. "But everyone's a hypocrite at some level, right? I know I am. I drop the ball all the time."

"Me too." He hesitated. "Can I get technical for a minute?"

"Please! I'm a detective. Technical is exactly what I want."

"It comes down to justification and sanctification."

Corrinne smiled. "Not that I don't know what those words mean, but, like . . . remind me what those words mean."

"Justification is when God declares us righteous based on the death and resurrection of Jesus. Our sins are washed away and when our perfectly holy God looks at us he sees the righteousness of Christ rather than our sins, which have been purged."

"And the other one?"

"Sanctification is the change in our lives as we more and more reflect the righteousness of Christ in what we do and say and think. Justification's instant. Sanctification is slow and often frustrating."

"But then it seems like the first one is just a legal fiction," she said. "It's not even real—if I'm righteous, but I'm still doing all this wicked stuff. What, I'm duping God? He's okay with us playing saint and he just goes along with it?"

"Let me illustrate."

"Oh, here we go."

"Shut up." Parker laughed. "We got the church building back, right?"

She nodded.

"So, we have a deed. A legal document that says the building belongs to us. Not a legal fiction—a reality. It's a church. But when you walk through it, there are still condom machines in the men's room, some pretty major damage to parts of the building. We've got no pews. I haven't gotten around to reassembling the pulpit. It needs work."

"Okay," Corrinne said, tentatively.

"But it still belongs to us. It's still the church's building. In fact, that's *why* we can do the work it needs. You follow?"

"Yeah, that helps," she said, her eyes still narrow. She thought it through again and nodded once, content. "Thanks."

He held up his half-empty glass. "Cheers?"

* * *

Parker sat in his study, staring at the wall. He had to make a decision, and very soon. Coffee with his wife had been amazing. They used to do that all the time, up until the last couple weeks. He needed that back in his life. He needed this case, which was piling tons of crippling stress, mortal danger, and spiritual crises on his wife's shoulders, to be over.

He looked down at his desk where the white polo sat, the iron-transfer paper still stuck to it. With his first attempt, he'd forgotten to flip the image horizontally before printing it out. This one was good, though. If he was going to do this, he was confident most people would buy the uniform without a second thought.

Grabbing his cell, he dialed up Father Michael.

"Go for Mike!"

"Hey, Father Michael. How's Panama?"

"Not what you'd think. I'm currently looking at a man with a rifle across his lap, cleaning a dead squirrel on a park bench—like ten feet from a playground."

"Really?"

"No joke. So, what's up?"

"I'm doing it."

"You're doing it? What are you—? No. Not the copier thing."

"Uh-huh. I'm doing it. Any advice?"

"Yeah. Don't do it," Father Michael practically yelled.

"It's already done. Look, Saturday night Corrinne said she had forty-eight hours to get evidence against Caraway or she'd have to let him go. That means they'll let him go *tonight*. I'm sure she's close to getting what she needs. If I can just give her a little boost."

"Let me ask you something, Parker. What did you preach on this Sunday?"

"James chapter three, why?"

"And how much of that sermon did your wife write for you?"

"You're forgetting that I've been an expert consultant for the police department. And Corrinne said herself, they never let me go. I'm still on the team."

"This is so stupid, man."

"I've seen you guys in action. I know how you do. And I've already practiced a bunch of times on our copier, from the same company. I can pop it out, copy it, and put it back in two minutes flat."

"Right, because it's a new copier," Michael said. "If there were thousands of images in that thing, it would take a whole lot longer."

"Okay, that's good to remember. Anything else?"

"You're gonna get caught," Michael said.

"No way. I've got the official shirt and a ball cap with the logo on it. The guy who installed mine didn't have one, but it looks pretty legit. I've even got a little name badge I printed up. I'm headed there when I hang up. If you have some helpful advice and you hold it back, well . . ."

"Okay, here's what you do," Michael said. "Pull the hat down low, over your eyes. And chew gum. Like obnoxiously. I mean, don't blow bubbles and attract attention, but rhythmically, relentlessly. I don't know why it works, but trust me, people won't remember your face as well if you're doing something obnoxious—assuming they don't recognize you as soon as they lay eyes on you."

"Gum. Check. Okay, I better go before I lose my nerve," Parker said. "Pray for me."

"Who's the patron saint of really, really bad ideas?"

18

The elevators in Bridgewater Place were far too fast. Parker had been hoping for a minute in there, alone, to get his head together and gather his wits. But the doors were dinging before he could even initiate a basic gut check. One minute he'd been noticing the marble floors in the lobby and the next he was hearing that horrible *ding* announcing that his stupid plan was about to commence.

On the drive over he'd been thinking of Father Michael—how he seemed to have endless courage and finesse and resourcefulness. Of course, he also had a partner in the equally effective Father Ignatius. Parker wished he had someone watching his back right now, ready to bail him out. But all his friends were either church members or fellow clergy. Not really an option today.

As he stepped through the propped glass doors into the lobby of Adler & Clark he felt a wall of self-doubt collapse onto him. This was idiotic. He wasn't Father Michael! His training had included theology, biblical languages, and counseling, not lock-picking, computer hacking, and espionage.

Then again, he had survived a serial killer's attack, defeated a legion of demons, and recovered the lost Crown of Marbella. This should be nothing by comparison. He pulled his hat down over his eyes, popped a stick of gum into his mouth and approached the desk, all confidence.

"I'm looking for the offices of FAR, Incorporated."

The receptionist directed him to the end of a long hall. "I'll call down there and let them know you're coming," she said.

Parker's confidence grew with every step. No one so much as glanced at him in these offices. The uniform—polo, hat, canvas tool bag, and covered metal clipboard—rendered him invisible. Ahead, a young man sat at a desk beneath a sign bearing the FAR logo.

"Need to have a look at your copier," Parker said between chomps.

The bored young man, whose nameplate identified him as Tannyr, looked up from his phone as if Parker's words had meant absolutely nothing.

"Your copier," he repeated, pointing at the logo on his shirt. He felt a twinge of regret for the deception, although the words themselves weren't untrue.

"What's the matter with it?" Tannyr asked.

Parker affected an annoyed sigh. "I don't know if you realize this," he said, "but if there's an issue with the copier—for example, the image transfer drum overheating—it wirelessly sends our office a repair request." Again, not a complete lie; Parker had learned this by reading and rereading the documentation that came with his copier on Saturday night. "It's all part of your maintenance agreement."

"I don't know . . ." Tannyr looked at Parker as if he were a suspicious e-mail, to be opened or deleted.

Parker flipped open the cover of his clipboard and squinted at the blank pages within. "Look, I can come back later," he spat, matching Tannyr's lack of charisma. "Or not at all. Doesn't matter to me, but make up your mind, because I've got other calls to make."

"No, it's okay. Follow me, Mr.—?"

Parker looked down at his name badge, which read CHUCK W. He hesitated. "Webis," he said. "Chuck Webis."

Webis?

"Webis," Tannyr repeated, leading the way.

The copier looked quite similar to the one Hope Presbyterian was now leasing. Parker smiled just a bit. He'd be in and out.

"You do know the machine doesn't belong to us, right?" Tannyr asked. "The law firm owns it. We're just renting."

Parker's calm confidence faltered. Somehow, stealing legal documents from an actual law firm seemed far more serious—more real, even—than copying the drive of a professional agitator. But of course, it was too late to back out now.

"Who do you think reported the problem?" Parker said. Could a question be a lie?

"I thought you said the problem reported itself."

Parker dropped the clipboard onto the top of the copier with a *clack*. "Do you want to argue with me all day or do you want me to keep your machine running?"

"Go ahead, I guess," Tannyr said. He made no move to return to his desk.

Reaching into his pocket, Parker pulled out a pair of latex gloves, which he stretched onto his hands. At the receptionist's inquisitive look, he explained, "A little trick I picked up. Keeps the toner off my fingers." He opened the access door at the front of the machine, revealing its inner workings.

The remainder of his cool crumbled. This machine looked nothing like the one on which he'd practiced. Where the hard drive should be was a latch that seemed to provide access to another, deeper recess in the copier's workings.

He studied the layout for a minute, trying to orient himself. Tannyr seemed to get bored with the proceedings and wandered back toward his desk. At least there was that. When nothing clicked in his mind, Parker began pulling levers, removing toner, opening every compartment he could. Still no luck.

Glancing at his watch, he realized he'd been here ten minutes already and hadn't even begun the duplication of the drive. And glancing at the copier and its component parts, now spread all over, he was sure it would take him at least that long to put it all back in working order—if he even could.

As he was beginning to toy with the notion of just bailing, he spotted a familiar rectangular module, situated almost to the back of the unit. He pulled the small screwdriver from his bag's pocket and freed the drive, tugging it loose from the grip of the ribbon cable. He held his breath and inspected the connectors on the back. It looked right. Not knowing if God would honor such a prayer, he tossed one up anyway as he snugged the cable from his own backup drive into place. Perfect fit. He pushed the button to commence duplication.

"Excuse me," a man said from behind him, "but what are you doing back here?"

Parker ordered his body to remain untensed, his breath unlabored, and his forehead free of sweat—all unheeded. He turned just enough to see the man who was challenging him and felt his pulse pick up speed like a freight train on a straightaway.

How could this be? Corrinne said she had forty-five hours. By Parker's count, it has only been 42. And yet, here he was, not only out of jail, but decked out in suit and sneakers, his hair painstakingly disheveled, at work.

"I said what are you doing there?" Caraway said.

"Diagnostics." Parker cringed. He'd moved into outright lies, which he realized was not much of a step down.

"Who made the service call?"

Tannyr materialized beside Caraway, saying, "Sorry, Sir. I told him it was okay. There's something wrong with—what was it, a roller?"

"Heat transfer plate," Parker said. "I replaced it. You're welcome." He looked down at the backup drive. It was only about a third done duplicating.

"Well, if there's a bill involved above the ordinary service agreement, you send it to John Slocum at Adler & Clark, you hear me? We're not covering it. We paid good money to sublease this machine and now it needs parts replaced within a week and a half?"

The weight pressing down on Parker doubled. If they'd only had the copier for a week and change, was it even worth cloning the drive? Yes. Yes, that would still overlap with the timeframe of the murders. The status bar was now at 50% and picking up speed.

"Are you listening to me?" Caraway demanded.

"Calm down, sir. It's all covered by your maintenance agreement. No charge."

Caraway nodded, pleased with himself as though he had just negotiated a million-dollar deal. "How much longer is this going to take?" he asked, leaning back against the counter opposite the copier, getting comfortable. "I want to make sure I get a copy of the paperwork."

The drive's display now stood at about 80% and did not appear to be moving.

"All done," Parker said, pulling the drive from the cable and sliding it back into its track. He figured the last 20% on the drive would be the oldest documents, not the most recent. If he was wrong, this had all been for nothing. He flipped open the clipboard and riffled through the papers. "Crud," he said. "I left a couple forms in the car. I'll be right back up."

He stuffed the partially cloned drive into the bag and headed back up the hall, toward the elevator, trying not to rush. As soon as the car began descending, Parker knew he wasn't going back up. He had told himself he'd leave the copier just as he'd found it, the drive reinstalled and no one the wiser.

Now they'd wait for him to return and when he didn't, their first call would be to Foster Copy and Print. And their next call would probably be to the police. If only he'd had time to think this through in the elevator on the way up. If only he'd listened to Father Michael.

He left the elevator, at ground level. This time he didn't notice the marble floors. Rather, out of the corner of his eye, he noticed a half-sphere mounted on the ceiling. And then another. Cameras.

* * *

When Vivian and Corrinne entered the Command Center that afternoon, they found Jackie studying the crime scene photos of Garrett Appelt, hanging in the orchard, skewered through the heart.

"I already solved that one," Corrinne said. "There's this sketchy guy who wears a St. Jude medal."

Vivien chuckled. It was the largest reaction Corrinne had managed to elicit from her.

Jackie wheeled, a bit embarrassed. The long bruise down the side of his face was just beginning to fade, resulting in a grotesque rainbow of colors.

"I don't even know why we wear them."

"It's kind of a funny story, really" Corrinne said. She was surprised to find that she actually missed the cockiness that now seemed muted after the incident at Anders's property. Jackie hadn't said a word about the incident all day, nor about the fact that the men responsible were now in the wind. "I was reading about it a couple days ago. Turns out St. Jude was one of Jesus' disciples. In the original language, his name was the same as Judas, the guy who betrayed Jesus."

She smiled, trying to project some levity onto Jackie. "But, even though they were two different guys, as patron saints were being assigned over the years, nobody wanted to pray to St. Jude, for fear of actually praying to the bad Judas, which I guess would bring some really bad mojo. So poor Jude was so needy up there in heaven that he'd jump at any prayer that came his way. Still, people would only pray to him when they were completely desperate. And so he became the last resort. Which is why he's the patron saint of lost causes or desperate causes."

"That doesn't explain why the Chicago PD claimed him," Jackie said.

"Does any profession involve more lost causes than police work?"

Jackie finally smiled. "You got a point."

"I've never understood the whole praying to saints thing," Vivien said. "You walk into a church, the first thing you see is a big cross with Jesus on it. And you kneel at a pew and say, *Let me pray to some other guy, so he can pray to Jesus*?"

"I take it you don't wear a medal?" Jackie asked. "No St. Christopher, nothing?"

Vivien shook her head. "No, but if I was going to, it would be tonight."

"What's tonight?"

"Seriously?" She looked from Jackie to Corrinne. "It's Devil's Night."

Jackie smirked, a little of the old smarminess seeping in. "I don't observe satanic holidays."

"He's from Chicago," Corrinne reminded her

"Oh, right." Vivien sat down on the table and crossed her legs. "Devil's Night started in Detroit, in the Thirties I think. The night before Halloween was dedicated to pranks—TPing trees, flaming bags of dog doo, whatever. By the Seventies, it was pure mayhem. Arson, vandalism, assault. They called it Devil's Night and it spread out to other cities. As a little girl in Saginaw, we stayed inside, doors locked, from dusk till dawn."

"So, it's like Gate Night, only . . . evil?"

"Gate Night?"

"Yeah, the night before Halloween. That's what we called it where I grew up. Ephraim, Illinois, outside Chicago. Kind of rural. We'd smash pumpkins, egg houses, you know."

"We?" Corrinne said. "I didn't realize you had such a rough past."

Jackie grinned. "Oh, I'm dangerous, honey."

Vivien checked the time on her phone. "While I could watch your clumsy, awkward flirting for hours," she said, "we have a long night ahead of us. Who wants to order in some Chinese?"

* * *

Fathers Michael and Ignatius pulled up in front of the church as the sun was beginning to set. They'd interviewed five people, all names Father Mark had given them—three who were close to the missing boy and two teenagers who had experienced odd phenomena in the church's sanctuary in the days since the disappearance. Apart from a small detail here and there, they had gleaned nothing new. Further, their many and varied attempts at contacting the parents of Brady Miller—the boy who had recently died—proved completely futile. It was almost as if they had dropped off the face of the earth.

Ignatius had just stepped out of the car and not yet shut the door when he whispered, "Stop." He tilted his ear toward the church. "Do you hear that?"

Michael closed his eyes and listened. "Yeah, someone's in there." He drew his gun and the two of them closed in quickly and silently. They found one door propped open. A hand signal from Michael communicated the plan and Ignatius slipped in to the Narthex, crossing over to the Epistle side of the church, gun in hand. Father Michael followed, coming right up the center aisle, ducking under the crime scene tape and staying low.

They could hear two men, up around the altar. The blue light of a camcorder illuminated their faces, which were practically pressed together. Michael approached them quickly, aimed his gun, and clicked on the flashlight mounted beneath the muzzle.

"Don't move," he commanded. The two young men froze in the beam of light. The camcorder clattered to the ground.

"What are you doing here?" Ignatius demanded from the darkness of the chancel. The two men flinched.

"Nothing! We're just . . . filming!"

"Why?" Michael asked.

"We're ghost hunters!" one of the two offered, his voice squeaking. "This place was just listed as haunted on midwest-paranormal.org."

"And what are you hoping to accomplish?" Ignatius asked from the darkness.

One of them looked up at Father Ignatius and said, "What is this, *The Exorcist*? We got an old priest and a young priest?"

"Answer the question," Michael said.

"We brought a UV filter. We just wanted to see if we could catch any footage of spirits. I mean, it's Gate Night, so—"

"Devil's Night," his companion corrected.

"It's Devil's Night, so paranormal activity is high. I'm sure we're not the only ones who will be here tonight."

"Leave," Father Ignatius said. "And do not return."

"Okay. Sorry. Thanks. Sorry." They recovered their camera and hustled out the back of the church.

"Devil's Night," Ignatius repeated. "Leave it to the American Middle West to preface Halloween with a more Satan-centric night."

"We can't allow a bunch of nerds to tromp through here, playing Ghostbusters," Michael said.

"Agreed. We will spend the night in the sanctuary."

DEVIL'S NIGHT
OCTOBER 30, 2017

18

The Tribunal tightened his grip on the condemned man's throat, struggling against him as he thrashed. It was The Tribunal's first waterboarding—was it still waterboarding if you didn't use water?—and he was pleased at how readily the old recliner leant itself to the practice.

He'd prepared the space by placing a large Rubbermaid tub beneath the chair to catch the pungent liquid as it cascaded down off the towel plastered to the man's face. The initial plan had been to subject him to a few rounds of this in order to illicit a confession before moving on to other means of torture. But the man had been slow to confess, drawing The Tribunal's rage to the surface.

Soon, he had stopped asking questions altogether and just continually poured the amber liquid down onto the towel, giving the man only the briefest of opportunities to catch his breath. As the last jug ran out, it was as if the gallons of liquid in the tub had called to him. The Tribunal grabbed the condemned man by the throat and thrust his head down beneath the surface, tipping the recliner back on its feet.

Having been slowly drowning by degrees for more than an hour, only to be revived again and again, the condemned man would now go under for good. His resistance was token at best.

The next thing the councilman knew, he would be standing before a just and wrathful God. There he would not be slow to confess.

* * *

The detectives had ordered five different dishes from the Ming Tree, all of which sat toppled, defeated, and mostly empty, along with cartons of rice and packets of sauce, all over the conference table.

"Okay," Corrinne said, "Let's walk through these scenes one at a time." She caught herself before the last word had fully left her mouth and shot a diffident look at Vivien. "Sorry. Habit. Go ahead."

"No, you start," Vivien said. "You get everything I sent you about Hannah Goodwin last night?"

"I did."

"Then walk us through the communion of saints here."

Corrinne looked around the room at the assembled information. "Well, the saint theory is still holding water," she said. "We've got a man who answers to the patron saint of discretion in the confessional, who covered up a church sex scandal. Then we've got this positivity guru who liked to beat up hookers, matched up with the patron saint of despairing prostitutes. The next victim— Garrett Appelt —gave me some trouble."

"Yeah, world's greatest grandpa," Vivien said. "Nothing in his closet that I could find."

"Then let me tell you a story," Corrinne said. "Appelt and his wife were foster parents—we knew that. And, based on the foster kids we've interviewed, they were supportive, loving, and all the rest. Even wound up adopting *eight* of their foster kids. But it was almost nine.

"There was a young teen in the late Eighties who was in the process of being adopted when the Appelts' house burned to the ground. Our vic insisted it was arson—that this boy had major emotional issues and had gotten angry about something and set the place ablaze. The boy insisted he had nothing to do with it. Fire marshal said it was inconclusive.

"When it looked like this boy might be stuck in juvie until his eighteenth birthday, our serial grandpa changed his story, said it had been accidental after all. The boy was released from the juvenile system, but he was no longer on track to be child number nine in the Appelt household. They gave up on him."

"A lost cause," Jackie said.

"That's great," Vivien said. "You talked to this guy?"

"One better," Corrinne said. "We arrested him."

Vivien's face fell. "Caraway."

"Yep." She turned to Jackie. "You get that juvenile record unsealed or what?"

"No. Captain Hillary killed the request."

"Exactly," Vivien said. "We're under strict orders to steer clear of this guy."

Corrinne shook her head. "But if the investigation takes us there, what choice do we have?"

"But it's not taking us there," Vivien insisted. "Caraway was in Florida when Leslie Doane showed up on the fountain. He was in jail when your buddy Donavan was attacked. And there's a young woman and a security camera on the south side that have Caraway very much engaged the whole night before Garrett Appelt's body appeared."

" . . . which had been frozen according to the M.E.," Corrinne reminded her.

"So?"

"So, what if Caraway killed him and put him on ice and someone else hung him in that tree? What if we're looking for two perps, working together, covering each other's tracks?"

"That's very thin," Jackie said. "I admit Caraway looked good when we picked him up. We had the list from his website with the first two vics, then he had motive with the third. But face it: the guy's not happening. Besides, he's got no connection whatsoever with victim number four, Hannah Goodwin."

"But he has every connection with victim number five. The one that got away."

"Again," Vivien said, "while he was in jail."

"That's why I'm suggesting two perps working together. What better way to exonerate yourself?"

"We're going in circles," Vivien said. "We'll keep him in mind, okay? Tell us how Hannah Goodwin fits in to the pantheon."

"She was the simplest one," Corrinne said. "Whipped to death according to the M.E.. The date on her phone was December 3. It looks like she was killed and her body staged beneath the museum a day earlier, which points to the second, feast day for St. Bibiana, who was also flogged to death."

"And what's her area?" Jackie asked.

"Among other things, she's the patron saint of those suffering hangovers, which I can't believe is actually a thing."

Vivien nodded. "Fits with Goodwin's record."

"What record?" Jackie asked.

"In '94, she was a school bus driver," Corrinne explained. "Got behind the wheel after a night of hard partying, ran a red light, and got T-boned by a garbage truck. Six children died. Goodwin did four years before she was paroled. More recently, she's been a secretary at a Kramer Elementary, where, by all reports, she was loved by student and teacher alike."

"So another 'whitewashed tomb' situation," Vivien said.

"What if we're being played here?" Jackie asked, abruptly.

"What do you mean, 'played?'"

"I mean, what if this is all misdirection? Think about it: every hour we spend talking about saints who died a thousand years ago, reading medieval garbage, and digging into the past lives of the victims, is an hour we're not spending on the actual perp—who he is, where he is, when he'll strike again. He picks the tune and we dance."

A deep silence hung in the room for half a minute.

"Not impossible," Vivien finally said. "But we can't just ignore the pattern." She gestured at Corrinne. "Last victim. Or attempted victim."

"Well, the prayer card you found in the trash was for Thomas More, patron saint of lawyers. He was executed for refusing to acknowledge the King of England as the rightful head of the Church. Donavan's a lawyer, of course. He represented Cates in the sex scandal lawsuit." She hesitated. "I don't know. There may be more to it; still need to think it through."

"My question," Vivien said, "is whether the perp even intended to kill Donavan. He cut the alarm, left the syringe there, like he wanted us to find it. Took off the moment someone showed up at the door, rather than just tying up the loose end." She glanced at Corrinne. "Sorry, Kirkpatrick."

"No, you're right. Leaving the syringe was out of character. Unless it's part of this body of clues he's leaving behind to taunt us."

"Or maybe he just panicked," Jackie said. "Maybe our perp's Johnny Freakin' Bravo when someone's drugged, tied up, helpless, but he's a skittish little mouse the rest of the time. Could be why he's doing all this—to actually feel powerful."

"Reminds me of someone we know," Corrinne said. "Preacher of hate who likes pointing guns at young girls."

"You don't think Anders stayed in town and went after the lawyer?"

"Probably not. But there were a number of men in that congregation—all brainwashed according to Wilson's profiler. Anders had a connection with November 2. I'd like to look a little closer at the lot of them."

* * *

Father Michael was just coming out of a power nap when the sanctuary lights came on. Disoriented and squinting, he stumbled to his feet. Ignatius was on watch and Michael had every reason to believe that, if an intruder had slipped into the church, the older priest was well aware and had good reason to let it happen.

"What're you doin' in here?" The words were shouted in the most Southern accent they'd heard so far in Panama.

"It's a church," Michael said, his eyes racing to adjust to the light. "I'm a priest. Do the math."

"It's a crime scene," the drawl declared. Michael could make him out now. A cop in a blue button up shirt, pinned with a star—like a medal for containing the ample gut within. He had his hand on a fat holstered revolver. "I already told you bead-fumblers, you can't be in here. Now Imma have to take you downtown."

"Look, this is a simple misunderstanding," Michael said. "Let me show you something." He reached into his back pocket for his documents.

"Hands where I can see 'em!" the cop shouted, drawing his gun.

"ID," Michael said. "I was getting my ID."

Father Ignatius emerged from the Narthex. "What is going on

here?" he asked. Michael could tell from the burning in his eyes that he already knew the answer.

"You! Over by your friend here! Hands behind your head."

The priests complied. "We are here as emissaries of the Vatican," Ignatius said. "We have full—"

"Shut your mouth! Your little costumes don't impress me and they sure don't put you above the law." The cop pulled Father Michael's wallet from his back pocket and flipped it open to examine the ID.

"Father Michael Gretzgy?" He snickered. "Like the hockey player?"

"Yes, like the hockey player. Did you think he was the only man in the world with that surname? Like he was spawned miraculously from center ice with no earthly family?"

The cop didn't answer, but absently ran his hand up first one side of Michael's torso and then the other.

"Now what do we have here?" he asked, smiling menacingly. He reached into Michael's coat and slid the handgun from its holster. The cop's approach was so sloppy that the priest had to consciously keep himself from disarming him.

"You carrying too, old timer?" he asked Ignatius. The old priest nodded. "Keep your hands on your head. I'd hate to have to drill you right here in the church." He set Michael's gun on the altar rail and fished out Ignatius's as well.

"What kind of creepy stuff are you into?" The officer studied the pearl handles of the two .45s, inlaid with the Jesuit seal—the letters IHS within a sunburst pattern."You two servants of God happen to have concealed pistol licenses?"

Michael smiled. "I don't suppose you'd believe me if I told you we have diplomatic immunity."

"Don't suppose I would."

"Well, you have my wallet. Just look in—"

A size 12 shoe between the shoulder blades caught Father Michael by surprise and sent him down to his hands and knees.

"Do not speak unless spoken to!" The cop chuckled. "You know, I was just going to give you a little wake-up call, put the fear of God in ya. Now you're gonna do some time!"

Father Michael squelched a smile. "I'm sorry; do some . . . *tahm?* Who's Tom?"

"Yeah, keep laughin'." He unclipped a radio from his belt. "Billy, you copy?" There was an unintelligible squawk from the speaker. "Head back to the station. I've got a couple priests for you to book. Yeah, you heard me."

"You're wasting your *tahm,* officer," Michael said. "We'll be walking out free and clear within the hour."

"I wouldn't bet on it." His eyes fell to Parker's file folder, setting on the front pew, where Michael had been perusing it earlier in the night. "This yours?" he asked.

* * *

It went right to voicemail again—the third time in an hour. Parker scowled. He wanted—no, he *needed*—to talk to Father Michael. To admit his plan had indeed been ill-advised and ask for absolution in the form of some sort of next steps, which might possibly salvage the whole stupid thing. Instead, he was leaving a message.

"Hey, Michael, it's Parker. I got a bunch of files off that copy machine. The dates range from this morning all the way back almost a year. But they don't mean anything to me. There's no JPEGs, PDFs, no pictures at all. I thought maybe you could help me have a look at them." He paused.

"I also just kind of wanted to talk. I'm worried about Corrinne—her emotional state. I guess her spiritual state. And her safety. These local militant guys that she arrested have escaped. I mean, they were last seen headed south through Indiana, so there's probably nothing to worry about, but . . . she's not here now. She's hardly ever here. I wish you weren't in Panama. Call me back when you get a chance."

19

Corrinne sat at her desk Tuesday morning re-reading witness statements. She was trying to distract herself from a troubling line of thought. From her earliest days solving cases, Corrinne had discovered that time to just sit and let her mind wander unchecked through the proverbial halls of evidence was a key part of her process. But today that had backfired.

It started with Donavan. Was he hiding something? Could he be guilty of something far worse than simply doing his job, something that put him on the level of Cates or Doane? Or was he just the victim of someone's misguided quest for vigilante justice? Her gut told her the former. But then the article had popped into her mind—the one from the Grand Rapids Press, all about Parker and the one year anniversary of Ketcham's killing spree, and mentioning November 2, when he would be the featured speaker at the Church Unity Revival at the Van Andel Arena.

That hadn't been the troubling thing, although it gave birth to it: why was Parker seemingly on the perp's radar, if not in his crosshairs? Was he hiding something as well? She had only known him a year, only been married to him for three months. As a detective, was she obligated to give him the same sort of impartial consideration she would apply to anyone else related to the investigation?

If anyone knew that spending hundreds of hours together, sharing secrets, even sharing a bed with someone did not guarantee that you truly knew them, it was Corrinne. She'd given Parker the benefit of the doubt because he was bumbling, seemingly innocent to a fault, and a man of the cloth. But Ketcham had been outwardly clean—to the point of teetotaling. Not to mention that she'd just broken the face of another so-called minister to save a girl's life.

It might be time to reconsider her presuppositions.

* * *

"How'd you sleep?" the cop asked, bounding into the small, quaint police station. Upon their arrival here last night, the other cop, Billy, had called the arresting officer Timmy. This did nothing to uproot stereotypes in Father Michael's mind.

Michael stood, leaning against the bars of the old-fashioned cell. "Not as well as the guard you had posted here, Timbo. Put his feet up on that desk and snored through the whole night. Except when he left for an hour and a half."

"You don't need to worry about Dewey," he said. "He's my responsibility."

"Yeah, I'm not worried about him. I'm worried about the diplomatic papers you took off us last night. Upon discovering those, you are obligated to call the State Department. Have you done that?"

"I'll tell you who I need to call: the Grand Rapids Police Department." The cop scooped up the file folder from his desk and began leafing through it. "Specifically, this Detective Kirkpatrick. He know you boys have files from an ongoing investigation?" He glanced from Ignatius to Michael. "Yeah, I didn't think so. You may want to get comfortable here. And I hope, for your sake, that this Kirkpatrick is a friend of yours."

"Oh yeah," Michael said. "Thick as thieves."

* * *

Corrinne breezed into the office of Holy Ghost Tabernacle. The place had become like a second home over the past year, as she'd popped in to visit Parker, down the hall. Dr. Watkins and his wife were undoubtedly the closest friends that Parker and Corrinne shared in common, frequently in each other's homes and even travelling together at one point. Twenty years older than Parker, they had also become de facto mentors to the newly married couple.

She waved to Tasha, the secretary, and knocked lightly on the pastor's door.

"Come in."

The older minister was reading a letter, a look of intense worry on his face.

"Everything okay?" Corrinne asked.

"Not exactly." He folded the letter up and slid it back into its envelope. "It's my nephew, Dante. He had a church in Detroit. Broadmoor, not a great area. He disappeared a couple years ago. I've been hiring PIs to track him down. Number three just told me it's a lost cause. Looks like he was in debt to some rough characters." He pushed the envelope away, as if it would carry the heavy thoughts with it, and looked up at Corrinne. "I'm being rude. How are you doing?"

"Stressed," she said. "Is that bad? Am I supposed to be too blessed for that or something?"

Charles laughed. "I hate it when people say that. I'll pray for you this afternoon. I miss seeing you around here. And Parker. What's he up to?"

"Doing rehab at the new church building."

"I didn't know Parker was handy."

"He's not."

Charles chuckled, his smile widening even further. "Where are my manners?" he said. "Have a seat. Tell me what's troubling you."

She collapsed into one of the leather chairs. "I don't even know where to begin."

***

Parker toppled a chair in frustration. He'd spent nearly an hour the night before carefully reassembling his grandfather's pulpit, applying wood glue to each piece and snugging them together. Lacking the right kind of clamps, he had pushed his desk up against the side of the pulpit, pinning it against the wall, hoping this would hold it in place while the glue dried.

It did not.

The pulpit was slumped oddly to the side—the type of podium best suited for use in a Dali painting. He opened an Internet browser and spent a few minutes reading about how to remove dried wood glue from precious antique wood. What he found was not overly encouraging. He would need acetone, which he certainly didn't have. Another trip to the hardware store. And now that his secretary Louise had moved her office to the original church building, he needed to make sure she didn't see this. Not that Parker would call her a gossip per se, but he knew how quickly word of his ineptitude would spread.

Grabbing his car keys and locking the study behind him, he popped his head into the church office and told Louise he'd be back in half an hour. As he headed down the hall toward the exit, he had a sudden sense of déjà vu and, with it, a feeling of warmth and peace. The frustration from his botched repair job faded as it dawned on him anew that they were back in the church building where he'd put his faith in Jesus. Where three generations of Parkers had ministered. A smile bloomed on his face.

This same sense of all-is-right had been filling him intermittently since returning to the original building. And each time it did, he'd returned to the sanctuary, looked around at its empty potential, and pictured how it had looked in ages past. How it would look again.

The moment he opened the double doors at the rear of the Nave, he saw him. His breath caught in his chest and his heart hung back for the space of a beat, before kicking back in, double-time.

On the steps up to the chancel, a man in a business suit lay, sprawled out.

Parker felt a charge of adrenaline. "Are you okay?" he asked, forcing himself to take a step into toward him. And then another. "Sir?"

The man lay completely still. No rise and fall in his chest. Nothing. As Parker took two more steps toward the man, he realized three things. First of all, this person was absolutely dead. Secondly, between the man's bangs, he could make out a hole in the middle of the man's forehead, from which a rivulet of blood bifurcated his face. And finally, Parker knew this man.

It was city councilman Max Van de Burg.

* * *

"I think it just boils down to the fact that I hate being rescued," Corrinne said. She'd been unloading to Dr. Watkins for nearly an hour in an unplanned counseling session, which had her feeling a bit lighter in spirit.

"That's just it, Corrinne," the pastor said. "If you're following Jesus, the whole point is that you have to be rescued. This is nothing you can do on your own. He washes us in his blood, he sanctifies us and makes us righteous. It's all him. You know, today is exactly five-hundred years since Luther nailed his protest to the church door. And one of his main beefs with the men in power was that they were teaching just do these little, outward acts of penance—pay some money, say some words—instead of living a whole life of repentance."

"Yeah, Parker was just explaining that to me. Justification. Sanctification. But, what about people who never seem to make it to sanctification? They say they've repented, but it's nowhere in their lives? They look like Christians from the outside, maybe even teach Sunday school, sit on a board of directors, help people. But deep down, they're no different."

"You're not describing yourself?"

Corrinne thought for a moment. "No. No, I'm definitely not. I can look back at even the past six months and see progress in my life. In my heart. But when I look around at so many others . . ."

"Don't sweat everyone else. The Lord Jesus told a parable about a man who was growing wheat in his fields. And one night, just to be a jerk, an enemy of his came and sowed weeds among the wheat. When they started growing up together, the man's servants asked if they should go and rip out all the weeds, but the owner of the field said no. They couldn't tell the difference for sure until harvest time. And besides, the roots might be entangled; by pulling up the weeds, they might uproot the wheat as well. So, they had to wait for harvest, which is of course the return of Christ, when he will separate them."

"That helps, Charles. Thanks." Whoever was behind this string of murders, they were clearly trying to pull up the weeds before the harvest, Corrinne thought. She wouldn't fall into the same trap.

"There's one more thing," she said. "I actually came by to talk to you about this revival on the second."

"What about it?"

"Well, I know it's your baby and I know Parker's really excited to speak at it. But I really don't think it's a good idea to go forward with it. Not right now. We have reason to believe that Jay Anders and his band of mouth-breathers were planning a terrorist attack on the revival. And Anders and his brother-in-law are still on the loose."

He shook his head, slowly. "We're not giving in to fear, Corrinne. God can protect us and we trust him to do so."

"What about just postponing it for a month or two? Give the marshals a chance to track these guys down."

"Sorry. I firmly believe that God would have us be a powerful witness to his power and might."

Corrinne felt her neck tightening up. This guy was more stubborn than Parker. "At least let the GRPD up security around the event. I'm sure my captain would authorize the expense."

Dr. Watkins smiled. "If it will make you feel better."

"A little better." Her phone buzzed the arrival of a message. Vivien. There was another body. This one at . . .

That can't be right.

20

Corrinne rushed into the old church, beating the other detectives. A single squad car was parked in front of the entrance, lights flashing. When a uniformed cop stepped into the doorway to block her access, Corrinne simultaneously lifted her badge and knocked him aside with a shoulder to his sternum. He should have been ready for it.

"Parker!" she called. No answer. Popping her head into the sanctuary, she saw the body, stretched out on the stairs. Looked like a bullet to the head. In her mind, she saw Van de Burg, the day before, glaring at her. No time for that now.

She found her husband in Louise's office, sitting in a folding chair, his face buried in his hands. He looked up when she burst into the room and reached out for her, pulling her into a hug around the waist. His eyes were red, but he didn't seem to be crying.

"You okay, hon?" Corrinne asked.

"Why would anyone do that? Why would they kill someone here?"

"I don't know, honey." She petted his hair. He always loved that and it seemed to calm him a bit. Corrinne, however, would not be consoled. She was just adept at hiding it, locking it down. The last time she'd seen Van de Burg was in a hospital room with Parker and Stephen Donavan. Now, not only had Donavan been attacked, but Van de Burg killed and dumped some fifty yards from Parker's office. There was no doubt; this whole thing had something to do with her husband.

Parker had not loosened his grip around her waist and Corrinne soothed him for another five minutes before Jackie appeared in the doorway. He opened his mouth to speak, then seemed to grasp what was going on and backed respectfully up to the wall outside the office door.

"I have to go now, Parker," she said, softly. "But I'm going to have a police officer come and sit with you, okay?"

He nodded and mumbled, "I love you" in to her abdomen.

"I love you too."

They were five paces down the hall when Jackie said, "So that's your husband."

"Yep."

"And he's the guy who took down your old partner?"

"Not exactly."

They found Vivien already taking notes in the sanctuary. "This is new," she said. "Going after a VIP."

"Who is this guy?" Jackie asked.

"City councilman Max Van de Burg," Corrinne explained. "Rich and powerful and knew it. And wanted everyone else to know it."

"Really? In a city this size? What do council members get paid?"

"About twenty-two grand a year," Vivien said. "But Van de Burg made his fortune in real estate in the Eighties. Owned quite a few rental units. More recently, he's given a ton of money to the under-privileged, the resettlement of refugees, the arts. That Artistry thing downtown? Van de Burg helped bankroll it, with a couple other big shots."

"We sure this is our perp?" Jackie asked. "He hasn't used a gun before."

"Still hasn't," Vivien said. "Look closer. His head was punctured with something sharp. Went in and came right back out. Something teardrop shaped."

Corrinne and Jackie hovered close to the body, examining the wound. The councilman's eyes were rolled upward, as if he too were trying to get a look at the blow that had apparently ended his life.

"You hear that?" Jackie asked.

"What?"

"It's like a hum."

Corrinne listened intently. "Yeah. Where's that coming from?"

Jackie pointed at the corpse before them. "I think it's . . . inside him." He took a step back.

Vivien stopped dusting for prints and joined the others. "What the heck?"

"Could be a bomb," Corrinne said.

Jackie balked. "In his *head?*"

"Wouldn't be the weirdest thing I'd seen this week."

Jackie stepped back up to the dead man. "It's weird," he said. "When you see a stiff, their mouth is usually hanging open. This guy's is closed tight."

"Careful," Corrinne said.

"We're not calling the bomb squad to come and open someone's mouth. Okay?"

Vivien gestured *he's all yours* and backed up a few paces.

Jackie swallowed hard, then reached his gloved hands up to Van de Burg's jaw, gripping tightly and pulling down. The dead man's lips remained tightly sealed.

"What is this, more symbolism?" Jackie asked. "Another guy who kept his mouth shut when he should have talked? Come on, Max, open up." He pinched the upper and lower lips and pulled them apart. They resisted for a moment, then separated. "Something sticky," he said. The buzzing got louder.

Jackie shouted an expletive and sprinted from the sanctuary. Corrinne had never seen him move that fast. She immediately saw why. Bees were pouring from the dead man's mouth. Angry, swarming bees. Trying to maintain some sense of dignity, Corrinne also retreated, Vivien hot on her heels, closing the doors behind them.

Vivien smirked at Jackie. "You gonna be okay, Reese?"

"I'm allergic," he said, with a bit too much conviction. "One sting and I can go into anaphylactic shock and die."

"Right." She threw up her hands in exasperation. "I guess we're on pause until we can get an exterminator in there."

"I'll make the call," Jackie said, pulling out his phone.

Corrinne watched a few intrepid bees make their way under the doors, out into the Narthex. "Who does that? Who kills a guy by stabbing him through the skull, fills his mouth with live bees, and glues his mouth shut?"

"You tell me," Vivien said.

"I plan to," she said.

Corrinne returned to the church office, remembering along the way that she'd failed to keep her promise and assign an officer to watch Parker. The office was empty. At the next door down, she found him in his study.

"Louise go home?" she asked.

"Yeah. Not much she could do here." A Bible lay open on the desk before him.

"Okay if I borrow your laptop? I need to do a little research while we wait for . . . a specialty team."

"Sure. It's right over there."

"Thanks, hon. Do you mind if I close the door on the way out?"

"Sure."

She lingered for a moment. "Also, you're not allergic to bees, are you?"

He shrugged. "No, why?"

"No reason." She grabbed the computer and withdrew to the old church library, where she stretched out on a comfortable couch and opened the laptop. The Wi-Fi signal was weak here, but she wasn't streaming video or downloading files. Just a simple search. "Saints Bees," she typed. An article popped up for St. Bees, "a coastal village in the Copeland district of Cumbria, England, on the Irish Sea." She added the word "symbolism" and ran the search again.

Great. Only 700,000 results this time. The first promising hit was Saint Bega, a virgin of the 9th Century. Oh, never mind. She had fled across the Irish Sea to St. Bees. She closed the window and continued combing through results. The name St. Bernard of Clairvaux popped up a number of times. She opened an article from a Catholic hagiography site. This was promising: Bernard was the patron saint of beekeepers.

Ten minutes of reading later, she was still unconvinced. Bernard's symbol and patronage were tied to honeycombs and beehives because his words had been so sweet. That might fit Van de Burg. Heck, it might fit Parker. But there was no connection with a puncture wound to the skull. She sent the article to the church's printer and clicked over to the next page of search results.

That's where she found it. St. Rita of Cascia. The heading "Mysterious Bees" jumped out at her. She read, "The day after her baptism, a swarm of bees, was seen buzzing around the peaceful face of the infant Rita as she lay quietly in her crib. Not only did the bees land on her lips without harming her, they were also seen going in and out of her mouth, which in her sleep was partly open. When her family saw that the bees did not harm her or even awaken her, they knew they had witnessed a sign from God, signifying that this young child would grow up to be a saint.

"These 750 years later, a swarm of bees still holds vigil in the convent where Rita's incorrupt body rests, just a short distance from her cell. They do not sting and spend most of the year as hermits, only coming out during Holy Week and on May 22—the feast of St. Rita."

Skimming through the biographical article, she quickly found what she was looking for. "After the death of her sons, St. Rita asked the Lord Jesus to cause her to suffer even as he had suffered. Immediately she received the stigmata of the head—not the marks of many thorns about the brow as normally manifested, but a single wound in the center of her forehead, which caused her great pain for the rest of her life."

She skipped to the end, which is where experience told her she would find, "Patronage: St. Rita is invoked for infertility, abuse, marriage difficulties, parenthood." She read that list again. Which of these applied to Max Van de Burg?

Ten minutes later, Corrinne headed back toward the sanctuary, looking for Allen and Reese. Instead, she found Captain Dunleavy. Or rather, the captain found her.

"Is there somewhere we can talk?" she asked.

"Sure." Corrinne led her back into the library and sat on the same couch.

The captain did not sit, which seemed a bad omen to Corrinne. "What's going on with you, Kirkpatrick?" she asked, only her tone did not invite a response. "I got a call today from a cop in some backwoods

Indiana town, said he had two priests in custody for impeding an investigation and carrying concealed weapons. Which sounds eerily familiar."

Corrinne bit her tongue. Nothing she wanted to say right now would help her.

"And one of these priests," the captain went on, "had a folder full of evidence, statements, photographs—you name it—all from this investigation. What do you think of that?"

"I didn't give any priests any evidence," she said.

"I didn't say you did. But your name kept coming up. Then we got a call an hour ago from some lawyer at Adler & Clark. Apparently, someone dressed as a copy repairman came in and boosted the hard drive in Don Caraway's office. The copier belongs to the law firm and they're treating it as corporate espionage. Reviewing the footage, it looks like a real pro. But your name came up then as well. Caraway's a bit paranoid when it comes to police."

Corrinne could feel it coming, like a herd of deer fleeing a wildfire a day before the smoke appears in the distance. Either she would be removed from the active investigation altogether—benched—or she would be suspended. Probably the latter, based on the captain's cagey body language. A ball of panic was filling her chest.

She was nothing if she wasn't a cop.

In an act of sheer preemptive self-preservation, she blurted, "Maybe I should take some time off."

Captain Dunleavy bit her lip, the gears turning—or maybe locked up—for a moment. Then she slowly nodded. "Yes, that might be a good idea."

Corrinne winced. What had she done?

"A week," the captain said. "Take a week. Clear your head. Jackie's doing okay. Vivien's got the case under control."

"Yes, ma'am."

"Would you like a security detail?"

"What for?"

"Anders, for one. Still unaccounted for. And then there's the fact that Van de Burg turned up here, at your husband's place of work."

Corrinne considered this. "You're not taking my gun are you?"

The captain twisted her lips up for a moment. "No."

"Then we're good. We'll hole up at home."

The captain nodded. "Anders is probably five states away by now, anyway. That little cult of his might be small, but has a network of followers all over the country. I doubt we'll ever see him again."

Corrinne grunted her agreement.

"By the way, the man you shot at Anders's place? They brought him out of ICU today. Looks like he's going to make it."

"My prayers have been answered," Corrinne mumbled. Then asked, "Am I dismissed?"

"Sure." As Corrinne gathered Parker's laptop, the captain added, "Tell me, is it going to be a problem to keep the auditorium closed off for a while?"

"No. Our services are at another building, a couple miles away."

"All right. Get some rest, Kirkpatrick."

Corrinne stood up, which took considerable effort. Her legs felt like they were made of lead. She knew she should confer with Allen and Reese before heading home, let them know about St. Rita and the connection with the councilman.

But she didn't.

ALL HALLOWS EVE
OCTOBER 31, 2017

21

The Tribunal sat on the hard metal of the recliner, feeling every edge, every point of contact.

He was alone tonight. No sentence to execute, no message to send. Soon, he would bring this Inquisition to its climax, revealing the meaning of it all to the world. The thought quickened him. Two more days. But tonight, he sat in his robe and hood, reflecting on this quest of his.

The irony was not wasted on him: a costumed man sitting in a secret chamber beneath the earth on Halloween night, while children walked the streets above in their own costumes, adorably scaring up candy. The children were fewer than they had been in recent years, and The Tribunal was probably to blame for that. If only they understood what he was trying to do, that he was harmless to the harmless. A little child wearing a mask would be safe, even here in this room with him.

Grown men and women wearing masks, on the other hand . . .

It was five hundred years ago today that Martin Luther had nailed his Ninety-five Theses to the door of the Castle Church, beginning the "Great Reformation."

Only, it didn't take.

In retrospect, it almost seemed designed to fail. The persecution was so heavy from those in power, the temptation to compromise so great. Luther should have turned it back on them with the same intensity. The same brutality. He should have funded the revolt of the peasants, not put it down.

As Jesus himself had taught, there was no room for half-measures. Pluck out the eye. Cut off the hand. In for a penny, in for a pound. Five centuries later and the Reformation was just a signpost on a road full of hypocrites, monsters, and opportunists. The Tribunal would do what Luther had not dared: turn the terror back on them with even greater brutality.

The woman, Bibiana, had begged him for mercy while he flogged her back open. But he saw himself clearing the temple with a whip, sending the wicked scattering into the night. His Inquisition was the cure for a cancer which was spreading rapidly through every member of the Body. This was chemo. This was a purge. A detox.

He smiled beneath the hood. It was All Hallows Eve. *Saints and angels, rest from your labors. The guilty will not escape.*

* * *

Corrinne followed Parker home, her eyes expertly searching for a tail or anything out of the ordinary. They'd met at the Clear Water Grill for dinner, during which no more than a dozen words were exchanged between the two of them. The sun was just now setting as they turned into the drive.

All evening she'd been wondering how long she would have to wait before unleashing her anger. She knew better than to bottle it up; that's what had dragged her father into an early grave via heart attack. But an hour ago, she was hugging him, comforting him. Some sort of transitional period seemed in order.

It happened sooner than she had planned. The moment they entered the house, Parker asked, "Why aren't you back at the church, working the case with the others?"

Before she could craft a response, she unloaded on him: the priests, the folder full of evidence, how she had narrowly avoided suspension and was now off the case for at least a week, stuck at home. Thanks to him. She stopped short of bringing up the copy machine and the corporate espionage. The thought of Parker pulling off something that smooth almost brought a smile to her face, even in the midst of all this. "Looks like a pro," the captain had said.

Parker flopped down on the couch. "I should have told you about the folder."

"No. No!" Corrinne stood over him, feeling oddly like the parent in this relationship for the second time today. "You never should have gone into my bag to begin with. And you certainly shouldn't have copied my files and handed them over to Father Fondue!"

Parker lifted his shoulders. "But didn't he help you out, a bit? The whole saint angle. I saw what you were looking up on my laptop, so I have to assume—"

"It doesn't matter, Parker! Think about this from my point of view, if you can! The FBI's breathing down the captain's neck because of me—that is if they can find another agent to throw at us—and the captain's breathing down mine! My last partner turned out to be a homicidal maniac, shot dead by a Vatican agent *in a church,* while he tried to kill you. And now I find out you copied confidential police documents while I was asleep in the bed we share and gave them to the self-same Vatican agent, who incidentally has been barred from ever entering the country again. How do you think that makes me look?" She shouted the last question before quickly regaining control of herself.

The doorbell rang and a chorus of "Trick or treat!" came trickling in from outside. Parker hopped up from the couch and opened the front door. A cheap plastic cauldron, full of fun-size candy bars sat on a small table beside the door.

"Look at you!" he said, smiling. "Are you a princess? Oh, a fairy princess! Very nice. That's the best kind. Happy Halloween." He shut the door and turned tentatively back to his wife, as if to see whether they were still fighting. His face fell at the sight of hers.

"Well, do you have anything to say?" she asked.

"I may have done some stupid things," he admitted, "but I did them for you."

"That's just it, Parker. I didn't ask you to do anything for me. I mean, do I get into the middle of your work and screw it all up?"

"Yes!" Parker brought his fist down into the candy bars, smashing a few. "Do you have any idea the fallout I've had to deal with, from you reading Ruth the Riot Act? It's every day now. I've got people who have attended Hope since LBJ was in office who are having second thoughts about me pastoring the church!"

The doorbell sounded again. "Trick or treat!"

Parker spun on his heels and opened the door. "Oh, wow! Are you Iron Man? 'War Machine?' That doesn't sound very nice. But you seem like a nice guy, so here's two. Have a happy Halloween!"

He shut the door, turning only halfway back toward his wife.

"I'm sorry about the thing with Ruth," she said. "I've been . . . dealing with some stuff. And she knows the fastest route to my last nerve. But that's no excuse. I could have handled that a lot better."

"Why didn't you come to me? I could have helped you."

"I don't know, Parker. Because I'm no good at this. I'm not cut out to be a pastor's wife." She dry-washed her face. "Besides, trust is part of the whole thing."

"I hope that doesn't mean you're questioning whether or not you can trust me. We're married. You know me."

"I knew Ketcham for ten years," she said. "I've known you for exactlyone."

Parker gaped, speechless, and Corrinne grabbed the opportunity to retreat to the basement. Stumbling over to an armchair, Parker flopped down. Surely, she hadn't meant it. She hadn't just compared him with the demoniac who had stalked, toyed with, and tried to kill him a year ago.

Like a drunk fumbling for the bottle, Parker pulled out his phone. He thumbed through his missed calls and dialed one from the day previous. It rang twice before, "This is Brenton Doyle."

"Hi, Brenton. It's Parker Saint. You called me a couple days ago about an interview for the *Press*."

"Right! You have some time free?"

"How about tomorrow?"

"I'm free at two," the reporter said.

"Great," Parker said. "Come by Hope Presbyterian. And Brenton? You can ask me anything. Nothing's off the table."

* * *

"Okay, he's gone," Father Michael announced. The lone officer had left the building at precisely the same time as the night before. "Hopefully he gives us more than an hour again."

"It's a woman," Ignatius said. "He'll be gone for some time."

Michael pulled a long metal pin from each of his shoes and inserted them both into the antique lock of the cell door. "How do you know?"

"I just know."

"Whatever." As he struggled with the lock, he asked, "Let me ask you something: how many times have you and I been locked up?"

"I'm not sure," Ignatius said. "Perhaps ten?"

"Try a baker's dozen. And what is the longest we've stayed behind bars? Three hours?"

"Approximately."

"And now we're coming up on twenty-four. And these Barney Fifes have zero interest in checking into our status or formally charging us with anything. Something's messed up here." The lock turned and the cell door swung wide.

Ignatius walked over to the desk where Officer Timmy had deposited their effects in the bottom drawer. It was unlocked. "I agree," he said, returning his wallet to his pocket, "and come morning I am leaving, with or without an official release."

"But what about the kid?"

"The Superior General will send a replacement team, while we return to Rome."

"That would take precious time," Michael said, pulling his phone from the desk drawer and powering it up. "If this kid's alive, we need to find him, like, yesterday."

"And how can we do that, languishing in a cell?"

"Good point." Michael pushed the desk phone over toward the old priest. "Make the call."

Ignatius scowled and began punching in a long series of numbers—calling card, country code, area code—while Michael punched a key on one of the police station's fifteen-year-old computers, bringing up a login prompt. He tried a password. Then another. Ignatius was speaking Italian into the phone now.

On Michael's fifth try, he found himself looking at a text menu. He searched by name: Griffin Matthews. The case file appeared and he began paging through it. Just then, his phone finished booting and chirped the presence of three texts and two voicemails—all from Parker.

Father Ignatius hung up the landline and announced, "Our release is forthcoming."

"How mad is the Big Man?"

"He'll get over it. What have you found?"

"Well, the password is PASSWORD1234, so we're not dealing with the most capable law enforcement we've encountered. Looks like a local lab confirmed the blood in the church is the same type as Griffin's. DNA testing is going on right now in Terre Haute." He paged down again. "Not a lot here." He opened an Internet browser. "That kid's gotta have a Facebook or Instagram account. Something. Yeah, here he is. No posts since the day before he disappeared. Looks like he has a gmail account. I should be able to crack that."

Father Michael snatched up his phone and opened an app called HolyHacker by tapping an 8-bit icon of the keys of St. Peter. Thirty seconds later, he was looking at an inbox. "Kid's got one message here. 'Your Interlibrary Loan Book Has Arrived.' Well, that cracks the case!" He tossed his phone to the desk. "We've got to get back out there."

"Soon," Ignatius vowed. "But if we're not leaving tonight, we should return to our cell."

"All right, but I'm bringing my phone."

They closed the drawer and arranged everything as it had been before locking themselves back up—which proved more difficult than unlocking the cell. Estimating they still had about a half hour before the cop returned from his tryst, Michael read and listened to Parker's frantic messages.

He replied with a text: "This is a link to my CloudCache account. Dump everything there. Then get rid of that drive. I mean burn it, melt it, microwave it. Then bury what's left. I'll go through the contents tonight. I've got nothing else to do."

* * *

Corrinne stared at the enormous corkboard. She'd picked it up from Staples ten minutes before they closed, lashed it to the roof of her Expedition, and mounted it on the wall of her basement office. While she and Parker both still referred to the room on their main floor as "our office," sharing it had never really worked well and she had been slowly moving down here for more than a month.

The board, six feet long, was covered with every photo, fact, and theory from the walls of the Command Center. Corrinne had conveniently forgotten to turn over her files before heading home for a week of R & R. It was now nearly two in the morning and neither R was on her radar.

Copious amounts of yarn linked photos, names, and locations, signifying any connection that might help move the investigation forward. Never much for things domestic, she'd had to buy a skein of yarn from a craft store. In two decades as a detective, she had never done this (the yarn) before, but it seemed the thing to do now, in her current headspace. She felt like a rogue detective in a crime movie, having been suspended in the third act and, therefore, about to break the case. Of course, she hadn't been suspended, and was actually just bivouacked in her basement, far from rogue, but that was just good maneuvering on her part.

She took two steps back from the board and absorbed the whole web at once. At the very top were mugshots of two men, one on the far left and one on the far right, and that was fitting. Caraway and Anders had exactly one thing in common—that they had been arrested and now walked free—but other than that, they were polar opposites

And yet, for some reason, Corrinne felt an overwhelming urge to run a long piece of yarn across the board, connecting the two men. These two contrasting suspects, to which every other item on the board could trace its lineage. There was no forensic reason to do this;

no reason at all. Just her gut. And, for Corrinne, that wasn't quite enough.

* * *

Father Ignatius was snoring. It was the sort of uvula-flapping bull-roar that could drive a prisoner to hang himself from the bars with his pants. But Michael was used to it. Besides, he was busy. He lay on his cot, the grimy, coarse army blanket over his head, focused on the screen of his phone, as he flipped through document after document from the photocopier's hard drive.

There wasn't a lot here. An unflattering picture of Don Caraway was emerging: a man who would sue anyone who dared pray in public, mention God, or reference religious values. At least he was consistent. Unlike most militant atheists, he was waging a secular jihad against all religion—Christian, Jewish, Muslim, Eastern, or Pagan. The sheer volume of motions, petitions, and letters, along with the time stamps on each file, made it clear that he was an absolute workaholic.

"Hey, Iggy," he whispered, knowing the hated term of endearment would bring the priest out of the deepest of sleeps. "You awake?"

"Mmm?" he answered, his voice ragged.

"Why is it that 99.5% of atheists are likeable people, good neighbors, mind their own business, but it's that point-five percent that gets all the attention?"

"That is beyond me. I find the same to be true of Baptists."

Michael snickered.

"Did the Protestant glean anything worthwhile?" Ignatius asked.

"Not really. And I'm back into the days when the law firm was using the thing. Not really a—" He froze. A simple memo filled the screen. No recipient named, no signature. Just one line: "It's been taken care of. Detective Kirkpatrick will not be a problem."

ALL SAINTS' DAY
NOVEMBER 1, 2017

22

Despite having dug the old cot out of their storage space and covered it with bedding, Corrinne had been up all night. And that was fine. Rather than lower the fog of sleep deprivation, each hour seemed to just focus her thoughts all the more. She'd worked her way through every crime scene, through the eyes of every person on the board, at least twice.

Today was All Saints' Day. And tomorrow, All Souls' Day. She could not afford to sleep.

For the past two hours, she'd been digging into the life of Max Van de Burg, looking for any hint of a scandal—a dark secret, particularly something that might tie him to Rita of Cascia, the patron saint of abuse, infertility, marriage difficulties, and parenthood. But she had found nothing. How could that be? The man had certainly made his share of enemies in the business world, and had been through two political campaigns—usually a guarantor that any skeletons would vacate the closet. But no. His character and integrity were rarely even questioned by his opponents or competitors.

Corrinne felt the disconnect from her team for the first time. She needed the kind of resources she couldn't access without risking a reprimand from the captain and attention she couldn't afford. Pulling her phone from her purse, she began composing a text to Jackie Reese: "I need a favor . . . "

* * *

Parker bounded out of bed at 6 AM. It was Book Release Day and he'd blocked it off entirely on his calendar. His secretary knew not to expect him at church, he'd set a temporary absence greeting on his voicemail, and he planned to devote every moment to the successful launch of *Faith of My Fathers: A Memoir* by Parker Saint.

After a breakfast of avocado on artisanal toast, he fired up his laptop, headed over to the BooksGalore site, and looked up his title, scrolling from the top of the page down to the bottom. He wasn't certain what he expected to find, but it wasn't this. Zero reviews. Zero ratings. Sales rank: 2,145,009. He refreshed the page. Nothing changed.

He checked the time: 6:25. Probably too early to call his agent. And his editor wouldn't be in the office for another hour and a half. What else had he been planning to do today? Visit some bookstores, just to take in the sight of his work on the shelf, maybe sign a few copies—a little surprise for his readers. Driving all over town just to see his work seemed a bit childish, but it was a reward he felt he deserved after all his hard work. He searched the hours for three local booksellers. The first one didn't open till nine. A feeling of helplessness descended on him. Was there nothing he could do before then?

Parker needed something to keep him busy. To keep his mind off the fact that Corrinne hadn't come to bed last night. Again. And the fact that his church was now a crime scene. If only he'd scheduled his meeting with that reporter over breakfast or early morning coffee. Too late now.

He clicked back to BooksGalore and refreshed the browser.

* * *

Officer Billy Bob, as Michael had taken to calling him, entered the station in stony silence. He spoke in in hushed tones with the only other officer in the building, before unlocking the priests' cell and gesturing curtly for them to leave.

"What happened?" Michael asked. "You get a call at home from the lieutenant governor or something?"

The cop stared at his feet. "I don't know who you boys are and I don't care. But I don't want to see you in my county again. You understand?"

Michael took a step out of the cell. "We'll take our documents and personal effects now."

Billy Bob opened his desk drawer and pulled out one wallet and one phone, which he plopped down on his desk. He dug around, looking for more.

"That'll do," Michael said. "And our guns?"

The cop finally looked Michael in the eye. "You go through my desk?"

"How could we? You've had a guard on us the whole time, right?"

"Beau, go get these gentlemen's pistols from the safe." He eyeballed the priests again. "You'll need to sign out."

"Gladly." Two minutes later, the other officer brought them a cardboard evidence box containing the two handguns.

"I'll ask you to leave them in the box until you're out on the street," he said.

"Fair enough," Ignatius said. "We'd like a ride back to the church now. We'll be there for at least another day. I hope you realize how pointless it would be to arrest us again."

"You heard 'em," Billy said. "Drop these two off at St. Michael's."

Once in the squad car, Michael checked his messages again. "Big Man says we've got to wrap this up soon," he whispered. "We head back to Rome in two days, whether we've found the kid or not."

"It looks like some of our ghost hunters may have been here after all," Michael said, walking through the now-broken string of yellow police tape. "Good thing Officer Billy Bob was keeping such a close eye on the place."

Ignatius grunted. He was once again inspecting each spray-painted symbol on the church walls. "We have two days," he said, "which leaves no time for sour bellyaching. Do you have a plan for how we can best utilize the time we have?"

"We start here. And I mean we start over. Fresh eyes. There's got to be something that we've overlooked."

"And if there's not?"

"Then we sit down with Father Mark and turn up the heat," Father Michael said, his jaw set. "We don't need two days. We're finding that kid before the sun goes down."

* * *

"What are you, living down here?" Jackie asked, glancing at the cot against the wall.

"Something like that," Corrinne said.

He raised his eyebrows. "Things not going well with the preacher?"

"Don't get your hopes up. I asked you here to fill me in. What have I missed?"

"Well, we've got a guy in custody, but it's more a preemptive thing. Jeremiah O'Dell. He has ties to Anders' group and he works at the arena. Vivien thought it would be smart to just hold him as a person of interest until after the big revival deal tomorrow night. In case he was planning on smuggling something in."

"What about Van de Burg?"

"Right. Potter did the autopsy last night. Turns out the hole in his forehead was postmortem. Cause of death was asphyxia due to fluid aspiration."

"So he drowned."

"Yeah, but not in water. His lungs were full of formaldehyde."

Corrinne flipped through a couple pages in her notebook. "That's the stuff of straight-up nightmares," she said, "but it makes some sense. St. Rita's body was found to be incorrupt. As in, miraculously preserved."

"What, it didn't decompose?"

"Right. She's on display in a shrine in Italy. In a church named after her."

Jackie scratched his chin. "You think the formaldehyde is some sort of sidelong reference to this St. Rita?"

"I guess. But why? I've been digging into Van de Burg's life half the night and I can't find anything to do with abuse, marriage difficulties, infertility . . . "

"We talked to his wife yesterday," Jackie said, "and they did struggle with infertility. But, according to her, he was nothing but supportive and wonderful through the whole thing. Now they've got two perfect kids, both in college. To hear her tell it, our boy Max was the perfect husband and father. So far, no one's contradicted that."

"Yeah, I couldn't find any dirt at all."

"Which is weird, right? Nobody's that clean."

"At least not in this case. I mean, with every other victim, we've found some sort of dirt swept under the rug—at least from our perp's point of view, they're all guilty. What are we missing here?"

"I thought you were taking time off."

"I am," Corrinne said. "When you stopped by, you found me binge-watching *Breaking Bad*. Remember?"

He smiled. "Right." He looked at the cot again and back to her. She'd just been stepping out of the shower when the doorbell rang and her hair was still wet.

"So, any theories?" she asked.

"Just one. And Allen wouldn't even hear it. But, what if this is political? What if our perp really just wanted to take out the councilman for some reason and killing all these other people in all these bizarre ways was just to mask what this really was: an assassination?"

Corrinne digested this. "It's possible. Raises the question: who would want Van de Burg dead?" She looked at the whiteboard and found her eyes drawn to Don Caraway, the councilman's nemesis and constant thorn in his side over the past year. Then her eyes drifted over to Anders and the old cliché came to the forefront of her thoughts: *the enemy of my enemy is my friend.*

* * *

Parker slipped into the church at about 9:30. A team of crime scene technicians was at work in the sanctuary. Corrinne had given them her key the day before and Parker had assured them they were could come and go as they pleased until the investigation was over.

The church office was dark, reminding him that Louise was back at their former office in Holy Ghost Tabernacle. Although this seemed a bit like the opposite of progress, he hadn't been willing to insist the poor woman return here all by herself the day after a dead body was discovered.

On the way in, Parker had stopped by Skyler's Books & Music, a local independent bookstore, only to find that they did not have his book on the shelf. He'd asked the manager, who said they had ordered a few copies, but wouldn't receive the shipment for at least a week. Defeated, he'd come here, where he was now distracting himself with another attempt to reconstruct the pulpit.

The removal of the wood glue had gone well, although the chemical he used had eaten away some of the stain as well. He'd have to sand it all down and refinish it, but that was something he'd actually done before. For now, though, he just needed to attach the pieces securely enough to withstand the occasional thump of his fist.

Wood glue was still in the mix. But now he was using the electric nail gun he'd bought on Tuesday to hold the wood securely together while the glue dried. He'd been itching to use it and now he savored the *ka-chung* it made with each pull of the trigger. Book Release Day was a wash so far, but it was early. If he could finish reassembling the old pulpit before he hit up the next bookstore, that would feel good.

All at once, Parker realized he wasn't alone in his study. The nail gun slipped from his hand and clattered to the floor.

"Sorry to startle you," Stephen said. "The door was propped open. The police, I guess."

"It's okay." Parker did a quick inventory of his person and found it pleasantly free of nails.

"And, uh, sorry to tell you, but . . . " he gestured at the front of the pulpit, where the sharp ends of at least six tack nails were poking through.

The lawyer ran his hand along the old wooden furnishing. "I haven't seen this piece in quite some time. I had assumed it was long gone."

Parker examined the new nail holes, two of them splintered. "Yeah, if I can actually put the thing back together without ruining it, this will really complete the sanctuary."

"Brings back a lot of memories," Donavan said. "Your grandfather baptized me. Married me and Constance, God rest her soul. Baptized young Connie too. I'm glad to see you wanting to preserve that legacy." He poked his finger against one of the errant nails. "When you decided to keep the new name, I thought maybe you wanted to distance yourself from Brian Parkers I and II."

"Absolutely not," Parker said. "And I've got a book that comes out today to prove it." *If I can find it anywhere.*

"Well, a little wood filler and no one will even notice these holes. And I supposed you've got plenty of time to finish things up here before anyone will see it. Any idea when we'll have access to the sanctuary again?"

"They say a week at most. That's about when the pews are supposed to be delivered."

Donavan nodded. "I really wish you'd called me yesterday. I had to learn about Max on the news." The corners of his mouth pulled down and trembled a little. "What a horrible blow."

"I'm sorry, sir. I was in shock. I didn't call anyone." Parker felt a wave of guilt, capped with regret. Since the death of his father, the falling out with Joshua Holton, and the death of Evert Carlson, he had very few remaining relationships with older men in the role of counselor and confidante. And with Charles now completely immersed in the planning and execution of the Church Unity Revival, Donavan was the only man who fit the bill. Parker really should have called.

"The last time I saw him, we were all together," Stephen said, musing sadly. Then his voice dropped to barely a whisper. "I've got to admit, Parker, I'm sleeping with one eye open. When I'm sleeping at all, that is."

"I know what you mean."

"At least you've got police protection at night. I thought about checking into a hotel, but I can't let some monster push me out of my own home. It's the principle of the thing."

"It's a horrible feeling," Parker said, "when someone violates the sanctity of your home."

Donavan nodded. "We need to take precautions. Have you considered withdrawing from this revival service?"

"What? No! I'm the keynote!"

"I understand how important this is to you. But your safety should be far more important."

"You sound like my wife."

Donavan chuckled. "I admit, she may have put me up to this. Still, I have to agree with her. With all this going on, it seems an unnecessary risk to bring so much attention to yourself."

Parker thought about the picture he'd seen in Corrinne's file folder. The one of David Cates's planner, in which the only intact page was the day of the revival. All Souls' Day.

"Tell me you'll at least think about it," Donavan said.

"Okay. But I make no promises."

"That's all I can ask." He looked at the pulpit again. "You want some help with this? I've done my share of woodworking."

"No thanks. I know it's kind of silly, but since it was my idea to put it up in the attic to begin with, I feel like I owe it to Grandpa to fix it myself."

"Not silly at all. I think that's laudable." He smiled, approvingly. "I'll leave you to it then."

He left Parker alone, wishing he wasn't. After surveying the damage wrought of his latest attempt to repair the pulpit, he began gently pounding the exposed nails back out. He planned to wipe off the excess wood glue with a damp cloth and start over. But when the heavy front piece came unfixed from the rest, Parker saw it, taped to the back: a prayer card.

"St. John Chrysostom, Pray for Us," it read. A very Byzantine image of the venerable doctor of the church had been altered by whoever left it here. Over the bearded man's face was pasted an image of Parker's own, printed out from the Hope Presbyterian website.

Chrysostom. It meant the *golden-tongued*. Patron saint of preachers. Parker only knew this because he had been nicknamed Chrys by his homiletics professor and classmates in seminary due to his skill and ease in the pulpit. Against his better judgment, he glanced over at his desk calendar. He'd last torn off a page yesterday morning. Now someone else had removed two more days, leaving the calendar at November 2.

His heart began to pound. In that moment, he knew what he had to do. First, he had to summon the crime scene technicians and show them this new evidence—no longer one step removed from him. This was personal. His own likeness, in his own study. Next, he had to get out of here. This building, which had so recently brought nothing but a pleasant sense of nostalgia for the past and hope for the future, now seemed unsafe and menacing.

And finally, he had to call Dr. Watkins and break the news that he would not be headlining the Church Unity Revival after all.

23

"Father Ignatius, have a look at this," Michael said, pointing to one of the symbols painted on the church wall.

The older priest sidled up to him. "The sigil of Decarab the Beautiful," he said. "Not a demon generally known to the casual occultist."

"But look at the top," he said. "It's supposed to be a circle, right? Rounded. But this one is squared off."

"You are correct."

"Which is weird, right? Because everything else is so precise."

"I agree." Ignatius traced over the occult seal with his fingers. "What do you suppose the significance is?"

"Could be some variation that we've never encountered, some idiosyncratic way of summoning the demon. But I'd say the simplest explanation is that whoever painted these things was too short to complete the full circle. Look around; this one goes higher than any of the others."

Ignatius glanced around the nave of the church. "You make a point. That would put Father Mark above any suspicion, of course. He's at least six inches taller than you."

Michael gazed at the stunted circle for a minute. "Come with me," he said. Father Ignatius followed him down the squeaky steps, back into the cellar of the church, where they had been two days previous. Michael found the string hanging from the nearest lightbulb and brought it to life.

"We've got three of these lights," he said, gesturing at the bare bulb, "all with pull chains or strings." He walked over to the next nearest light, currently dark, and touched it. "It's warm," he reported.

Father Ignatius drew his gun. "Are you thinking that the presence we felt down here may have been human after all?"

"I am." Michael gestured at the wall next to the stairs. "If all these lights turn on the same way, what's that light switch for?" Ignatius walked over and flipped the switch. Nothing seemed to happen.

"Look," Michael said, pointing up between two rafters. A faint red light now glowed where there had been none. Ignatius flipped twice more, causing the red light to blink out and back on. The two priests approached the source of the red glow, which turned out to be a chrome-colored device mounted up against the subfloor of the church.

"The WeBeJammin2000," Michael read. "Seriously?"

Ignatius wrinkled his brow. "What on earth is this contraption?"

"It's an old cellphone signal jammer. We're almost exactly beneath the altar here. There's your interference. The 'strange occurrence' as Father Mark put it. Remember, he said the former priest used to come down here regularly. Must have mounted this device here and turned it on during mass so no one's phone would ring."

Ignatius nodded his approval. "Good for him."

"But somebody flipped that switch recently, trying to turn on the light." An epiphany flashed onto Michael's face. He pulled his phone from his pocket and began to type.

"What are you doing?" Ignatius asked.

"Just checking some e-mail." Michael's face lit up. "Here, have a look at this." He handed the phone to Ignatius and headed for the stairs. "Wait here. I'll be right back." As he mounted the steps, he called back, "And put that hand cannon away!"

Michael ran out the door of the church and across the street to Coney Heaven, where he ordered one Ultradog with everything, one plain hot dog, and a large Coke. He paid and waited what seemed like an inordinately long time for the dispassionate teen to deliver his order.

His arms loaded down with food and drink, Michael returned to the church, where he found Ignatius waiting at the top of the stairs.

"Did you read Griffin's e-mail?" he asked.

"I did," Ignatius said. "But I don't fully understand."

"Everyone told us he was a bit of a nerd. Super-studious. Don't you get it? His best friend died. The only other kid who ever really got him. Even after Griffin spent hours and days and weeks here, praying for Brady to get better. He wanted to lash out at God. But he couldn't just do it halfway. Not this kid. He got a book, to study up on it. What was it, *A Dictionary of Occult Symbolism and Demonology*? Had to wait three days for it to come by interlibrary loan."

"Yes," Ignatius said. The two priests descended the stairs, hot dogs and soda in hand.

"Griffin," Michael called out, "come on out here. No one's angry." There was no response. "I've got hot dogs. You must be hungry, right? I assume you ran out of food a while ago if you resorted to communion wafers. Like Styrofoam, am I right?" He looked around, expectantly, but there was still no response. "I understand why you were so angry. And why you felt like you had to hide after you did what you did. I promise, you won't be in any trouble. Your parents love you. Your church loves you. Jesus loves you. And they all forgive you."

"I'll go to the rectory and summon Father Mark," Ignatius whispered. He ascended the stairs and returned a few minutes later with the lanky priest.

"Griffin?" Father Mark said. "Son, if you're here, please come out. I've called your parents and they're on the way over. They've been so worried about you."

There was a quiet scuffle from above the boiler and the face of a young boy appeared between two rafters, his hair wild and greasy and his eyes red with tears. Father Mark rushed over and helped extract him from the narrow space. It was so tight that all three priests had dismissed it as a possible hiding place.

As he emerged, the boy wrapped his arms around the priest's neck and began to weep into his shoulder, a deep hiccupping cry. He was bare-chested, his T-shirt wrapped around his arm and caked with dried blood.

"I know, son," Father Mark said. "I miss him too. It's okay. It's okay to cry. It's okay to be angry. God understands."

The stairs squeaked and complained as Cliff and Gloria Matthews rushed down into the basement. They'd made the five-minute drive in less than three. At the sight of their son, they covered the ground between them and Griffin in a second, pulling him close and covering him in kisses.

Michael grinned. "Well, this one turned out okay" he said,

glancing at his partner. "Father Ignatius, are you crying?"

"No."

"Don't lie to me; I'm a priest."

Ignatius rubbed his sleeve against his face and suggested, "Let's give them their privacy, shall we?"

The Jesuits Militant waited in the sanctuary for nearly twenty minutes. When the family and their parish priest ascended the steps back into the church, Griffin's eyes were still red and puffy, but his mouth bore the telltale signs of Coney sauce.

"He cut his arm on the glass case," Father Mark said. "That's where the blood came from. It seems to be healing all right, but we're going to have a doctor take a look at the wound and give him a general checkup, just to be sure. And then we're going to have a private mass for the Matthews family. But first, I believe someone would like to thank you."

Griffin's parents gushed all over the priests until both were embarrassed at the attention.

"Just doing our job," Michael said. "You have a good church here and a good priest. And a good son. It was just a bad situation." He looked over at Griffin, who stood stock still, fighting back tears once again, his eyes fixed on the broken head of Christ at the foot of the cross.

"Don't worry about that," Father Mark said. "We'll fix it. And you can help paint over the marks on the walls if you like." The boy nodded, unconsoled.

"I think we can help out a little more," Michael said. "Father Ignatius, why don't you call the Knights of Malta. Tell them they can square us by donating a new crucifix to St. Michael the Archangel Church in Panama, Indiana. Make it a nice one."

"Right away."

"It should be the same one," Griffin said, his voice quavering. "The same one I broke."

"You heard him," Michael said.

When the Matthews and Father Mark had left for the local clinic, Michael and Ignatius cleaned up the broken glass, scrubbed the blood stain on the floor until it was gone, and began clearing away the crime scene tape.

"You realize what this means," Michael said, as he balled up the last of the yellow tape. "We're not expected back for two days."

Ignatius gave him a dubious look. "What are you suggesting? You want to remain in Panama? Have a short holiday?"

"Yeah, right. I don't think I'm exaggerating when I say this place is literally the worst."

"What then?"

"It's providence," Michael said. "Parker left me a voicemail about these fundie whack-jobs who went after his wife. She put them behind bars, but they escaped, killed some federal agents. Now they're on the lam."

"How is that providential?"

"Well, it looks to me like these guys might have some kind of vendetta against her and maybe against Parker too. And according to the AP, the last place they were seen was about an hour and a half drive from here."

"No," Ignatius said, firmly. "We've finished our assignment and now we report to the Superior General."

"But don't forget: until we do that I'm still in charge. Right?"

Ignatius frowned, and said nothing.

"That's what I thought. Now, I'm getting me one of those Coney dogs across the street and then we hit the road."

24

"What do you have there?" Father Ignatius asked.

"Just a little parting gift," Michael said. He shut the trunk of their rental car and got into the passenger seat.

"Was that the contraption from the basement?"

"You mean the WeBeJammin2000?" He laughed again at the name. "Yes. Those things are illegal. Can you imagine what Officer Billy Bob would do to that poor priest if he somehow found it?"

"Good point."

Michael opened a map on his iPad and tipped it toward the driver's seat. "So this Anders guy seems to be stealing a car, driving a stretch, ditching the car, stealing another . . . Rinse and repeat. So far, he's eluded the FBI, U.S. Marshals, and at least two state police forces. The last car they found was about here," he pointed at a map of Indiana on the tablet's screen, "just off I-65, outside a town called Martinsburg. Let's head that direction. You drive. I'll dig."

"I would like to restate my original objections to this," Ignatius said, pulling slowly away from the church.

"Noted. Now be quiet. I've got to make a phone call."

* * *

Corrinne was on the verge of an epiphany; she could feel it. It was as if the yarn and paper web had emerged from the board in glowing 3D, floating there in midair, and she was able to turn it in different directions like Tony Stark—see it from different angles. Or maybe she was just really, really tired.

Her phone rang and the whole thing fell apart.

It was a long distance number she didn't recognize.

She answered, "What."

"Hi, Corrinne. It's Father Michael."

She said nothing.

"Right, so I just wanted to give you a little heads up. It looks like a lawyer at Adler & Clark law firm in Grand Rapids must have either hired someone to 'take care of you' or maybe knew somebody with some juice or, I don't know. Anyway, there was a memo that said, 'It's been taken care of. Detective Kirkpatrick will not be a problem.' That's you, right?"

"What are you doing?"

"You keep asking that. I'm helping you out, sharing information. Also, we're trying to track down Jay Anders and his buddy for you. The one that got away. Call it a late wedding present."

"No, what are you *doing*? With my files in some police station? Sticking your creepy little nose into my life? How do you know about this memo? Did you steal that hard drive from the law firm?"

"Please," he said. "I was in a jail cell when that went down. And I'm sorry about the folder. That was sloppy and I thought that—"

"If I find out you were involved in any way, I will nail you to the wall, immunity or no. Do you get me?"

"I was just—"

"Do you get me?"

"Yes, ma'am."

"Good. And I told you, don't ever call me again."

"Come on, Corrinne. Don't be like that. We should be friends. I was at your wedding."

"Yeah, well you won't be at the next one," she spat.

"Hold on, now. Let's not say things we'll—"

"And *seriously*? A fondue pot? It's not 1978!" She hung up, tasting her anger on her tongue. The doorbell rang. For just a moment, she thought it might be Father Michael. No, that was unlikely. She looked through the peephole.

Worse. It was Ruthless Ruth. Standing on her doorstep. Holding a teapot in one hand and two cups in the other.

* * *

"Okay, so look at this," Father Michael said, tipping the iPad toward Ignatius.

"One moment. Let me pull over."

"Just glance at it, man."

Ignatius pulled to the side of the highway and put on his flashers.

Michael rolled his eyes. "Okay, so, I poked my head in a couple law enforcement e-mail servers. And it looks like the marshals are splitting all their eggs between two baskets. Obviously, these guys were headed south and they've got pretty significant followings in Louisville and Birmingham. They've had plenty of time to reach either, so that's where they're searching. But," he said, expanding the map and dragging it west of the freeway, "*this* is where they ditched the car: Martinsburg. It's way further off the exit than either of the others. Maybe they're just being more careful, or . . ."

"Or maybe they had no intention of getting back on the interstate," Ignatius said.

"Exactly. So I brought up all of Anders's event invitations for his funeral protests and all that shiny, happy stuff, and I geomapped all the comments and RSVPs. This is all in a closed group, so no critics are posting, just supporters. And look what happens when I map them near where they found the last car." He tapped the screen a couple times and a cluster of red dots appeared ten miles northwest of Martinsburg.

"That's Stick Creek," Michael explained. "Seriously, that's the name of the town. Anders has a relative there. A cousin? I don't know, with this guy, it's probably a cousin-slash-uncle-slash-brother. Anyway, they've had two protests in Salem, and in both cases, they met *here*: at a Walmart parking lot two miles from the cousin's home."

"You think this cousin may be harboring him."

"Definitely worth a look."

* * *

Ruth hadn't said much of anything yet.

When Corrinne answered the door, she'd lifted the teapot feebly and asked, "Do you have a moment for some tea?" Of course, Corrinne had exactly zero moments for Ruth or tea today, but in light of Parker's revelation the night before, she couldn't very well send her away. Besides, there was something oddly pathetic about the sight of this prim and proper woman, hat in hand, teapot in hand, showing up unannounced.

And so now they sat, in the dining room, sipping tea. Corrinne had found a half-empty package of Milanos and dumped them onto a plate. They'd been sitting, sipping, and nibbling for nearly twenty minutes and the only topic of conversation had been the tea, the cookies, and the weather.

"Well, this has been nice," Corrinne said. It had been painfully awkward, of course, but she was truly thankful that a truce had been reached. Restoring the status quo was *something*, even if the status quo had been passive-aggressive comments and backhanded compliments.

Ruth nodded, but made no indication that she might leave anytime soon. Corrinne picked up another cookie and took a small bite, her eyes flitting around the room. She had a sudden, troubling thought. What if this was all just Ruth's way of fishing for an apology? What if she'd come here under cover of olive branch, intent on staying until Corrinne said she was sorry for her outburst. Granted, she *was* sorry, but that was not the sort of thing she could easily say.

The clinking of the old woman's spoon seemed to fill the room, announcing the close of trading. Ruth cleared her throat and looked from her tea up to Corrinne's face.

"We had an unfortunate interaction recently," she said.

"That's one way of putting it."

"And I admit that I was angry afterward, because I was hurt." She paused, visibly gathering her thoughts. "But I was reading the Scriptures this morning, in Titus chapter 2, where it says that older women should reverently encourage and train younger women to be more faithful followers of Jesus, better wives and mothers . . . "

She seemed to lose track of her thoughts for a moment. "Well," she said, "the Holy Spirit convicted me. I haven't been very kind to you. I've treated you like an outsider instead of welcoming you in. I've gossiped about you." She clamped down on her eyes and mouth for a moment, holding back tears. When they passed, she folded her hands gently in front of her and asked, "Can you forgive me?"

Corrinne just nodded. She was smiling, a first in the company of Ruth. "I can. And I'm sorry for the rotten things I said the other day. I'm still new to this. All of this."

"We're all here for you," Ruth said, squeezing her hand. She dabbed at her eyes with one of the cloth napkins she'd brought in her purse. "Pastor Parker loves you very much. That's clear. And that should have been good enough for me from the very beginning." She stood and smoothed her clothes. "I'm glad we did this. We should do it regularly."

"I'd like that." She was surprised that she meant it. "You want some help bringing all this out to your car? You had kind of a tenuous hold on the way in."

Ruth smiled. "No, they're for you dear. You keep them." She took a deep breath and let it out. "You know, the one thing the enemy wants most is to divide us. When we're unified, we're powerful. But when we're divided . . ." She shook her head, sadly. "Well, I don't want to be divided anymore."

Corrinne saw her out, the words ringing in her ears: "the one thing the enemy wants is to divide us." The Church Unity Revival was less than twenty-four hours away. Saints of all stripes gathered together on All Souls' Day, a feast devoted to the saints who had died. She thought of the gulf between Anders and Caraway and the expected 10,000 Christians from all over the state packed in to the arena.

She practically ran back down the steps to the basement. Tea time was over. She had a case to solve.

25

"We've been driving now two and a half hours," Father Ignatius complained. "This seems increasingly less providential."

"No, *you've* been driving two and a half hours. If I was driving, we'd have been there forty-five minutes ago."

"I'm hungry," Ignatius said. It was the first time Michael had heard him utter those words.

"Should have had a Coney dog. They were dope."

Ignatius twisted his face up. "You treat your body like a garbage dump."

"Okay, this is it," Michael said. "1244 10 Mile Road. Wow, what a crap hole."

They turned onto the dirt drive and came to a stop. Both men pulled the tabs from their clerical collars and folded them down inside their shirts. Father Michael reached into the backseat and unzipped the top compartment of his suitcase, pulling out two white dickies with black neckties attached. Moments later, the priests exited the car, no longer looking like priests.

They carefully picked their way around mud puddles and dog feces, heading for the door. Michael rapped a couple times. A minute later, the door opened and a ragged woman appeared. She might have been thirty or fifty. It was impossible to tell. But definitely a smoker.

Michael displayed a gold badge and said, "Hello, my name is Agent Gretzgy. And you are Mrs. Mooney, I presume?"

"Uh-huh."

"I was wondering if your husband was home. We have a few questions about Jay Anders."

The woman's face fell. "Marshals were already here yesterday," she said. "They searched the whole place. Didn't find nothin'."

"I'm sorry, so your husband *isn't* home?"

"No. He's at work."

"When is the last time you saw Mr. Anders?" Ignatius asked.

"February."

"I see. And when do you expect your husband home?"

"Late. He works second shift."

"Alright then," Michael said. "We'll be on our way. Thank you for your help." He stepped quickly back to the car, covering his shoes in mud, but beating Father Ignatius to the driver's seat.

"She's not lying," Ignatius said as the car backed out of the driveway.

"No. But Anders could still be around here." He checked his watch. "We don't have time to head to Louisville. I suggest we search every sad little motel and flophouse in a twenty-mile radius."

"I don't expect that would take long."

"You're right. We've also got a dozen other people who've attended his protests down here. Couldn't hurt to swing by, have a look at each place. Searching for a needle in the hayseeds kind of thing, but what else can we do?"

"We can return to the Vatican and make our report."

"You were a hall monitor as a kid, weren't you?"

"A *what*?"

* * *

Parker felt a brief, diluted rush at the sight of his book. There it was, finally, at the fourth store he checked: three copies! Granted, they were hidden away in the "Inspirational" section in the back corner of the store, but still. He turned a few Joshua Holton books spine-out to make room, and faced two of the three copies of his own memoir.

Stepping back, he took in the sight he'd been longing for as long as he could remember. It was underwhelming to say the least, which was apparently the theme for the day. An e-mail from his editor had wished him a "Happy Release Day" at nine that morning, but nothing else had marked the day with anything but disappointment. Even his big interview with Brenton Doyle hadn't panned out, as a local college student had saved a woman from choking at Panera and that somehow outweighed Parker's life's work.

Upon finding no copies at the second store, Parker had called both his agent and his editor, neither of whom seemed surprised or concerned—or even interested. Corrinne didn't even seem to remember that the book allegedly came out today, at least not during their two minutes of interaction that morning. He wandered over to the bookstore's coffee shop and ordered a decaf caramel macchiato.

As he sipped, he Googled "book release day" and thumbed through several articles about what authors should expect and what they should do on the day their book came out. They all had one thing in common: plan some sort of elaborate launch party. Parker had chosen to forego a dedicated event, since he was scheduled to speak to 10,000 people the very next night. Not anymore, though.

It was horrible that someone was murdering people, disfiguring them, and leaving their bodies on morbid display. But in that moment, the worst thing the monster had done was steal Parker's spotlight. The grotesque selfishness of the thought brought guilt and shame, bubbling up to the surface, mixing in with his bitter disappointment. At least it was some variety.

Then he remembered the card taped to the pulpit, presumably by the same man—Parker's face on the patron saint of preachers—and a familiar fear was added to the cocktail. He glanced around at all the other tables. No one suspicious, no one familiar. No one even seemed to notice him. When he'd shown the card to Det. Allen, she had urged Parker to go home and stay there. He wasn't sure why he hadn't taken the advice.

The clock on the wall told him it was nearly six. He would normally be headed home right now, for dinner. But he doubted Corrinne was expecting him.

***

The Lucky Strike Motel was situated next door to a boarded-up bowling alley and just outside the twenty-mile radius the Jesuits had established. But they'd checked seven other motels, four them actually functioning, and had a look at a dozen private dwellings, most of which were in a single trailer park and none of which was a likely hideout for two wanted fugitives. Besides, it had become quite clear that the U.S. Marshals had already visited each of Anders's known associates. So here they were.

It was almost ten and the only visible light came from the mercury vapor lamp in the parking lot, two rooms, and the motel office. The three cars in the dirt lot corresponded to these lights. Michael texted the plates to one of his contacts and found that none had been reported stolen.

"This is the last," Ignatius said. "Agreed?"

"Yeah, we're just burning perfectly good gas at this point."

The door to the office was locked. Michael tapped on the window with his badge. A slob in a tight-fitting, multi-stained T-shirt stumbled groggily up to the door. He squinted at the badge and let them in.

"I'm Agent Gretzgy," Michael said. "We're looking for two men who would have come by here in the past couple days. Paid in cash. One of them has kind of a torn-up face, might have waited in the car while his companion rented the room."

"Haven't seen anybody like that," the manager slurred, settling back into a threadbare easy chair, eyes glued to an old tube TV.

"You sure?"

"Look, I got two guests right now. That's the most I've had at any one time in three years. I think I know who's staying at my place."

"Do you mind if we have a look at the register?" Ignatius asked.

The slob shrugged and pointed lazily at the front desk. "Sure. Help yourself. Both guests have been here almost a week."

"What room are they in?" Michael said.

"Two and three."

"No Jay Anders or Timothy Philips?"

The man swallowed, visibly. "Don't know those names."

Michael smiled, impatiently. "You've got two people on the books, two lights on out front. But three keys missing from the board over here." He pointed and reached into his jacket, hand-on-gun. "Besides, you're like a walking billboard for flop sweat, all of a sudden."

"I'm just trying to run a business, make ends meet. I don't want any trouble."

"And we don't want to give you any trouble. Just tell us, are they in there now?" He looked up at the empty hook on the wall. "Room Six?"

"I dunno. Probably."

"You stay in here," Michael ordered. "And if you don't want the door kicked in, why don't you slide me the extra key for that room?"

Ignatius took the key and the priests left the office, quietly approaching the dark motel room, guns drawn. Sliding the key smoothly into the lock, the old priest counted off three and the two of them burst into the room. It took less than three seconds to sweep it.

"Bathroom clear!"

"Closet clear!"

Michael dropped to the filthy rug and shined a light under both beds. "There's no one here," he said.

"But they've been, recently." Ignatius gestured at the two duffle bags, open on the dresser. "Let's have a look."

Michael kept an eye on the parking lot while Ignatius systematically went through both bags, coming up with a short stack of documents, two boxes of .45 caliber ammo, and four tear gas grenades.

"Hey, we've got a car pulling in," Michael called from the window. "Let's get ready. Wait." He pulled the curtains back further and craned his neck. "Oh, crap. You know that cousin of Anders? Mooney?"

"Yes?"

"I think we already met him." Outside the motel office, he could see the manager talking to two men—the three of them silhouetted—pointing back toward room #6. Their car was still running, exhaust blowing up into the beams of the headlights. The men made a dash for the car.

Michael burst out the door, gun raised. "Freeze!"

The two men crouched and ran in a zig-zag toward the sedan—the stuff of backwoods do-it-yourself military drills.

For a second, Michael lost them in the headlights. Then he heard a gunshot and the window to his left disintegrated. The priest dropped into an Isosceles Stance and returned three shots. There was a cry of pain from near the car before the doors opened, illuminating the interior.

Michael rushed out toward the vehicle. He could clearly see Anders's burned and lacerated face as the car lurched forward. The image blurred behind the front sight of the gun as the priest took aim.

"Down!" Ignatius yelled. Michael fired a shot through the windshield and dove to the ground, covering himself in red dirt, as another, deeper, gunshot rang out near the office. The car, a late-Nineties blue Bonneville, picked up speed and disappeared down the road.

Michael pulled himself to his feet, his clothes filthy. Ignatius now had the manager pinned to the ground, gun to his head. A sawed-off shotgun lay three feet away.

"You missed," Michael said. He saw faces peering out from behind the curtains in the two occupied rooms. He held up his badge and shouted, "Please remain inside! Everything is under control!" Then to Ignatius, "Let's go."

"We can't catch them."

"If I drive, we can!"

"Drive what? That car?" The older priest pointed at their rental, it's rear driver's side tire shredded by buckshot.

"So we take his car," Michael said, pointing at the manager.

Ignatius shook his head. "No. We change our tire. We drive to Indianapolis. We catch a flight."

"You want to let these guys get away?"

Ignatius jerked the manager to his feet and shoved him into his office, commanding, "Sit. Stay." He swung the door closed and pulled a stack of loosely folded pages from his back pocket. "We know where they're headed."

Michael shined his flashlight onto the top page: a schematic of Van Andel Arena in Grand Rapids. "It was a fake-out," he said. "They were never really headed down South. Just planning to lay low a couple days and then double back for the big day tomorrow. We're lucky we didn't miss them. Must have been gassing up and getting supplies."

Michael dug out the spare tire from the trunk. "Okay, so we may have lost the trail, but we can beat them back to Michigan."

"No," Ignatius said again, retrieving the scissor jack and four-way. "We're done with our unauthorized side adventuring. It's time to receive our next assignment."

"Father Ignatius," Michael said, loosening the first bolt, "don't make me pull rank. It's so awkward for me."

"I've played along with these silly games long enough. Your command ended when we left Panama. You must choose now whether you are an obedient priest or a rebellious child."

Michael stopped turning the wrench for a moment. "Okay, fine. I'll call Parker's wife and warn her to be on the lookout for these clowns. If she'll even take my call."

"Why don't you just call Saint and have him relay the message?"

"Because Parker's acting completely *loco* lately! Mid-life crisis or something. The last thing I want to do is pour fuel on that fire." He loosened the last bolt and gestured for Ignatius to begin raising the frame.

"You said you were hungry hours ago," Michael said. "You must be famished by now."

"I could eat," Ignatius agreed.

"Okay. On the way to the airport, let's stop at and get a bite. That'll give me some time to run through the rest of Parker's files before we move on."

Father Ignatius nodded. "Acceptable."

* * *

That night, Corrinne gave up.

There was only so much one could do from a basement with no new information and no real resources, save Reese dropping by with the occasional update. Around nine, after finishing the last of the leftovers from Parker's bulk Thai purchase, the floor of the basement littered with empty cartons and her mind running on fumes, she'd called it. Her investigation was over.

It was a rather peaceful death. She didn't rip all the photos from the corkboard or punch the wall. She just turned off the light, crawled onto the cot, and closed her eyes. It was actually kind of liberating. The sun would come up tomorrow, All Souls' Day, and she'd deal with whatever the day held then. She'd keep her gun on her hip and her husband in sight.

She had finally drifted off to sleep when the ringer of her phone yoinked her back to reality. She found it in the pocket of her pants, crumpled on the floor, and waited for the display to come into focus. That 410 number again. The priest.

"Are you kidding me?" she answered.

"Look, I know you don't want to hear from me, but—"

"Do you have any idea what time it is?"

"Um, I've got 11:41. Why, were you asleep?"

She sighed angrily into the phone. "What do you want?"

"I thought you'd want to know that we made contact with Anders and Philips. I think I winged one of them."

"I cannot be hearing this! You know what I'm supposed to do with information about unsanctioned international operations on U.S. soil?"

"No. What?"

"I don't know," she raved, "I'm seriously asking!"

Father Michael chuckled nervously. "What you really need to know is that they're headed back your way."

Corrinne was silent for a moment. "What?"

"We found some detailed blueprints for the arena, some e-mails, all coded, but the IP addresses put them in your neck of the woods."

She sat up on the cot and processed this for a minute.

"Hello? I think she hung up on me."

"No, I'm still here," she said. "Look, Mike, I couldn't do anything about this even if I wanted to. I'm taking some time off. Thanks to you. Why don't you call the tip line?"

"Will they believe me?"

"Probably not. I'll tell you what, I'll pass this on to a colleague of mine. Okay?"

"Thanks a lot, Corrinne. I like it when we get along."

She ended the call.

* * *

To Father Michael, the diner seemed a lateral move from Coney Heaven, but Father Ignatius clearly approved, ordering his usual—a veggie omelet with a side of bacon—and continually singing its praises. Michael, on the other hand, was full-on depressed, poking at his chicken sandwich, barely eating.

"You are moping," Ignatius observed. "I have never seen this."

"I'm bummed, okay? I feel like I'm letting Parker down just when he needs my help the most. Probably because *I'm letting Parker down just when he needs my help the most*."

"Your loyalty is to the Order and the Holy Church, though. Not to this Protestant, as much as we both may like him."

"You don't get it. You pulled me out of boarding school at sixteen, threw me into training programs and seminary. I knew I was giving up the normal teenage stuff, college life and all that, but come on—I've never even had a real friend."

Ignatius looked up from his meal.

"Oh, don't give me the sad basset hound eyes. Yes, you're my friend. But you're like a *thousand*. Parker's the only guy somewhat close to my age that I've had a normal connection with."

"What about Father Andrew? You had an awful lot of fun with him in Santiago last year."

"We took down a guy who was mutilating cattle."

"You seemed to enjoy it."

"Look, I'm sorry I'm a little mopey tonight. Just let me mope through it. It's a long flight. I'll come around." He turned his attention back to his phone and the files Parker had sent him. He wasn't expecting to find anything else, having worked his way back to before the recent murders had even begun, but it was better than trying to explain himself to Father Ignatius.

"I'm going to the restroom," the older priest announced, sliding out from the booth. Michael waved weakly, his eyes still on his phone. He swiped through another legal brief. Then a bunch of copies of the same letter addressed to ten different people.

Father Michael sat bolt upright. What was this? He stood as he read, his heart pounding. He had to get this information to Corrinne. He doubted she would even answer another call from him tonight. He could text it, but what if she deleted the attachment without opening it? Plausible deniability and everything.

He rushed up to the cash register and slapped a quarter down on the counter. "Can I have twenty-five pennies?" he asked the clerk.

She stopped chewing her nail long along to pop the drawer and begin slowly counting them out.

"Eleven . . . twelve . . . "

"I'm sorry, but could you do it a little faster?"

She actually slowed down. "Sixteen . . . Seventeen . . . "

"That'll do. Thanks!"

Michael grabbed the pennies and raced over to the unisex bathroom. He tried the door handle: locked. Perfect. He could hear water running. Pushing all his weight against the door, he forced a stack of six pennies between the door and jamb, a foot or so above the knob. He did the same thing a foot below the doorknob.

"Father Ignatius, I just want to say, I'm sorry," Michael yelled, through the door.

"What?" Ignatius was rattling the door, torqueing on the handle.

"You can't get out. Not until someone clears these pennies."

The whole door began to shake.

"Seriously, you're stuck. We used to do this to each other at Stonyhurst. There's a motel half a mile from here. I'll come back for you. I promise."

"Release me at once!" came the muffled voice of the older priest.

"Look, I love you like a father. Or, ya know, a great-grandfather. But Parker needs me. I gotta go!"

"I order you to open this—"

"I'm really sorry! I'll catch you at confession later!"

"You insolent little—"

Father Michael stepped out into the cool night. He checked his watch—1:30 AM. It was a six and a half hour drive up to Grand Rapids. He could make it in less than six.

ALL SOULS' DAY
NOVEMBER 2, 2017

26

The Tribunal was on his fourth piece of toast, covered in bacon and eggs.

He'd awakened ravenous, as if his body knew he'd need the extra fuel today, staying power to see this all the way through. He sat at the dining room table, looking out at the shed. His hood and robe were locked away in there, and yet, in this moment, he was absolutely The Tribunal—the very manifestation of purging the Church with fire. Any lines of demarcation were beginning to fade away. Thankfully, he only had to keep it steady for another twelve hours.

Today was All Souls' Day. The day he would kill the final Saint. He gazed at the photo, lying on the table next to his plate. The preacher, his wife the detective, and an old family friend and parishioner. He tilted his head, looking at the old man with the pointless crusade. The Tribunal had left the syringe in the trash can and Parker's friend on the linoleum floor in order to make a point: *I can get to you and yours whenever I want.*

Now it was time to make good on that promise. Before he killed Saint, he'd take everything from him. And everyone.

* * *

Father Michael gave his face a violent rubbing. Late fall road construction had slowed him down considerably, drawing out his drive time to nearly seven hours. He hadn't slept in more than twenty four.

The cool morning air streaming in through the open windows helped. He chugged the remainder of his third Wattage energy drink and cranked up the music. MxPx. A rare treat, as Father Ignatius would only endure Gregorian chant or, if he was in a contemplative mood, Enya.

On the seat next to him, his cellphone announced another voicemail. No need to listen. Ignatius had already left him four since freeing himself from the diner restroom: the first two in English, the third in Spanish, and the fourth in Latin—increasingly irate.

The GPS in the dash spoke, mostly drowned-out by the music: "After two hundred feet, you have reached your destination." He slowed. To his right, a heavy gate blocked off the drive, chained closed.

Michael pulled the car off the road about fifty yards past the driveway in the dappled shade of an enormous orange maple. He stepped out of the car and jumped the fence around Anders's property, stealthily making his way up toward the side of the house. He flattened himself against the siding next to an open window. A woman's voice wafted out into the morning. One side of a conversation; must be on the phone.

"I don't want to see you until you've made it right," she was saying. "No. No! If you can't manage by then, Tim and Aaron can handle it." Her footsteps clapped against the floor, louder then quieter, like she was pacing while she listened. "I'm sorry, *who* put it together? Yeah, that's what I thought." He heard the phone clatter down on a hard surface and the woman muttered a series of expletives as her footsteps faded toward the back of the house. Then he heard the back door open.

Michael took off toward the front of the house, rounding the corner just as the woman stepped out into the open. The priest peeked around the corner, catching a glimpse of her from behind. She had brown hair down to her waist, tinged with a mousey gray, and wore a frumpy ankle-length dress. He watched her disappear into a pole barn a stone's throw from the house.

Despite seven hours on the road with nothing to do but formulate a plan, Michael was not quite sure how to proceed. It was possible that Anders and Philips were inside the house even now. Surely, the woman—presumably Anders's wife—hadn't been speaking to him in that tone. The easiest way to get a look inside a given dwelling was usually to knock on the door and flash the badge. But that hadn't worked too well for the last people who tried it here.

Still, what choice did he have? Continue skulking around the perimeter in broad daylight? Michael made up his mind; he'd knock on the door and charm his way in. Then he'd deal with whatever he found. If only Father Ignatius were here.

Turning back toward the front door, he froze. And raised his hands. A young teenage girl stood ten feet away, pointing a double-barrel shotgun at Michael's chest.

* * *

Parker was unpacking the first of ten boxes he'd brought over from the Hope Presbyterian office. When he'd come down the stairs that morning, Corrinne was already showered and dressed, suggesting they go out for breakfast. She was wearing a T-shirt and jeans, her badge and gun attached to the belt.

Over omelets, Parker told his wife about the card he had found taped inside the pulpit the day before. She nodded and chewed slowly as he described it. Parker feared she would flip out on him forholding back the information, but she said nothing about it. Perhaps Det. Allen had already told her.

They'd finished their breakfast by eight, at which point Corrinne had asked, "Where to now?" It was obvious she was babysitting him. And so, Corrinne being allegedly on vacation and Parker very much not, he'd suggested the church, which seemed to please her. It sat well with Parker too, as it allowed him to keep busy and forget about what was increasingly looking like a viable if vague threat on his life, while also being protected by a trained and armed police officer whose only concern for the day was keeping him safe.

Once he was locked securely in his office, Corrinne headed out to "check the perimeter," although Parker guessed she was actually in the sanctuary, having the detailed look at the crime scene she'd been denied two days earlier. This gave Parker a chance to remove the misfired tack nails and apply some wood filler. He also dumped a package of screws he'd bought specifically for this job on the floor, ready to be affixed.

A rotten feeling gripped him around the middle: he had no idea what he was doing. This physical manifestation of a three-generation ministerial legacy would likely not survive another failed attempt at restoration. Before his mind could turn this into a metaphor, he turned to the stacks of boxes, making slow progress. Each one contained some items to be junked, items that belonged somewhere else, and items that sent him on tangents of reading and reminiscing.

Tearing open a new box, he found himself looking at a scrapbook with the words "Five Years of Abundance" stenciled on the front. Paige had presented him with this album on the fifth anniversary of the television program. He flopped down in his desk chair and began flipping through it. The pictures were all image-conscious smiles and intentional projections of success.

He flipped quickly through the headshots, publicity stills, and seflies with fans, landing on a photo of himself and Joshua Holton sharing the stage for the very first time. All at once, an avalanche of memories crashed in on him. TV appearances. Packed houses. A book in the works, guaranteed to occupy Barnes & Noble endcaps and feature tables. Parker felt a sudden urge to call Holton up, try and mend the fences. Instead, he turned the page. A picture of Paige, beaming, pressed up against his side. They were both dressed to the nines, although he couldn't remember what event it had been. But oh, was she young and beautiful! And passionate. And easy to talk to.

What was he thinking? He stood and took a step back from the book, as if it might actually suck him in. Wavering there, between the pulpit and the scrapbook—representing two roads coming up from the past, each calling him to a different future.

Paige was dead. And Parker was dead to Holton. Living in the past was stupid. What he needed to do was reconcile with his wife, who was not only alive but somewhere in the building, physically close, if not emotionally. That charming young man in all the pictures, with his slick smile and smooth words—he needed to update his goals. Parker Saint, who had built a nationwide following on television, would rekindle the flame with his wife, woo her anew. And he knew exactly how.

Pawing through the stacks of junk on his desk, he located the framed and matted marriage license. Today was the day he had planned to give it to her. The three-month anniversary of their wedding, which he had foreseen taking place at Van Andel Arena, amidst a whirlwind of autographed books and applause for his moving address, rather than here in the church, on high alert.

Remembering her emphatic command not to leave the office without informing her, he texted Corrinne. "Come here when you get a chance. I have something for you." Then he remembered the box of gift bags and wrapping paper, left over from a fundraiser years earlier. That would make it all the more funny-slash-charming. He pulled the lids off three boxes before finding the stash.

He was in the process of fluffing the tissue paper just so when Corrinne walked in, asking, "Everything okay?"

"Just one second," he said.

She wandered over to his desk. "This is what you wanted to show me? A picture of you and your old girlfriend?"

"What? No, that was just . . . in a box." What a moron. He couldn't close the book?

Corrinne leaned closer to the glossy photo. "Quite a body on her. Very feminine. She's your type, right?"

"No. I mean, she was. Sort of. We didn't even really date. It was kind of platonic."

"Kind of platonic."

Flustered, he tried and failed to put just the right words together. Instead he just held out the gift lamely and said, "Happy Anniversary."

She accepted the bag, tossed the tissue paper to the floor, and removed the framed document. "What is this?"

"It's our marriage license."

"Don't I already own this? Like isn't it half mine?"

"Yeah, but I had it framed. For you, for the three-month thing. You know, because we both think it's stupid."

"We think this is stupid." She stared at the gift.

"Celebrating three-month anniversaries. We were talking about it last week. You said you thought that was cheesy."

"Right. I'm not sure what I'm supposed to do with this."

Parker snatched it back from her. "Nothing. Never mind."

"Well, don't make me the bad guy. I don't get what you're doing."

"It's fine. You can get back to whatever. I'm going to work on the pulpit."

She glanced at the half-assembled item. "I wouldn't use those," she said. "They're drywall screws."

27

There were at least six ways Father Michael could disarm this kid. But she was a kid. And she'd caught him sneaking around her home, so he couldn't exactly blame her for pulling a gun. In fact, he was rather impressed that she'd been able to get the drop on him.

"I'm going to reach into my pocket," he said. "Please don't shoot." He pulled the out the gold badge and waved it. Had she looked closer, she would have seen the words *Societas Iesu* along the top and the motto, *Ad Maiorem Dei Gloriam* along the bottom. But no one ever looked closer.

She lowered the gun a few inches.

"I'm here because I'm afraid Jay Anders is planning something horrible. And I can't imagine how you'd feel if you could help me stop him, but you chose not to."

Her chin quivered a bit.

"What's your name?"

"Esther," she answered, little more than a whisper.

"And are you related to Mr. Anders, Esther?"

She nodded, barely. "He's my uncle."

"Do you know what's going to happen today?"

Again, she nodded, lowering the shotgun entirely.

"He's going to hurt a lot of people, isn't he?"

"Yeah. That's why I called the police."

Michael reached over and gently removed the gun from her hands. "When and where?"

"The arena, downtown. They call it Judgment Day."

"Is he here right now? Or Timothy Philips?"

She shook her head. "No. I think they're going to meet at the arena later today."

"Are you going along?"

"Uh-uh. We're having a prayer meeting in the chapel. Everyone will be here, except the four horsemen. And Aunt Lonnie."

They heard the door slam at the rear of the house and Esther's eyes went wide with fear.

"You can come with me if you want," Michael. "If you don't feel safe here."

She shook her head. "I need to go back inside."

"Okay," he whispered. "But I was never here. Understand?"

He popped open the break-action of the shotgun and handed it back to the girl.

* * *

"Hey, Sister," Dr. Watkins called out, smiling and making his way over to Vivian Allen.

"Hello, Pastor," she said. They hugged briefly.

He surveyed the dozens of uniformed cops and the K9 units moving to and fro. "This seems like a bit much. I mean, the arena's got pretty heavy security to begin with: X-ray machines, metal detectors."

"Yeah, Kirkpatrick was a little over-the-top about all this. But it's my squad now."

"Still, all these cops," he said. "And dogs. Not exactly the welcome I was hoping to extend. Brings back bad memories for some of us. Kind of the opposite of what we're about here."

"I know. You hear about anything shady going down, bring it to me. I won't tolerate it."

He nodded. "What exactly are you looking for, if you don't mind my asking?"

"Serial killer. Crazy white boys looking to kickstart the Apocalypse. Like that."

"And the dogs can smell that coming?"

She smiled. "You'd be surprised."

* * *

It was either a late lunch or an early dinner.

"How's your sandwich?" Corrinne asked, wiping mustard from her mouth.

"Pretty good," Parker said through a mouthful of pastrami and sprouts.

They sat on either side of Louise's desk, eating subs they had ordered online. Corrinne had practically frisked the poor kid who delivered them, then forgot to tip him.

"How about yours?" Parker asked, grateful for a benign topic of conversation.

"It's fine."

The *ding-dong* of the intercom filled the room.

"You expecting someone?" she asked.

"Nope." Parker rolled Louise's chair over a few feet and peered into the black and white display. "No way," he said.

"What?"

"I think it's Michael." He punched the talk button and said, "Hello?"

"It's Father Michael." His voice filled the air by way of the scratchy speaker. "Do you know where your wife is? I checked the police station and your place. Can't find her."

Parker looked up at Corrinne, not sure what to do.

"Actually, I know she's there," Michael confessed. "I triangulated her cell."

"Keep him there," Corrinne whispered. "Which door is he at?"

"I can totally hear you, Corrinne. Hi."

"What are you doing here?" she asked.

"Just came by to leave you this." He held a small object up to the camera. "It's a thumb drive. I'm setting it down on the intercom."

"Do I dare ask what's on it?"

"Documents. From that law firm's copier." He threw up his shoulders. "I admit, I had a friend of mine duplicate the drive. But you're going to want to see this."

"I can't look at it. There are rules."

"I broke the rules; you didn't. Just think of me as an informant."

Corrinne said nothing as she chewed this over.

"Let me ask you something," Michael said. "A man was killed here a couple days ago, right?"

"Yeah. So?"

"Invoking Rita of Cascia, patron saint of marriage problems and abuse. You find any marriage problems or abuse?"

"No," she admitted.

"Exactly. The guy's squeaky clean."

"So what are you getting at?"

"A simple question. What ties together a bigshot like Max Van de Burg and some paramilitary messiah who wants to watch the world burn? These guys should be poison to each other. Or, maybe I should say, *who* ties them together?"

"I hate riddles, Michael. If you know, why don't you just . . . wait." She pushed Parker and his chair out of the way and leaned into the intercom. "Slocum. He was tight with Van de Burg, but he was also representing Anders."

"Bingo."

"Save me some time," she said. "What's on the drive?"

"Letters. Someone was blackmailing the councilman. What for, I don't know. But the guy's not as clean as he looks."

"Was it Slocum?"

"No, but it was almost worse. Slocum was helping the blackmailer—sold him the information to begin with. Then he turned around and handled the payoff for the councilman. Real Judas, this guy."

Corrinne felt the familiar rush—a case was coming together. It was something she hadn't experienced in weeks.

"You want me to drop in on him?" Father Michael asked.

"No. I'll do it." She leaned heavily on her elbows, thinking. This was dangerous territory. She'd avoided suspension so far, but putting pressure on Slocum would violate a direct order. She'd *actually* be going rogue. Then again, the lawyer's leverage had died with Van de Burg, his get-out-of-jail-free card. There was no one to put pressure on her superiors, no real reason to give him a pass.

"You still there?" the priest asked.

"Yeah. Thanks for the tip, Michael. I'll take it from here."

"If you want, I'll stay and keep an eye on Parker."

"No," she practically yelled. Then quieter, "No, I have it covered."

"You can't leave him alone today."

"I know. Shut up."

"I take it he's not speaking at the rally tonight?"

"That's correct," Corrinne said.

"Tell me something: how well did they publicize that? Parker's pulling out?"

"Not well, I guess," Corrinne said. "They'd already printed all the flyers and even the program for the event."

"I see." He furrowed his brow a moment, making him look very dangerous in the black and white screen. "Who's in charge of security?"

"Detective Allen. Vivien Allen."

"Is she competent?" the priest asked.

"Yes."

"Do you trust her?"

Corrinne hesitated. "Yes."

"Okay. You have my number. I'm going to have a look at that arena." He disappeared form the frame.

Corrinne could feel Parker behind her, wanting to ask what we she was thinking, what she was going to do. She pulled out her cell and tapped the screen a couple times.

On the fourth ring, a semi-hushed voice answered, "This is Reese."

"It's Corrinne."

"I know. I had to duck into a supply closet. We're not supposed to loop you in on anything today. Captain's orders."

"I need you to do better than loop me in. I've got a lead I need to follow up on. Now. But I can't leave my husband alone today."

"Who are you talking to?" Parker whispered. She ignored him.

"What, you want me to abandon my post and come babysit your husband?"

"Yes."

"No way," Jackie said.

"Some might say you owe me."

"Hey, I already stuck my neck out for you yesterday."

"Seriously, Reese? I saved your life, you stopped by my house for ten minutes and told me stuff I already knew."

"What do I tell Allen?"

"I don't care. You forgot to give your dog his vertigo medicine. You've got diarrhea. How many friggin' cops are there right now? I can't imagine you'll be missed."

"Is this more of that flirty banter?"

"If that'll get you here."

He chuckled. "I choose to believe it is. You at home?"

"No, the church. Where we found Van de Burg."

"Give me twenty minutes."

"Okay. And Jackie? I need you to bring me something."

* * *

Michael was trying to keep his speed under control as he zipped up Union Avenue, toward Fulton. While Father Ignatius's driving was maddening, stopping at every yellow light, never exceeding the speed limit, the other extreme was no good either. Police attention, traffic stops—it all got very complicated for a Vatican agent working in the U.S. under an assumed name.

He stomped on the brakes, bringing the stink of hot rubber off the blacktop. A soft drink delivery truck tooled out in front of him, blocking the narrow lane, the driver oblivious. Michael punched the steering wheel, bringing a feeble little *bleet* from the horn. His reflexes were not at one hundred percent after a night of no sleep and lots of driving.

As the delivery truck picked up speed, a sudden insight came into focus, as if the cloud of blue exhaust, now dissipating, had been obscuring it.

Father Michael pulled to the side of the road and fished Parker's folder from the back seat, flipping quickly through dozens of pages until he found it. The truck parked beside Anders's farmhouse. At first, Kirkpatrick's notes indicated her suspicion that he had stolen it from Fresco Food Service and used it to transport the massive mill wheel. When the plates came back clean, she amended the theory, assuming he'd purchased a decommissioned truck from the company's fleet.

His thumbs flew over the phone as Father Michael brought up AutoFacts, a website that allowed users to check the ownership of a vehicle going all the way back to manufacture. There it was: Fresco Food Service had never owned that truck. Which meant that someone else had painted the logo on it. A quick search revealed that Fresco was a major regional distributor, providing food to a majority of the restaurants in the area. Such a truck would provide easy access to almost anywhere you could buy a hot meal. Anders had purchased it three weeks ago, only to see it destroyed during his escape.

A renewed urgency filled Father Michael. The police might have total control over those entering the arena. Bomb sniffing dogs and metal detectors could keep new dangers out. But that didn't matter. Because whatever Anders needed to bring about his "Judgment Day," it was already inside.

28

Jackie, who had asked for twenty minutes, took more than an hour to arrive. Intermittent texts during that time continually delayed his getting away, related his trouble in securing the file she wanted, and reminded her that he was taking a risk here. But, true to his word, he did finally pull into the parking lot.

Corrinne was waiting by the door. She'd expected him to be annoyed at the very least, but he got out of his car with the smarmy grin plastered on his face. She was glad to see that the old Jackie was back. An ordeal like what he'd been through could steal part of you if you let it.

"Allen give you any trouble?" she asked.

"Not really. She said, 'If you leave, don't come back.' So, I guess I have the rest of the day off. Here's what you wanted." He handed her a case file.

"I really appreciate this."

He looked around. "What's the security situation here?"

"There are six doors to the outside, all locked. The two facing the parking lot have a camera-equipped intercom security system. The best 1993 had to offer. You can buzz people in from the office. But it's an old church, meaning everyone and her brother has a key to this place in their junk drawers at home. I've been doing regular perimeter checks."

Parker wandered up from the direction of his study.

"Hon, this is Detective Reese. He's going to stay with you for a bit while I check into something."

Jackie nodded at him. "Hey."

"Hon," Parker said, "can I talk to you a minute?"

"No," she said. "I've got to go. Promise me you'll do what Jackie says. He can keep you safe." She turned back to Jackie and said, "Thanks again, Reese."

"This squares us, right?"

She laughed. "You wish."

Parker studied the floor.

Then she was out the door, leaving the two men separated by ten feet of palpable awkwardness.

"Why don't you show me where you'll be?" Jackie asked.

"Sure. Follow me." Parker led him down the hall to the pastor's study, feeling uneasy. There was something about this man that he disliked intensely, and it wasn't just the way he'd looked at Corrinne.

"This is my study," Parker said. Jackie poked his head in and looked around.

"No windows," he said. "Good."

"So I'll just be in here . . . working."

Jackie pointed at the pulpit and the pile of tools next to it. "You know those are drywall screws, right?"

* * *

The sun was beginning to dip as Corrinne pulled into the parking ramp of Bridgewater Place. She quickly crossed into the building proper and waited for an elevator to belch out half a dozen people before getting on. She hit the button for the seventeenth floor.

Her heart was thumping as she stepped out of the elevator car and through the glass doors. She flashed her badge at the young receptionist and chugged right past the desk. She'd seen Slocum down the same hall that led to Caraway's operation. Of course, that didn't mean his office was necessarily down here. She slowed. This is right where he'd been, smirking and sneering, showing off those ridiculous white caps. There were six offices. Four doors open. No Slocum.

Coming to a stop, she closed her eyes and listened. Behind the door to her right, a woman droned on about billable hours, pausing every couple seconds. A phone call. No sound came from the door to her left. Well, now was no time to go indecisive.

She tried the knob and the door swung open. One of the women she'd seen draped over Slocum the week before sat at a small desk, typing, beyond her another closed door. Of course Slocum had a private secretary. And of course she looked like a cross between Jessica Rabbit and Hello Nurse.

"Is he back there?" Corrinne asked quietly, pointing at the badge on her belt.

"What did he do?" The secretary seemed a little tickled at the thought of her boss in hot water.

"Is he back there?" she repeated.

"Yes, but I'm not supposed to disturb him."

"That's okay. I'll do it." She brushed past the secretary and tried the door. This time the knob did not turn. It was a cheap, hollow interior door, though, and a firm *whump* from her shoulder was all it took to pop it open.

"Hey. John-boy," she said.

Slocum looked up from his desk, eyes and mouth round, white powder dusting his nose.

"Remember," Corrinne called back to the secretary, "he doesn't want to be disturbed." She shut the door.

"You can't just barge in here!" the lawyer growled, wiping frantically at the desk before him.

"Seriously? Coke on the leather desk blotter? Did you take a DeLorean here from 1985?"

Slocum rose to his feet and Corrinne put her hand on her gun. "You want to be on the news tonight? Like, next to the word *arrested*? Or *police shooting*?"

He sank back into his leather chair. "I heard you were suspended."

"You heard wrong. I've still got a badge and a gun. And you're going tell me everything I want to know."

* * *

Lonnie Anders passed through the metal detector and gathered her purse and keys from the plastic on the conveyer belt. She wore a black blouse with a clerical collar and a ruffled front. She'd bought it online a few weeks earlier. A ticket taker scanned her pass and welcomed her to the event.

At a table marked "Clergy/Press Registration" a middle-aged volunteer asked, "What church are you with?"

"My name's Lara Chappell. I'm with *The Ecumenical Post,*" she said, smiling. She was wearing foundation and a bit of rouge, which she hadn't done in years. "Here are my credentials." She pulled a laminated press pass from her purse.

The volunteer dug in a box beneath the table and came up with a lanyard bearing three more laminates. "Here are your event passes," he said. "You're allowed backstage, but there are two rules: don't talk to the VIPs, don't bother the VIPs. Understood?"

"Absolutely." She passed between two heavy black curtains and descended a long concrete staircase to field level. The place was filling up—about half the seats taken—and a praise band was howling their way through a repetitive chorus. She walked toward the loathsome noise, breaking left at the stage and flashing her press credentials to a fat security guard with a dimpled head. He nodded and stepped aside.

Once backstage, the blare of the music became tolerable. Above her a third of the arena's seating was empty, cordoned off. She quickly climbed up into section 116, row F, and made her way to the seat Jeremiah had prepared for her. No one was watching up here. The few roadies and sound techs moving about at ground level were immersed in their own tasks.

Lonnie squeezed her belt buckle and felt it release and come out in her hand, half a razor blade emerging from the cold metal disk. She sliced into the upholstery of the seat, tracing it over several times, before reaching into it. She glanced around in the low light for anyone who might be watching. Seeing no one, her fingers closed around the object and she pulled. The seat seemed to vomit out orange foam and, behind it, a pistol-grip stun gun. She smiled. Silent and efficient. They may have locked up Brother Jeremiah, but not before he'd given the Four Horsemen everything they needed.

She clicked the blade back into her belt and descended the stairs to the mouth of a tunnel, which led down to the locker room level. There, another security guard held up a hand to stop her.

Smiling, she waved her laminates at him. "I've got a press pass," she said. "And I'm scheduled to do an interview in the green room in about ten minutes. Can I get by?"

The guard shook his head. "Sorry. You need Level 3 clearance to go down there."

"Oh, I think I've got that," she said, digging into her purse. "Is this what you're looking for?" She stepped up to the man, wrapped her arm around his neck, and buried the stun gun in his hip, holding it there for a few seconds before the man tumbled backwards to the ground. She landed on top of him and continued to engage the weapon into his hip until she'd counted three-Mississippi.

Grabbing him by the wrists, she dragged him behind a large, rolled up mat, three feet tall. The guard was thin, but his dead weight was still a challenge. Lonnie grunted as she pulled him the last three feet, into total darkness. She hesitated a moment, waffling over what to do with him. He'd be dead before long anyway. And she couldn't have him coming to and notifying the police, complete with her description.

Lonnie took a deep breath and pulled the blade from her belt.

* * *

Corrinne leaned over the desk and locked eyes with Slocum. "I need to know what Van de Burg was hiding."

"I want my lawyer."

"You *are* a lawyer, moron."

"I'm entitled to representation," Slocum insisted. A shadow of the smirk returned to his face.

"You want to go that route? How much cocaine you got there?" She nodded at an open paper bundle on his desk. "This can be a few simple questions or a whole lot more . . . official."

"You can't ask me to break attorney-client privilege."

"No. But the councilman wasn't your client, was he? He was your daddy's college roommate. Besides, he's dead now."

Slocum half-shrugged. "I'm not sure what you're even looking for."

"Marriage problems. Abuse. Infertility."

A crack appeared in the veneer and Slocum began rubbing his meticulously trimmed beard. "If you already know, why are you asking me?"

"Pretend I don't. Pretend I just know that you helped blackmail him. And then you helped him deal with the blackmailer. These felonies are starting to pile up."

"Nothing will stick. I've got witnesses that will attest to the fact that you've been harassing me."

"I've got a witness too," Corrinne said, dumping the folder onto the desk. "Open it."

He obeyed. Right on top was a surveillance photo of Slocum in his car, Corrinne leaning partway in. Then one of her on her back. Then the Benz pulling away with Corrinne trapped in the window.

"This is all out of context," Slocum snorted, flipping to the next photo. Corrinne, standing against a cinder block wall, wearing a bright orange tube top, her hair a cross between a beehive and the Bride of Frankenstein. A nasty bruise extended up from beneath the orange spandex like tree roots wrapping around the hot pink strap of her bra.

Slocum picked up the print. "Can I keep this one?"

"You want to make jokes?" she said. "See that DVD? That's a video of the whole thing. Decent sound quality too. I'll bring it directly to the prosecutor. And if she won't pursue it, I'll go to the press. Everyone will know that you like picking up hookers and beating up women. Can't be good for business, John."

He slammed the folder closed. "I didn't blackmail anyone."

"Who did?"

"Your buddy. Caraway. He couldn't find any dirt on the guy. So he offered me a little on the side for any useful information."

"And you just turned on your friend. Your friend who stuck his neck out to keep yours out of an orange jumpsuit."

"You don't get it. Fifty grand is nothing to him. It was only afterward that Caraway demanded he step down from the city council."

"And how did Van de Burg deal with that?"

"He . . . explored his options," Slocum spat.

"Meaning . . . ?"

"You're a cop; read between the lines. What do powerful people do when someone threatens to expose them?"

"He was going to have Caraway killed."

Slocum nodded. "Maybe the guy beat him to it."

"I'm going to ask you this one more time: what was the information you gave Caraway?"

He crossed his arms. "Don Caraway actually *is* my client. We're protected."

"But you're going to turn on him to save yourself, aren't you? Just like you turned on Van de Burg. Tell me the truth and you don't have to do a perp walk through the office this evening." Corrinne could feel him break. It was beyond satisfying.

"You said it yourself," the lawyer mumbled. "Infertility. They tried and tried to have kids. Doctors and specialists. There was even a prayer group set up on AOL." He snorted derisively. "But it didn't work. She wanted to adopt, but you gotta realize, this was back before that was fashionable. Max thought it would hurt his image."

"But they've got two kids."

"When you have enough money and influence, you can buy anything, Detective."

"Who else knew?" Corrinne demanded.

"Other than me and Caraway, I have no idea."

"Is Caraway in his office?"

"I saw him passing through a couple hours ago."

"You're going to stay in here while I have a chat with him." She unplugged the cord from his desk phone. "Give me your cell. I'm not going to risk you calling to warn him."

Slocum stood. He was four inches taller than Corrinne and a lot broader than she remembered. "You can't deprive me of my property. You wanted your little answers and now you've got them. Get out of my office."

"The cellphone," she said again. Slocum cracked his knuckles. "Johnny, we've been on this ride before and we both know how it ends. Don't be stupid."

"I see you coming this time," he said. A fierce, detached malice settled in behind his eyes. She'd seen it before, the night he came charging out of his Mercedes, frothing and punching. She may have broken the man, but the wild animal inside was untamable. She still had the bruises to prove it.

"I'm done playing," she said. "Turn around and put your hands behind your back."

Slocum leaned forward, his eyes growing even more wild. With a flick of his wrist, he tossed the paper bundle of coke right in her face. Her eyes clamped shut and his hands closed around her neck.

29

As she strode down the tunnel to the locker room level, Lonnie pulled the clerical collar from her shirt and dropped it to the floor. Papist garbage. The tunnel leveled out into a blindingly white hallway, like a spaceship from a Sixties sci-fi movie. Framed posters on either side of the hall celebrated bands that had played the venue, the Griffins hockey team, and the now-defunct Grand Rapids Rampage football club.

Removing her shoe, she withdrew and unfolded a schematic, following the path Jeremiah had laid out for her. The original plan had been for the five of them to use Jeremiah's key card to come in through the service entrance. But with so much heat on them, they feared the authorities would be monitoring its use. And so Lonnie followed the specified route down another hall, this one unfinished—exposed ductwork, electrical conduits, and pipes hanging from the ceiling.

After another fifty feet, she entered a vast open area with concrete walls, packed with hundreds of folding chairs, heavy equipment, huge spools of electrical cords, and a golf cart tricked out to look like a Humvee. There it was: Emergency Exit. She padded over to it and reached up next to the hydraulic arm to unscrew the end of the cable, disabling the alarm.

Lonnie pushed the door open, revealing Timothy Philips and two other men—both named Tyler—all of them dressed in head-to-toe black like Halloween ninjas. She waved them in.

"Here you go," Philips said, handing Lonnie a Glock M/27.

She slid it into her waistband at the small of her back and said, "Get to work. We purify the Church tonight."

Philips produced his own schematic, this one marked with a different path, and led the two Tylers down a corridor lined with caged storage compartments. They moved quickly, slaloming around a rack full of beer kegs, a forklift, and several pallets of food, wrapped in heavy plastic.

"This is the one," Philips announced. He produced a key from his pocket and unlocked a padlock before swinging the cage door open. "Should be the bottom box over here." He indicated a stack of boxes that read, "Styrofoam Cups – 400 Count." His two companions toppled the stack and ripped open the box, casting columns of cups out onto the floor.

"Got it," the shorter Tyler said. He pulled out three army-issued metal ammunition boxes, each with a set of initials scratched into the lid. He handed one to each of his companions.

"Here, here, and here," Philips said, indicating points on the schematic. "We all meet back by the little Hummer exactly ten minutes from . . . *now*." The three of them depressed buttons on identical watches.

Timothy's location was closest to the cage: a steel I-beam stretching across a concreate support column. He could take his time, which suited him fine. The gunshot in his arm had been a through-and-through, but it still screamed with pain. The Tylers would have to go aboveground, into the crowd, to set their charges. He gave each of them a 50/50 shot at making it back in time. Didn't matter.

Timothy opened the latch on the ammo box and swung the lid open. He smiled. There was nothing sexier than C-4.

* * *

Corrinne cranked her shoulders up and her chin down. Her airway was already closed off; she had to act quickly. But she also had to keep her head. Her hands ran along Slocum's long fingers, searching out the loosest one—his left pinky. Wrapping her fist around the single digit, she wrenched it down backwards, feeling it snap as she pulled the hand down to her waist. Slipping his grip, she low-stomped his left knee, driving it into the floor.

Throwing both arms up and roaring like a professional wrestler, Slocum rose again, teeth bared. He tackled her around the middle, slamming her into the drywall. They fell to the ground together and he straddled her body, landing a punch to her jaw.

"I'll tell them how you attacked me," he said through clenched teeth. "You pulled your gun on me." His hand went to the holster at her side. She pinned it there with her own arm. For just a moment, it occurred to her that this was just like the fight with Anders, only in reverse. Then the training kicked in. Her edge.

Corrinne wrapped both hands around Slocum's elbow, her fingernails digging through the Valentino shirt. She then trapped his ankle with both her legs and bucked her hips, sending him sprawling beside her. Rolling quickly to her feet, she drew her weapon and took aim.

"I will shoot you," she said. "Turn around. Hands behind your back. Now."

Slocum froze, halfway to his feet, and raised his hands. "You can't shoot me. I'm unarmed."

"Watch me."

The lawyer wavered for a moment then seem to come to himself, the coke-fueled rage subsiding. He turned his back and assumed the position. "Yes, *ma'am,*" he spat.

"'Yes, ma'am.' I like that," she said. "Some women don't. I do." She holstered the gun and clicked the cuffs onto his wrists before reaching into his pocket and confiscating his cellphone.

"You've got me in a bit of a spot here, John," she said. "I'll send someone to get you, but first I have to take care of some business. So you're gonna wait in here." She steered him toward a closet in the corner of the office and opened the door. It was packed with file boxes and a few garment bags hanging from the bar, but there was just enough room to deposit one scumbag lawyer on the floor.

"Do not come out until the police arrive," she said as she swung the door shut. She wedged a chair beneath the handle, then slid his entire solid wood desk up against the chair.

Corrinne took a moment to straighten herself up in Slocum's full-length mirror before walking back out into the secretary's office. The woman beheld her with a sense of awe.

"Everything okay?" she asked.

"Your boss is cuffed in the closet. Some police officers are going to come and pick him up soon." She dumped Slocum's cell and his desk phone on the secretary's credenza. "For now, though, I need you to make sure he stays in there, okay? He comes out, you dial 911."

A broad smile slowly spread over the woman's face. "No problem."

Corrinne stepped out into the hall, intent on charging down to the FAR offices and going at Caraway just as hard. But something made her stop short. In the back of her mind, something was bothering her after learning what she had from Slocum. Parker was safe, so that wasn't it. For all his smarminess, Jackie was a good cop and he knew what he was doing. He'd attacked two armed men in his underwear to give Corrinne an out, for crying out loud.

Then it hit her. If Caraway was taking out his political enemies and the people he'd shamed on his index of hypocrites, what about the one man who fit both descriptions? The man who had already been attacked once? How had she failed to think of Donavan as November 2 dawned? Only now as evening descended did it occur to her to keep him safe. What if she was too late?

"Are you all right?" the secretary asked.

"I just need to make a phone call." She tried Donavan's cell, knowing that he left it home half the time. It was a running joke.

Just as it was about to go to voicemail, he picked up. "This is Stephen Donavan."

"Stephen, it's Corrinne. Where are you right now?"

"I'm at home. Why?"

"Can you do me a favor? Get in your car, lock the doors, and drive to Hope Presbyterian. The old building. Parker's there and so is a police officer name Detective Reese. Just hang with them for tonight. Please?"

"Should I be worried?"

"I don't know, Stephen. Maybe. I'd just feel a lot better if I knew you were somewhere safe."

"Right," he deadpanned. "Who could even imagine a crime being committed at our church?"

Corrinne sighed. "I know it's not where you want to be right now. But please? As a favor to me?"

"Honestly, my home doesn't feel overly safe either, for obvious reasons. I'll take the crime scene with police protection over the crime scene without."

"Thank you, Stephen. I'll call a little later and check in."

She ended the call and dialed up Jackie.

"It's me," she said. "How are things going there?"

"Dull. I've made my way around this place so many times I'm getting dizzy."

"Well, things are about to get a little more interesting," Corrinne said. "I've got another guy coming to the church. Stephen Donavan."

"Oh, come on Kirkpatrick! Now I'm babysitting a preacher *and* a lawyer? I can't stand lawyers."

Corrinne laughed. "Just try not to shoot him, okay?"

"Fine. But you owe *me* now."

"Shoot me a text when he gets there."

"You got it."

Corrinne pocketed the phone and marched fifty feet down the hall to the offices of FAR, Inc. Tannyr's desk was unoccupied and Corrinne pushed forward, through the empty cubicles and past Caraway's office, also empty. She found the woman with the blue hair sitting in the cramped conference room where she and Jackie had questioned Caraway.

"I'm looking for your boss," Corrinne said.

Blue Hair glanced up impassively and said, "As you can see, he's not here."

Corrinne cracked her neck. She was in no mood for this. "Tell me where he is or I'll run you in for obstruction."

It was an empty threat and they both seemed to know it. Still, the woman said, "He sometimes goes out on the balcony to have a cigarette. And think. And not be harassed by one of the police officers in the city council's pocket."

"I've got nothing to do with the city council," Corrinne said. "Now how do I get to this balcony?"

* * *

Father Michael was actually quite impressed by the security situation at the arena. Having read that the revival was a free event, he'd strolled up to the door, wearing fresh clericals, only to find that he needed a ticket all the same. And that the event was "sold out." No problem, though. He made a careful circuit of the building, probing for weaknesses. A few years earlier, Michael had gained access to Madison Square Garden through an air intake vent—took him all of ten minutes. But this place was sealed up tight, with cops making the rounds, in either direction, at irregular intervals.

Twenty-five minutes later, he found himself back at the entrance on Fulton Street, his frustration mounting. That's when he saw the woman holding a cardboard sign. I HAVE X-TRA TICKETS, it read. He rushed over.

"How much for a ticket?"

She looked offended. "I wouldn't sell them. They're free. I just ordered too many for our small group. Here you go, Father."

"Thank you so much." There was no longer a line to get in and Michael was able to walk right up to a metal detector, dumping the contents of his pockets on the way. He'd left his gun locked in the trunk of the car in a public lot two blocks away.

Michael rushed through the door just in time to hear an announcer proclaiming, "Some traditions call November 2nd All Souls' Day, a day of remembering the saints who have died. But tonight, we're thankful for you, the saints alive, who make up the living Church!"

Holding out his ticket for the scanner, Michael began to take in his surroundings, building a model of the arena in his mind.

"Welcome to the Church Unity Revival," the ticket taker said, smiling.

Father Michael smiled back, but he wasn't feeling it. Sure, he was in, but unarmed. He had no idea how to locate Anders in this sea of thousands of people. And the clock was running down.

***

Stephen Donavan gripped the wheel of his Cadillac DeVille, feeling the pounding of his heart in his white knuckles. He was headed to the place where he had always felt safest. As a boy, it was where he and his mother would go when his father had too much to drink and turned violent. It had always been a sanctuary, a haven. Of course, given all that had happened, it made sense that it didn't quite feel like that tonight.

Donavan turned left onto Jefferson. The car behind him followed. He scrutinized the sedan in his rearview mirror. It had followed him through the last least three turns at least. And it was hard to tell in the waning light, but it almost looked like there was a bullet hole in the windshield.

30

The balcony in question was actually the roof of the office tower's second tier, jutting out to the south, covered in stone tiles. Two potted trees and a few round picnic tables failed to sufficiently fill the vast open space.

Caraway was the only one out there, leaning against the low wall, which served as a safety rail. His back was to Corrinne. But the gray suit and the blue sneakers were a giveaway. She opened the door quietly and began walking toward him, her feet clicking against the tile floor despite her efforts. It was twilight now and light shined down from the much taller River House Condominiums building, kitty-corner from the office tower.

As she approached, hand on her gun, Caraway stiffened.

"So you've finally come to do me in," he said, his voice empty, defeated. "What took you so long?" He turned to face her. "Oh. It's you, Detective."

"Who were you expecting?"

Caraway chuckled, darkly. "Let's just say, when you make a deal with the devil, the devil eventually comes to collect his due."

"I thought you didn't believe in the devil."

"I don't believe in your God. But I see the devil in all of us." The fingers of his right hand began to slowly disappear into his suit jacket.

Corrinne remembered the gun she'd confiscated and pulled her own. "Let's keep your hands where I can see them."

Caraway laughed. "You've said that to me twice now. Do I seem untrustworthy?"

* * *

Jackie was finishing yet another perimeter check when he came face-to-face with an older man shuffling along in khakis and a button-down shirt.

"Whoa! Stop!" Jackie drew his gun, pointing it two inches shy of the man's feet. "Who are you and what are you doing here?"

The man threw his hands in the air and shouted, "I'm Stephen Donavan! I'm Parker's friend! His wife told me to come here. A cop. She is. A cop!"

Jackie holstered the gun. "How did you get in here?"

"Parker buzzed me in."

"Come with me," the detective spat, leading the man by the arm down the hall to Parker's office. He found the door locked, like he had instructed Parker, but it still annoyed him. He pounded on the door, which then opened an inch, through which Parker peered. Seeing Jackie with Donavan behind him, he opened it wide.

Jackie gestured at the newcomer. "What do you think you're doing, Parker?"

"What do you mean?"

"You buzzed him in? Did I tell you to buzz people in?"

Parker wrung his hands a bit. "No, but the cord was long enough to bring the intercom in here. And I couldn't leave my friend standing outside. What if it's not safe?"

"You could have gotten him shot, bringing him in here without telling me." He looked over his shoulder at Donavan and seemed to soften a bit. "Look, if I'm going to secure this place and keep you safe, then I have to be in complete control over who comes and who goes. Understand?"

Parker nodded. "Got it. Sorry."

Donavan was squinting at the cop. "Have we met before?" he asked. "You seem familiar to me."

"I doubt it. Why don't you wait in here with Parker? Don't buzz anyone in, don't call anyone, don't answer the phone unless it's Corrinne. Okay?"

Donavan offered a little salute. Parker just studied his shoes like a chastened child.

As Jackie was about to shut the door, Donavan asked, "Is this really necessary? Shutting us in here like this?"

"Kirkpatrick just wants to keep you safe," Jackie said. "You of all people should appreciate that. Since someone already made a run at you."

Donavan nodded, thoughtfully.

"By the way, I should ask: did you notice anything unusual on the way over? Cars following behind, maybe the same car popping up more than once?"

"I couldn't say for sure," Donavan said. "I actually did think someone was following me for a few blocks. But then they turned off, and I chalked it up to nerves."

"I'm going to check the perimeter again," Jackie said.

* * *

"Are you going to shoot me, Detective?" Caraway asked. He slowly pulled his gun out, finger off the trigger, barrel down.

"Drop it, Caraway. I will fire!"

He brought the gun up, slowly, to his own temple. "Do me a favor. I've grown bored with all this. It was exciting for a time. But now it's just stress and fear to the point of monotony."

Corrinne lowered her gun, but not much. "Please just drop the gun, Mr. Caraway. If you need help, we'll get you help."

He laughed, mirthlessly. "You're here to arrest me. We both know that. Because we both know something neither of us is saying."

"What do we know?"

"That I killed Garrett Appelt." He sniffed. "You wouldn't get it. You and your preacher husband and your law and order. Your liberty and justice for some." He read the shock in her expression. "Oh. You didn't know." He laughed again. "I guess that makes sense. You couldn't tell who was who because, once you start pulling at a single thread, the web of hypocrisy expands to include everyone. That's why my work is so pointless. At the end of the day, we'd all be caught up in the web. Chaos."

He turned his back to Corrinne and looked out at the city, the gun still at his head. She slipped out of her shoes and took three silent steps toward him.

"I let him use me," Caraway said. "Me. How did that happen?"
Corrinne took another step.

* * *

Michael spotted him right away. If only there were as many cops in here as there had been outside, one of them would have noticed the guy too. Way up in the nosebleeds, moving along the press box, which was dark and unoccupied, toward the empty seats backstage. He wore all black and moved along quickly, hunched over so that the seatbacks largely hid him from view. Michael began moving quickly up the steps, toward the top level, slipping through the foot traffic. Ahead, his current path would take him under the upper level and out into the concourse. Instead, Michael jumped up and grabbed the handrail above, pulling himself over, drawing looks from everyone in the vicinity—a mixture of awe and disapproval.

He continued climbing, his eyes never far from the man in black, now descending the stairs to field level, backstage. He seemed less concerned with stealth now and more with speed. As he neared the front row of seats, a muscled-up man in an orange vest came out from the tunnel, holding up a hand and saying, "hold up" and "let me see your pass." Instead, the black-clad man jumped up, grabbed the railings on either side of the aisle, and slammed both of his feet into the security guard's chest, sending him sprawling to the ground, his head cracking against the concrete floor.

The man in black landed practically on top of the guard, retrieved an item from his pocket, and pushed it into the guard's neck, sending him into spasms. Michael quickened his pace, shuffling free of the row of seats, and began to run down the stairs toward them. The guard's body was still jiggling. Finally, the man returned the stun gun to his pocket and began dragging the neutralized guard back behind an enormous mat, rolled-up near the side of the field.

Michael sailed over the last railing and hit the ground running. The man in black and his victim had disappeared behind the mat. The priest crossed the floor at a full sprint. As he slowed himself, approaching the mat, the man sprung out from behind and jabbed the stun gun into Michael's shoulder. He felt the pain—both dull and sharp at the same time—involuntary seizing muscle for only a second before he slammed his fist into the weapon, sending it clattering to the floor.

A wave of nausea rose up and then subsided and Father Michael stumbled back a step. Most stun guns approached a million volts and would incapacitate even the largest of men for up to half an hour. But part of Michael's training had been repeated exposure to this sort of weapon and he remained on his feet, although he teetered a bit.

The man in black finally seemed to get a good look at him, squinting in confusion at the collar, before slamming his weight into Father Michael, knocking the priest back, and continuing into the tunnel. Michael bounced on the concrete, made a full roll, and popped back up, already moving in pursuit. The effects of the electricity were all but gone now and he tapped into his strength and speed once again.

He saw the man in black turn left up ahead and followed him.

* * *

Jackie clicked off the safety on his Beretta. He could have sworn he'd just heard a noise coming from the sanctuary. He did not want to go in there.

Not that he was afraid or anything. It just gave him the willies. Over the past ten years he'd been around dozens of stiffs. A hundred maybe. But there was something about the body with the mouthful of bees in the old church. Even the memory of it got a rise from the hairs on the back of his neck.

He opened the heavy wooden door and began moving up the center aisle. There were no pews lined up, creating hundreds of shadowed recesses from which someone could attack. For that he was grateful. In fact, the place was more or less empty and it took him only a few minutes to search it back-to-front.

As he came out of the sanctuary, he felt a sudden chill. Cold wind, blowing in from outside. He followed the chill to its source: a perfectly round hole, six inches in diameter, cut from one of the windows. The lock, which Jackie had double checked not half an hour ago, was now disengaged.

* * *

Michael was surprised at how little he was gaining on the man in black. His mile was closer to four minutes than five, and yet he'd closed less than half the distance between himself and his quarry. *The guy must be a sprinter.* The man turned left again and Michael followed, six paces behind.

Then he saw red. Fire Extinguisher Red. And went down.

The world came slowly back into focus. The fluorescent lights directly above him and a bunch of Ethernet cords, zip-tied together, snaking along the ceiling. Then he saw three faces peering down from all around him. Two men and a woman. They were smiling.

"Nice shot , Tyler," Philips said. "This is the guy who put a bullet in me." He squatted down, got right in Michael's face. "Eye-for-an-eye time."

* * *

"I didn't even want to do it," Caraway said, turning back toward Corrinne. "Hey!" he shouted, and pulled back the hammer on the gun, still pointed at his head. "I said stay back!" He climbed up onto the low wall, a step single away from a 250-foot drop to his death.

"Sorry," Corrinne said. She holstered her gun. "You didn't want to do what?"

"Any of it. Blackmail Van de Burg. Kill Garrett Appelt. I mean, I wanted to, but . . ." He squeezed his eyes shut and gave his head a rough shake. For a moment, Corrinne thought he might jump. Then it passed.

"I got home one day and Garrett was there, tied up on my couch," Caraway said. "Bound and gagged. And he said it was my chance to set things right. An eye for an eye, he said. He was wearing a robe and a mask. It didn't even seem real. He thought I wouldn't know him in that costume." Caraway began to cry, distorting his words. "I thought my luck had changed back then, you know? They took me in. The Appelts. And they were going to adopt me. They said they loved me. And 'God' loved me. Then one day they caught me with Dean and immediately disowned me."

"And you tried to burn down the house."

"No! It was an accident. Mrs. Appelt caused it. But it was a convenient way to get rid of me while saving their reputation. Sure, he changed his tune, but only after I'd spent a year in juvenile detention. And after that, I was too high-risk for foster parents. No one wanted me. My life was ruined.

"And when I saw that man, there in my home, his eyes pleading for mercy . . . This guy who had given me none! I just lost it. Suddenly, I had this sharp thing in my hand and I shoved it into his chest. And then another, and then another. He just kept handing them to me, egging me on. And then I belonged to him. There was DNA everywhere. I had to go along with him after that."

"Who?" Corrinne shouted. "Who was it?"

"Like I said, I made a deal with the devil."

"Anders?"

"What difference does it even make?" Caraway pulled the trigger and Corrinne let out an involuntary shriek. It took a moment for it to register: he's still standing there, smiling that sad smile. There'd been no bang. No blood.

"Not loaded," Caraway said. "I hate guns."

Corrinne saw her chance and rushed him, wrapping her arms around his thighs and throwing her hip, dumping him to the floor of the balcony. Caraway popped back up and lunged for the sky beyond. She followed, slamming her body into his, pinning him down to the ledge. She pulled his right arm behind his back.

"Stop struggling," she commanded, closing the cuff around one wrist. He would not die. Not on her watch. For a moment, Caraway obeyed. But as she reached for his other arm, he slammed his body back into hers, pushing her just a step. He threw his legs over the ledge, casually, like he was hopping into a pool. His body dropped.

Corrinne gripped the cuffs with both hands, bracing herself against the barrier. "Help!" she called. But no one had been near the exit to the balcony when she'd come out. And she saw no one back there now. Caraway's shoulder had dislocated, she could see that, as he pulled and kicked against the outside of the low wall, his arm stretching where the ball and socket had parted.

"Quit fighting!" she shouted, wrenching on the metal chain. "You don't want to die." She was toying with the idea of cuffing him to her own wrist. But that would be irreversible. If he went down, so would she. If only the balcony had an ordinary railing, she could cuff him to that.

"What kind of deal did you make with Anders?" she asked, amid grunts.

Caraway stopped tugging for a moment and locked eyes with her. He looked bizarrely like a man reclining in an invisible lounge chair, his feet flat against the wall. "I know you want answers," he said. "You want everything to make sense. But you can't have it."

Caraway kicked her square in the face with his bright blue sneaker, blasting her to the ground, and simply disappeared. He didn't scream on his way down, at least not that she could hear.

But he was gone.

31

Jackie forced himself to put one foot in front of the other, moving toward Parker's study. The metal of his gun felt like it was bending beneath his Kung Fu grip. He needed to call for backup, but he didn't dare take out his phone and divide his attention. Not out in the open. No, he'd have Parker call instead. It was only another twenty feet.

"Drop the gun," a gravelly voice commanded from behind him. Jackie froze. The familiar voice said, "You want to die, cop?" Jackie cursed and tossed his gun to the floor and looked back at his attacker.

"Oh, it's you." Anders laughed. "You get disarmed a lot, don't you fancy-pants?" When Jackie didn't answer, he said, "You're not going to cry and beg this time? You grow a pair? Put your hands behind your back."

Jackie placed his hands on his head.

"I said behind your back! That's right, and interlace your fingers. Good." Keeping his gun trained on the detective, Anders kicked his discarded weapon, sending it skidding off into the distance. "You got another woman lined up to come to your rescue?" he taunted, disappearing behind Jackie again.

"You mean the woman who did that to your face? You look like a friggin' nightmare, by the way."

An explosion of pain in the back of his head—metal meeting skull—sent Jackie lurching forward. He failed to disentangle his hands fast enough and his right cheek broke the fall. Another explosion in his abdomen as Anders' foot connected.

Jackie cried out in pain and tipped onto his side, curling up in a fetal position.

"There's someone else out there," Donavan said, his face going white. "Call the police!"

"Reese *is* the police," Parker said.

"Call the rest of them!"

It sounded like a good idea to Parker. But first, he double-checked that the door to the study was still locked. Then he picked up the phone on his desk. No dial tone.

"It's dead," he announced. A little whimper escaped Donavan's throat. He looked to Parker like a scared child, sitting on the floor, against the wall, his knees gathered to his chest. He was holding Parker's nail gun up like a pistol, as if he could take out an intruder coming through the door from ten feet away.

"Do you have your cellphone?" Parker asked.

Donavan checked his pockets. "No. I left it at home. I'm sorry." There was another cry of pain from out in the hall, this one louder than the last.

Parker checked his pockets. No phone. Had he left it charging in the church office next door? Or maybe in a desk drawer. He began rifling through them. Nothing. There were so many boxes and piles of papers and books around, it could be anywhere.

He felt a sudden flashback to the previous October, running through the dark halls of an old church building, being stalked by a killer. And now he had his neighbor and friend to protect as well as himself. At least he was here in a well-lit office, door locked, under the protection of a man Corrinne trusted, with training and a gun. Then again, Paul Ketcham had been a man Corrinne trusted, with training and a gun.

Parker slid down the wall and sat next to Donavan, who was shaking and gasping for breath, still holding the nail gun up, pointing it at the door. Reaching up gently, Parker removed the battery from the tool and placed it on the floor between them.

***

At the woman's command, Tyler began dragging Father Michael down the hall. He was incredibly strong and, between the stun gun and the blow to the head, Michael was not at his best. His feet slid along, shoes squeaking against the tiled floor, then scuffing as the group moved off the beaten path onto concrete.

Apparently happy with where they had arrived—a darker, semi-secluded dead end of a hallway—the man dumped Michael to his knees and Philips pointed a .357 right in his face. He had a dumb face, but he knew enough to keep the gun beyond Michael's reach.

"Be not afraid of desolation," the woman said, "for the wicked shall not see it coming."

"What is that supposed to be?" Michael asked. He was fairly sure this was the woman from Anders's house that morning.

"It's Proverbs," she said. "You'd know that if you learned the Bible instead of all that hokus-pokus-wafer-god filth."

"That's nothing, though. You're thinking of Proverbs 3:25. 'Be not afraid of sudden fear, nor of the desolation of the wicked falling upon thee.'"

The woman haltingly tried on and discarded a catalog of phonetic sounds before declaring, "You won't confuse me, devil."

Philips looked around, shifting nervously back and forth. "I say we off him and get out of here."

"Hey, where's your boss?" Michael asked. "Scarface?"

The woman spoke. "My husband is tying off a loose end. We don't stand for loose ends."

* * *

"Speaking of the lady-cop," Anders said, "where is she?"

Jackie groaned in agony. Anders had kicked him three times and he was quite sure his spleen was ruptured. Out of the pain rose up a realization. "Wait. You're here for Kirkpatrick? Not Parker?"

"Parker? Who's Parker? Focus! The lady-cop! Where do I find her?" He hung over Jackie in anticipation for a moment. "I get it. You need a memory booster."

Another blow to the stomach was almost more than the detective could bear. He curled up into an even tighter ball. That's when his fingers brushed against his ankle and he remembered what was there.

"She's . . . in . . . " Jackie emitted a manufactured grunt against very real pain, as he reached under his pant leg, pulled back the hammer of the snub-nose .38 in his ankle holster, and pulled the trigger. Anders' foot exploded, blood gushing form a wide hole in his leather boot. He cried out in pain.

Jackie cleared the gun and rolled onto his back, firing twice before even taking aim. Both shots missed, but as the two men locked eyes, Anders dropped his gun and placed his hands on his head.

At the sound of the first gunshot, Donavan had begun to hyperventilate, sucking air but seeming to get none. Parker gave his shoulder a squeeze, while the next two shots sounded and then resumed the frantic search for his phone.

He thought of Paige. Being close to Parker had cost her her life. Would it happen again? Donavan's head was down between his knees. Parker prayed it was only panic and not a heart attack. The lawyer was older, but fit—always exercising, jogging every morning in his corny bright white sneakers.

Then again, it seemed like he always heard about health nuts downing granola, heading off on their daily jog, and keeling over dead—while the guy who smokes and drinks with abandon lives into his nineties. Depending on how this played out, it might be the better option for Donavan to simply fade out, rather than face whoever was out there.

Parker picked up the landline again. Still dead.

* * *

Anders was lying on his stomach now, hands behind his back. Barely able to stand straight, Jackie didn't dare get close enough to cuff him. Instead, he tossed the handcuffs onto Anders' back and ordered, "Put them on tight. Back there."

It took the fugitive a minute, but he managed to get them secured. Keeping the .38 trained on Anders's head, Jackie reached down and tightened them. He forced himself to stand tall, despite the pain in his stomach. This was a moment of victory. The man who had humiliated him in front of Kirkpatrick, dehumanized him, put a gun to his head then crawled inside it, from whence he had kept Jackie from a single decent night's sleep since . . . that same man was now cuffed and neutralized at his feet.

"Took your advice," he said. "Got a backup piece." He wished he had a cooler line, but that would do.

Walking the ten feet to Parker's study, Jackie banged on the door a couple times. "Parker, it's me! Open up!" he said. Then looked at the defeated man lying on the ground and allowed himself a smile.

* * *

"I told him," Anders's wife sneered, "no kind of man gets arrested by a woman cop. And he's not to come home until he makes it right."

"He's gone to find Corrinne Kirkpatrick?"

"How do you know that name?" the woman asked, leaning in close. "Who are you?" The blush on her cheeks, combined with the hate in her eyes, brought a chill to Father Michael. He smiled all the same.

"You'd be surprised what we know. Jack Chick was right about us Jesuits. It's no fundie conspiracy theory. We're always watching. And listening. The Holy Father has microphones everywhere." He looked furtively left, then right, and whispered, "And there are spy satellites in your teeth."

Philips slammed his fist into Michael's temple, knocking him to the floor.

"Gonna be loud," Tyler said. "Should we wait for Tyler?"

"No," Philips said. "He knew the plan. Anyone gets caught, falls behind, gets to be a martyr."

"Wait," Michael said. "I'm so confused. I thought *you* were Tyler."

"We're both named Tyler," the man in black offered, helpfully.

"Enough," Philips said, leveling the revolver at Father Michael. "Goodbye, priest."

* * *

"Parker, it's me! Open up!" It was Jackie's voice and, presumably, his fist pounding on the door.

The ball of dread and fear in Parker's chest dissipated. He abandoned the box he was digging through and scrambled over to the door, to unlock it. As he swung it open, he saw Jackie leaning against the doorframe, not looking well. His left hand cradled his abdomen and his breath seemed labored. Still, he was smiling, and that was something.

"You call 911?" he asked.

"No. The phone's dead." Parker poked his head out the door. "Is *he* dead?"

"No, he's okay." The cop looked over at his prisoner. "Won't be running any marathons, though, will you?" He pulled his cellphone from his pocket.

Parker stumbled back and collapsed against his desk. His heart hadn't even begun to adjust. "Tell them to send an ambulance for Stephen, too. He's in bad shape." He looked back to where his friend had been sitting; Donavan was gone. Then a *ka-chung* from the doorway grabbed his attention. Jackie fell hard to his knees, eyes wide. He stared up at Parker in abject confusion.

Ka-chung. Ka-chung. Ka-chung. Donavan fired three more nails into the top of the cop's head. Parker opened his mouth to scream, but had no breath for it. A trickle of blood, like a single tear, rolled from Jackie's eye and down his cheek, and he tipped forward onto the filthy carpet.

"Oh, this moment," Donavan said. He was using two fingers to check his pulse. "I've thought about this for so long." Stooping down, he pried the cop's gun and phone from his lifeless hands. "I'm going to send a little message to your wife." He pointed the gun at Jackie's lifeless body and added, "You drag that into the closet. Then get your coat; we're going for a ride."

"Stephen. What are you—"

"All in good time. For now, do as I say or I'm going to get angry."

Parker grabbed Jackie around the wrists and pulled him over to the closet, struggling to fit his entire body in. He forced the door closed and turned around to see Donavan drop Jackie's phone to the ground and crush it with his heel. He then pulled another phone from his jacket pocket and held it up. "Looking for this?" he asked before also crushing it beneath his shoe.

The lawyer bent down and picked up both phones, tossing them into one of the many open boxes. Nudging the gun at Parker, he said, "After you . . ."

As they walked out into the hall, Donavan paused and peered down at Anders, cuffed and whimpering. "What have we here?" he said. "You're on my list. I had something wonderful planned for you. Oh, well. You saved me a trip."

He pointed Jackie's gun at Anders's head.

"Cover your ears, Parker."

32

Corrinne opened her eyes. She felt as though she'd been lying on the cold tile floor for an hour. But a look at her phone told her it had been only minutes. Important minutes, though. Below, she could hear sirens approaching. She could imagine crowds of onlookers. Chaos.

But up here, it was silent and still. Caraway was gone and everything had changed. It was as if the kick to her face and the contact of her head with floor had jarred everything loose in her mind. As she lay there in pain and grief, her first cohesive thought had been about how this whole thing had begun with a man knocking her down to the hard ground. And now here she was again.

But then all those pieces of the puzzle—now jarred free—began to fall together and click into place. Who was 'the devil' in Caraway's eyes if not Stephen Donavan? Publicly the two men despised each other, but then an attack on Donavan helped to clear Caraway's name. It all started to make sense in a nonsensical way. Garrett Appelt had probably been the first one killed according the M.E.—then put on ice.

Once Caraway had murdered the man, he was entirely at the mercy of his nemesis. Not only had Donavan forced him to blackmail the councilman, she could see now that it was Donavan who called the news crew to his own mother's funeral. It was probably Donavan who ordered Caraway to show up as well.

Their public feud was so personal, so vicious, that no one would have suspected them of covering each other's tracks. As long as neither man could have committed all the murders, they were safe. There was just enough evidence at the end of the day for Caraway to be the fall guy. Which he had become—literally.

As her mental fog dissolved and her epiphany cemented, she felt a sudden shot of panic and sat bolt upright. Jackie and Parker were with Donavan. Now. On the night of All Souls' Day.

And they had no idea.

She checked her messages. Two unread, both from Jackie. The first just said, "Lawyer is here," with a puking face and a party hat-confetti emoji. The next read, "Something came up. Dropped Parker and the lawyer off at home. Sorry. –Jack"

Corrinne felt as if she was the one in freefall.

Jack?

* * *

The sound of someone approaching grabbed the attention of Lonnie and her men. Their guns swung up in the party crasher's direction. He looked like some sort of hunchback, shuffling toward them from the dim light beyond.

Philips narrowed his eyes. "What the—?"

As the man shuffled closer, bent down, Michael saw that one side of his face had taken a brutal beating. He was wrapped in athletic tape, securing his hands to his side, his thighs to each other, and something large and bulky to his back. Another piece of tape, wrapped around his head, kept his mouth shut. Behind him, he was dragging something big, black, and square.

"Tyler?" Philips said.

"What's that tied to him?" the other Tyler asked, his gun once again poked up to Michael's head, but his attention on his prodigal companion. "Is that his C-4?"

A blur of black came roaring in from behind a stack of empty cardboard boxes and collided with Philips's face, crushing bones and flattening him to the floor. Grabbing the distraction, Father Michael turned, rose, and disarmed Tyler, shooting his knuckles into the man's throat and sweeping his legs from beneath him.

Philips was already rising to his feet, gun still in hand, his face a mess of blood and broken skin. Michael took aim at him, but the Tyler he'd just disarmed was grabbing at his gun, struggling for control of it. From behind the pile of boxes, a man rushed out, hurling another black object like a discus, before taking cover behind the taped-up hunchback. Philips sidestepped the object, which slammed into the wall, bounced off, and slid along the floor. A 15-pound free weight.

The mystery man raised a pistol in each hand and looked out from behind his human shield. Only his eyes and a shock of white hair were visible.

Father Ignatius.

* * *

Parker was riding in the trunk of Jackie's car.

Donavan had smiled—a benign, childish, pleased-with-himself smile—while he forced him in at gunpoint, promising that their big night was just getting started. They'd been on the road maybe two minutes and Parker felt a strange and unexpected calm, which he was trying to convince himself was more the result of his experience in surviving such ordeals and less the sort of "give up and play dead" tactic people used on grizzly bears.

It's a just a man this time, he reminded himself. Not a legion of demonic host. And a senior citizen at that. And, of course, his good friend. But he couldn't explore that right now. What he needed was some kind of weapon with which to overpower Donavan. He was sure the best chance—perhaps the only chance—he would have was the moment the trunk opened up. He would be ready to spring into action, with a tire iron or a crowbar, or . . .

Nothing. Parker thought about the time he had spent face-down in the grass next to the car. Clearly, Donavan had removed anything useful. He'd have to. This was a cop's car, after all. Corrinne kept a loaded shotgun in the back of hers.

But it was possible Donavan had overlooked something. Parker felt around in the inky blackness. If this were a movie, the inside of the trunk would be awash in a dim blue light. But it wasn't a movie and there was nothing but pure black.

He was lying on carpet, which he pulled away, folding it down under his own body. The car took a sharp turn and Parker slid against the side with the momentum, his head crunching against the inside of the trunk. He shook it off. Beneath the carpet was a sort of false bottom for the trunk itself—a thin wooden board cut to exactly the right shape, beneath which the tire and jack were stored. It was the same in his own car.

It took some painful gymnastics, but Parker was able to wedge his arm beneath. He groped, twisted, contorted. If there was a tire iron down there, he couldn't reach it. The spare was clearly screwed down, probably along with the rest of the equipment.

Then his hand touched something soft. There was a flap at the front. He pulled and heard the unmistakable sound of Velcro opening. A roadside emergency kit! Perhaps there would be scissors inside. Or a heavy flashlight. Or . . . his hands closed around two cylinders.

Parker pulled them up into the trunk proper. They were about nine inches long, each with a plastic cap at the end.

Road flares.

* * *

With a kick, Father Ignatius launched his bound and gagged hostage sprawling into Philips, just as Michael brought his elbow up to Tyler's eye and wrenched down on his gun, securing it. There was shouting and chaos, echoing through the concrete hall.

A single gunshot got everyone's attention. Lonnie Anders held a compact pistol in one hand and a chunky burner phone in the other. A small cloud of concrete dust swirled down from a hole in the ceiling. She leveled her pistol at Father Ignatius, who returned the favor with his own gun, while holding another—presumably taken off the unluckier Tyler—on Philips.

"Looks like we've got a Mexican standoff," Michael said. "Wait, is that offensive? Can you still say that?"

"We've got no such thing." Lonnie waved the phone back and forth, for both priests to see. "I push this button and the whole building goes *boom.*"

"Lonnie," Philips said.

She ignored him. "We're willing to die as martyrs for our cause. Are you?"

"Without question." Father Ignatius stepped closer to her.

"You think I won't do it?" she yelled. "You have three seconds to lay down your guns or I swear I'll bring this whole building down on our heads. *Three. . .*"

"Wait!" Father Michael said. "Just wait . . . Is that one of those old-people Jitterbug phones? Father Ignatius, don't you have the same one?"

"*Two . . .* "

"Lonnie, what are you doing?" Philips said, lowering his gun. "This was never the plan."

"Have some conviction, you coward," she spat.

"I'd run if I were you," Michael said to the Tyler on the floor before him. "Go."

Tyler scrambled to his feet and took off frantically down the hall. Father Michael re-centered his aim on Philips.

"*One.*" Lonnie squeezed her eyes shut and pushed the button. In lieu of a *boom*, the phone beeped loudly, three times.

"Whoops," Father Ignatius said, snatching the gun from her hand and crumpling her to the floor with a punch to the nose.

"Drop it, Hoss," Father Michael ordered, cocking the pistol, "or I'll put another one in you." Philips obeyed. "How about you lay down by your friend here?" Michael said. He peered down at the object taped to the prone man's back. An electrical cord, wrapped in more tape, ran down to the car battery. "Is that the WeBeJammin2000?"

The older priest smiled, but just for a second. "I've got plenty of tape," he said. "After we restrain these devils, you may summon the authorities."

* * *

It took Parker almost five minutes to figure out how to light the flare in the dark. The plastic cap contained a smaller cap, under which he found a rough surface, not unlike the strip on a box of matches. By striking it against the end of the flare, he finally got it to come to life, filling the trunk with a flickering red light. He read the print on the other flare. It claimed to last twenty minutes. But he had no idea where they were going or how long he'd be in the trunk.

As if to answer that particular question, he felt the car slow, turn, and come to a stop. There was a rumbling sound, which Parker identified as an electric garage closing. Feeling a burning anxiety he hadn't experienced in a year, Parker lit up the second flare with the first and waited.

33

Parker heard the trunk lid click open and saw a rim of low light appear. Now. It had to be now.

Bursting forth from the darkness, he sailed through the air, leading with the two burning flares. He landed on the cold epoxy floor of a two-stall garage. Jackie's car was parked next to a newish Chrysler 300.

"Heroic," Donavan said, drily. He was leaning against the wall of the garage, the keyless-entry remote in his hand.

Parker pivoted and threw himself at his neighbor, driving the burning flares at the man's eyes. Donavan caught him by both wrists and turned the flares back on Parker, slowly overpowering him. The red flames got closer and closer to his face until he dropped them both. Donavan buried a fist in his stomach, doubling him over. It was so much harder than he'd expected. Almost as hard as a blow from Ketcham and his demonic horde.

Donavan laughed. "Oh, you're going to burn. Don't worry. But not yet." He grabbed Parker around the throat, dragging him to his feet and then bodily out the back door of the garage and into the cool, dark night. Parker tried to scream, but his throat was caving in on itself. They made their way to the back corner of the yard where Donavan opened a shed and pushed Parker inside.

* * *

Michael walked through one of a dozen glass doors, bearing the words NO RE-ENTRY in large, block letters. It was strange to suddenly be standing in the lights of downtown, cars passing by, people milling about. Spotting a group of cops chatting, Michael walked up and said, "I'm looking for Officer Allen."

"I'm Detective Allen," a pretty young woman said.

"Huh."

"Can I . . . help you with something?"

"Oh, right. This is going to sound a little weird, but you know those fugitive terrorists you've been looking for? They're in the arena. Down below. Tied up."

Vivien nodded. "You got a weird sense of humor, padre."

"I'm not kidding. Also, there's a bunch of guns and explosives, so you may want to check that out. Probably evacuate the building. Come on, I'll show you."

* * *

Donavan shoved Parker down into the hard metal of the La-Z-Boy and zip-tied his wrists and ankles. It was all sharp edges and right angles.

"Make yourself comfortable," he said, throwing the lever, violently tipping Parker back.

"Please, Stephen. We're friends. I don't understand."

Donavan put a finger to his pursed lips. "Do not speak unless asked a direct question," he said. "The Tribunal is in session." He walked over to a small wardrobe in the corner and withdrew a long leather robe and hood, which he donned. The raw fear in Parker's chest double in volume, threatening to crush him from the inside.

"You want to know why. Of course, I'll tell you. It would be unjust to execute a man without rehearsing his crimes. This is a just Inquisition, after all." He smiled at Parker's abject confusion. "I suspect you think I've changed. But I never changed. I just woke up after a long slumber. In truth, I started on this path decades ago.

"If you had known the twisted piece of work that was my father, this would all make more sense. Some men are fun drunks. Some mean drunks. My father became creative, artistic. And his chosen medium was pain. He rarely came after me, though. My mother was usually his canvas. He hated her, hated her forgiveness, hated her talk of God. Despite his inebriation, he always managed to confine his artwork to the hidden parts. She too kept it hidden." He stepped over to an old workbench and fingered a number of blades and tools.

"One day, though, she buckled under the pressure and confided in a friend what she'd been enduring. Not just a friend—a man she trusted intrinsically. A man of God. Her employer. Her pastor." His eyes burned from under the hood, meeting Parker's. "Your grandfather."

"She told him everything, breaking down and weeping. She was humiliated, but unburdened. I know because I sat just outside the office and heard each and every word." He plucked up an X-Acto knife from the bench. "And do you know what the good reverend told her?" He waited, as if Parker might already have this knowledge. "He said, 'Jesus was abused too, and perhaps this could be your life's ministry.' You know, turning the other cheek. Giving in to his every demand and suffering every insult and blow. And when she shared her fear that doing so might mean her death, your grandfather said, 'But think of what a witness for Christ that could be.'"

"That's unforgiveable," Parker said. "Horrible. I had no idea."

Calmly, Donavan made a small cut along Parker's cheek. "Silence. Unless asked a direct question. Show some respect for the proceedings." He took a step back and took in the sight. "Your beautiful, handsome face. Not for long. I know that your grandfather didn't kill my mother. Not with a dagger to the heart. It was death by a thousand cuts. And that's how you'll die too. A thousand little cuts. And when you're fading away, Chrysostom, I'm going to cut out that golden tongue of yours."

* * *

Corrinne stomped the accelerator, her phone pressed to her ear.

"This is Detective Reese with the Major Case Team. I'm unavail—"

She hung up. Jackie hadn't sent that message. Or if he had, signing it 'Jack' was his way of telling her that he was in trouble. And he certainly was. Possibly dead. Which meant Parker was—

She pulled the plug on the thought.

The red light on her roof flashed as she slowed just enough to take the corner. *Forget the phone.* She dumped it on the passenger seat. Multiple calls to Jackie, Parker, and Donavan had come up with nothing but voicemail boxes. Likewise, their home landline and the one at church had gone unanswered.

Corrinne needed to get to the church. But first, she'd pass by her house on the way. It was a longshot, but maybe Parker really was home. Maybe he was sleeping and missed her calls. Maybe he was bleeding on the floor, unconscious.

The Expedition screeched to a stop. There was their house, dark and closed up. Two doors down, there were lights on at Donavan's place. She wavered. If Donavan saw her enter her own house, it would give him a window of escape. That wasn't going to happen.

* * *

"My mother took that horrible, satanic advice. She would be a martyr, a punching bag. Perhaps that actually was the silver bullet that would change my father's shriveled heart. And then one day, he cracked the plaster in their bedroom with her head. And while she didn't die, she was never the same. She couldn't speak. Couldn't care for herself. Couldn't be a mother to her son." Donavan made three quick cuts down Parker's forearm. Parker could only gape at the blood, eyes wide.

"The day I turned eighteen, my father disappeared. The police assumed he just left town, tired of caring for his sickly wife, now free of the burden of fatherhood. But in reality, he's buried right next to this shed. I cut out his tongue too. If she couldn't speak, neither could he. Neither can you." He flicked the blade downward, cutting both of Parker's lips.

"But then I went to law school, and went to sleep. Perhaps I could honor my mother by defending the Church against her enemies. Men like my father, who lash out against the faithful. It wasn't until I defended that monster, Cates, that I began to stir. And when a third generation Rev. Parker had risen to fame and prominence, celebrated as a hero in the press and the pulpit, just as my dear mother was dying, it woke me up entirely. I realized I'd been off-track, trying to defend the Church against men like my father. When what was really needed was to purge the Church of men like your grandfather."

He opened a drawer, mounted beneath the workbench, and pulled out his advance copy of Parker's book. He laughed and tossed it onto Parker's lap. "How fitting that your little book singing the praises of that horrible man came out today: the anniversary of the day my mother's life was stolen from her. The day I'd already chosen for my revenge."

He made a few more lazy cuts on Parker's neck and ear. "I almost let you skate by," he said. "Can you believe that, Saint? After all this, I almost gave you a pass. Because we're friends." He laughed again.

Parker racked his brain for the right thing to say. He remembered a counseling class from seminary and lamely asked, "How does that make you feel?"

"It doesn't."

* * *

Corrinne finished a circuit of Donavan's house, ending where she'd begun, right where the front walk met the sidewalk. She'd seen no one inside, although there were plenty of lights on. As she mounted the stairs to the front door, she considered calling for backup. But then a wave of doubt overtook her. Caraway hadn't actually named Donavan. At best, he'd implied it. Or she'd just inferred it. And her epiphany had indeed coincided with what was likely a mild concussion.

If she called for backup now, begging her colleagues to ignore the captain's orders, she'd be playing her last card. If Parker wasn't here, then what? She couldn't afford to roll those dice. Corrinne reached up and pushed the doorbell.

* * *

The Tribunal had now completely overtaken Stephen Donavan. And he could now see that it was something else, alive in him. He gave himself over to it completely. He'd always known it was there, beneath the surface. From the moment he first put on the robe and hood. His hatred for Parker had appeared in that moment, and he'd been able to see how his neighbor was as good as responsible for everything his grandfather had done. Surely, The Tribunal had hated Parker Saint before Stephen Donavan ever did.

He gazed down at the preacher in the chair and felt a warmth inside. Yes, it was revenge, but it was something much deeper at the same time. Saint was bleeding, enough to create panic in his fragile little mind, but not enough to cause any real damage. He would make this last until the sun came up.

On the workbench, a cellphone came to life with a familiar repetitive tone. The Doorbell App—a clever little tool to keep an eye on things from a safe distance. The Tribunal picked up Donavan's phone. The image of Saint's wife standing there did not surprise him.

He pressed the X-Acto knife to Parker's throat by way of warning, then pushed the Intercom button and said, "Mrs. Saint, how may I help you?"

"It's Detective Kirkpatrick, actually. I'm looking for Parker."

"Haven't seen him. Not since your friend dropped me off. Parker was still in the car then. I think they were headed back to the church."

"How about you come to the door and talk to me?" Corrinne seemed to notice the camera, mounted discreetly in a corner of the porch.

"I'm in bed," he said. "And I don't feel well. We can talk tomorrow. Best of luck finding him." The Tribunal ended the conversation with a push of another button. Then he stared at the phone for a moment. The police could likely triangulate its location if he kept it turned on. *We can't have that.* He popped the battery out and set it atop the phone on the workbench.

"Now," he said, "where were we?"

34

"Hello?" Corrinne shouted. "Stephen!" No answer. She looked at the front door and thought about the concept of probable cause for just a second before drawing her gun and kicking the door open. An alarm console on the wall began beeping loudly, demanding a disarm code. She ignored it and began sweeping the house.

It only took a couple minutes to clear the main floor: bedroom, den, living room. As she entered the kitchen, she thought of how easily Donavan had manipulated her. Just wait till he heard a knock on the door, inject the drugs, trash the needle, slam the back door. And then lay down, looking pathetic. He'd meant for his daughter to find him, she now realized, but Parker randomly showing up was even better as a cover. Corrinne swore to herself that she would not be played by this man again.

She ascended the steps to the second floor, finding three freakishly neat bedrooms, to the point where she could barely tell which one Donavan occupied and which were guest rooms. The basement was an even quicker search, yielding nothing you wouldn't find in the average retiree's home.

Returning to the kitchen, she spotted something that chilled the blood in her veins. A tasteful Audubon Society calendar hanging on the wall, its colors complimenting the paint of the room. November 2 was circled in thick red marker. She couldn't help but wonder if, had she only flipped the page from October to November as she stood in this room on Sunday afternoon, might she have seen this then? Nausea threatened to overtake her and she leaned against the sill of a small window.

Her eyes drifted out into the backyard and fell upon a shed. She'd never noticed it before. It was small—an unlikely hiding place. But she would have a look all the same.

* * *

Parker estimated he'd been cut fifteen or sixteen times. He feared that Donavan knew exactly the number of cuts, because he was keeping count, on the way to literally one thousand. Each individual slice did not hurt much, but he could feel blood soaking the collar of his shirt and his left pant leg, and a dull burning pain was overtaking his skin. His heart was chugging to keep up with his sense of terror, not helping the problem.

"I'm sorry for what my grandfather did," Parker said, "but I'm not him."

"No. You're worse. Remember the Scriptures? 'The world is full of those who, knowing the judgment of God, that those who commit such things are worthy of death, not only do the same, but give approval to them that do.'"

Parker couldn't help himself. "That's way out of context."

"I'll give you some context," Donavan said, turning the knife slowly in his hand.

* * *

The doors of the old shed were secured with a combination padlock, but the wood of the doors was old and soft. Corrinne dumped a hummingbird feeder, mounted on the side of the shed, to the ground and slid the long metal hook from its bracket. Inserting it between the door and the latch, she pried down, easily pulling the screws from the rotting wood. She redrew her gun and, looping the hook through the latch, pulled one of the doors open, ready for a man to come charging out at her.

No one did.

She reached into her pocket for a small LED flashlight and clicked it on. The shed was every bit as unremarkable as the house had been. Packed full of stuff: a lawnmower and snow blower, aerater, stacks of various large bags—seed, rock salt, soil, concrete. She stepped inside, slipping around a wheelbarrow, making her way back.

At the very back of the shed was a big, old, rather feminine suitcase, propped up on a stepladder. This didn't belong here. Corrinne grabbed it down, popped the latches and opened it up.

* * *

"Do you believe in justice, Parker?" The Tribunal asked. He was trying to keep his prey, who was clearly a bit woozy, from passing out. "I do. Especially poetic justice. This shed, behind my mother's house, is such a fitting place for so many hypocrites to die. I used to hide in here when things got too scary. And that chair you're sitting in—the skeleton of the very recliner where I found my mother, unconscious, barely breathing. 'She fell in the shower,' he told the police. And no one asked how she got dressed and into that chair."

He smiled and shook his head, as if remembering something pleasant. "So much has happened there since. I pulled dear old Dad's tongue out in that chair—the first subject of my Inquisition—and now you'll be the last, tied down, unable to speak on your own behalf—slowly, slowly bleeding out. Isn't that beautiful poetic justice?"

The Tribunal's face lit up, as if by an invisible lightbulb turning on above his head. "I just thought of something even better," he said. "I'll be right back."

* * *

Corrinne pawed quickly through the contents of the suitcase. It was a go-bag, containing everything Donavan would need to start over: clothes, a gun, keys to a Ford Something. She'd never seen him drive anything but his Cadillac. A gallon-size Ziploc bag contained a number of documents, including a Maine driver's license with Donavan's picture and a different name, a degree from a law school in New Hampshire and a law license, both bearing the same name, and an old black and white picture of a pretty young woman and a little boy, standing in front of a modest house.

Clicking the suitcase shut, she pulled her phone from her pocket and took a step toward the dim moonlight of Donavan's backyard. Time to call in backup. She would have a citywide manhunt underway within half an hour. The case was as solid as it would get. Her foot sunk down slightly at the next step and she felt a distinct *click-click* beneath it.

She froze. Turning her head as little and as slowly as possible, she looked behind her. Mounted there on a large metal tool chest, semi-obscured by the handles of a dozen garden tools, was a Claymore mine.

Corrinne could just barely read the words, FRONT TOWARD ENEMY in the dim light. Her mind raced. She'd never seen one of these in real life. But if television was to be believed, any movement, any shift of her weight would cause this deadly device to tear her to pieces. She was suddenly very aware of the heavy suitcase in her left hand and felt an urge to chuck it out into the yard. Of course, that would be a fatal move. No, she had to hold it exactly still, exactly where it was at this moment. Or she'd die.

She did have her phone in her hand, though. That was good fortune. Or a gift from God. She raised it up from her side, swearing she could feel half a *click* through the soles of her feet, if that was even possible. She brought it to life with her thumb and missed a breath. Every tiny move was potentially deadly.

Her feet were already falling asleep, but she dared not shift in any way. Even the movement of her thumb as she pushed the telephone icon seemed like a wild upending of her center of gravity. Her fingers were sweaty and the screen of the phone slippery. The pressure plate was creaking now, beneath her.

Corrinne's call history appeared on the phone's screen. A whole bunch of outgoing calls to Jackie, Parker, and Donavan, none completed. A single icon next to each would redial the number, but they were all useless. She needed to call 911, get the bomb squad down here. Now. She reached her thumb slowly up toward the 'Keypad' button, way at the top left corner of the screen. It felt like twenty feet. Halfway there, she gave up. The phone was in danger of slipping out of her sweaty hand, which would mean her death. She chuckled hopelessly at the irony: holding a cellphone, but not daring to dial a three-digit number.

Then she saw the very last visible call on the log: incoming, from an unknown number. Father Michael. The little "call" icon was right beneath her thumb and she pressed it firmly.

35

The attendees were filing out of the arena while the bomb squad prepared to enter and remove the explosives. Philips had disclosed the location of all three charges and volunteered several times to "flip" on his companions in exchange for a lenient sentence. The police had seemed less than interested.

"Don't you go anywhere," Vivien said to Michael. "I need to talk to you." She pulled out a notepad. "What's your name?"

"Father Michael Gretzgy. I'm from Da Church of da Pleasant Manners. It's in Vancouver."

"Right. You seem kind of young to be a priest."

"That's what they tell me."

She smiled and jotted something on the pad.

Michael was quietly chanting under his breath, "Vow of chastity, vow of chastity, vow of—"

"What's that?"

"I said, *Wow, that's nasty*. These guys were going to blow this place right up, with all these nice people inside. It really does shake my faith in humanity."

"Uh-huh."

Father Michael's phone rang in his pocket. He ignored it.

"You need to get that?" Vivien asked.

"Nah, I'm sure it's—" He pulled it out and saw the name on the screen. "Yeah, I actually better. Oh, and that guy Tyler I was telling you about? That's him right there. Orange coat. You probably want to arrest him." Vivien followed his finger into the distance and then ran off in pursuit of the terrorist.

Michael crossed the street, toward Father Ignatius, answering his phone as he trotted along.

"Hey, Corrinne! I knew you'd come around."

"I need help," Corrinne gasped. She was sobbing. "Parker and me both. I'm afraid we're going to die tonight."

* * *

The moment Donavan disappeared up the metal staircase, Parker turned his attention to his right hand. It was slick with blood and he'd been surreptitiously testing it against the plastic zip tie holding his wrist to the chair. The restraint was tight and unyielding, but he felt like the blood might just lubricate it enough to slip free. He pulled with all his might, backing off when the sharp edge of the zip-tie pulled at one of his open cuts.

He gritted his teeth and pulled again. His hand, even slicker now, came halfway out. With a final burst of strength, he wrenched it free, leaving some skin in the zip tie. What now? He could try to free his other hand, then his feet, but without a tool that would likely be impossible. He looked longingly at the selection of cutting implements on the workbench four feet away.

Parker reached as far as his arms would allow, shifting in his seat. "Please God, help me. Help me get out of here," he prayed out loud. His outstretched fingers missed the corner of the workbench by six inches. If only his other wrist weren't holding him back, he could—

Idiot! Reaching down to the side of the chair, he grasped the lever and pushed it forward, un-reclining himself. Upright, he could now touch the corner of workbench, but the tools were all still beyond his reach. Then he saw the phone, its battery stacked on top.

"I'll be right back," Donavan had said. How long ago was that? Parker unbuckled his belt and pulled it free of the loops. Holding it by the end, he cast the metal buckle out onto the workbench like a fishing line, landing it right on top of an old hacksaw. He pulled gently, a few inches at a time, praying for that perfect balance of speed and finesse.

It was working, and better than he could have hoped. The saw inched toward him, pulling a long butcher knife along, which in turn drew the phone ever nearer. He glanced up toward the staircase. Still no one. No light. No sound. He could see an avenue of escape opening: quickly call the police, cut away his bonds, choose from a whole assortment of weapons with which to defend himself until help arrived.

The belt buckle was so close now, bringing the saw, the knife, and the phone with it. Just another few inches and Parker thought he could reach them. Then, disaster. The belt slipped off the saw, spinning it thirty degrees and pushing the knife off the edge. It clattered to the ground.

Still, all hope was not lost. Parker reached for the phone and felt the tips of his fingers just barely close around it. He began to carefully pull it back to the chair in his slippery fingers, balancing the battery on the screen.

* * *

Father Michael opened the closet in Parker's study and Jackie Reese came tumbling out. Michael side-stepped the corpse, almost putting a bullet in him. He slipped the gun back into his shoulder holster. According to Corrinne, the real danger was this Donavan character. But what had happened here? It looked like Anders had shown up, looking for . . . something, and the cop from the closet got the drop on him. And then Donavan made his move.

Corrinne had already checked his home. That's where the Claymore was, which Ignatius was hopefully defusing now, tapping into all that military experience and knowledge of explosives.

So where had this Donavan gone? And was Parker still with him?

* * *

Hand shaking, Parker dumped the phone and battery onto the surface of his own hardcover book, resting on his lap. He brought the phone over to his restrained left hand and deftly pulled the back off of the device, then reinserted the battery. He clicked it back together and powered it up. A logo appeared on the screen for a few seconds, followed by the words "Loading Operating System" and a status bar that creeped slowly along, one tiny tick at a time.

36

Father Ignatius sprang from the driver's seat and sprinted into Donavan's backyard, clearing the fence like a teenager. He saw the shed Parker's wife had described and rushed to the door.

Corrinne stood there, tears streaming down her face. Her legs were beginning to wobble and he could see the trial it was to simply continue holding the suitcase at her side.

"Who are you?" she asked.

"My name is Father Ignatius. I am a friend of Father Michael's and I'm here to help you."

"Please tell me you called the police."

"You don't need them. You need me."

"*What?* I need the bomb squad, not some geriatric priest!"

"The bomb squad is busy, dear, at the arena. Besides, this is not the first time I've dealt with an antipersonnel mine. He craned his neck around her form and saw the Claymore. "Monstrous device," he said under his breath, carefully picking his way back, around the wheelbarrow, the same way Corrinne had initially gone.

He crouched down and studied the mine.

* * *

The Tribunal threw another box across the room, in a rage. Where was it? He'd packed it up not two months ago, along with all sorts of his father's effects, while the hospice nurse had bathed his mother: the very belt with which his father used to beat him. It would be such perfect symmetry to give Parker a taste of the same punishment.

He'd already searched through half a dozen boxes and wasted a good deal of time. Now he'd have to rebuild his momentum. And it had been going so well, too. He ripped open another box and smiled. There it was, coiled up like a snake waiting to strike, atop his father's old bathrobe. He grabbed it and turned out the light.

The doorbell sounded, echoing through the house.

The Tribunal froze.

Who would be here, after dark, knocking on a dead woman's door? And what should he do? He couldn't very well pretend no one was home, since whoever it was had just seen an upstairs light shut off. Looking down at his current dress, he realized he couldn't answer the door either. Not like this, anyway.

Grabbing the bathrobe, he pulled it on over the old leather cloak, stuffing his hood into the robe's pocket. In the dim light of the bedroom, he caught his reflection in the mirrored closet door and shuddered. Wearing his father's bathrobe, holding his father's belt, he looked all too much like the man. But he was not his father. He was the very opposite.

Creeping down the stairs, he could see the silhouette of a tall, broad man through the glass block windows. At least it wasn't Corrinne. He opened the door, tentatively, and gawked.

Why was there a priest standing on his mother's front porch?

* * *

"Can't you just turn it backwards?" Corrinne asked, her back to Father Ignatius.

"Too risky," the priest answered. "The gyroscope from a ten-dollar cellphone can be used as a failsafe. Tell me, did this Donavan serve in the military?"

"I don't think so."

"Good. Let's hope he doesn't know any field tricks. I am going to remove the detonator. It's very important that you stay perfectly still a while longer."

"I'll try," Corrinne croaked.

Ignatius pulled firmly, careful not to tip the explosive device. It didn't budge. He pulled a pair of reading glasses from his breast pocket and propped them on his nose, letting out a disappointed sigh. "The detonator is epoxied in place."

"Is that bad?" Her voice wavered.

"Nothing to worry about, dear." He pulled a multitool from a leather case on his belt and flipped open the pliers. "I'll just have to use a little brute force." He crossed himself and whispered a prayer before gripping the ignitor and pulling it free of the mine. The tension left his body in a deep sigh.

"Are we good?" Corrinne asked, a hint of hope in her voice.

"Stay very still. It's out, but the detonator could still badly injure or even kill you." Father Ignatius buried the charge between two bags of concrete mix, then piled half a dozen plastic sacks of topsoil on top.

He made his way back around the wheelbarrow and to the door. "I'm going to count to three," he said. "One." He wrapped his hand around Corrinne's wrist. "Two." The priest flung her out of the shed. A muted *bang* sounded from inside. Corrinne landed on her stomach in the cold grass. She rolled over and looked back into the shed, where the air was thick with concrete dust.

"Three," she said. Closing her eyes for a moment, she almost felt like she could drift off to sleep, exhausted in every way. Then she remembered. Parker. This wasn't over.

Forcing herself to sit up, she saw the suitcase, lying open, its contents strewn along a short debris field. The plastic bag of documents was closest to her, and she dumped it out, pawing through it.

It was clear Donavan was planning to come back here at some point, to gather these things. Or maybe he thought he'd truly get away with it, let Caraway take the fall, and he was planning on sleeping in his own bed tonight.

None of that helped. She flipped through the IDs and fake degrees, and came to the old photo. This must be Donavan and his mother. Yes, that house looked familiar. A couple weeks ago, she and Parker had stopped by there for a prayer service after the viewing. It was only about a five-minute drive from here.

She rushed to her feet, her legs almost giving way beneath her. She kissed Father Ignatius on the cheek. "Thanks so much. I gotta go!"

* * *

"Can I help you with something?" The Tribunal asked.

The young priest smiled. "Yes, I'm looking for my friend, Jack. I think he's somewhere around here."

"Wish I could help, but I'm afraid I don't know any Jack. Sorry." He began to shut the door, but the priest's foot stopped it.

"Thing is, his car has one of those police GPS trackers installed in it, and it's somewhere very close by."

The Tribunal breathed in slowly through his nose and out his mouth. He didn't have time to deal with this rude young cleric, as much as he wanted to. Besides, he might look like his father, but he was nothing like him. It was never rage that made him kill. It was justice.

"I certainly hope you find him, but I'm on my way to bed." He gestured around him. "And there's no one here but me."

"Okay," the priest said, withdrawing his foot. "Thanks anyway."

The Tribunal closed and locked the door. Then, retrieving the belt and hood from its pockets, he stuffed the bathrobe into a waste basket.

* * *

Despite himself, Parker thought of that stupid movie Paige had made him watch—the one with the TPS reports, where the computer took forever to power down.

"Come on," he said through gritted teeth as the status bar ticked along. He could feel it; now was when Donavan would come back, carrying whatever tool of torture his sadistic mind had dreamt up. Now, when he was so close.

But he didn't. And the status bar suddenly picked up speed, zipping up to 100 percent. Parker's hope rallied. A generic background appeared, slowly populated by a grid of icons. Just when it seemed ready to go, the screen changed. "Enter Access Code," it read, foll-owed by the numbers 0 to 9.

His heart withered in his chest. He tried a few different codes, only managing to smear blood all over the screen. Then he saw the words at the bottom of the screen, in tiny print: "For Emergency Call Touch and

Hold," it said, with a small red icon. Yes!

No. He heard Donavan returning. The opening of the trap door above. Parker mashed the little red phone icon. He'd dial 911, then toss the phone behind beneath the workbench, out of sight. They'd have to trace the call if—

"To make a call, disable airplane mode first," the screen read.

Then footsteps.

37

The Tribunal was halfway down the steps when he spotted the phone in Parker's hand. "Very clever, Saint," he said. "I'm afraid that won't—"

He stopped descending the stairs. And listened. Something was wrong. Parker had one hand free, but that was nothing to worry about. All of the blades and tools were precisely where they should be, except for one saw, slightly askew and a butcher knife on the floor.

No, it was behind him. He turned back in time to see a large black shoe connect with his chest, launching him out from the staircase. For a half second he seemed to hang in mid-air before landing in a tangled heap on the hard floor, his robe all around him. The attacker took the stairs in two strides, drawing a pistol from under his jacket.

The Tribunal laughed out loud. It was the priest. Down here, where the Inquisition was reaching its climax. It was perfect. More poetic justice.

The young priest took aim and said, "Get up, step away from Parker, and put your hands on your head. Or I will shoot you." As he stood, The Tribunal's hand closed around the butcher knife's wooden handle.

"Come toward me," the priest ordered.

"Father Michael," Parker wheezed, "he has a—" The word evaporated as soon as the tip of the blade touched his throat.

"'Father Michael.' You two men seem to know each other," The Tribunal said. He smiled maliciously at the priest. "You shoot, I fall, he dies."

Father Michael took a step toward him.

"That's close enough. If you want Parker to live, you'll drop your gun. I won't ask again."

The priest complied.

"Now kick it over to me."

Michael sent the pistol sliding under the tool chest and took another step forward. "He gets so much as one more little nick and I'll kill you with my bare hands."

"So, you do care about this man?"

Father Michael nodded.

"Then you won't want to waste any time." The Tribunal buried the knife in Parker's left thigh and gave it a hard twist as he pulled it out. Blood spurted up from the artery. The priest was at his side in a moment, leaving no one to stop The Tribunal from clanging up the metal stairs.

He ran toward the garage, his robe flapping in the breeze. He climbed quickly into his mother's Chrysler and popped the visor down, dropping the keys into his lap. As he backed out of the driveway, he chided himself for going off-plan. The suitcase should be with him, leaving him free to disappear. But it wasn't, and now he had to risk capture just to collect it. For all he knew, Corrinne had a dozen police officers combing his house and yard. Or perhaps she had broken into the shed and paid the ultimate price, meaning crime scene investigators would be collecting her in little plastic baggies. He loved the thought, but he hated the uncertainty.

His original plan had involved luring both Parker and his wife into the shed behind mother's house. But he'd improvised when she begged him to go the church and he would improvise again. If the next twenty minutes went his way, he could disappear with ease. He had it all lined up: a new vehicle, a new identity, even a new job waiting for him. And, of course, another Inquisition.

He pulled into a community college parking lot to the darkest point between two lights and killed the engine. His backyard was visible from here and nothing seemed amiss. Certainly no flashing red lights or cops milling about. If he was going to do this, he needed to do it now.

Leaving the car, he stepped into a thick grove of trees and jumped a chain link fence—no small feat in the vestments. He'd thought about losing the robe in the car, but decided against it. After all, Parker and his friend were otherwise engaged and no one else knew to look for a robe. And The Tribunal was still in session, after all. Besides, from a distance it didn't look much different than a long trench coat.

For thirty seconds he stayed back in the shadows, studying the yard—particularly the shed. He'd moved the suitcase out here just before staging the attack, in case the police got overzealous in their investigation within the walls of the house. Now, it was just twenty feet away. He would make it. Divine Justice demanded that he be rewarded for what he'd done.

Emerging from the stand of trees, The Tribunal walked quickly to the door of the shed. He began dialing the combination into the lock, but stopped when the whole latch and hinge pulled free of the wood. What was this? He held the knife at the ready and opened the door.

The interior of the shed was in disarray. Someone had apparently ransacked the place, breaking open bags of sand and concrete in the process, spilling them everywhere. The Claymore and its rig were nowhere to be seen.

His face darkened. Corrinne. It had to be her.

Spotting his go-bag, still up on the hanging ladder, he rebounded. She'd missed the most important thing once again. Climbing over the plundered contents of the shed, he snatched the suitcase.

Right away, he knew: it was too light. He popped it open and found his worst fears confirmed. Empty.

* * *

Corrinne was a block from Beverly Donavan's home when a text bleeped in from Father Michael: "We are in the shed. Help on the way. Hurry." She drifted a bit on the turn into the driveway and her bumper made contact with the garage door. Within half a minute, she was racing into the backyard shed, not even registering how odd it was that the thing had a basement.

All she saw was Parker, bleeding profusely. Father Michael hovered over him, wearing a wife-beater and pressing his black shirt onto a wound in Parker's thigh.

"I tied it off," he said to Corrinne, nodding at Parker's belt, which had found yet another calling, this time as a tourniquet.

"It hurts so bad!" Parker shouted, squishing his face together with the heels of his hands.

"Knife wound?" Corrinne asked.

"Yeah. It's bad. Thank God it missed the femoral artery. But Parker's complaining about the tourniquet, aren't you buddy? I told you, if it's not that tight, it won't stop the blood flow." To Corrinne, he said, "Paramedics should be here any second."

"Am I going to die?" Parker asked.

"You're going to be fine," she assured.

"She's right man," Michael said. "We got to it quick enough."

Corrinne realized she was doing that cop thing—detaching herself from the victim, all business, and reminded herself this was her husband. Taking his hand in hers, she kissed it and squeezed it and let him squeeze hers to the point of crushing the bones. For some reason, she thought of the old lady named Marty at church and how bad she wanted the pastor and Corrinne to have children.

"I love you," she said. "I'm sorry for . . . you know."

"Me too," Parker grunted. "I'm an idiot."

"Me too."

"It's Thursday night," Parker said, grunting in pain and laughing at the same time.

"Yeah?"

"Date night."

The sound of an approaching siren got louder and louder until it cut out just beyond the house.

"That'll be the ambulance," Father Michael said, "but I'm guessing it would be best for you, Detective, if I weren't here when your colleagues arrive." He took Corrinne's free hand and pushed it down onto the blood-soaked shirt.

"Thank you," she said. "I owe you. Again."

"Maybe we can bust out that fondue kit sometime."

She laughed through her tears. "Oh, Michael. I brought that thing to Goodwill, like, the day we got back from Cancun."

The voices of two paramedics echoed down from the shed above.

"Parker, I'll visit you in the hospital before I go," Michael said. He stepped back into the darkness behind the stairs until the medics were tending to Parker. Then he slipped out into the night.

Corrinne stepped back to give the paramedics room. One checked his vitals while the other inspected the tourniquet. "Nice work on this," he said to Corrinne.

"It's too tight," Parker said. Then he looked up at his wife. "Did you get Stephen?"

"Don't worry about that now, honey."

Fear washed over his face. "You didn't get him?"

She thought of the suitcase in the shed. "I know where he's going," she said. "I can call my—"

"No. You do it. Go get him."

Corrinne hesitated. "Do you mean that?"

"Did you mean it when you said I wasn't going to die?"

"Of course."

"Then go," Parker said. "Get out of here!"

"I'll see you soon." She was already rushing up the stairs.

* * *

The Tribunal was at a loss.

Looking from the empty case to the hood in his one hand and the bloodied butcher knife in the other, he felt suddenly silly and unprepared. Kirkpatrick was still here, somewhere. She had to be. And he'd brought a medieval robe and a six-inch blade to a gunfight. His theatrics and poetic justice would do him no good now. His only firearm had been in that suitcase, which he had believed to be almost too well-protected.

Forget the plan; it was time to run. Turning on his heels, he angrily knocked a stack of empty milk cartons out of his way and lunged for the shed door—then came to an abrupt halt, catching a heavy wall-mounted hook to stop his forward momentum. Standing frozen, he looked down and felt his chest begin to constrict. There, beneath his feet: the pressure plate. He'd felt the telltale *click-click,* indicating that it was now armed.

This was all wrong. The Claymore was now situated in the doorway of the shed, pointing in. FRONT TOWARD ENEMY. Someone must have silently set it up while he was occupied with the suitcase. A man stepped up behind the explosive device, silhouetted against the light of the moon, which was one night shy of full.

As his eyes adjusted, The Tribunal could make out a gun in the man's hand. And a white tab collar around his neck. Who were these priests, showing up at the worst moments, foiling his meticulously laid plans? It was as if they somehow knew he was running an unsanctioned Inquisition and couldn't bear the competition.

"I wouldn't move if I were you," the priest said. Unlike the man at mother's, this priest was old. But his eyes were sharp, alert, boring into his own. The Tribunal had to look away. He was squeezing the knife and the hood in twin death-grips, afraid of loosening his grasp, lest he trigger the device.

"Three of my ancestors sat as Grand Inquisitor," the priest was saying. "How could you think yourself worthy to wear that hood? You do not understand justice any more than you understand grace. You like killing hypocrites? Perhaps you should have started by killing yourself." He began to close the doors. "If Parker Saint dies, we will meet again. Otherwise, enjoy spending your golden years in prison." The doors closed and the shed went black.

The Tribunal weighed his options. They didn't weigh much. When he had initiated the Inquisition, he'd known that martyrdom was not impossible, but it was never anything he'd seriously considered. Certainly not something he desired. But now it might be his only real option. Oh well. In for a penny, in for a pound.

A wall of cold air came wafting in as the doors were again thrown wide. Standing where the old priest had been was Corrinne Kirkpatrick, gun drawn and trained on him.

"Detective," he said. "How's your husband?"

"He'll be fine. You, on the other hand—you're facing more capital charges than I can even keep track of. But don't worry, I'm sure prison is like one big Chuck E. Cheese ball pit for a sixty-something lawyer-turned-serial killer. You'll make lots of new friends." A smile tugged at the corner of her mouth.

The Tribunal made a decision. He slowly raised the hood over his head and pulled it on, centering the holes over his eyes. He would not go to prison. He'd spent ten years in the prosecutor's office early in his career. The most violent of those offenders would still be in the prisons to which he'd sent them.

He closed his eyes and stepped off the mat, surprised at how seamless it was, stepping into the next life—no pain, no suffering, no…

No, he was still in the shed. He opened his eyes to see the butt of Corrinne's gun connect with the bridge of his nose, crushing cartilage and burbling blood. The hood spun on his head and the knife clattered to the ground.

Corrinne dragged him out onto the lawn and roughly pulled his hands behind his back, cuffing them in place.

"No chance you're getting off that easy," she said. "You're under arrest for the murders of David Cates, Leslie Doane, Hannah Goodwin, and Maxwell Van de Burg. You have the right to remain silent."

The Tribunal could hear many sirens approaching, then footsteps and cops talking to one another. Beneath the hood, he smiled. The trial would be a circus. And he'd still have the chance to explain the poetic justice of what he'd done to the world and, more importantly, to the Church.

Whatever happened, he was sure of one thing: he had begun a movement.

38

It was nearly midnight by the time Corrinne got to Hope Presbyterian. Parker had spent more than an hour in surgery. She'd been allowed to see him in the recovery room, where he'd been looped out of his mind and just kept telling her that she was, "Pretty, but not as pretty as my wife, Corrinne." When she'd kissed him, he pointed to his wedding ring and warned her not to fall in love with him because he was married to the most amazing woman ever. She'd be back in the morning.

Tonight, though, she just needed to pick something up. Entering the building, she flashed her badge to a uniform she sort-of recognized as she brushed past Anders's body, surrounded by a little city of cardboard evidence tags. Entering Parker's study, she nodded a sad greeting at Alvarez. Jackie's body had been taken away, but there were plenty of reminders all around.

Corrinne reached up to the shelf above the credenza and pulled something down.

"Kirkpatrick," Alvarez said, holding up a hand, "gloves."

"It's not evidence." She showed him the framed document and he nodded his understanding.

Corrinne passed back through the flurry of police activity and got in her car, where she sat and studied the marriage certificate. She thought about her coffee with Parker, when he'd explained justification, in which God declares us righteous, and sanctification, the slow and frustrating part. He'd illustrated it with the church building. They had the legal document in hand. It was theirs. But there was still a lot of work to do.

She gently placed the certificate on the passenger's seat. It would hang over her desk, in her basement office. She and Parker had the legal document saying they were one.

And now they had some work to do.

* * *

The Jesuits Militant were back in the Amway Grand Plaza Hotel, staying in the very same room they'd inhabited the year before. Father Ignatius had checked them in by phone and Michael did not ask whether it was nostalgia or a very unlikely coincidence that had landed them back in that room. After returning Father Ignatius's rental car, they'd enjoyed a meal at Café 37. It was late as they stepped onto the elevator and began the ride up.

"I swear," Father Michael was saying, "if you really forgot your CPAP machine, I am going to literally smother you in your sleep."

Ignatius scoffed. "Even in my sleep, I would make short work of you. And just because we haven't discussed it, don't think I've forgotten what you did to me—leaving me in that God-forsaken diner."

"Forgive me father, for I have sinned," Michael said.

"I will forgive you. But I will also be assigning your penance."

Michael laughed. "How about you go light on me and I don't tell anyone you punched a woman? Like, sucker-punched her. Right in the nose. Man, she went *down*."

"Very amusing."

"I'm just saying, I think you might have actually knocked her unconscious. She didn't talk for like five minutes. That's so bad for you. Probably has brain damage."

"That's enough," Ignatius said. The elevator doors opened and they stepped out into the hall.

"But seriously," Michael continued, "she'll probably be the slowest woman in her cell block. Real shame. Seemed like such a sweet lady."

"*I* had no choice in what I did."

"You realize that if I hadn't ditched you, Parker, his wife, and thousands of innocent people would probably be dead right now."

"It's your insubordination and lack of discipline that concern me. My ancestor, Rodrigo Pérez, led hundreds of men into battle at Coimbra. Had his men disobeyed him at will, the cursed Moors would still control Iberia." He slid his card into the lock, resulting in a green light and a click. Father Ignatius opened the door.

A man was standing just inside, like he'd been waiting for them. Dark-skinned. Middle Eastern. Both priests drew their guns.

"Who are you?" Michael asked. The man held up his hands.

"I am a friend," he said with a subtle accent. The sleeves of his loose cotton shirt fell to his elbows, revealing a tattoo of the Jesuit seal.

"Okay. What do you want, *friend*?"

"I assume you have heard about the latest pronouncement from His Holiness."

"We've been a little busy, actually," Michael said.

"Well then, I am happy to bring you good news. It seems that our order will continue on, after all. At least for the foreseeable future."

The man dropped his hands to his sides.

"My name is Father Ali, and I am to be your third."

Bonus Material

I first had the idea for the following short story a couple months after my sophomore novel *The Last Con* came out. I wanted to write something that would promote my books, link the two worlds together (namely, by teaming up the Jesuits Militant and the Knights of Malta), and set up the *Playing Saint* sequel, which was already coming together in my mind.

I've always loved stories that fill in gaps in an earlier story and thought this was a great opportunity to do that sort of thing, for a book that hadn't even been written yet. i.e., What exactly happened between Parker's airport meeting with Ignatius and Michael and their arrival in Panama, now carrying a couple chips from Father Sacha?

I wrote the story (which originally appeared in a collection called *God Rest Ye Motor City*) really fast and was very happy with it. But then I made a decision that complicated matters: the *Playing Saint* sequel would not be a Christmas story after all. The idea of a serial killer thing set against the celebration of the birth of Christ just didn't sit well with me. And so I bumped it back to the neighborhood of Halloween, leaving one Christmas-themed short story that doesn't quite fit the novel and is probably not canon (although, between you and me, this *is* pretty much what our favorite Jesuits did to land the Knights of Malta in their debt), but will hopefully entertain you all the same.

CRYING HE MAKES

A Story of the Jesuits Militant

By Zachary Bartels

When people say they're "flying out of Detroit," they're really not.

The international airport is actually located in Romulus, Michigan, a smallish city twenty-five minutes' drive from Detroit proper. It was there that Father Sacha Katrakis and Joe Duncan were hoping to catch, not a plane, but two secretive Vatican agents on layover whose connecting flight had been delayed, quite by design.

The drive in had taken longer than usual and their search of the sprawling airport longer still. In a moment of frustration, Sacha had removed his tab collar—something he rarely did in public—before sheepishly replacing it and crossing himself.

"There," the priest said, pointing to a booth belonging to a crowded chain coffee shop, spilling out into the concourse. "The protégé. But who's that with him? He's no priest."

Duncan consulted a tablet computer, flipping his way through several files. He wore a very serious gray suit, set off by a red necktie, the knot of which was perfectly dimpled. "Found him," he said, pointing at a dossier. "Parker Saint, formerly prominent pastor from Grand Rapids, now better known for his role in taking down a man the press had dubbed, 'The Blackjack Killer.'"

"Hmm." Father Sacha mopped his damp graying hair back off his forehead. "And based on his present company, we can assume he had help in that matter. What do you think? Should we approach him now or wait until we locate his mentor?"

"Now is fine." The voice came from behind them, bringing a start from Sacha, but not Duncan.

"Father Ignatius," Sacha said, dipping his head slightly. "It's been . . . some time."

"It has." The old priest wore full clericals—crisp and without wrinkle, in contrast to his disheveled white hair, wizened skin, and untamed eyebrows. "You should know better than to sneak up on one of the Jesuits Militant."

Duncan shrugged. "You sneaked up on us."

Ignatius frowned. "Sacha, you should keep a tether on this layman or he may find himself subject to discipline."

Duncan met his gaze, wordlessly, for what felt like much longer than it was, while Father Sacha—six inches shorter than either of them—nervously checked his watch. "I'm afraid we're on a bit of a schedule," he finally said.

"As are we. Our flight will be boarding in a few minutes. This has been pleasant. Perhaps we can do it again some time."

"I'm afraid your flight's been delayed by six hours," Duncan said, biting down a smile. "And that we haven't just happened upon you today."

Ignatius nodded, thoughtfully. "The plane. Your doing?"

"I'd rather not say."

"Unusual for a Knight of Malta. Your order is typically so eager to trumpet its little victories, especially when they involve subterfuge and—"

"We need your help," Sacha blurted. "We need you to come with us, back to the city."

Ignatius scowled. "I see." He craned his neck, peering around Duncan, to where Father Michael and Parker were well into their third frothed-over coffee drinks. "It seems we have some time on our hands, thanks to you. If it will serve the Holy Church, we will help you."

"Thank you," Father Sacha said, letting out a sigh of relief.

"But first, you have to apologize."

Duncan folded his arms over his chest. "And what wrong have we allegedly done?"

"Not you personally. Your order. The Knights of Malta acted shamefully, treacherously against us. And now it seems you need us."

"You can't possibly be angry about the Jesuits being expelled from Malta." Duncan laughed. "That was 250 years ago. That's absurd!"

The deep lines in the old priest's brow deepened, but he said nothing.

"We are sorry," Father Sacha said with a little too much conviction. "You're right. It was uncharitable and underhanded, hardly becoming of us."

Ignatius grunted. "Exactly what I would expect from an order that puts laymen above priests. Let's collect young Michael and be on our way." He strode over to the booth, spry for his apparent age, and placed a hand on the young priest's shoulder. "We are needed elsewhere, my son."

Father Michael drained his coffee. "Alright, then." He slid his athletic frame from the booth and gave Parker the briefest of hugs, more a chest bump and whack than a real embrace. "Good to catch up. Tell the wife I said hi. And let me know how this thing works out." He indicated the file folder.

Parker offered his hand to Ignatius, who clasped it firmly and resisted his attempt to shake it. "Christ be with you, Protestant," he said. "And good luck with the serial killer."

"You say that like it's normal."

"As long as I've known you, it has been."

Parker chuckled darkly and walked off toward the short-term parking.

Michael hefted his carry-on to his shoulder. "What's up?" he asked his companion.

"The Knights of Malta need us."

"That's a good one," Michael chuckled. "Seriously, though. What's up?"

* * *

"I heard you had been defrocked," Father Ignatius said from the backseat of the Impala, his first words since leaving the airport.

"Yes," Father Sacha answered. An awkward silence spread through the car for a few seconds before he added, "I was refrocked."

Michael checked his watch. Quarter of six. It was already dark—the joint product of Daylight Saving Time and the tilt of the earth in relation to Michigan on December 21st, the longest night of the year. He surveyed their surroundings. The neighborhood had been steadily declining for at least ten minutes as they'd driven deeper into the city. The young priest habitually touched his fingers to his side where his Colt 1911 would be if it weren't locked in his luggage in the belly of a grounded plane.

"Where are we headed?"

"A church," Sacha answered from the passenger seat. "Just up ahead here. The next street."

"Stop. Now." Michael was opening the door and stepping out of the car, even as Duncan pulled up to the curb.

"What are you doing?" Duncan called.

"A kid," Michael shot over his shoulder. He backtracked to the last street they'd passed, rounded the corner, and locked in on his target: a pale man in a puffy red jacket, wearing shorts in late December. The man had a broken beer bottle in one hand and the collar of a young boy in the other.

"Hey!" Father Michael called, the word visibly jetting from his mouth in the cold air. "Tag me in, kid."

"Get lost, Father," the thug said, glancing at Michael with beady eyes, barely visible beneath a stocking cap. "Private matter. Kid owes us money. You want no part of this."

"You called me Father," Michael said, taking another step toward him. "Now I'm bound to offer you some spiritual guidance." He leaned back, easily avoiding the jagged glass, and snapped his knuckles up under the man's ribs. The bottle flew out into the street with a harmless *tink* and the man went down to one knee. He cursed.

Father Michael glanced up, expecting to see the kid disappearing into the distance. Instead, he stood planted there, a bewildered grin plastered on his face.

The thug was rising now, a chintzy 9mm gangbanger special in his hand. Michael tensed. Disarming this zero would be nothing. Less than nothing. But the kid was six feet away, which complicated things. The sound of approaching footsteps echoed in from behind him and for just a second the man's vacant eyes flickered off into the distance. It was all the opening Michael needed.

He sprang forward and jerked the man's hat down over his face, securing it there with a fist. The gun came up, swinging blind. Michael trapped the man's wrist, broke the pistol from his grip, and dumped him on the concrete in a heap.

"Impressive," Duncan said, striding to the prone form of the thug. Behind him Ignatius seemed to catch himself smiling proudly and resumed his standard scowl. Duncan stooped down and pulled the knit cap from over the man's head, revealing a broken nose burbling blood. He produced a badge from his belt and said, "Name's Special Agent Duncan. And you just assaulted a young boy and a priest on a city street, with three witnesses, two of whom are also priests and one of whom works for the FBI." He chuckled. "Sure you don't want to steal some candy from a baby while you're at it?"

"Maybe punch a kitten in the face?" Michael offered.

"I got this, Father Michael. Thanks."

Flashing blue light filled the street and an unmarked car pulled to a stop near them. A rumpled man in a cheap suit emerged. He walked up to the odd crowd, gestured at the bloodied man at the center of it all, and asked simply, "So what's this?"

Duncan stood and again displayed the badge. "Agent Duncan, FBI. And you are . . . ?"

"Marion, narcotics. I thought I recognized you. My partner and I worked with you on the Canadian pipeline thing last year. You remember?"

Duncan nodded. "I do. And to answer your question, our friend here just assaulted this priest and this child, before being subdued."

"What child?"

Duncan looked back where the kid had been.

"Must have gotten scared and ran."

"Yeah, kids do that in this neighborhood." Det. Marion nudged the perp with his foot. "So you want me to book this guy or what?"

Duncan rubbed his chin. "Fortunately for this young man, we're on a bit of a schedule and don't have time to give statements and deal with the logistics of an arrest. So, unless he wants to file a complaint against us . . . "

The thug shook his head no and wiped his bleeding nose on his sleeve. The detective pulled him to his feet.

"I know who you are, punk. I don't want to see you around here again. Understood?"

The man nodded, pulled his blood-stained stocking cap back on, and took off running.

Marion watched him disappear down an alley half a block away, then turned back to Duncan. "So I have to ask: what's with the priests? The bureau changing things up?"

Duncan courtesy-chuckled. "No, these men are friends of mine. We were just on our way to St. Lambert's Church."

"I thought they closed that place down."

"It's . . . complicated. Anyway, it was nice to see you again, Detective. We'd better be going."

"Word to the wise," Marion said. "You priests stay close to this guy. This neighborhood is an open sewer. Drugs are everywhere all of a sudden and we can't pinpoint the source. Homicides are up. Believe me, those collars won't protect you anymore. I think you learned the hard way, they'll just advertise that you're an easy target."

"Truly a shame," Father Ignatius said. "We will be careful. Thank you for your concern."

"No problem. But trust me—careful won't even cut it. Heck, lately even the Blessed Virgin is fair game. Seems like God has left the building." He waved and got back into his car, killing the blue light and driving off.

"The Blessed Virgin?" Michael repeated. "What a weird thing to say. Right? That's a weird guy right there."

Duncan sighed. "If you follow me, I'll show you what he meant." They began plodding down the sidewalk in the direction they'd been driving. "Did you keep the gun?"

"Yeah," Michael answered. "It's a piece of junk, though. Jenner 9mm, mass-produced weapon of choice for thugs and loser. Always jamming up, misfiring."

"Well, I didn't see a thing," Duncan said, clearing his throat.

"So that badge is real, huh?" Michael asked.

"Of course."

"I have one sort of like it, but it doesn't say FBI. It says SOJ. For Society of Jesus? Most people don't look very closely at it. They just make assumptions and tell us what we want to know."

Duncan shook his head and picked up the pace. "One of the advantages of being a lay order, Father Michael, is that the Knights of

Malta have members in almost every agency, military, and government. We don't need to impersonate law enforcement. Which is good, since, unlike you Jesuits Militant, we can't hide behind diplomatic immunity as Vatican envoys. Here's the church, just up ahead."

The boxy, nondescript building, three stories tall, was only identifiable as a church by a single metallic cross, mounted between two windows which were, like all the building's windows, boarded up.

"So it *has* been closed down."

Father Sacha nodded. "The parish was merged with St. John the Baptist and the building deconsecrated two months ago."

"And I imagine," Ignatius said, "that it's hard to sell a building this size in this neighborhood."

"There was one prospective buyer, but unfortunately they could not secure a loan."

"Fascinating," Michael said, dryly, mounting the stops to the front entrance. "So *why* are we here?"

"Remind me never to watch a movie with you," Duncan said, holding the door open.

"What's that supposed to mean?" They followed Father Sacha through a door into a stairwell. "Seriously . . . what do you mean by that?"

They arrived in a large open hall in the church basement, converted into a make-shift auditorium, complete with dais, podium, and about two hundred chairs.

"This is why we're here," Sacha said, stepping up onto the platform.

"There's a group still meeting here," Father Ignatius observed.

"The Broadmoor Burmese Community Church. About 175 Christians—all refugees—and growing every week."

"Protestants . . ." Ignatius said under his breath. "At least the church has been deconsecrated."

"Ignore him," Michael said. "So this Chinese church—are they squatting?"

"Burmese," Duncan corrected. "And no, not exactly. The church is really the only thing going for the immediate neighborhood, in the midst of all the drug traffic and violence, which I'm afraid Det. Marion was possibly understating. Despite being refugees themselves, they feed a hundred people a week, among other ministries. They've got very little savings and no credit to rent a facility and no one else has offered them anywhere near enough space."

"The young boy from the street," Ignatius said, "he was Burmese, no?"

Father Sacha nodded. "I suspect so. Most of them live in tenement housing a block away."

"So the diocese just keeps paying the bills?" Michael asked. "Utilities, insurance, inspections . . . "

"At the moment, yes," Sacha said. "Because of this." He gestured at a large, very Seventies nativity scene—Mary, Joseph, and Child—arranged to the right of the pulpit. "This set belonged to St. Lambert's and it was set up outside until two weeks ago, when, as the detective alluded to, all of the Marys in the neighborhood began to disappear."

"I've heard of frat boys stealing the baby Jesus," Michael said, "but never Mary."

"Well, it's because of Jesus that we've brought you here today, my Jesuit friends," Duncan said.

"Ohhhh." Michael nodded, knowingly. "You guys don't know Jesus? Okay. Lemme see, where to start . . . "

"Father Michael," Ignatius said, pointing at the babe in the manger, "look."

"What?" The young priest approached the figure slowly. The statue's left hand was reaching out, index finger extended like his Father's on the chapel ceiling, the paint rubbed from the fingertip to reveal the aluminum beneath, as though it had been worn smooth by the touch of countless pilgrims. "I'm trying not to make an E.T. joke here," Michael started to say. But then he noticed the tears streaming down the baby's cheeks. "Oh."

"That's why the Burmese church is still here," Duncan said. "A miracle was reported to the diocese, triggering an investigation. You know as well as I how long that can take, and their congregation will continue to meet here in the meantime."

Michael nodded. "Any chance this is a ruse on their part? A way to keep the space a while longer?"

"It's possible," Duncan said. "The tears first started flowing two days before the group was to vacate. Now they have an indefinite reprieve."

"And the prospective buyer, the one who couldn't get a down payment together . . . ?"

"It was the Burmese church. They did their best to raise funds, but in six months had only succeeded in gathering $30,000. The Knights of Malta offered a grant of another ten thousand. But the church grounds encompass this entire block and neither the newly formed congregation nor its refugee members have much in the way of credit. The bank rejected their loan as too risky and said they wouldn't reconsider unless the church brought $125,000 to the table. Later that same day, the tears were first discovered."

"Seems like you could just *give* them the church," Michael mumbled.

"Believe me, I would," Sacha said. "But these things are above my pay grade."

Father Ignatius grunted. "Neither Father Michael nor myself is in a place to question the decisions of the Church. We do, however, wonder what your purpose was in bringing us here."

"Your reputation," Sacha said, gesturing at the Baby Jesus. "Your team is known for authenticating or debunking this sort of thing."

"When we were three," Ignatius said. "No longer."

Sacha nodded solemnly. "I heard about Father Xavier. My condolences. And I did not realize that he possessed all your expertise on the matter. I see they haven't replaced him."

Michael scoffed. "Nope. Seems we're being phased out."

"It's true," Ignatius said. "Even with a Jesuit on the Chair, I'm afraid young Michael will be the last Jesuit Militant to take the oath."

There was a moment of mourning for the old ways.

"Wow, that killed the mood." Michael hefted the Baby Jesus from the aluminum manger and looked it over. "I don't see anything weird. I mean, Xavier could have had a whole lab constructed by now and run all sorts of tests. But to me, it looks solid. Huh. The tears stopped when I picked it up; that's something. Although they don't seem to be coming out any holes or anything. Condensation, maybe?"

Father Sacha and Duncan exchanged a disappointed look. "Well," Sacha said, "I'm sorry that we—"

"Ah, we have company!" A well-dressed young man smiled his way into the room. "Good to see you, fathers. Allow me to introduce myself. I am Biak, the pastor of BBCC." His accent was light and his step lighter. "Pardon me if we've met before. You people all look the same to me." He laughed at his own joke.

"Nice to meet you, Biak. I'm Father Michael." He cradled the babe like a football and gave the pastor's hand a pump.

"I see you're looking at our little miracle. Are you here to authenticate it?"

"I'm afraid not," Sacha said. "These men are . . . just friends. Where is Pastor Hrang?"

"Hrang was called to a church in Indianapolis," Biak explained. "I am his replacement."

Another man, clad in work clothes, came rushing into the room, speaking a mile a minute in Burmese. He gestured at the priests, at Biak, and repeatedly at the aluminum Jesus in Michael's hands as his voice grew in volume. Biak answered him, meeting his intensity, causing him to fall begrudgingly silent.

Biak smiled apologetically. "He said you should not be handling these things because they are holy things. I explained that the nativity belongs to you and that you are holy men."

In the distance, Michael saw something moving. Someone beckoning him from the mouth of a hallway at the far end of the basement, beneath a RESTROOMS sign. The kid from the street.

"I need your facilities," he said to Biak.

"You need what?"

"Restroom."

"Sure. Just over there."

He found the boy hiding in a toilet stall. "He's not our pastor," the boy said. "And that man wasn't angry you were touching the Baby Jesus. He's a deacon and he was asking you to make Biak go away. We all want him to go away."

"If he's not your pastor, who is he?"

"He works with Cutter."

"Who?"

"The guy you beat up. They sell drugs from the church when people come in for food. And they keep their money here. And Pastor Hrang isn't in Indianapolis. We don't know where he is. He disappeared one day and the next day Biak showed up. Once a week, Hrang calls one of us and tells us to do whatever Biak says, but he does not sound happy and he will never say where he is."

"You think Biak has done something to him?"

"Yes. Everyone is afraid of him. Except me."

Father Michael smiled. "Is that why he sent his friend after you?"

The boy puffed out his chest. "I took some of their money. I found where they kept it, in the bell tower, and I took ten percent and put it in the poor box. If they do their business in a church, at least they have to tithe."

"How much was ten percent?"

"Four-thousand, two-hundred dollars. I should have taken all of it. Then we could have bought the building. But with Biak here, there's no point." The kid clenched his fists in frustration.

"I don't suppose they still keep their money in the bell tower."

"No, they moved it. I don't know where. But if I find it, I'll take all of it."

Michael smiled. "What's your name, kid?"

"Van."

"Well, Van, this Cutter guy—you know where he lives?"

"Yeah, in a big old house. Only a block from me and my mom."

Father Michael rubbed his jaw. "You think you can get outside without being seen?"

* * *

"What was so important, Father Ignatius?" Duncan asked. "That was a rather rude exit." They stood at the corner near the rear of the church, having been not-so-subtly herded out by the old Jesuit.

"I'm not sure. Father Michael used a code phrase, indicating that we needed to leave." The three men looked at him expectantly.

"Hold on, here he comes," Michael said. Van was running stealthily up from the side of the church building. "Okay, kid. How far to this Cutter's place?"

They walked about two blocks through the night, in and out of the streetlights, though more out than in, as the city had removed every other bulb—a cost-saving measure, Father Sacha explained.

Van pointed at an apartment building. "Me and my mom live there," he said. "And Cutter lives there." The house was leaning slightly to the left and shedding paint.

"Okay, Van. We're going to pay Cutter a little visit. I need you to promise me you'll go home and lock the door. Stay inside, okay?"

"Okay." He took off running.

The four men surveyed the dilapidated house from across the street, standing in the void between streetlights.

"Looks empty," Michael said. "Let's have a look inside."

"Can't do that," Duncan said. "I have to have probable cause to go in without a warrant."

"Like if someone was breaking in?" Michael asked.

"Don't even—"

"Give me two minutes." He jogged off around the block, cut between two houses, and jumped the fence into Cutter's back yard. At the rear of the house, he found a storm cellar, locked with a chain and padlock. From his pocket, he retrieved a small leather manicure kit he'd stashed in his carry-on—a trick Father Ignatius had taught him. He quickly found the right lock pick and tension wrench and had the doors open within a minute.

Michael dropped into the basement and clicked on a small LED flashlight affixed to a pair of tweezers, also housed in the leather case. They'd been a gag gift for Father Ignatius the Christmas before, but had proven useful more than once since. The weak beam made a sweep around the unfinished basement. He pulled out his phone and dialed Ignatius.

"Hey, I'm in the basement. No drug lab or anything. Just a couch and a TV. Video games. A freezer. A cot. I'm going to head upstairs." He silently ascended the steps to the first floor, stepping out into a grimy kitchen. Four pizza boxes were stacked on a chipped Formica table, surrounded by dozens of empty booze bottles. Passing into the living room, he stopped short.

"Whoa."

"What is it?" Ignatius asked.

"I think I know what happened to all the Marys."

There were almost twenty of them, lined up in two rows on either side of the room, varying in size and material, all crossing their arms over their breasts, treasuring this bare, bleak house in their hearts. "And I think I've got a verdict on our alleged miracle." He squeezed the phone between his head and shoulder, freeing both hands. "Looks like our guy was practicing on these statues, trying to perfect the crying game. Ha! *The Crying Game*."

"What?"

"Never mind." Father Michael tipped a lightweight plastic Mary back to reveal a large dry cell, some tubes, and a motor housed inside the hollow figure. He connected a loose wire to the battery's positive contact and the motor began to whine, sending a stream of tears down the Madonna's cheeks from two rather obvious pinholes.

"Looks like these are some early attempts," he said. "Pretty rough work." He turned his attention to the next one, a more expensive acrylic model. A toggle switch turned this one on and brought a thicker, red substance flowing from her eyes. "Ugh. That's super creepy. Why would anyone . . . ? You know what, don't bother coming in, guys. Place is dead. I'll be back in a minute."

Michael emerged from the basement, replaced the chain on the cellar doors, and circled back to the others.

"So they were working on a few different prototypes in there," he reported. "Some even cried blood. Look at this stuff." He handed Duncan a half-liter glass bottle. "Some fingerprints there for you. Stuff's called Ultraviolet Red Dye Gel No. 14. Do the tears glow in the dark? That's a little Trent Reznor, right?"

The three men stared back at him.

"Anyway, I'm thinking Biak and this Cutter had a good thing going with that church, a good cover for their illegal activities. And so they wanted to keep it in play as long as possible. Kind of a clever move, you ask me. Not much that's slower than church bureaucracy. And when the diocese finally caught on, they could just abandon the place and start dealing somewhere else." There was a murmur of agreement and Michael added, "I'd like to have a few words with this Biak guy."

"Someone should keep eyes on the house as well," Father Sacha said, "in case one them returns. I'm very concerned with the disappearance of Pastor Hrang."

"I'll stay," Father Ignatius offered.

"Not a good idea," Duncan said. "You heard Detective Marion. That collar won't protect you in this neighborhood. What if someone attacks you?"

Michael laughed. "Then they'll get trounced by an old man. Which, ironically, *never* gets old."

"At least take this." Duncan pulled up his pant leg and drew his backup pistol, holding it out to the old Jesuit.

"Thank you, Agent Duncan. I'll wait at the bus stop here. Should anyone arrive, I'll call you."

"I'll wait with you," Michael offered.

"No, you'll go with them."

"You forget, Father Ignatius. The Superior General may have put you in charge for our last assignment, but this one's off the books. Neither of us is in charge. Weird, I know."

"My son, this Cutter has seen your face up close," Ignatius said. "Besides, someone needs to keep an eye on the Knights of Malta. The last time we looked away, they had us expelled from Malta and closed our college."

"What was that, like, 250 years ago?"

"Yes," Ignatius said, his eyes stern.

"Ooookay, I'll go with them. But you text me if anything happens and I'll be here in a second."

Ignatius nodded.

"What's his deal?" Duncan asked as the three of them made their way back to the church.

"His deal?" Michael echoed. "He's the greatest priest—no, the greatest man—I've ever known. That's his *deal*."

"You know what I mean," Duncan persisted. "It's like he's stuck in the Middle Ages."

"Yeah. Isn't it awesome?"

* * *

Father Ignatius had been sitting at the bus stop only fifteen minutes when Cutter appeared from the direction of the church and let himself in the front door of the house. The priest considered calling Father Michael but, knowing that such a call would bring the whole trio tromping back, decided against it. Better to get a look at what was happening inside. Perhaps a little one-on-one time with the young hoodlum. Based on what he'd seen earlier, it would not be too difficult to extract the information they wanted.

"OUR FRIEND FROM STREET NOW HOME," he texted, only missing the "STOP" that would make it a full-on telegram. "HAVING A CLOSER LOOK."

He circled around, just as Michael had earlier, and entered the basement.

* * *

The church doors were still unlocked, though there was no one in the Burmese worship space. Returning to the Baby Jesus, they found him crying once again. Michael held his ear up to the figure, listening intently for the faint sound of a pump or motor, but hearing nothing.

"I say we look for the cash hoard," he said. "We get that, we have leverage. And I'm thinking, if they peddle their junk here and they were keeping the cash here, it's probably a convenience thing. Meaning there's a good chance it's still somewhere in the building. Did the church have a safe?"

Father Sacha thought for a moment. "No."

"What about the host? Did they keep it somewhere secure they might have repurposed?" His blood boiled at the thought of drug money languishing where the consecrated bread of Holy Communion had once been kept—deconsecrated or not.

"The host was reserved in a beautiful locked tabernacle, but that was removed when the altar was stripped." He held up a short finger. "There *is* an ambry on the wall though, where they kept anointing oil. I believe it also locks."

"Worth a look." They made their way up to the bare Nave of the church and on to what had been the sanctuary. The door to the ambry hung wide open, revealing nothing inside.

"You're back," came Biak's voice, the kindness now having left it. He sauntered in from a set of double doors near the front of the Nave. "Is there something I can do for you gentlemen?"

Duncan pulled his badge out again and half waved it in the man's face.. "We're just trying to find where you keep the drug money, Biak."

* * *

Having adjusted his eyes to the low light, Ignatius made his way along the block wall. For all of Michael's strengths, the young man was still not as observant as he should be and when he had the chance Ignatius usually double-checked his work.

Apart from the entertainment center, the only appliance in the basement was a large chest freezer. Father Ignatius had encountered a nearly identical freezer in a basement two years earlier and discovered a frozen, frostbitten corpse inside. He cracked the lid, expecting the worst.

No light came on, and no cold escaped. Ignatius opened the lid entirely. Inside were military MREs—freeze-dried rations—as well as handcuffs, ropes, several rolls of duct tape, and two cases of water.

Father Ignatius pulled the small revolver from his waistband and, in that same moment, felt a presence behind him, Someone was there, someone who must have been there all along. He turned quickly, just in time to see the two-by-four connect with his face. The floor came up to meet him.

* * *

"Drug money?" Biak screwed up his face. "What are you talking about?"

Duncan pulled back his coat, revealing his sidearm. "Keep your hands where I can see them, preacher."

"I have no idea what—"

"Don't be coy," Father Michael chided. "You work with that wannabe gangster Cutter. You forced your way into the church, intimidated these people, and now you're using the place as your own private drug store. Just one question, though: where's the money? And what did you do with the old pastor? Two questions, I guess."

"It's true," Detective Marion said, coming in through the same door. He was massaging his neck. "They're using the church as a front. But you're missing an important piece. Biak's my informant. Ya see, Pastor Hrang didn't tolerate drug activity in and around his church. He made some noise, even confronted some dealers. And they took a shot at him. Now we've got him in protective custody. And we're getting close to taking the whole operation down. So I'm asking you, Agent Duncan—I'm begging you—don't arrest anybody yet. Let this thing ride."

Michael's phone buzzed. He glanced at the text. "Cutter's home. Maybe we should all go have a word with him."

The cop waved his hand dismissively. "That punk is nothing. Street level. We're in this for the big fish. They're moving a lot of drugs in this neighborhood, with no competition. Trust me, that takes more than a couple of punks. That takes some real muscle."

* * *

Cutter was dragging Ignatius up the stairs by his ankle. In his years of service in *El Mando de Operaiones Especiales* and his decades with the Jesuits Militant, he'd been knocked down many times. But he'd never been knocked unconscious. And it was killing him that this street trash had come the closest to date to breaking that unblemished record. The priest was woozy, docile, going in and out. The only thing he could focus on was Cutter's right arm with its ugly purple veins showing through the skin, dragging him up a step at a time like a bag of concrete mix. *Thud. Thud. Thud.*

The next thing he knew, he was in the living room amidst all the Blessed Virgins. He could hear the electric pumps whirring and he could feel something around his wrists and ankles.

He had passed out.

Determining not only to humble this unspeakably lucky and undisciplined whelp, but also to never, *ever* tell anyone about this, Ignatius gave his head a quick shake, instantly regretting it as a wall of pain collapsed in on his skull. Surveying his situation, he found that he was in an antique chair—rather a nice piece, actually—his wrists secured to the wooden arms with a few heavy-duty plastic zip ties, and his ankles liberally duct taped to the front legs of the chair.

"Shoulda sent your friend," the young tough said. "That Kung Fu priest. He's got some moves. But *you,* old man . . . You got nothin'. Funny, I only came back here to burn this place down. Now I get to burn you with it. And your friend is next." He laughed and smashed his fist into the side of the priest's head, knocking him and the chair over.

"But you don't have to burn up alone." You can hail Mary and Mary and Mary, all the way around. Look how sad they are for you. Breaks my heart."

His vision swimming a little less, Ignatius took in the sight of the stolen Marys, all crying—some of them transparent tears, some of them appearing to weep blood. A few of them glowed from within.

"How did you know a crying statue would keep the church open?" he asked.

"My partner told me. Pretty smart, huh? But we weren't the only ones who thought of it. That foreign pastor musta had the same idea, beat us to the punch." He picked up a red plastic gas can from behind a brown-skinned Mary. "This one was my favorite," he said, indicating the large fiberglass figure. "I would have put her in the church. Oh well." He sloshed gas onto the statue and then across the room to the other row of weeping Virgins. Then he disappeared behind Ignatius. The smell of the fumes was nauseating and overpowering.

Three minutes later, Cutter reappeared, now back in the puffy red jacket. "I wouldn't bother praying, Father," he said. "Fire department doesn't come out for abandoned houses around here. You see, when they burn, it saves the city the money of tearin' 'em down. In a few weeks, someone might come sifting through the ashes and find you. Maybe."

He pulled a book of matches from his pocket. "By the way, that kid you rescued? He's in my trunk, tied up like what. Imma use him to get your friends right where I want them. And then I'm gonna kill all of them. With your gun. How about that? Enjoy the barbecue. Gotta go." He struck a match and tossed it into the pool of gasoline. A moment later, Ignatius heard the back door slam shut.

***

"But what about the church?" Father Michael asked. "They're already struggling, they're going to lose their building, and now you're stringing them along like this as a pawn in your War on Drugs? These people have been pawns in enough wars."

Biak snickered. "Let me tell you something: In Burma, half my town went blind from drinking jet fuel. It's true. Someone stole a truck labeled 'Power Alcohol' and everyone who drank it lost his sight. Now some of them have made it to America, where there is alcohol that won't steal your eyesight. But there are also these monsters who will sell poison to kids, get them hooked from a young age, even kill them if they get in the way. And people are just as blind as they were in my village. It needs to stop, Father."

"That's great," Michael said, "but we actually believe in something bigger. You let this church die on the vine, and it doesn't matter how many drug dealers you take down."

Marion tipped his head toward the back of the church. "I want to show you gentlemen something in the basement. Might change your mind."

***

The heat of the flames was jostling for the air around Father Ignatius. *You got nothin', old man.* The words echoed in his ears. They would be his way out. Even after the beating Father Michael had handed him, the sight of a white-haired man in clerical clothing filled the hoodlum with overconfidence. And the fact that he'd easily overpowered the priest had only cemented that, informing the way he had bound his hands and feet.

Despite his recent defeat, though, Ignatius knew he was quicker and stronger than almost any man in his prime—perhaps even young Michael. The strength training regimen he'd begun decades earlier and continued every day of his life with the same religious zeal that drove his prayers and devotional reading had ensured him of that. He thought of how he must look now, bloodied and beaten, attached to the chair, knocked carelessly to the ground—helpless while the fires advanced. Experimentally flexing first his left leg, then his right, then each arm, the old priest looked for a weakness. The chair was solidly built—American Colonial, probably as old as the house.

But it was just a wooden chair.

The right arm. That was the weak point. In addition, his weight was resting on that arm, which he could use. Eight feet away, the first of the Marys began to melt, the pigments of her face blending into her red tears. Her mouth opened macabrely, drooping down to her waist. Others were beginning to melt as well.

Sweat was pouring off of him now; if he couldn't break the chair, he might be able slide his arm out from under the six zip ties holding it there. That would take some skin with it, though. No, his pride had taken all the damage it would tonight

He began rhythmically pulsing his core muscles, focusing them down into the point where the arm of the chair made contact with the oak floor, while simultaneously pulling up with his arm. His clothing was getting hot, stinging him where it made contact with his flesh. One of the Marys closest to him—made of something dangerously synthetic—burst into flames, producing an unnerving high-pitched scream as it burned.

His head swam. In just a few moments, the heat would overtake him and the smoke would also begin to take its toll, even down here at the floor where it was clearest. This could be it. After a long and successful career defending the Church against heretics, frauds, persecutors, and all manner of demonic conspiracy, he would be snuffed out by Cutter the street youth, cooked like a Christmas ham. He could imagine the crowd gathering outside to watch the house burn, unaware of the man roasting inside.

Ignatius began the rhythmic flexing again, but with a fraction of the commitment. Despite the glowing flames, darkness enveloped him. He had always assumed he would die in the midst of glory—perhaps a martyr for the faith or sacrificing his own life to save others. Failing that, he would have taken death at the hands of a worthy opponent—one who allowed him to smoke one last Montecristo. But this death would accomplish nothing and leave young Michael with no one to train and guide him.

A sudden *crack* sounded from beneath him, not unlike the crackling of the fire, but louder. Closer. There was some give in the arm of the chair now, although it remained attached. Father Ignatius rallied, reciting a prayer for strength and endurance. He pushed the chair's weakened joint again until all at once it gave out, turning Ignatius another ninety degrees. Now face-down to the hardwood floor, still taped and tied to the chair, he wondered if this was really progress.

* * *

Marion led the group back down into the basement. "Let me get the light," he said.

As the fluorescent bulbs flickered on, they could see that many of the chairs had been cleared from the middle of the floor and a large plastic sheet had been spread out.

"There were three priests earlier," Marion said, coming up behind Duncan. "Where's the other one?" Biak's eyes flashed back and forth between Michael and Duncan, something crazy flickering behind them.

"Let me ask you something first, Detective Marion," Duncan said. "You mind if I see your badge?" He rolled his forearm along his jacket, pulling it back from his weapon.

"My badge? Why?"

"I showed you mine. You never showed me yours. That's not fair."

"You know I'm a cop. You said you remember me."

"I know you *were* a cop. But I also know that your friends were using UV Ultraviolet Red Dye Gel No.14 as tears for their statues. Thing is, I've only ever seen that particular dye used by law enforcement, for marking suspects in riot situations. Stuff's not cheap. Where would these street punks procure such a thing? That got me thinking about cops who help themselves."

Marion shifted from one foot to the other. His suit seemed to be rumpling more by the second.

"You see, I don't think you *have* a badge. I knew your face was familiar, and from more than just that case a couple years back. I read about you. You were caught with your hand in the creamer and they fired you. But no one around here knows that, do they? They've seen your badge and your gun and your flashing blue light and they're all still afraid of what you could do to them. These poor refugees probably think you can throw them in jail without cause or send them back to Burma. Like you said, it takes muscle to move that much product, but that doesn't necessarily mean a lot of guys."

"You think you know stuff, huh?" Marion's hands were shaking as he rubbed them together. Then he locked eyes with Biak and gave a slight nod.

Michael saw the gun coming up in the poseur's hand and cleared his own weapon a half-second faster. Or rather, Cutter's weapon. The piece of junk misfired. Biak got two shots into Duncan before Michael's hands snapped the gun from him and brought it hard into the man's throat.

"Drop it, Father!" Marion ordered from behind him. Michael obeyed. "What kind of priest *are* you?"

Father Michael smirked. "You don't want to know."

* * *

Just eight more feet to the kitchen, with its many drawers, at least one of which must contain a knife. Father Ignatius could feel the flames licking at his heels as he pushed himself up as high as he could with his now-freed right hand and lurched forward, gaining another foot and a half, but breaking the fall with his already-raw right cheek. Behind him, something was loudly whistling and popping within the Mary Inferno.

Three more lurches forward and Ignatius was able to pull himself, chair and all, up by the kitchen counter. Beyond, the back wall and door of the house were engulfed in flames. Smoke was burning in his lungs.

The kitchen countertop was bare. No knife block, no blades of any kind. He began rifling through drawers, turning up a kitchen towel, two bottle openers, a variety of lighters, and finally a pair of children's safety scissors.

Thirty seconds later, Father Ignatius was free and forming a plan of escape. He held the towel under the faucet and turned the knob. Nothing. The flames were closing in now.

Oh God, who knowest us to be set in the midst of such great perils . . . Getting low to the ground, beneath the brunt of the smoke, he found himself face-to-face with a cabinet door . . . *that, by reason of the weakness of our nature, we cannot stand upright* . . . A rare smile spread over the old priest's lips as he spotted the fire extinguisher beneath the sink, then faded as he noticed the words "Replace Feb 2006." More than ten years ago.

Grant us such health of mind and body . . . He stood, spraying the foam into the flames, clearing a narrow path . . . *that those evils which we suffer for our sins we may overcome through Thine assistance.* The extinguisher sputtered and gave up the ghost just as a large window came into view. He hurled the extinguisher through the glass as the flames began to move back in, and took three steps back. *Through Jesus Christ, Our Lord. Amen.*

It would later occur to Father Ignatius that, even with the pathetic amateurism that had marked his time in this house, jumping through *fire,* out a window, and landing with a tight roll amidst broken glass balanced the whole thing out. He stood and crossed himself, walking away from the inferno without looking back.

* * *

Father Sacha knelt at Agent Duncan's side, praying fervently for him. He had rolled his friend onto his back, only to find his crisp white shirt soaked through with blood, the stain slowly expanding. Michael was on his knees as well, fingers interlaced behind his head as the disgraced detective and the imposter preacher had commanded.

"I'm gonna ask again," Marion said. "Where's the other priest?"

Michael smiled. "You're right. That is absolutely what you need to be worried about right now. Where *is* Father Ignatius?"

"He's dead," Cutter announced, sauntering into the church basement, his puffy jacket swooshing. He walked right up to Father Michael and pointed Duncan's backup piece in his face. "I get to do this guy."

"Sure," Marion said. "But not yet. Where's the kid?"

"In the trunk. I didn't know where we were doing this."

Marion pursed his lips, thinking. "Here's what we'll do . . . We take care of these Jesus freaks and the kid right here on the tarp, grab the money, and burn this place down too. Maybe we light a couple more houses, just to throw off the scent. We divvy up the cash, wait a couple months, and find a new base of operations. By then, demand will be higher than ever. Sound good?"

The two mooks nodded. "What about Hrang?" Cutter asked.

"Fire and brimstone," Marion said. "He'll be the first house we light up. This is gonna bring some heat, so no throwing money around. Take it easy. Remember what size cell you two'd be rotting in if it weren't for me. Now go get the kid."

Cutter mounted the stairs to the back entrance of the church and walked out into the frigid night. His car was parked at the curb, in a dark spot. He looked around for any witnesses and, seeing none, lifted the trunk lid.

Empty. The kid had gotten out.

"Hello, my son." Cutter turned to find Father Ignatius, his face streaked with soot and blood, glaring at him. "It's good to see you at church."

* * *

"I know you're not a real pastor, Biak," Michael said, "but are you really okay with this? Killing priests, burning down a church? Neither of you is worried about the toll this will take on your souls?"

"It's no longer a church," Biak said, shrugging.

"It is to 175 Burmese Christians. You know that better than I do."

"Right," Marion said. "And your people were ready to kick them out if it hadn't been for some bogus miracle. The church is a racket." He shook his head, as if he thought it was a real shame. "I mean, we got you two priests here praying away, but you can't help your friend, can you? He's bleeding out and you're helpless."

Father Sacha doubled the fervency of his prayers.

"Tell ya what," the detective said, "if you can get the Big Guy to fix Agent Duncan here, I'll let you all live. Heck, I'll let him cuff me."

He waited silently for a moment, getting no response but the weak, pained gasps of the FBI agent. "Guess I don't have anything to worry about," he said.

Then his mouth slowly fell open, wider and comically wider as he watched Duncan stand up, shoulders back, and straighten his necktie over the blood-soaked shirt. He smirked at Marion.

Biak lowed his gun for a moment and took two involuntary steps back.

"What the . . ." Marion took aim, but hesitated. "Hey Cutter," he called to the man in the puffy red jacket, swishing up behind him, "are you seeing this? Cutter?" He turned to his partner. "Where's the kid? Wait—who are—?"

Father Ignatius glowered at him from between the knit cap and the big red coat. "Not Cutter." He snapped Duncan's revolver into Marion's temple, dropping him to the ground, and kicked the former detective's pistol, sending it skidding along the plastic sheeting to Father Michael. While Sacha descended on Marion, pinning him down in an arm lock, the two Jesuits took aim at Biak, fanning out to forty-five degrees and approaching steadily in perfect sync.

"Love that look, Father Ignatius," Michael said. "Very street."

"We will never speak of this again."

Biak swung his aim from one priest to the other. "Back off!"

"I don't want to do this, little man," Michael said. "How about we cut a deal? You drop the piece, tell us where you're keeping the pastor, and we all live to see another day."

"What did you do to Cutter?" he asked, taking another step back, off the plastic drop cloth.

"He's doing penance," Ignatius answered, "in the trunk of his car."

"Is he dead?"

"Nothing a couple of casts won't fix. In time."

Biak hesitated another moment, then dropped the gun and put his hands up.

"Would you like to cuff him, Agent Duncan?" Ignatius asked. Duncan took an experimental step, then grimaced in pain and lowered himself as gingerly as he could back to the ground.

"I believe I have some broken ribs," he said. "Here." He held up a pair of handcuffs. "You do it. I'm guessing Marion has a pair too."

Michael took the cuffs. "I've got sort of an awkward question for you," he said. "How are you still alive?"

"Kevlar vest." Duncan pulled open his shirt. "Fifth time one's saved my life."

"But you're bleeding, like, a lot."

Duncan reached into his suit jacket, wincing in pain, and withdrew a shattered fragment of a glass bottle from the interior pocket. "Red UV dye concentrate. Bullet went right through the bottle. I guess we're—"

A gunshot rang through the cinder block basement. The revolver in Father's Ignatius's hand chugged smoke and a bullet hole leaked blood from between Marion's eyes onto the plastic beneath. In his lifeless left hand was a snub-nosed .38.

Father Sacha released the dead man's arm and took a few steps back. The three priests knelt down and crossed themselves, praying for the corrupt man whose arc had taken him from upholding the law to defying it.

"Your firearm, Agent Duncan." Ignatius said, handing it over.

"Thank you." He secured it back into his ankle holster. "A clean shooting. Unfortunate, but clean. Going to be a lot of paperwork though."

Michael checked his watch. "I don't think we're going to make that flight."

"So sorry," Father Sacha offered.

"No problem." He pulled Cutter's hat from his mentor's head. "You're freaking me out with this thing, man. Where's Van?"

"I sent him up to the bell tower. The police will want to speak with him of course, but no reason he should have to see this." He gestured at Marion's body.

With Sacha's help, Duncan rose again to his feet and approached Biak, whose hands were now cuffed. "Before I call this in, I need you to tell me two things: where's Pastor Hrang and where's the money?" Biak glared at him. "We've got you on a whole buffet of charges here, from attempted murder and unlawful imprisonment to conspiracy and carrying a concealed weapon, but if you don't tell us where the pastor is, it can actually get worse. You'll never see the outside of a prison again." He gave him a moment to think on that before adding, "You help me, I help you. And you want my help. I'm the guy you *shot*."

"Hrang's in an abandoned house. Three doors east of the place Cutter burned down. Number 624."

"And the money?"

Biak sneered. "The priest just shot the only man who knew that. Maybe his house. Maybe somewhere in the church. It's a big building. Good luck."

"Get it straight," Duncan said. "*I* shot Marion."

* * *

Father Michael had only intended to grab a power nap.

When the yellow crime scene tape had been wrapped, the respective FBI and police personnel had set up camp, and the endless questions and witness statements had finally come to an end, it was after 2:00 AM. Another hour and a half went by while the crime scene technicians did their thing and the coroner removed the late Detective Marion.

Shortly thereafter, the members of the Broadmoor Burmese Community Church had begun arriving, having been turned away from the police station due to their numbers and exuberance and showing little concern for the active crime scene. Pastor Hrang had promised to return to the church as soon as the police finished their questioning, which prompted an impromptu worship service, full of music and prayers and rejoicing, showing no signs of waning. Michael, already jet-lagged, had leaned back in an old padded pew along the west wall of the basement auditorium and fallen asleep, despite the revelry.

It was December 22 now and they had been through the longest night of the year. When Michael opened his eyes and rubbed his stiff neck, the sun was shining in through the east windows of the church basement. Van was slumped against him, snoring and drooling. And up on the platform, a thin, young Burmese man with round glasses was preaching passionately in another tongue.

When he saw Michael stirring, the pastor cut out mid-sentence and came rushing down.

"I am Hrang," he said in a thick accent, shaking Michael's hand. "I have already thanked your friends. And now I thank you. I am free because you cared about us."

Van rubbed his eyes and sat up. Seeing his pastor, he instantly awoke and rushed over to hug him in a vice-grip around the waist.

"You see? We're all so happy," Hrang said. "Even the Baby Jesus is no longer crying."

Michael put a hand on Hrang's shoulder. "Cutter seemed to think you might have rigged that up. If you did, we understand. All is forgiven."

"'Rigged up?' I don't understand," Hrang said, confused.

"Never mind. I'm glad you're safe. Why don't you get back to your service?" Hrang shook the priest's hand again and bowed slightly before returning to the pulpit and resuming his sermon.

"Hey Van," Michael said, beckoning. "Come here a minute." The boy followed him over to a door that bore the words "CCD Supply Closet." Projected there on the lacquered wood, about eye-level for Michael, was what appeared to be a glowing image of the sun, not unlike the image on the Jesuit emblem. Michael craned his neck, looking back up at the platform and found that the sunlight was glinting off the bare metallic fingertip of the babe in the manger, throwing a distinctive reflection onto the door, which he opened, letting the light into the shallow closet. The image of the sun now appeared on the side of a cardboard box.

Or maybe it was the image of a star.

The priest pulled the box down from the shelf and was opening it when he noticed the little plumber access panel on the wall, where the Star from the East now hung, perfectly centered for just a moment, before blinking out as someone pulled the curtains. Michael pushed on the access panel and it gave way.

Counting the money took some time, and Michael did it twice. Eighty-five thousand dollars exactly. He weighed his options. He could turn it in as evidence. Or, along with the thirty grand the Burmese church had raised and the ten from the Knights of Malta . . .

He stooped down to look Van in the eye. "I'm going to put this money back," he said. "Sunday morning, I want you to come get it and give it to Pastor Hrang, okay?" Van nodded. "You can help this neighborhood. Show them Jesus's love."

As they stepped back into the worship service, which now smelled quite strongly of cooking meat and Eastern spices, they bumped into Father Ignatius.

"There you are," he said. "Father Sacha is ready to drive us to the airport. We've been called to Panama."

"You're leaving?" Van asked.

Michael nodded. "I'm afraid so." The boy hugged him tight for a few seconds, then locked Father Ignatius in a hug, before running off to join a group of other children.

Ignatius smiled. "A good lad." He cleared his throat. "I will pray that their church continues to thrive, wherever they wind up."

"Well," Michael said "Who knows how long we'll be in Panama. And I'm going to be really busy for a while when we get back. I mean, I haven't even bought you a Christmas present yet. I highly doubt I'll get around to filing the report of our findings until at least the first of the year. In the meantime, my money's on a Christmas miracle."

They headed for the street, where they could see Father Sacha's car waiting in the falling snow.

Father Ignatius frowned. "You really haven't bought me a Christmas present yet?"

ACKNOWLEDGEMENTS

This sequel was a long time coming, but in no way a foregone conclusion. It first took the form of a loose outline and book proposal, sent to my editor at the publisher who put out *Playing Saint*. They were pretty much like, "Hard pass," so I moved on to other things. But the story kept coming together without my permission. Parker, Corrinne, and the Jesuits Militant would not leave me alone. And so Gut Check did sixty-three feasibility studies and decided to put out the book.

As a result, my heaps of gratitude this time around are divvied up between fewer people. First and foremost, my wife Erin Bartels. She's a publishing professional with a fulltime job, a growing freelance business, and her own multi-book contract with a major publisher, and yet she freely offered her time, skill, and expertise to make sure this book was as good as it could be. I'm an insanely lucky man. Sorry about all the commas.

Others who helped with proofreading and continuity include Jen Colin, Shelly Bartels, and Noel Harshman. Thanks to Sam White and Jeff Martin for the technical advising. And to Kara Peck for being the whole Street Team.

Also, big thanks to Ted Kluck, Cliff Graham, Jay Casten, and the whole Gut Check Army; join me in blowing the victory shofar and applying the Musk of King David. And of course everyone who has been listening to the Clinch Podcast, especially those who tweet about the suspense killing them and stuff. You know who you are.

Ad Maiorem Dei Gloriam,

Zach

About the Author

An award-winning preacher and Bible teacher, Zachary Bartels has served as pastor of Judson Baptist Church since 2005. He holds degrees from Cornerstone University and Grand Rapids Theological Seminary.

Zachary lives with his wife and son in the capital city of a mitten-shaped state, where he enjoys film, fine cigars, stimulating conversation, gourmet coffee, reading, writing, and cycling. He also hosts *Clinch: A Podcast of Fiction and Not-Fiction* and co-hosts *The Gut Check Podcast* (www.zacharybartels.com/podcasts).

You can find more information about Zachary (as well as follow his blog, Twitter, and Facebook) at www.zacharybartels.com.